For Murray Pollinger

THE SILENT LAND

Sally Spencer

This first world edition published in Great Britain 1996 by
SEVERN HOUSE PUBLISHERS LTD of
9–15 High Street, Sutton, Surrey SM1 1DF.

British Library Cataloguing in Publication Data

Spencer, Sally
  Silent Land
  I. Title
  823.914 [F]

  ISBN 0-7278-4868-2

Typeset by Palimpsest Book Production Limited,
Polmont, Stirlingshire, Scotland.
Printed and bound in Great Britain by
Hartnolls Ltd, Bodmin, Cornwall.

Remember me when I am gone away,
Gone far away into the silent land.

Christina Rossetti, *Remember*

My past haunts me and my future terrifies me.

Peggy Calvert Woods

Chapter One

When he's not serving customers, Ali likes to stand in the doorway of his shop and watch the world go by. Sometimes he watches me – watches my painful progress up Matlock Road – and then, when I'm close enough to hear, he calls out, "Good-morning, Princess! Want any help, Princess?"

He always smiles as he speaks. His mouth widens to reveal pearly-white teeth, his brush moustache stretches to its limit. He's mocking me, but only in a friendly way. I've been 'Princess' to him – this little brown man who lives in a climate which is no more his than it is mine – ever since the day we finally laid Gregory Lozovsky to rest.

How long ago was that? A year? Two? No, it was four long years ago.

Highgate Cemetery, that March morning in 1985, was so cold that the wind seemed to slice through what is left of my flesh and chill me to my crumbling bones. Since most of Gregory's friends were long since dead, it had fallen on me – one of his sworn enemies, albeit his last mistress in exile – to supervise the arrangements. The only other mourner was Demetri, Gregory's part-time, unpaid valet. Or so I thought at first.

Having lived the life I have, it didn't take me long to spot the watcher. He was standing three graves away, but he was looking at *us*. He was in his thirties and wearing a white trenchcoat. Apart from his eyes – which were keen and calculating – he seemed an unexceptional sort of man.

Special Branch? I asked myself.

Surely, as old as I was, I no longer merited surveillance. I turned back to the grave, imagining how it would look with

1

the headstone, a two-headed Russian Eagle perched on top of a slab inscribed:

'General Gregory Borisovitcha Lozovsky 1899–1985 Loyal Soldier of the Tsar and Defender of the Fatherland'.

So few words, yet an essay on the delusions through which people like Gregory lived out most of their lives.

General Lozovsky? He was a lieutenant in the Guards when Nicholas abdicated. The title 'General' was bestowed on him by one of those crazy emigré groups who for years sat around in London and Paris, plotting their triumphant return. And 'Defender of the Fatherland'? Well, he died in a Whitechapel nursing home – thousands of miles from the sacred soil he had sworn to protect with his life.

When it was over, Dmitri put his hand respectfully on my shoulder and said in Russian, "Allow me to take you back to your residence."

My residence! What a way he had with words, this small, insignificant man who worshipped the Russia he'd only known as an infant.

"Princess, it's time to go."

Looking down at his thatch of thin, grey hair, I felt a wave of disdain sweep over me. Why should a man – any man – act like a lackey through choice?

"It is cold," Dmitri said insistently. "I must drive you—"

"To my residence," I agreed. "119 Matlock Road, the door next to the communal bathroom. But first, I must visit Marx's tomb."

"I don't think—"

"Correct," I snapped. "It isn't a servant's place to think."

And I almost laughed when he nodded his head gravely, accepting the rebuke.

A sheen of frost glittered on the paving stones and clung to the lichen-green gravestones. We made our way slowly to the final resting place of the political visionary whose words had sustained me throughout the bitterly cold winter of 1917.

A group of young Chinese in boiler suits stood around the tomb, jabbering excitedly and pointing their cameras. I looked up at Marx's bust, and it gazed back – as if daring me to speak.

2

"Workers of the World, Unite," I said softly. "You have nothing to lose but your hopes."

As I turned, I saw him again – the man in the trenchcoat. He had followed us, and it was me, not Dmitri, who he was watching. I stared defiantly at him as I'd stared at Marx. His eyes were puzzled – questioning. I thought of challenging him then and there, and would have done if it hadn't been Gregory's funeral. Or perhaps I'm only fooling myself. I've seen much horror and faced death many times, yet this man frightened me, not so much the man himself, as what he represented. Even though I had no idea where he was from, or what organization he belonged to.

He looked at me for a little longer, then walked away. I let out a sigh of relief. "You can take me back to my residence, now, Dmitri," I said.

We drove home in Dmitri's rattling, coughing Mini. He grasped the wheel as if it were the reins of a coach and four. At the corner of Kilburn Lane, I said, "Would you like to come in for a cup of tea?"

I don't know why I made the suggestion. Maybe it was because I'd just buried a man who – however ridiculous he'd been – was my last real friend in the world. Perhaps I just wanted to shock Dmitri, to jolt him back to reality with the sight of my drab, dark room where the damp-soaked walls shed paper as a snake sheds its old, tired skins. Or I may simply have been unnerved by the man in the cemetery, whose look had seemed to be weighing me, assessing what of value could still be extracted from my ancient carcass. Whatever the reason, I made the offer, and threw Dmitri into a panic.

"I don't know whether it would be proper . . ." he began, flushing.

"It would be if I say so," I told him.

My voice was harsher than I'd intended, but it was so hard to be civil with this little man who drew his self-respect only from his respect for others.

As we drew level with Ali's store, I remembered I'd used my last spoonful of tea that morning. "Pull over here," I said. "I won't be a minute."

3

He didn't wait in the car, of course. He just had to come into the shop with me. And while my arthritic hands were struggling with my purse, he reached into his pocket and pulled out some notes.

"Allow me the honour of paying, Princess Anna," he said, and for once the fool chose to speak in English.

Ali heard, and was amused. He chuckled as he handed Dmitri the change, and the joke has never lost its appeal. Now all the people who nod to me in my small world, which reaches from Kilburn Lane to – on a good day – Harrow Road, call me 'Princess'.

It's useful for them, you see. They need to classify everyone they meet, and with the old, who no longer merit serious consideration, they want a quick, easy label. What better than 'Princess' for an aged lady who walks stiffly but with bearing, who wears tailored costumes which were once smart but now are old and long out of style. What they mean, when they call to me across the street, is that I act as if I really *were* an ancient princess. If only they knew the truth.

It is Thursday, the 2nd of February. In my homeland, a man called Gorbachev thunders on ineffectually about *glasnost* and *perestroika*, while here in the land of my exile we are sliding – lurching almost – into the tenth year of the Gospel According to Thatcher. There may yet be hope for both of my homes – but not in my lifetime.

I'm awake, though I keep my eyes tightly closed. Some mornings, I like to play a game with myself. Lying perfectly still in my bed, I remember all the different ceilings I've looked up at during the course of my long existence. The thatch of the *izbá* where I spent much of my childhood. The painted plaster ceiling in my room at the Big House. The majestic carving which dominated my bedroom in the palace on the Neva. Ah, Russia, Russia.

"What was it like in Russia?" they ask me in the saloon bar of the Vulcan, when they find the time to talk to a crazy old lady.

It was extreme, I want to tell them. Extreme heat and

extreme cold. Extreme idleness in the winter, extreme activity in the summer. But above all, it was very, very hard.

Yet how could I ever begin to explain to these smug islanders what it was like to live in a country where there were no horizons, only a great empty flatness which stretched to the edge of the world? How is it possible to make people who spend their lives in this insipid drizzle – which the English call 'weather' – understand what a real climate is?

Winter! Short, bitterly cold days. Snow. Not the slush they – we – have in London, here today, gone tomorrow, but feet of the stuff, white and powdery and wonderful. Days spent on the toboggan, nights around the earthenware stove that took up a quarter of our tiny hut.

Spring! In England, the spring comes as if it were an old woman like myself – hesitant, tottering, wondering whether it is yet quite warm enough to venture out. In Russia, the spring is a tiger which has unexpectedly escaped from long confinement in the iron cage of winter.

How could the English imagine ice so thick it bore the weight of a locomotive and yet vanished over-night? But it did. In the evening it was there, in the morning it was gone. Gone – all gone – save the floes trapped in the middle of the river like forgotten islands. And even they did not remain long. The angry water gripped them and dragged them downstream. Ruthlessly it used them to crush everything in their path. Remorselessly it forced them to gouge chunks from its own banks.

The land changed, too. Where the day before there had been a carpet of white, there was now only demanding greenness.

Consider the words. The English call it a thaw, making it sound more like a speech impediment than a bursting forth of nature. But in my native Russian it is *otterpel* – powerful, aggressive. Enslaving and liberating at the same time.

God, how we worked after the *otterpel*, even the children. In the factories of St Petersburg and Moscow they toiled for eleven hours a day all the year round, but out there in the fields, we slaved for as much as eighteen during the growing season.

"I'm tired, Mama."

"Keep planting, Annushka, keep planting."

"Where's Papa?"

"Working on the Count's land."

Using wooden ploughs, we turned the earth and sowed the spring oats. The oats came up and we harvested them, ploughed the earth once more and planted our winter crop of wheat. And even when we were so exhausted we could hardly stand, we still had to find the time to cultivate the garden plots outside our huts. If we had let ourselves neglect the cabbages and cucumbers we grew there, we would have had nothing but black bread to eat.

What *was* it like in Russia? There's much I could say to these kindly people who stop to have a word, but I know they're not really interested. So instead I take the bottle of Guinness they offer me, smile vacantly and say, "It was such a long time ago. I don't remember."

But I *do* remember.

I lie still a little longer, knowing that when I move it will hurt, yet knowing too that movement must come, because this withered, defective machine which imprisons my soul is already making demands on me. If I don't go to the bathroom soon, my bladder will give. And my great-granddaughters, Sonia and Jennifer, who visit me once a week – and today is that day – will see the stains when they change the sheet and take it as proof I can no longer cope. Then, finally, they'll have the excuse they've been searching for, and lock me away in an old people's home with clear consciences.

I twist my aged body and feel my feet touch the cold floor. It will be better now. If I take it slowly, if I do not let my natural impatience force me too suddenly to my feet, I should be able to avoid a further onslaught of agony for several minutes.

While I gather my strength, I look around the room. The bed takes up a great deal of the available space, and the rest is occupied by an old chest of drawers, a battered wardrobe,

6

and a single chair. Sordid and cramped as it is, I suppose I'm lucky to have it really. The *izbá* of my childhood was no bigger, yet my whole family lived in it.

The clay stove dominated the room. It was our heater, our bakery, and at night, when we climbed on top of it, our bed. Next to the stove were the bench and table, where we ate our frugal meals and made sweat-shop gloves for Peter during the long winter months.

At the other end of the *izbá* was the 'Beautiful' corner, where we kept our icons. We were great ones for religion, we *muhziks*. We hardly considered God, except as the bringer of bad luck – but how scrupulously we observed the ritual! Church every Sunday. Two fast days a week – Wednesday and Friday. Three major fasts which lasted for several weeks *each*, during which we were not allowed to eat any animal products – not even milk. And after the Revolution, when we were told that religion was no longer necessary, we discarded it all as easily as if it had been a rotting potato.

Sundays were for purifying our souls, but Saturdays were when the real cleansing took place. The whole village visited the *hammam* – the village bath-house. There we would sit, sweating, as water was poured over the oven to produce steam. There, we beat each other with twigs and put on a change of underwear. It was the only time in the week when we, or our clothes, were completely clean. And in summer . . . ? In summer, though we worked all day under a boiling sun, there was no time for bath-houses. In summer, we stank.

I was not always a withered old woman. Once, I was beautiful – and I can prove it. One of my few mementos of Russia is a photograph taken outside our *izbá*. I don't remember exactly when the picture was taken, but we are all barefoot and have puttees wrapped around our legs, so it must have been in summer.

The photographer was a friend of the Count's, anxious to capture a little true ethnicity before it all disappeared. That's why my father is wearing his high felt hat, though his normal headgear was a peaked cap. That's why my mother has on her *kokóshnik* – a tall head-dress decorated with fake pearls and gold, which she only usually got out on Sunday.

My father, Vladimir Alexovich, was a short broad man with a bushy beard – a typical peasant. In the photograph, his expression is one which at the time I took for granted, but in later years – when I saw it on the faces of other *muhziks* – would drive me to an emotion somewhere between rage and despair. The look is specially posed for the Count's fancy friend, and is a mixture of deference and idiocy. However much my father might attack the *dvorianstvo* behind their backs, he was, like all peasants, humble in their presence. He called the other members of the *mir* 'brother' – *brat* – but anyone of obvious social standing was always addressed at *otets* – 'father'.

"Yes, *otets*," my father would mumble. "No, *otets*. Whatever you say, *otets*."

And as he spoke, he would he look at the ground and fiddle with his cap, acting as if he were retarded. But God, how he and his *brats* could lie to the *otets*. And cheat him, too, if they were given the slightest chance. There is no more accomplished dissembler in the world than the Russian peasant.

Next to my father in the photograph stands his eldest son, Alyosha, almost Papa's double. He did not have long left to live – the Russo-Japanese War would see him off. Then come my two other brothers, one scarcely out of the cradle, both destined to meet their end fighting the Germans. My mother is beside the older of the two, her arm draped over his shoulder. She is still a pretty woman with large eyes, high cheekbones and an oval chin, yet already there are indications that after one or two more harvests she'll begin to look old.

Finally, little Annushka. I don't seem to belong in the photograph at all. True, it's possible to see a facial resemblance to my mother, but there's nothing of my father in me. And my build's all wrong. Many peasant children are skinny like I am, but it is plain that when I fill out, I'll still be nothing more than slender. I lack the *muhzik* woman's hips, on which can be carried a whole sackful of wheat. There are no signs of future thick legs, which will anchor themselves to the ground during the backbreaking task of harvesting the crop. I'm a freak, a huge practical joke of mischievous fairies.

Did my father notice that I was different? I think so. And did he know why this should be? Again, I think so. It is very difficult to keep secrets in the small universe of the *mir*.

I remember sitting with him on the long winter evenings, sewing gloves by the flickering light of an oil lamp. Often, we would work in silence, but sometimes – occasionally – he would tell me his version of our history, the only story that he knew, the only story his peasant imagination could comprehend.

"Your grandfather was a serf, Anna," he told me, "but the Tsar, our Little Father, freed him."

"Why, Papa?"

"Because the Little Father loves us. And he hates the *dvorianstvo*, who cannot plant and cannot plough."

"Is the Count a *dvoriane*?" I asked, five years old and ignorant of the ways of the world.

"He is, my child. He rides on his fine white horse when we don't even have a bony nag to pull our plough. He pays others to work in his fields instead of doing it himself as any real man would."

"Why does he do that Papa?"

My father shrugged. "Because that is what the *dvorianstvo* do. But one day, one day, Annushka, I will go and see the Tsar myself, and tell him all about it."

"Where does the Tsar live, Papa?"

"In St Petersburg. In a house that is even bigger than the Count's."

"And where is St Petersburg?"

He pointed vaguely. "Over there. More than sixty *versts* away."

Sixty *versts* – forty miles. The distance seemed as inconceivable to me as it did to my father. If either of us had been told the truth, that St Petersburg was over a thousand *versts* away, we would not have believed it – the world was simply not that big.

"And what will you do when you reach the Tsar's house, Papa?"

"I'll knock on the door. The front door. He'll not make me go around to the side as the Count does. And he'll say, 'Come in, Vladimir Alexovich.'"

"He will know your name, Papa?"

My father snorted at my ignorance.

"Of course he'll know my name. He is the Little Father."

"And what will happen next?"

"We'll sit by his stove drinking *kvass*, and I'll tell him that no man should have more land than he can farm himself."

"And what will he say?"

"He will agree. And he will take land off the Count and give it to me."

Oh yes, my father was a naîve fool, But he was not alone. There were few men in our *mir*, or in any of the hundreds of thousands of *mirs* scattered throughout the Russian Empire, who didn't think as he did. They were convinced that the Tsar knew them, just as the elders of the *mir* knew them. And they were monarchists to the extent that they felt the Tsar was on their side, and would eventually give them the land they hungered after. But that was as far as their loyalty went. Once the redistribution was completed, he could go hang himself for all they cared.

Land, land, land. It is the only thing the *muhziks* could understand.

"Another man's tears are only water," they used to say.

Because the man matters less than the rich, brown earth, the man is nothing when compared to crumbly soil. They had only one real love, those *muhziks* – one real loyalty – and that was for the land. To fail to understand this is to fail to understand them.

I tried to explain it – to Trotsky, Zinoviev, Bukarin and Kameniev – to all the members of the intelligentsia who made a revolution in the name of the People.

"The *muhzik* doesn't give a damn about the international

10

workers' revolution," I argued. "He knows nothing about solidarity. The *mir* is all that counts for him."

They listened – Trotsky stroking his thin beard, Zinoviev nodding his head sagely – because I had earned my place in their councils. But they never understood. How much more these wild-eyed idealists might have learned if, instead of studying Plekhanov in some foreign library, they had attended one meeting of the *mir*.

Picture the scene. A rough wooden table set up in the village street, a street which is dry and dusty in the summer, but a quagmire in winter. Behind us is the village inn. To the left is the church, distinguished from the *izbás* only by its onion-shaped dome. The men sitting around the table are dressed in full-length sheepskin *shoobas* and felt *valenki* boots. They all have long hair, full beards, blunt features and low-cunning eyes. To the people from the Big House, they will all look pretty much the same, differing only in age and size, like pigs or oxen. Even I, a *muhzik* myself, notice the similarity – the land is a great equalizer.

The air is thick with resentment and tension. The *mir* has been convened to discuss the periodic redistribution of farming strips. A village elder, grey-haired and bowed, is addressing one of the younger peasants.

"You must take the rough with the smooth, Anton Pavolovich," he says. "Your strip in the field by the wood is bad, but the one near the village is good."

"They're both bad. I'm always given bad land."

"It has been decided. There is no more to be said."

But there's always more to be said.

A recent widower is the next to be dealt with.

"Now that the fever has carried off your wife and children, Nicolai Ivanovich," the elder tells him, "you must give up some of your holding."

Nicolai's face is flooded with grief, though it is not the loss of his family which is tormenting him.

"I'll marry again, I'll have more children," he says desperately, looking around at his brethren, calculating which of them has a daughter of marriageable age, wondering how

11

soon he can acquire a new breeding machine so that he can claw his land back.

"When you marry, when you have more children," the elder says heavily, "we'll talk again."

And what am I doing here, little Annushka, only five years old? Why am I sitting cross-legged in the dirt and watching the whole proceeding? Is it because, even at such a young age, I am interested in village politics? No. I am here because, in the midst of this homogeneity of appearance and outlook, there are two men – Peter and Sasha – who are different. And I'm drawn to them as irresistibly as a pin is to a magnet.

I wish I had a photograph of Sasha and Peter, taken at the same time as the one of my family. It's so very difficult at my age – and after all the changes in my life – to separate what I know now from what I knew in the past. So though I can close my eyes and see the two of them at the *mir* meeting, I can never be certain whether I am seeing them then, or later, when our fates became inextricably bound together in St Petersburg.

Let us say it was then. Sasha has a thin, intense face with a slim, almost artistic nose and deep blue eyes. He reminds me of an *icon* of the suffering Christ. Peter has the peasant squareness, but in him it has been altered in subtle ways – his nose, though blunt, is not shapeless, the cunning in his eyes is deeper, more far-seeing.

In my mind, I picture them glaring at each other across the table. "We sh. . .should get rid of the strips altogether," Sasha is saying.

His stutter, which he never lost, is a sign of nervousness, but also of excitement and intensity. It gives his voice an earnest quality which unimpaired speech would not. It makes people realize that he is serious, but suggests, too, that the thoughts he expresses are only vaguely connected with the real world.

"If we ha. . .have just one big field and all work it together, we can make great improvements," he continues. He holds up a book. "It's all in h. . .here. Agricultural improvement schemes, drainage plans – everything we need."

The other peasants are impressed. Sasha has always been the clever one. Sasha, with a little help from the village priest, has taught himself to read. Nicolai, who has just lost some of his land, nods his head in agreement. Anton Pavolovich, who always gets – or at least believes he gets – the worst strips, is as deep in thought as a peasant can be. And yet there is a general feeling of unease. The *muhziks* know there's some flaw in Sasha's plan, but they can't yet place their work-gnarled fingers on it. It is left to Peter to put it into words.

"How do we share out the crop?" he asks.

"E. . .equally," Sasha replies passionately. "Each m. . .man will get the same, each woman the same, each child of a certain age the same."

Peter pretends to think about it. Sasha looks at him hopefully.

What a fool you are, Sasha! Peter already has land, bought from the Big House, which belongs solely to him and is not subject to *mir* redistribution. Nor is that all. During the winter months, half the village works for him, making the gloves which he then sells in Nizhni-Novgorod. But rich as he is by peasant standards, Peter is still cautious. What concerns him most at the moment (though of course, I, a child, do not realize it) is how he can ingratiate himself with the other peasants because without permission from the *mir*, he can't leave the village – however wealthy he is – can never lose his peasant status and become a *mestchanin* – a burger of some large town.

"Why should I labour hard on the land if I know that my neighbour, doing less than me, will get the same?" he says finally, playing on the peasants' greed.

Peter, you hypocrite! You no longer labour on the land *at all*. Others do the work for you – day labourers.

Yet the other peasants nod their heads in agreement, casting their limited imaginations into the situation he's described, knowing that if they couldn't have all they produced, they would not work as hard as they do now.

But it's not just the words – the argument – which has had an effect. Sasha is earnest almost to the point of fanaticism, but Peter has an energy, a power, which is overwhelming. I remember – and this, I am sure, is a real memory – that even then, when Peter looked at me I felt my stomach stirring. I was later to love Sasha – deeply. But it was always Peter I lusted after.

Chapter Two

They'll be here later in the day – Sonia and Jennifer – and there's much to do before they arrive. My room must be dusted. The window needs polishing. I must search around on my arthritic hands and knees for any odd scraps of food . . .

This last is very important. Sonia, who but for her social snobbery would be happiest as a housemaid, once found a few cake crumbs on the floor.

"You'll have to be more careful, great-grandmother," she told me. Slowly, as if I were a child in need of instruction. "Food on the floor attracts all kinds of vermin."

And Jennifer, standing near the door, nodded her head in agreement – though carefully, so as not to disturb her immaculate hair-do.

I'd have had more respect for them if they'd say what's really on their minds. "You're an embarrassment to us, old woman. Why don't you do the decent thing and agree to go into the nice Home we've found you. Then we can pay other people to go through all this."

Yes, I must clean the place thoroughly. But first, I will have breakfast. A cup of Russian tea and a slice of toast covered with Lyle's Golden Syrup. And as I spread the syrup on the bread, I think of the first time I tasted it, over eighty years ago, in the Big House near my *mir*.

The first time I saw the Big House was in 1904. I was just seven years old – and there on business.

It's impossible to imagine the effect it had on me unless you, too, can see it through the eyes of a small girl from a primitive peasant village in which even the church is

15

little more than a shack. Think of it, walking away from the muddy village street and reaching those wrought-iron gates. In the distance, at the end of the long drive, was a white, three storey mansion. It had a veranda at the front. A terrace ran the length of the first floor and was supported by eight magnificent, carved columns.

And the windows! They weren't poky little things like the one in our hut. They were wide and spacious, letting more light and air into the house than a peasant would have ever dreamed of. Some of them on the terrace went right down to the floor, I noticed, and opened just as if they were doors.

Even the Tsar himself can't have an *izbá* like this, I thought to myself.

And there was more – much more.

In front of the house was a large flower bed. The potted plants in it were laid out to form the date, and so, of course, were all changed every day. I didn't know that then. I didn't even know what a date was, nor would I have understood its value if it had been explained to me.

At the side were strange sheds made almost entirely of glass, in which flowers were being grown. I wondered why anyone would bother to do that when there were plenty of flowers in the woods. Beyond the glass sheds were more gardens, one with a pond in it, though I could not see the stream which was providing the water.

Just visible behind the house was the orchard, where cherries, apples and pears were cultivated – unknown, exotic fruits which formed no part of the peasant diet – and beside the orchard were the stables, in which the Count kept his wonderful, wonderful horses.

Was I overawed? Yes. Did I understand any of it? No. It was as alien to me then as Mars is now.

I made my way up to the front of the house and then, as my father had instructed me, walked around the side. Outside the pantry stood Zossim, the Count's cook, a bald man with a head like an upturned pear. From behind him wafted the delicious smell of bubbling jam. In front of him was a table on which sat a set of scales.

I held out the basket of wild strawberries I had spent all

16

day picking. Zossim didn't speak, or even look at me. He simply took the basket, emptied the contents into the pan and placed a weight on the other end of the scales.

"Watch him, Annushka," my father had warned me. "He'll try to cheat you. They'll *all* try to cheat you."

"Twenty-five *kopeks*," Zossim said.

He took the pan off the scale and reached into his apron for the money.

I heard the sound of hooves on the cobblestones behind me, but much as I loved horses, my eyes remained fixed on the scales.

"It's not enough," I said.

Peasants may be uneducated about most things, but we soon learn to assess weight, and I knew that though the scales had balanced, they *shouldn't* have done.

"It's a fair price, you urchin," Zossim said. "Take it or leave it."

The clatter of hooves had stopped, and I could hear the horse snorting.

"Weigh them again," I said.

Zossim was reddening with anger, his pear-shaped head turning the colour of an apple.

"Be off with you," he shouted, "or you'll feel the back of my hand."

"Weigh them again," a deep masculine voice said, "and this time, keep your finger off the balance."

I did turn this time, I couldn't help myself. The deep voice belonged to a man sitting on a bay horse. He was in middle age, and his hair was already greying. He had a strong athletic body, a long, straight nose and a neatly trimmed beard. He looked vaguely familiar, although I was sure I'd never seen him before.

"Weigh them again," the Count repeated to his servant.

Zossim put the pan back on the scales and then lifted his hands clear to show that this time he was not interfering. The scales did not balance. He put another weight on.

"I made a mistake," he mumbled. "It should have been fifty *kopeks*."

"Give her a *rouble*," the Count said, and though his voice was stern, I felt that he was trying not to laugh.

"A *rouble*," Zossim protested. "But then, master, you'll be out of pocket."

"No," the Count replied. "*You'll* be out of pocket. And that's what comes of trying to cheat a poor peasant girl."

Zossim reached into his apron and pulled out four twenty-five *kopek* coins. I took the money hesitantly, not daring to look into his angry eyes, but the moment it was in my hand, I made a tight fist around it.

The Count had not moved on, so etiquette required that I stayed where I was, too. Also according to etiquette, my eyes should have been fixed on the ground – where a *muhzik's* eyes belong – but try as I might, I could not keep them there. I found my gaze wandering along the flank of the horse, up the Count's lean body and finally resting on his face. He was smiling.

"What is your name, little girl?"

"Anna, *otets*."

"And your mother is . . . ?"

It struck me as strange that he should ask Mama's name instead of Papa's. In the world of the *mir*, the men were the ones who mattered. I almost asked why he wanted to know, but it was not done to question a *dvoriane*.

"Her name, child," the Count said. Impatiently, as if he was really interested in the answer.

"Elisabeth Ivanova, *otets*."

The Count nodded. "Would you like to ride back to the *mir* on my horse?"

How can I describe my emotions at that moment? Me – on the Count's horse. I tried to speak, but the words would not come, and in the end I merely nodded.

The Count patted the side of his beast. "Come over here, then."

My body had gone numb but I forced myself to move until I was standing where he had told me to. The Count reached down and hauled me into the air. I spread my tiny legs and he lowered me over the neck of the animal. I clamped on tight.

So many new sensations assailed me – all at once. I was riding on a real horse. I was looking at the countryside from an entirely new perspective. I was breathing in the smell of the Count, not sheepskin and sweat but polished leather boots, starched serge uniform and eau de toilette. We were half-way back to the *mir* before I realized that I had somehow managed to lose the four coins which Zossim had paid me, but I could not really bring myself to care. I'd never been so happy in my life.

As we trotted down the muddy street of the *mir*, it was almost like the arrival of a circus. Other children ran along beside us, screaming and shouting excitedly. Adults stopped what they were doing and looked on in astonishment. And I sat astride the horse, as proud as the Tsar himself.

Word had reached home before we did, and my father was waiting in front of the cabin. "This is an honour, *otets*," he muttered, keeping his eyes pointed at the ground.

"I am prepared to honour you further," the Count said. "I wish Anna to come and stay in the Big House."

Panic engulfed me. The Big House was a fine place to look at, but how could I possibly give up my cosy cabin and go and live there? I started to struggle, trying to get the right leg over the horse's neck, so that I could drop to the ground. I felt the Count's hand on my shoulder, restraining me.

"Let me go!" I screamed.

For the first time, my father raised his head. "Anna," he said, "you mustn't talk to the *otets* like . . ."

"It's all right," the Count reassured him.

Strong arms lifted me into the air and deposited me on the ground. I ran to my father and buried my head in his sturdy thighs. The old comforting feeling, the old reassuring smells.

"You want Anna to live in the Big House?" Papa asked. "As a servant?"

"No. As a companion to my children."

Companion? My father must have been as mystified as I was. In our harsh peasant world, there was no room for such a luxury. Everyone had to work, and the results of that

19

work could be seen and touched, eaten or used. For us, the word 'companion' simply had no meaning.

"She would take lessons with my children," the Count explained. "She would eat with them and play with them. She would be better off than she is here."

I felt my father's legs tense against me. A romantic would say it was at the thought of losing his daughter, but that would only show how little he understood *muzhik* men. Papa knew – or at least believed – that if the Count wanted me to live in the Big House it would come to pass whether he opposed it or not, and he accepted the fact with the fatalism which has led the Russian masses to their deaths in innumerable wars. But he knew, too, that the Count would not expect to get me for nothing. Cunning peasant that he was, he sniffed a deal.

"The girl is useful to my wife," he said. "And if she goes, the *mir* will take some of my land off me."

"You shall not lose out of it," the Count replied. "You'll no longer have the expense of feeding and clothing her, and I'll pay you a hundred *roubles*."

"A hundred *roubles*!" my father said, trying to keep the greed out of his voice.

I'd been frightened before, but now I was terrified. One hundred *roubles*! Was there that much money in the whole world?

I could feel my father quivering in anticipation.

"Are we agreed?" the Count asked.

Say, no! I pleaded silently.

"We are agreed," my father replied.

I let go of the legs which would no longer protect me, and rushed into the cabin. My eyes were full of tears. I wanted to find my mother, wanted to tell her that Papa had just sold me.

Once, in the depths of winter, hunger drove a wolf into our *mir*. It cornered Mama and me on our way to sweep out the church. Its glassy eyes fixed on me and saliva dribbled from the corner of its mouth. As it tensed to spring, I knew that my last hour had come.

Beside me, a voice – Mama's voice – suddenly screamed, "No! No! I won't let you take my child!"

The wolf shifted its attention from me to Mama, and Mama ran at it, swinging her broom.

A full grown wolf is of awesome size and weight. It could easily have held its ground – but it didn't. It was faltering even before Mama cracked the broom over its muzzle, and then it turned and ran. Perhaps hunger had made it too weak to fight, but I think it more likely it was intimidated by the passion of a mother defending her cub.

That was how I expected Mama to react now, when I sobbed out the story of my father and the Count. She *was* angry, as angry as she had been with the wolf, but her anger was directed at me. She knelt down, placed her hands on my shoulders, and shook me.

"You little fool!" she hissed. "Can't you see how lucky you are?"

"I want to stay with you and Papa."

She swung me round so I was facing the stove, then turned me again until I was looking at the cupboard. "You want to stay with *this*?" she demanded. "When you have the chance to live in the Big House?"

"Y . . . yes, Mama," I gasped through my tears.

She shook me again, even harder this time, until my teeth rattled. "I would have done anything – anything – if only he'd have let *me* . . ." she began. She let go of me. Her face was still red, but her blazing anger had left her and her eyes were as cold as ice.

"Mama—"

"If you won't go," she said, "then you're no daughter of mine. You can wander the countryside until you die!"

At that moment, I think she really hated me. Hated me for not seeing the opportunity when it was offered. Hated me for being lucky enough to have it offered at all.

We set off for the Big House the next morning, Mama and I. The sun was shining and the birds were singing. Insects,

21

hidden in the grass, made strange rasping noises. I watched other children swinging their strawberrying baskets, and I thought my heart would break.

I was wearing my best Sunday dress and head-square. In my hands, I carried a cloth parcel containing all my worldly possessions – my wooden spoon and bowl, my sheepskin *shooba* and felt *valenki*.

We reached the cast-iron gates, and Mama stopped. I had hardly spoken to her since her ultimatum, and it was only fear which made me speak now.

"Shall we go on, Mama?"

"No, my child."

Joy of joys! She had changed her mind.

"You must go the rest of the way alone," Mama said. She knelt down beside me as she had done the day before, but this time there was no anger in her eyes, only a deep sorrow. "This is for the best," she said. "A few more harvests and I will be an old woman. And after that, there is only death."

"No, Mama!"

She put her fingers to my lips. "Shush, child. A *muzhik*'s time on earth is hard, yet it is mercifully short. But for you, there will be a better life." She paused. "Remember the wolf? How he ran when I hit him!"

She laughed, and I laughed too, although we were both crying.

"He had his tail between his legs," I said, "like a beaten dog."

"I would have given my life for you that day. It would have been easier than what I am doing now."

"Can you . . . walk with me to the door?" I asked, trying to grasp a few extra minutes with her.

Mama shook her head. "There was a time when I might have done, but not now. Look after yourself, my Annushka."

As I watched her disappear into the distance, the bundle in my arms took on the weight of lead. I wanted to put it down, but I knew that if I did, I'd never have the strength to pick it up again.

I waited until my mother was completely out of sight, then turned my back on the *mir* and headed slowly, reluctantly, towards the Big House.

Chapter Three

The staircase was incredibly wide, and the red carpet which covered it tickled the soles of my bare feet. When we reached the top, the man in the frock coat, who had been escorting said, "Wait here."

He knocked gently on the nearest door and then opened it. "The girl is here, master."

"Bring her in."

I walked timidly to the opening, clutching my bundle tightly in my trembling hands.

The room took my breath away. Everything was strange and wonderful. The shining parquet floor. The windows, seeming even bigger looking out than they they did looking in – and with *curtains* hanging beside them. The furniture, delicate polished wood, so different from the rough benches of my *izbá*.

"This is Anna."

The Count's words snapped me back to reality. He was sitting at a round table in one corner of the room. He was not dressed in his riding uniform, but instead was wearing a suit, shirt and bow tie. He did not seem so commanding as he had done the day before. His glance flickered back and forth between me and one of the women on his right, his voice had lost the assurance it had when he was talking to my father.

To his left sat two children, a boy and a girl. The girl was perhaps a little younger than me, the boy a little older. He was dressed in what I later discovered was a sailor suit, she in a pretty blue and red check dress that I would have given my soul for.

Of the two women it was plain, even to my untutored eye, that one was important and the other wasn't. The unimportant one was young and wore a dark skirt with a pale v-necked blouse. The older woman was taller and more imposing. She had on a long white dress with a high collar. Around her neck was a string of pearls.

"This is my son Misha," the Count said.

The boy rose to his feet and bowed in my direction.

"My daughter Mariamna . . ."

The girl frowned at me, sulkily.

". . . and Miss Eunice who is their governess and will be giving you lessons too."

Miss Eunice smiled, and though she was not pretty, the smile made her face look warm and welcoming.

"And this is my wife, the Countess Olga."

The tall woman stood up, walked across the room until she was only a few feet from me, then slowly and calculatingly looked me up and down. Unlike the governess, Countess Olga was pretty, almost beautiful, yet her features seemed unnaturally pinched.

I had no idea how to react to a lady. *Muzhik* men bowed to each other, but I knew of no polite method of greeting women, so I made the only formal sign I knew – I crossed myself.

The Countess laughed, and the sound was harsh and grating. Then she spoke to me, very quickly, in what sounded like gibberish.

I looked down at the floor and mumbled some sort of reply. "I . . . I don't . . . I'm sorry . . ."

"Good heavens, child," the Countess said, "don't you speak French?" Without waiting for a reply, she turned to her husband and, still in my native tongue, told him of my deficiency.

"Be reasonable, my dear," the Count pleaded. "Of course she doesn't speak French. She's a peasant girl."

"Exactly," the Countess replied triumphantly, still in Russian to make sure that I understood. "This mad idea of yours can never work. Look at her! Smell her! She stinks!"

"All peasants stink," the Count replied, "but it's only because they're dirty. Give her a bath and she'll be just like Misha and Mariamna."

"She will *never* be like Misha and Mariamna," the Countess

25

said, and with a swish of her immaculate white dress, she left the room.

Children, they say, have great resilience to suffering. Perhaps that's why we Russians have allowed ourselves to take so much punishment – never having really grown up, we accept pain and discomfort as a way of life. And though I endured a great deal that first day at the Big House, I was both a child and a Russian, and it never occurred to me to run home to Mama.

My first ordeal was a tub of hot water. I'd never had anything but a steam bath before, and the idea of immersing myself in water seemed as dangerous as it was novel. "I'll drown," I complained to Elena, the fat old peasant women who served as the children's nanny.

Elena laughed. "You won't. Lots of people get clean this way."

Lots of people drank vodka until they fell over, I thought, but it still wasn't a very sensible way to behave. Still, I climbed into the tub and let the nanny scrub away my dirt.

Once my skin was pink again, I was given an old dress of Mariamna's to put on. The cloth was so smooth that it felt uncomfortable, and I began to itch.

"Time to get rid of the bugs in your hair," Elena said cheerfully.

What for? Everyone had bugs. Didn't they?

I sat there patiently while Elena dragged a brush through the knots in my hair and rubbed a burning lotion onto the scalp to kill the lice. "There's a positive army of them in there," she told me, "but this stuff'll soon shift 'em."

I endured it all with a peasant's resignation. Only over the shoes did I revolt. "They don't fit," I protested.

"Yes, they do," the nanny assured me, running her finger along the gap between my foot and the side of the shoe. "There's more than enough room."

It all seemed crazy to me. In the winter, when the ground was frozen, I wore my boots. That was only sensible. But in the warmer weather, why should I make my feet prisoners? Because the Countess and Mariamna did?

26

That wasn't a good enough reason for me and I told Elena so.

Though we were alone in the room, the nanny looked around her before lowering her head until her lips were almost touching my ear. "Listen, little one," she whispered, "you have an enemy in the mistress, and she'll do everything in her power to get rid of you. Don't even give her the tiniest excuse."

"But why do they want me to act like them?" I demanded. "Why am I here at all?"

"Hush, child," Elena urged. "There are some things it's better not to talk about.

"Do *you* know why I'm here?" I persisted.

"Yes, Anna. Everybody does. That's the problem."

When I was finally presentable, the nanny took me back down to the ground floor, into a room just off the main hallway. "You'll be sleeping here with the servants, instead of upstairs with the family," Elena explained. She sniffed. "That's one battle, at least, that Madam has won."

I looked around for the stove, and could find none. Instead, the whole room seemed to be filled with long, thin, iron tables, all covered with blankets. "*Where* am I to sleep?" I asked.

Elena stripped the blankets off one of the tables. "Here," she said. "In this bed."

"Bed? I don't understand."

The nanny sighed with exasperation. She had forgotten what it was like to be a *muzhik* and to see the world through simpler eyes. "This is the bed frame," she said, tracing it with her finger, "and this is your mattress. This is where you'll sleep."

It seemed very strange that anyone should wish to sleep on mattress suspended above the ground when they could just as easily, and more cosily, lie down on the stove. But I was coming to accept that people in the Big House always did things in a much more complicated way than normal folk.

"Wait here until they call for you," Elena said briskly. "I've other duties to attend to."

And she was gone, leaving me sitting on the edge of

my new bed, and wondering how things could possibly get much worse.

It must have been an hour before fat Elena came to see me again. "They want you upstairs," she said. "Or at least, *he* does. You've to have dinner with them. Come on. Don't keep them waiting."

I quickly rummaged through my bundle, pulled out my wooden spoon and ran after Elena, who was already waddling her way upstairs.

Having once visited the room in which the family lived – though I had seen neither stove nor beds there – I expected to be returned to it now. So I was mystified when Elena led me to another one, even larger than the first.

The family and Miss Eunice were sitting at a long table, as long as the one which the *muhziks* used for a meeting of the *mir*. I would have thought it strange that they needed a table of such a size, had it not been for the quantity of things piled up on it. There were glasses, plates and dishes, any number of knives, forks, spoons . . .

I became aware of the wooden spoon in my hand at the same moment Mariamna did.

"See, Mama," the girl said gleefully. "See what she's holding."

I put my hands quickly behind my back.

"You look very nice, Anna," the Count said.

The Countess twisted her lip into a sneer. "She looks like a peasant who has been scrubbed and dressed in Mariamna's old clothes."

The Count pretended not to understand. "Tomorrow we will take her into town and buy her some clothes of her own from the Jewish shop." He smiled at me. "Come and sit down, Anna."

I walked timidly towards the table. A servant – there were three of them in the room – stepped forward, and for a moment I thought he was going to block my way. But he didn't. Instead, he pulled out a chair between Mariamna and Misha. I was not used to sitting on chairs, and anyway, this one was rather high. As I struggled to climb on it, I was aware of all the family's eyes on me, and of Mariamna's sniggering.

"Help her," the Count ordered.

The servant put his hands under my armpits and swung me up. Even then my troubles were not over – I could hardly see over the top of the table.

"Cushions," the Count said crossly. "Like you bring for the other children."

The servant fetched some, lifted me, and placed the cushions beneath my bottom. I took the opportunity to surreptitiously drop my wooden spoon on the floor.

"You may serve now," the Count said.

In my long – too long – life, I have seen many terrible things. I remember a steppe village during the war in which the peasants, starving to death, had eaten the bark off the trees until there was none left, and then resorted to cannibalism. I remember a small town in Spain where the Nationalists, in revenge for a Republican atrocity, had slaughtered every man and mutilated every woman. Yet my most recurring nightmare is not of death and destruction, it is of that meal over eighty years ago.

Knives, forks, spoons, glinting at me – accusing me in my ignorance.

"Just do what I do," Misha said. And under the table, I felt a small hand squeeze my knee.

"Tell us," the Countess said, "what is life like as a peasant?"

I could think of nothing to say. Life was life. Cold in the winter, hot in the summer. Difficult when there was a poor harvest, better when nature was merciful. What could I explain? There *was* nothing to explain.

"The child is stupid as well as barbaric," the Countess announced.

"All she needs is time, my dear," her husband said soothingly.

The Countess answered him in gibberish again, though she never took her eyes off me. This was to be her tactic from now on. Speaking in Russian when she wished

29

to humiliate me directly. Switching to French or English when she merely wanted me to know that she was talking *about* me.

The food arrived – *borscht*, our national soup. I was surprised that there were so many implements on the table, just to eat *borscht*. My wooden spoon would have done the job perfectly. I was surprised, too, to find the family eating the same food as the peasants – though I had no real idea of what else they would eat.

I realized I was very hungry, and, using my spoon the same way as Misha did, began to ladle up my soup. It was delicious, the best, the most extravagant, *borscht* I'd ever tasted. Soon it was all gone, and my stomach was completely, satisfyingly full.

The servant took our bowls away and returned with even more food – a variety of fish dishes served with salted cucumbers and marinated fruits. I gazed at it, unable to understand how anyone could eat any more.

"Have some fish, Anna," the Countess said. "It's only proper manners, and if you're going to live with us, proper manners you must learn."

I think it was her calling me by my name which put me off my guard. That and the fact that she talked about me living in the Big House as if she accepted it.

I wanted to please her. I carefully forked up a piece of fish and put it into my mouth.

"More," the Countess urged. "You're eating like a mouse."

I saw the Count smiling with relief. He, too, was taken in. I forced a little more down, though I didn't really want it. I was relieved when the fish was taken away, but horrified when the servant brought more food. It was roasts this time – chicken, turkey and goose with apples.

"A young lady always takes a little of everything," the Countess said. "Don't you want to be a young lady?"

I nodded my head, and ate a little of the meat.

It was the cakes and pastries which were my final undoing. "One slice, Anna. You don't have to eat it all."

But one *mouthful* was enough. I had been brought up on a diet of black bread, cucumbers and cabbage, with a little tough meat on Sundays and at the end of fasts. All this richness was just too much.

A heavy, uncomfortable feeling had been growing in my stomach, and the cake was a signal for it to erupt. I'd seen men vomit after two or three days of steadily drinking vodka, and I knew I mustn't do it here. I fought back the bile and climbed off my chair.

"Do you want to be excused, Anna?" the Countess asked, and even through my discomfort, I noticed a triumphant gleam in her eye.

I didn't stop to answer. I turned and ran for the door. I was half-way there when the pain hit me, and I fell to my knees. My stomach heaved again, and I gave up the battle. My mouth opened, my body shook, and I was violently sick.

My body was out of control, but my mind was still working and I heard everything that was going on around me. Misha's gasp, Mariamna's laughter, Miss Eunice's, "Oh dear!"

And the Countess, talking to her husband. "Can you see now that all this is pointless?"

"It's bound to be difficult at first."

"Difficult? Impossible! Whatever you do for her, she'll never be any more than a *muzhik* – a brutish beast."

Chapter Four

Imagine this – knowing nothing beyond the world of the *mir*. Worse, imagine being completely incapable of seeing the point of knowing more. The Russian peasant had no interest in what the sun was made of, or why it appeared in the east and set in the west. For him, it was enough that it did appear, and he could build his life around that simple fact. Nor did the peasant speculate on what made an automobile move without a horse to pull it. The vehicle would amuse, even amaze him, much as would the antics of a dancing bear, but what had that to do with planting crops or fermenting bread to make *kvass*? Such was the state of my mind when, on my first morning in the Big House, I climbed the stairs to the second floor, where the schoolroom was located.

It was a square room, middle-sized for the house. At one end was Miss Eunice's desk and behind it a wall-mounted slate board. Facing the board were the pupils' desks. A table rested against one wall with a hand-written notice above it. When I learned to read English, I would discover that it said 'Nature Table', but for the moment I was merely mystified by its collection of birds' eggs, animal bones and dried flowers. Why would anyone wish to keep such rubbish inside the house?

Mariamna, Misha and our governess arrived together, and we all sat down. "Until Anna has learned some English, we will sometimes have to speak in Russian," Miss Eunice said.

Her Russian was slow and careful, and though she made mistakes, it was not a lot worse than that spoken by the family, who only used the language when they were addressing servants.

"Let us see what you know, Anna," she continued. "What is that on the wall?"

I looked at where she was pointing. It was a picture, obviously, but it was not a picture of anything I could recognize, just a series of different coloured shapes which seemed to slot together.

"Is it an icon?" I asked.

Mariamna burst into laughter. "It's a map, stupid!"

"How could she know that?" Misha asked quietly.

Poor, little Misha. Always so willing to defend me, and yet always so meek in that defence. A knight in shining armour who carried a flower in his scabbard.

"Mariamna," Miss Eunice said severely, "you will not be rude to Anna. She has not had the advantages you've had."

To my surprise, Mariamna bent her head and said, "Sorry, Miss Eunice."

"It is not to me you should apologize. It is Anna you have insulted."

It seemed my powers of astonishment were to be stretched to the limit that day. Mariamna turned to me and, red-faced, and with eyes full of hatred, mumbled, "I'm sorry, Anna."

"I can't hear you clearly, Mariamna," the governess told her.

"I'm sorry, Anna." Louder this time, almost shouting.

"And I'm sure Anna accepts your apology. Now, look at the map and watch my finger." Miss Eunice traced around one of the shapes. "That is Russia."

It seemed particularly imbecilic to me to say that a shape on a picture could be Russia, but I was learning it was wiser to hold my tongue.

"Mariamna," Miss Eunice said, "show us where Great Britain is."

Mariamna stood up, walked to the map, and traced her finger round a smaller shape.

"Mariamna can cut out all the countries of Europe and fit them back together again," Miss Eunice told me. "Just like a jigsaw puzzle."

She was trying to be fair – Miss Eunice always tried to be fair – compensating for her earlier rebuke with well earned

33

praise. It had little effect on me. I had no idea what a jigsaw puzzle was, but I couldn't see why anyone should bother to cut something up just to put it back the way it had been in the first place.

The map game continued for quite a while, and by the time it ended I was able to trace several countries successfully, though as far as I was concerned they might as well have been called Meat and Potatoes as Germany and Italy.

At the end of the exercise, Miss Eunice set the others some reading to do, and came and stood over me. "Do you like doing this, Anna?" she asked.

What could I say? What did she want me to say? "It's . . . it's very nice," I stuttered.

Miss Eunice smiled, but in that smile there was as much command as in Lenin's hard stare or Stalin's frown. "Don't lie to me, Anna," she said softly.

"It's . . . I don't see why we're doing it," I confessed.

"You will – if you give it a chance. I can open up a whole world for you, Anna. Will you let me?"

Those were probably not her exact words, of course, but knowing Miss Eunice they must have been something like that. And though I didn't understand, I could feel her intensity, sense that what she had to offer was wonderful.

"You must not neglect my children for the sake of the peasant girl, Eunice."

The Countess, terrifying and magnificent, was standing so close that she could almost touch us. I felt a sudden chill overcome me, as if my very life were at stake.

Miss Eunice rose to her feet. "I would never dream of neglecting any of my charges, Madam." There was deference in her tone, but there was also anger. "Misha and Mariamna are making good use of their time."

If the Countess was offended, she did not show it – except perhaps for a slight narrowing of her eyes. "I am going to Kiev next week," she said. "I think you could use a new dress. Velvet would be nice. You'd like that, wouldn't you?"

Miss Eunice gave a short curtsy. "Thank you, Madam."

The Countess was almost at the door when she stopped and turned round. "I don't think this peasant girl will ever learn anything, Eunice," she said. "It's a waste of both her time and yours. I wish you would tell my husband so."

Miss Eunice gazed down at her sleeve, as if she had discovered a loose thread.

"Don't you think it is a waste of time?" the Countess persisted.

"It's too soon to know, Madam," Miss Eunice replied.

The Countess's eyes narrowed even further, and her mouth tightened until her lips were almost puckered. "Are you happy working for us, Eunice?" she asked.

"Yes, Madam."

"There are a great many British governesses in Russia. Most of them, I imagine, would be more than willing to change places with you."

"I'm sure that's true, Madam," Miss Eunice replied dully. "I am well looked after here."

"So you'll speak to the Count?"

Miss Eunice stood with her feet wide apart, her hands bunched into small, angry fists. "I will do my duty," she said.

"I see," the Countess replied, and swirling round in her practised, haughty way, she left the room.

Miss Eunice did not lose her position, but neither did she receive the velvet dress she had been promised.

Oh, Miss Eunice, how much I owe you. What doors you opened for me. Did you ever think, when you left your comfortable bourgeois home in Glasgow and made the long journey from Tilbury, up the Kiev Canal to St Petersburg – did it cross your mind even for a moment – that you could have such an effect on a child as you had on me?

I can picture her now, her small, wiry body, her hands waving wildly as she made a point. Sometimes, the Count came into the schoolroom and watched our lessons, nodding gravely when we got the answers right, frowning when we failed. Occasionally, the Countess would pay us a visit – mainly to laugh at my ignorance – but as both my confidence and knowledge grew, so the frequency of these visits declined.

It didn't matter to Miss Eunice who was there. The

schoolroom was her little kingdom in which she bestowed her precious gifts on her small subjects – and she bowed her head to no one.

It was a strange life I led, with the children in the daytime, the family at meals and the servants at night. Some of the maids were suspicious of me at first, thinking I'd repeat what they said to the Countess, but once they'd heard the way *she* spoke to *me*, they realized there was no danger of that.

As their trust in my discretion grew, I began to learn almost as much from the servants as I did in the schoolroom upstairs. I discovered, for example, that the marriage between the Count and his wife had been far from a love match. The Mikloshevskys were a much older, more noble family than Countess Olga's, but they were poorer, too.

"He needed the money," Tassaya, one of the kitchen maids, whispered to me in our room one night. "But even with the dowry, he's finding it difficult to make ends meet."

I found that incredible. The Count was the richest man in the whole world. There was always meat at the table, fine horses to ride, the grandest clothes to wear.

"They've been selling off their farming land," Tassaya continued. "It's nearly all gone. Soon it'll be the timber forests, too – and then the Count will have nothing."

"Yes," giggled Natulia, another of the maids. "Already Peter owns almost as much land as the master does."

"Peter Vassilyevich?" I asked. Peter from the village who made my stomach turn in a way I didn't quite understand? "But he's only a *muzhik* like my father."

"It'll be a lucky girl who marries him," Tassaya said, ignoring me. "And in more ways than one."

"Well, it won't be you," Natulia replied, rather nastily. "Vodka once drunk is nothing but piss."

"Better piss than horse shit," Tassaya retorted.

The two girls folded their arms, turned their backs on one another and lapsed into a sulky silence, leaving me, sitting in the middle, completely mystified. There was much about big people I still didn't understand.

*   *   *

The events which were to change Russia – and the world – really began in the Autumn of 1905. There had been grumbling earlier in the year – when the Tsar's soldiers fired on an unarmed demonstration – but it was the printers' strike in Petersburg which first threw the country into a chaos it would not emerge from for another twenty years.

"And it's not just the printers who are on strike," the Count complained over breakfast, as he read a report from a newspaper published in strike-free Kiev. "The Petersburg lawyers are refusing to work, and so are the bank employees. Even the *corps de ballet* have come out in sympathy."

"And what is the government doing about it?" Countess Olga asked.

"Nothing!" the Count replied in disgust. "The whole city's in the hands of the workers' soviet."

"The workers' soviet," the Countess repeated, her disgust matching her husband's. "They're nothing but anarchists and should be hung from the nearest lamppost."

Soviet! There are some words which seem to have a magical ring about them, which roll around the mouth like a ripe strawberry. Soviet was such a word for me and though I had no idea what it meant – and knew I would get no satisfactory answer at the Count's table – I wanted to find out more. And so I went to see the one person in the *mir* – apart from my mother – who still seemed to have time for me. I went to see Sasha.

I ambushed him by the well at the edge of the village, and fired my question at him. He put his bucket on the ground and squatted down, so that our eyes were at the same level.

"The S. . .Soviet is rule by the workers, f. . .for the workers. Can you understand that?"

"I think so," I said dubiously.

"Each f. . .factory elects a man to it. The Soviet controls the st. . .strikes and demonstrations. But it also distributes f. . .food."

"What does 'distributes' mean?"

"It sees to it that p. . .people get food, and that each person gets a fair share."

37

"You mean that if we were living in Petersburg, my mother and the Count would get the same?"

"Ex. . .exactly."

What a wonderful thing the Soviet seemed to be.

The meetings at the well became a regular part of our lives. Sometimes Sasha would talk about politics, and though much of what he said was above my head, I was content just to listen to the sound his voice. On other occasions, I was the one who did the talking. I would tell him about life at the Big House, and he'd nod his head in disgust at the luxury and extravagance of it all. I would repeat my lessons, and he'd greedily absorb the information at second hand.

They were peaceful, happy times. We were careful to go to the well only when we were sure there would be no one else there, for though we had never discussed it, we both *knew* we had a pact to keep our friendship secret. And so our meetings remained a secret – until that fateful day in late autumn.

It was Sasha who was doing the talking that day. He was sitting on the ground, legs stretched out and back leaning against the well. He had a radical newspaper in his hand, and he was telling me about an article he'd just read. And I, sitting cross-legged and so close to him that my knees almost touched his feet, was eager to listen, eager to learn if I could.

"The Tsar's s. . .set up a *Duma*," Sasha said. "An elected parliament."

"That's good, isn't it?"

"N. . .no. Because he's not given it any real power. He st. . .still controls the army and f. . .foreign policy and the police. And when the *Duma*'s not meeting, the government – and that means Nicholas – rules by decree."

"So what will happen to the Soviet?" I asked.

"The Soviet," a new voice said, "will collapse."

We looked up, startled, to find Peter grinning down at us. What was he doing there? He didn't fetch his own water, he paid other people to do it.

A few moments earlier, Sasha had been relaxed, despite the earnestness of the conversation. Now he tensed up, and when he spoke again, his stutter had got worse.

"T. . .the S. . .Soviet will g. . .go on," he said. "It w. . .w. . .won't give in. It kn. . .knows that Tsar h. . .hasn't g. . .given m. . .much away."

Peter's grin widened.

"You're such a fool, Sasha," he said. "The Tsar hasn't given away much, but it'll be enough for the liberals. They're like donkeys – just letting them see the carrot is enough. They'll go over to the government, and the Soviet will be finished."

"N. . .no!" Sasha said.

"Y. . .y. . .yes!" Peter countered.

They may have said more, things that were beyond my comprehension. I simply don't remember. But I'll never forget their expressions as they looked at one another, Sasha squatting on the ground, Peter towering over him.

On Peter's broad, chiselled face was a look of complete complacency, a look which said, 'I will always be right, you will always be wrong. I will always win, and you will always lose.'

Sasha's expression was more intense, but there was none of the gentle, suffering Christ in the *icons* about him now. His eyes blazed with hatred for everything Peter was – everything he stood for.

Peter was right about the Soviet. The liberals withdrew their support, the strike collapsed and the government of the workers, by the workers, fell with it.

As for the meetings by the well, they stopped as abruptly as they'd started. It wasn't just that Peter had spoiled the place for us – though he had – Sasha seemed reluctant to meet *anywhere*. I think he felt he'd been humiliated, and that our relationship could never return to its former state until he had done something to redeem himself. Which is just the sort of foolishness that men *do* indulge in. I recognized it then as clearly as I recognize it now, and I have never, ever, been able to understand it.

In our snug, smug little world, seven hundred miles from the centre of great events, there was scarcely a ripple of discontent – not then. The young men who had survived the Russo-Japanese War had no time to gripe; there was a harvest to be reaped and memories of battles were soon smothered by their struggle against time and nature.

I, too, had obstacles to overcome, battles to fight. I learned how to ignore the hostility of Mariamna and Countess Olga, or at least to insulate myself so that their barbs did not prick quite so deeply. I learned how to behave at table, cutting up all my meat with a knife, then placing it on the knife rest and eating with a fork only. I learned history and geography and English, and basked in the warm glow of Miss Eunice's approval.

And so the autumn slid into winter – double windows sealed with moss, hot soups and stews, tobogganing. Then it was spring again, with crocuses pushing their heads out of the soil almost as soon as the snow had gone, to be quickly followed by blue asters and flowering lilac. It was not until the spring of 1906 drifted lazily into summer that the trouble started.

It began as rumours. *Muhziks* in a village some hundred *versts* away had revolted, killing the landowner and his family and slaughtering all their beasts.

"How did it happen?" I asked breathlessly from my bed in the maids' room.

"They slit their throats from ear to ear," Natulia told me in a tone which lay somewhere between relish and fear.

"No," Tassaya countered, as she always seemed to do on principal. "They locked them in the house and set it on fire. They were roasted alive."

The troubles got closer. On still summer evenings, we could hear distant church bells ringing out the *tocsin* to warn of fire. The Count unlocked his armoury and issued every servant who had served in the forces with a rifle. Dressed in his Guard's uniform he marched his reluctant troops into a fallow field and watched as slowly – clumsily – they regained their old skills. For three whole days all other tasks around the house were neglected, until finally he was satisfied that his private army was ready to deal with any disturbance. After that, there was nothing to do but wait.

It was two o'clock on a summer's morning when something

finally happened. I remember it all vividly, even now – the dry taste in my mouth, the stickiness of my eyelids, the reluctance of my body to move despite Tassaya's urgent shaking.

"Get dressed," she kept saying. "There's a fire in the lower barn."

I struggled into my clothes and ran through the warm night air towards the amber glow. The barn was made of brick, or it would have burned down before anyone could reach it, but the thatched roof blazed away with tremendous force. The oxen, rescued from their stalls, had lost their normal placidity and shuddered nervously. The villagers, as was their duty, had all turned out with a bucket or a shovel to give their assistance. Firemen on their wooden truck were pumping furiously and a jet of water shot from the end of their hose onto the burning roof. I watched everyone I knew in the whole world fighting the fire – and wondered which one of them had started it.

There were my mother, father and young brothers; here the thin, intense Sasha who I had not seen for nearly a year; over there the burly, powerful Peter, swinging the heavy fire buckets as if they weighed nothing. And suddenly, though I could not have explained how I knew, I realized that the fire was Peter's work.

It was an hour before the blaze was extinguished and we could return to the house. I climbed back into my narrow bed but though my small body cried out for rest, my mind buzzed with fear and excitement, and sleep would not come.

I could smell the smoke in my night-dress. As I tossed from side to side, the straw in my pillow crackled like the flames which had greedily eaten up the thatch. I wondered if there would be more fires, or if we'd be murdered in our beds as the maids had darkly predicted.

The morning, like so many mornings which follow nights of childhood fear, was an anticlimax. The servants, though looking sleepier than usual, were carrying out their normal duties. I sat at the breakfast table with the Count and his family, as I always did. In through the long windows shone an untroubled sun.

"It's a good day to start the harvesting," the Count announced cheerfully, and as if to give ourselves fresh

41

courage, everybody, including the bad-tempered Countess Olga, agreed that it was.

We were excused school during harvest time, and when breakfast was finished we all went down to the pantry door where the bailiff had set up his table. We were waiting for the *muhziks*. Few of them grew enough to feed their families, and most were forced to work as labourers for the Count and the richer peasants like Peter. Soon, they would appear at the gates and shuffle uneasily around to the side of the house to make their marks in the bailiff's ledger.

An hour passed, and not a single peasant appeared. "The idle dogs," the Count said. "Just because they were on fire duty last night is no excuse for sleeping in this morning." His voice was gruff, as if he were annoyed. Yet I thought I could detect a underlying hint of unease.

It was another hour before a solitary figure appeared at the gate. He was thin for a peasant and he didn't walk down the drive with the hangdog attitude favoured by most of the *mir*, but instead moved with the purposeful, yet awkward gait of a reluctant hero. Even before we could see his face clearly, I knew it was Sasha.

It seemed to take forever for him to arrive at the table. Once there, he stood squarely before the Count and his bailiff.

"You're late to sign on for work," the Count said.

"I haven't come to s. . .sign on, *otets*."

Father! How ingrained are our habits, even in the souls of revolutionaries.

"Then why *are* you here?" the Count demanded.

"As a re. . .representative of the U. . .Union of Peasants."

"You mean, the *mir*,' the Count sneered.

"No," Sasha insisted, "the U. . .Union of Peasants."

"And what does the U. . .Union of Peasants have to say?" the Count asked mockingly.

"That we're t. . .tired of seeing our children go hungry, of w. . .watching our wives grow old before their time. That this year, we w. . .want to keep more of what we h. . .harvest for ourselves."

42

The Count had been sitting, but now he sprang to his feet. "You *dare* to threaten me?"

Sasha didn't retreat – not an inch. Never in my life had I seen a peasant behave like this in the presence of the aristocracy. "I'm not here to thr. . .threaten," he said. "I'm here to n. . .negotiate."

The Count picked up his riding crop from the table and slashed it through the air. Sasha reeled backwards under the blow, and fell to the ground. His face had turned deathly pale save for the angry red mark which ran from his cheekbone to his mouth.

Slowly, Sasha climbed to his feet and dusted himself down. "You can h. . .hurt me," he said, "but you can't h. . .hurt us all. If you don't n. . .negotiate, your crops will rot in the fields."

Only half a century earlier, the Count could have had Sasha *knouted*, until his back ran red with blood – until he was dead. But now the serfs were emancipated – now he could only stand there in helpless rage.

"I'll starve rather than give in," he shouted. "I'll see my family starve rather than give in."

Sasha turned his back and began to walk away. He hobbled somewhat, as though the blow had injured his body as well as his face. No one tried to stop him.

"Saddle my horse," the Count said finally, when the *muhzik* was only a small shape in the distance.

"Are you going riding?" Countess Olga demanded sulkily. "At a time like this?"

"I'm not doing it for pleasure," the Count snapped. "I'm going to the town to telegraph the dragoons. They'll soon break this Union of Peasants."

Chapter Five

There have been perhaps seven or eight occasions in my life when I've known, with absolute certainty, that there was something I had to do. They flit through my mind now, almost as if I were watching them on the flickering screen of the Bolshoi Cinema. Making a furtive assignation with a sex-crazed, fanatical holy man called Rasputin. Joining the Bolshevik Party. Forcing myself to pull the trigger of my pistol that night in the Crimea . . .

Seven or eight occasions only. There may be one more. I will *not* let my great-granddaughters, my mock-solicitous, insufferable great-granddaughters, put me in a home. I, who have seen the vastness of the Russian Steppes, who have openly defied Joseph Stalin, will *never* allow myself to be confined to a narrow cell, granted freedom only at the whim of some uniformed matron.

Sonia and Jennifer will not succeed in breaking my spirit now. Rather than submit to their tidy plans, to their desire to sweep an old woman under the institutional carpet, I'll kill myself. I'll wait until everyone else is out of the house, then put my head in the gas oven and turn on the tap. I'll lie in the tepid water of the communal bath and slit my wrists. I'll . . .

Pull yourself together, you old fool! That isn't what you meant to say. Not what you meant to *think*.

Start again.

There have been seven or eight occasions in my life when I've known, with absolute certainty, that there was something I had to do, and the first of these came that day when I saw the Count ride off to telegraph the dragoons.

I told no one of my plans and it was only when I'd said

44

good-night to the family that I made my move. By the time I reached the *mir*, a pale summer dusk had fallen and the *muhziks*, returned from the fields, sat outside the village inn, sipping tea. They would have preferred vodka, but drinking is a serious business in Russia requiring three days – one to get drunk, one to *be* drunk, one to sober up – and during the harvest there was no time for such luxury.

The men looked at me as I walked past them, and I was almost on the point of speaking when they turned their heads away. I was not one of them any more. I'd been away for less than two years, and already I was a stranger.

A dog howled, a baby cried. I marched steadfastly down the unmade street. The *izbá* I wanted was at the far end of the village. I knocked firmly on the door, and when it was swung open I saw Sasha standing there. The slash mark across his face had turned an ugly black. He looked down at me and smiled uncertainly.

"Annushka! What are you d. . .doing here?" he asked.

"The Count has sent for soldiers."

Sasha nodded his head gravely. "I th. . .thought he would."

"You must go!"

"Go wh. . .where, little one?"

"Anywhere! As long as it's away from here."

"Whatever h. . .happens, I have to stay," Sasha said. "There's n. . .no choice."

"If you run away," I blurted out, "I'll go with you."

Sasha squatted down beside me, as he'd done so often in the past, so that our faces were almost touching. For a while, neither of us spoke. What was he thinking? It's hard to be certain, I can only say that in his eyes I read a sorrow as deep as the village well.

It was Sasha who finally broke the silence. "Your path has been chosen for you," he said, and his voice had a mystical – almost priest-like – quality about it. "Perhaps it will cross mine again in the future, but for the moment it must travel a different way. Go back to the Big House, Annushka."

He said it softly, but it had the force of a command – and he hadn't stuttered once.

I kissed him quickly on the cheek, then turned and ran.

45

The Big House was in darkness when I returned. I climbed in through the dormitory window and buried myself under the blanket on my narrow bed.

The dragoons arrived the next evening. They didn't come directly to the Big House, but instead rode up and down the village several times, glaring at the peasants who stood impassively in the street.

"A show of force," the Count said triumphantly.

But against what? No more buildings had been burnt and the *muhziks* were sullen rather than defiant.

The dragoons were divided into units and each was quartered in a different barn or outlying farm on the Count's estate. And there they sat for two more days, waiting for something to happen, while all the time the wheat in the Count's fields was growing dangerously towards over-ripeness. Even someone of the Count's influence could not have kept the soldiers there indefinitely, especially since there was real trouble in other parts of the country. Had events been left to themselves, the dragoons would probably have gone away and the Count would have been forced to give in to the peasants' demands. But that would not have suited Peter – and Peter was never a man to leave events to themselves.

He made his move at the end of the second day of our military occupation. I was lying on my bed when I spotted him coming down the drive. Sasha had been open in his approach, but the muscular Peter moved like a wolf, powerful but wary.

I wondered who he'd come to see. Most of the servants had been dispatched to deliver rations to the soldiers, and the rest were away carrying other errands. Even the Countess and her children were absent. Under an escort of dragoons, they'd gone out for a ride in the *drozhky*.

I don't know whether it was curiosity or fear which made me move away from the window. Perhaps it was both. I heard Peter's stealthy footfalls crushing the gravel, getting closer and closer, and then a voice saying, "Well, Peter Vassilyevich, this is a sorry state of affairs indeed!"

The Count. Sitting on the veranda. Almost as if he had expected the peasant to call.

"A sorry state of affairs, *otets*?" Peter asked, as though he didn't know what the Count was talking about.

"There are no *muhziks* to harvest my crop, and even if there were, much of my seed was destroyed in that unfortunate fire."

"It may yet turn out to have been *fortunate* fire," Peter said.

"Indeed? How could that be possible when it has almost ruined me?"

There was none of the surprise in his voice I would have expected. They were both *acting*, I suddenly realized. They were just like the cockerel and the hen in the mating season, each one involved in an elaborate ritual – each one knowing all the time what the end would be.

"I hope you'll think of me as a friend," Peter said.

"A friend?" the Count replied with obvious distaste.

"Or an ally, at least."

"An ally. Yes."

"Then as your ally, I'll see to it that you have the money to replace your equipment."

"At an extortionate interest rate, of course."

"At the fairest interest *you'll* get from any one," Peter said. "Now about the other problem, the striking *muhziks*. I have a way to solve it that will benefit us both."

"Come and look at the barn," the Count said, "then we can discuss exactly what I need."

I heard his chair scrape along the floor, then the sound of two sets of retreating footsteps. When Peter and the Count next spoke, they were too far away for me to distinguish the words. I wanted to follow them and listen to the rest of their conversation – to learn how a fire could possibly be fortunate for *anyone* – but they were out in the open and would soon spot me. I would just have to wait for my answer, I thought.

He came in the middle of the night, tapping desperately on the window like a trapped, frightened bird. At first I thought the noise was only in my dreams, but slowly I forced my eyes open and looked around me. The maids were all asleep,

47

little Tassaya no doubt dreaming of marrying Peter, the more practical Natulia snoring loudly.

I climbed out of bed and made for the window. The hand continued to tap and beyond it was the pale face of Sasha. He saw me and stopped knocking. I pulled back the bolt and slid up the window as quietly as I could.

"What do you want?" I whispered.

"You've got to h. . .hide me," he gasped. "The dragoons. Th. . .they're out looking for me."

I raised the window higher so that he could climb in, then took his hand and led him through the maze of beds to the corridor. "Why are they looking for you? Is it because the *muhziks* won't work?"

"No. Th. . .they say I burnt down the C. . .Count's barn."

"But you didn't. I know you didn't."

"Two of th. . .them came to arrest me. I knocked one out with my sh. . .shovel and beat the other one until he ran away. I'm st. . .stronger than I look."

How absurd men – all men – are. So proud of their physical prowess that they'll brag about it even in times of crisis – even to little children.

I led him up the wide staircase.

"Where are we g. . .going?"

To the most precious place in my small world, to my Aladdin's cave – the schoolroom.

I opened the door and motioned him inside. "You'll be safe here. When we don't have lessons, I'm the only one who visits it."

I closed the door again and crept downstairs. I had only just returned to my bed when I heard the heavy knocking on the front door.

There were six dragoons in the party. They'd followed the trail of a fugitive barn burner. They were sure he was in the house, and they wanted to search every room.

"How can he be here?" I heard the Count demand. "Ever since you arrived, I've made sure that every window, every door, was locked. If he'd broken in, there would be some evidence of it."

48

"It is the only place he can be, Your Excellency. And it *is* on your behalf that we're acting."

"Very well, search. But start with the servants' rooms. I do not want my family disturbed unless it is absolutely necessary."

They searched our room while Natulia and Tassaya, sleepy-eyed and clutching their night-dresses tightly to themselves, looked on and giggled. They checked the bakery and the carpentry workshop. Then they moved upstairs.

Sasha was trapped. There was no way out but the window, and it would have been suicidal to jump from that. There was nothing for him to do but wait while they searched the first floor, checking the Count's bedroom and the Countess's, looking under the dining table and behind the chairs in the ballroom. He could only hope that by some miracle they would decide not to check the second floor. They did, of course, and there he was, caught like a rat in a trap. Nose pressed against the dormitory window, competing with the maids for space, I saw him led away in chains.

I didn't dare cry until I was once more alone, shrouded in my blanket, but then the tears flowed freely. I sobbed quietly for most of the night and it was with a puffy face that I reluctantly dragged myself up to family breakfast the next morning.

No one noticed me at first, all eyes were on the Count, who looked as grim as I ever remember seeing him. "Someone let that man in last night," he said. "I don't expect loyalty from the *muhziks* . . ."

"Animals are never grateful," the Countess commented.

". . . but I do insist on it from my servants. Whoever is guilty will be punished."

"None of them would have the nerve," Countess Olga said, tossing her head imperiously. "They have too much respect for you. Too much *fear* of me."

Misha turned to look at me. "What is the matter with your face, Anna?" he asked worriedly. "Have you been crying?"

"Her!" the Countess screamed, pointing a finger at me. "She did it. She's a swill-guzzling peasant just as he is. She let him in through the window of the maids' bedroom. Well, now we can finally send her back to her hovel."

"I'm sure Anna wouldn't—" Miss Eunice began.

"Do you deny it, you little guttersnipe?" the Countess demanded.

"She did it, Mama," Mariamna chanted. "She did it. You can see it on her face."

I was not ashamed of what I'd done. I wouldn't deny it, whatever the punishment. "I—" I began.

"Hush, Anna," Misha said quickly. "I let him in."

"You!" the Countess said, incredulously. "Why would you let a pig into our house?

"I . . . I couldn't sleep. I saw him from my window – outside. He looked so afraid. I let him in through the front door. I must have woken Anna. She saw us. That is why she's been crying."

"I don't believe you," the Countess said contemptuously.

"It's true."

The Count looked squarely into my eyes. "Is it, Anna? Is it true what Misha says?"

"Yes."

"Can't you see what he's doing?" the Countess asked. "He's covering up for that little sow."

"I choose to believe my son when he confesses to a crime," the Count said with dignity.

"Do you? Do you? Then punish him. Punish him as you said the guilty party should be punished."

"How?"

The Countess picked up her husband's riding crop, which he never kept far from him, and waved it in front of his eyes. "Tell the servants to stay outside – and beat him."

The heavy silence which descended on the room seemed to last for ever. I didn't want to look at any of the others, but my body betrayed me, turning my head even as I tried to resist the movement.

Mariamna had a wicked grin on her face, a grin which said that she was confident, one way another, that she was going to enjoy herself. Countess Olga was looking steely and determined, watching first Misha, and then me, waiting for

50

one of us to break. Miss Eunice had suddenly found her hands very interesting. Misha was trying not to cry.

And the Count? He gazed at his wife with pure loathing, and if he'd thought he could get away with it, I'm sure he'd have killed her then and there.

"Well, are you going to punish the boy yourself?" the Countess demanded finally. "Or must I call for one of the grooms?"

The Count rose heavily to his feet. "I'll do it," he said.

I heard a gasp, and realized that I'd made it myself. Though I hadn't even known I was doing it, I must have been holding my breath.

"Don't come in until I tell you to!" the Count called to the butler and upstairs maids who were waiting outside the door. He turned to his son. "Bend over, my boy. And remember that you're a Mikloshevsky. Whatever happens, *keep quiet*."

Misha bent, his hands resting on his knees, his slim legs trembling. The Count raised his crop and brought it down with a heavy thwack across Misha's behind. I remembered what no fiercer a blow had done to Sasha's face, and I shuddered.

"Harder!" Countess Olga demanded.

The Count raised his crop again, and landed it with a blow which sounded like the splintering of bones. He lifted it for a third time, and was just about to strike when the Countess shouted, "Stop!"

Relief engulfed me like a tidal wave. I'd felt Misha's pain like it was my own, and now I offered up a silent prayer of thanks that his mother had chosen to show mercy.

Misha started to return stiffly to an upright position.

"I didn't tell you to rise," the Countess said, her voice as cold as the winter frost. "Bend over again." She walked across the room until she was standing in front of him, grabbed his hair in her hand, and lifted his head. "Who let the filthy peasant in? Was it you? Or was it that little bitch?"

"Me, mother."

She released his hair and his head flopped down. "Beat him again! Harder!"

At the third blow, Misha's knees began to buckle, yet somehow he managed to hold his position.

51

"Who let him in? You or her?"

"Me, mother. It was me."

"Hit him again! Harder!"

How many times did that wicked crop slash through the air? How many times did Misha wince and gasp with pain before his mother finally gave up and called for the servants to carry him to his room? Ten? Fifteen? I have no idea. After the third blow I no longer counted, no longer thought. I saw the scene, but only through a red madness brought on by anger and shame and sorrow.

I'd wanted to confess. To spare Misha the pain and take it on myself. But I couldn't. When the Count had asked me if I'd let Sasha in, I'd seen a look in his eyes which overpowered me. He was a proud man from a proud family. He'd never openly begged for anything in his life. Yet his eyes were begging then. Begging me to let Misha take the blame. Begging me not to say anything which would give the Countess the excuse she'd so long sought to send me back to the *mir*. I couldn't refuse him then, and if I were to live it all through again, I wouldn't be able to refuse him now.

How easy it must have been, in a peasants' court over which the Count presided as Land Commandant, to find Sasha guilty of burning down the barn. There were witnesses, men who worked for Peter, who swore that they had seen Sasha do it, but even without them the case was a foregone conclusion. He was sentenced to *katorga* – hard labour – in Siberia. The sentence was twenty years, but it might as well have been a hundred. Those who used *katorga* workers knew the authorities would never complain about the way they were treated, nor inspect the conditions under which they were living. Long before his twenty years was up, Sasha would be dead.

The strike crumbled. Almost as soon as the trial was over, the *muhziks* went back to work in the Count's fields. Through solidarity there is strength, but who was prepared to be the next martyr to that solidarity? Who else was prepared to suffer Sasha's fate? No one!

The dragoons took Sasha away the next morning. I stood at

the edge of the *mir* and watched them go. He didn't have a
horse – why waste one animal by having it carry another?
– so his chains were fastened to the saddle of one of the
soldier's mounts. They set off at a trot, and he was forced
to run desperately behind. If he'd fallen, I don't think they'd
even have bothered to stop so he could struggle back to his
feet. After a few miles of being dragged, he'd probably be
dead – but so what? Now or later – did it *really* matter when
he died?

I ran back to the Big House, knowing what I had to do.
Though I'd never dared face up to the Count before, I had
no choice now. I climbed the stairs to the first floor, turned
the handle of the study door and marched in, feet stamping,
arms swinging, chin jutting forward defiantly.

The Count was working on his papers. I came to a halt
directly opposite his table, my eyes only just able to see
over the edge. The Count put down his pen and looked at
me. "Yes, Anna?"

"You must have Sasha brought back. He didn't burn
the barn."

The Count looked at me oddly, as if he didn't know quite
how to react. For a moment, I thought he was going to order
me out of the room. But I wouldn't go! I wouldn't! Not until
he had promised to save Sasha. Then he smiled, and the smile
was strange, too. If I'd had the vocabulary, I would probably
have called it wearily cynical. "I know Sasha didn't burn
down the barn," he admitted. "It was Peter."

"Then how could you—"

The Count pointed to a footstool.

"Sit down, little Anna and I'll tell you a part of your history
that you'll not have learned from Miss Eunice."

I put my hands on my hips and stamped a small, angry foot.
"I don't want a history lesson. I want to talk about Sasha."

"This is about Sasha," the Count assured me.

"How can it be?"

"Sit down," the Count told me, "and you'll find out."

I sat, uncomfortably and aggressively, on the edge of the
footstool.

"Many years ago," the Count began, "long before your

grandfather's grandfather's time, the people of Uglich were called to the town square by the frantic ringing of the cathedral bell. Prince Dmitri, the Tsar's half-brother and heir, was staying in the town at the time, and the bell was to announce his sudden death."

"How does Sasha—"

"You'll soon see. A rumour spread that Dmitri had been killed on the orders of the Regent, Boris Godunov, so that Godunov could rule once the Tsar was dead. The townspeople went mad. They killed the Prince's alleged murderers and looted houses. Are you following this, Anna?"

"Most of it."

"A commission was sent to Uglich to investigate—"

"What's a commission?"

The Count smiled, warmly this time. "You're so clever that I sometimes forget just how young you are," he said. "A commission is a number of wise men who meet to decide certain things. This particular commission was sent to Uglich to find out how Prince Dmitri died. And do you know what they discovered?"

"No."

"That he hadn't been murdered at all. He'd died during a fit. The townspeople felt very foolish. And the Regent was faced with a problem, just as I was with the *muhziks*."

"What problem?"

"He didn't want to punish the townspeople. He badly wanted their support. But the death of his servants had to be avenged. So he sent orders to the commission – which is not so different from a court – as to where the blame should lie. Can you guess what those orders said?"

"No."

"Think! Who, or what, started the rioting?"

The townspeople came to the square because they had heard the bell ringing and once they were there . . . "The bell!" I said.

"Exactly. The bell. It called them to the square in the first place, so it was to blame. It was sentenced to transportation to Siberia. It's still there. Do you understand the story, Anna?"

54

I did, but I struggled desperately to find the right words to express myself.

"It was more con . . . con . . ."

"Convenient?"

". . . convenient to punish the bell than to punish the townspeople."

"And that's just what happened here. Peter is guilty. He took advantage of *muzhik* unrest to burn down my barn because he thought it would put me more in his power. And his plan has worked. I've lost equipment and livestock and I've no money to replace them. I must borrow from him – there is no one else who would lend to me. And how could I do that if he was in Siberia?"

"You could just take his money."

The Count laughed. "He's not foolish enough to keep his money in the *mir*. Besides, I understand Peter. He's a greedy man, and I can deal with greed. But Sasha? Sasha's too honest. He's a man who works for the benefit of all, a great bell who rallies the people. I don't want him here, and neither does Peter, who will soon own the whole village now that Sasha can no longer protect it. So you see, it is far better for both of us that Sasha should be the one to go."

My heart was thumping and my face burned red. "It's not fair!" I screamed.

"Of course it's not fair. Life is not fair."

"I hate you!" I told him. "I want to go home. I want to go back to the *mir*."

The Count sprang to his feet. He was going to hit me like he'd hit Sasha, but I didn't care. I wanted to be hurt. I wanted to suffer as Sasha suffered. And I would fight back, kicking with small feet, scratching with small nails.

He didn't strike me. Instead, he grabbed my hand in his and dragged me roughly out of his study, along the corridor and down the stairs. Servants stood open-mouthed as we rushed past, but I don't think he even saw them. Only when we had reached the veranda did we stop. Even then the Count did not release my hand, and though he was squeezing it so tightly that it hurt, I refused to show my pain, refused to ask *him* for anything.

55

"The *mir* is over there," he said, pointing. "But where is London, Anna?"

"In England," I replied, mystified. "It's the capital city."

He let go of my hand at last. "Write 'London' in the air for me, Anna?"

"Why should I?"

"Just do it!"

"In English or in Russian?"

"English."

I traced out the letters with my finger.

"How far is London from here?" the Count asked. "Thirty *versts*?"

I laughed, in spite of myself. "Of course not. It's thousands of *versts*."

"Does your mother know that?"

"My mother doesn't even know there is a place called London."

"No, she doesn't, does she? Go back to the *mir* if you want to, Anna, I won't stop you. But if you do go, you can never come back here again. There'll be no Miss Eunice for you. No schoolroom. Nothing. You'll be as much an exile as Sasha is."

Just two days earlier he had begged me with his eyes not to give his wife cause to send me back to the village. Now he didn't need to beg. Now he was confident that I wouldn't – couldn't – give up the great treasure which he had made possible. And I knew that he was right. I felt tears of shame and humiliation running down my face. I took one last look in the direction of the *mir*, then turned and fled back into the house.

Chapter Six

By ten o'clock, I am ready to face the world. Leaning on my stick, I open the front door and make my way painfully towards Ali's grocery store. Today the narrow sky of London is almost clear. Frost has formed a smooth, glittering skin on the pavement and the cold stings my cheeks. Careful, old woman! Don't slip now. Don't shatter any of your already crumbling bones. Once you let yourself be taken to hospital, you'll never again be allowed to return to your 'residence' in Matlock Road.

I reach Ali's shop and open the door. Ali gives me a gap-toothed smile. "Earlier today, Princess."

Am I? Was my ancient body a little more efficient this morning? Another small victory. Making my way over to the freezer chest, I'm already starting to feel better.

"I am sick and tired of the bloody weather in this bloody country," Ali tells Winston, his dreadlocked assistant. "I will sell the shop and go back to Pakistan."

"Got any beaches there?" Winston asks.

"Very fine beaches," Ali says defensively, as if Winston had meant to cast a slur. "Very fine beaches indeed. All around Karachi."

"We got beautiful beaches in Jamaica. Miles and miles of 'em."

"Miles and miles in Pakistan, too."

The conversation continues as I search through the freezer, unable to decide which is best value – pork chops or mince.

". . . and the end of Ramadan is a big party, not like the bloody poor affairs they have round here."

". . . should see a Jamaican carnival, man. Leave Notting Hill standin'. Steel bands? Let me tell you . . ."

57

It's only talk. They'll never go home, either of them. And it's strange to me how this talk seems to focus on landmarks – special times like festivals and celebrations – as if the rest of their lives were merely journeys between these mountain tops and had no significance of their own.

Yet who am I, of all people, to criticize them for that? What do *I* think of when I cast my mind back to the years between entering the Big House and my marriage? Do I remember my gradual mastery of the written word, my growing command of arithmetic and geography? Do I recall the slow filling out of my peasant frame and mind until I became, physically and mentally, one of the pampered? No! It's the peaks at which I gaze. Easter, Epiphany, the grand ball, the wolf hunt.

Perhaps that's not so unreasonable after all. It is at these peaks that we have time to stop, to reflect on where we've been and look ahead to where we're going. And perhaps, because we have this small respite, we can take the time to *choose* to make things happen, as I did in the barn with Misha, in the Easter of 1907.

Oh, those Russian Easters. How can anyone brought up in this prepackaged, convenience food society ever begin to understand what is was like in a Russian household – even a humble one – at Easter? Seven weeks we fasted – and then we went wild. *There* was a feast to rival the end of a Pakistan Ramadan, Ali. *There* was a carnival which, despite the absence of steel drums, could match any of Winston's sun-soaked memories.

Excitement was already in the air when we walked to church on the Sunday before the Resurrection. In Palestine, they had waved palms that day eighteen hundred and seventy-four years earlier, but we carried catkins, a symbol that, after the death of winter, the land would be reborn and flourish once more.

In the week which followed Pussy Willow Sunday the staff of the Big House threw themselves into the feverish, frantic preparations for Easter Day. In the kitchen, *paskhas* – special Easter cheeses – were being made. I watched, fascinated, as the servants filled a large tub with wheyless curds, added butter, whipped cream, sugar and vanilla, and then stirred – endlessly.

"Is that enough, Zossim?" I heard a tired servant girl ask after she had agitated the mixture perhaps five hundred times.

And pear-headed Zossim, a tyrant in his little empire, inspected the tub and found that it wasn't.

Hours passed, more stirring – and more – before the cheese was mixed to the cook's satisfaction, and could be poured into the muslin-lined cones which were kept in the cool pantry.

Nor was the bakery a safe haven from the madness of the kitchen. The Count's confectioner baked and iced, baked and iced, turning out scores of *kulich* cakes decorating them with 'KV', the first two letters of the words *Khristos Voskryese* – Christ has risen. Cakes for the family, cakes for the guests, cakes for the servants – cakes for the whole world.

What smells filled the air. Almonds, saffron, nutmeg, sunflower oil – blending together for a moment, then drifting apart. And how we worked with Miss Eunice in the schoolroom, painting the Easter eggs – green eggs, red eggs, yellow eggs, eggs of every colour and mixture of colours imaginable.

The eggs went on the Easter table, but they did not sit there alone. There were hams, joints of glazed veal, baby sturgeon in aspic jelly, salmon, caviar, pickled mushrooms, salted herrings . . . each with its own special place, all part of the celebration of the Saviour's triumph which would go on for several days.

On Holy Thursday, the family and guests rode to evening service in the *lineika*. Night had already fallen, but the church, lit by the candles that all members of the congregation carried in their hands, was bright as day. We stood in silence while the priest read twelve passages from the Gospel on the Passion of Jesus Christ, and impious little Anna found her eyes, and her mind, wandering.

I gazed at the stony faces of the *muhziks*. What did these people, who saw nothing beyond the *mir*, make of the story of the strange man who died in a hot land they couldn't even picture? How much of what they were doing now was merely habit, something to be endured, uncomplainingly, just as war and famine had to be endured?

My mother and father were there, along with all the rest. When Papa saw me looking at him, he turned his eyes to the ground – just as if I was one of the *dvorianstvo*. But Mama didn't look away, and I could see that she was crying, though I was not sure whether they were tears of pride or sorrow.

On Good Friday, we stood on the same spot and watched the life-sized *icon* of Christ being lifted from the Cross. The face *was* Sasha's, and like Christ, he, too, had suffered for these peasants. It was nearly a year since he had been dragged off in chains to his Siberian exile. I wondered if he was all right and knew, of course, that he wasn't.

The *icon* was laid at the gate of the Holy of Holies. We stepped forward and placed flowers at its feet. Then it was the *muhziks'* turn, and they shuffled forward and laid their offerings. They were paying homage now, I thought, because they knew that Christ had triumphed. But how many of them would have helped Him at the time, and how many would have deserted Him, just as they deserted Sasha?

After the midnight mass on Saturday, the *muhziks* went home to collect the food which the priest would bless. When they returned, they were weighed down with cheeses, sausages and suckling pigs. They had gone forty-nine days without eggs, meat or dairy products and when they looked down at their hoards, their mouths salivated.

The blackness beyond the church windows slowly changed to a soft blue and finally became a bright crimson as the morning sun began its climb.

"Christ is risen!" the priest intoned.

"Indeed He is risen!" the *muhziks* chanted, in much the same tone of voice as they would use eleven years later to proclaim, "The Tsar is dead! The Tsar is dead!"

The harshest fast of the year was over. The longest orgy of drunkenness was just about to begin.

We sat around the Easter table, the Count, the Countess, the house guests and we children, all eating as only Russians can. It was a warm day and the windows were open. Occasionally,

60

when the wind blew in the right direction, we could hear the sounds of celebration wafting in from the *mir*.

I could picture what was going on there. Having had their fill of food by now, the peasants would be attacking the vodka, not simply with the fierce dedication of the men sitting around our table, but with a passion which verged on insanity.

"Do you think your father will be paralytic yet, Anna?" the Countess asked me.

How, I wondered, was she always able to read my mind so easily? "I . . . I don't know," I stuttered.

"Don't you? I do! He'll be lying under the table at the tavern, covered in mud, with his face buried in his own vomit."

"He works very hard," I protested. He needed to. The money the Count had given him for me had been long since frittered away.

"Our horses work hard," the Countess said viciously. "So do our oxen. But yet they behave less like animals than the *muhziks*."

I glanced nervously up the table. If the Count had heard, there'd be trouble. He wouldn't publicly rebuke his wife, but later he would talk to her and she would find a way to make me suffer for it.

"Don't you agree, Anna?" the Countess persisted.

I breathed a sigh of relief. The Count was in deep conversation with one of his guests.

"It's bad manners not to speak when you're spoken to! I asked you whether you agreed that the behaviour of the *muhziks* would put most animals to shame?"

The Countess was out for blood, and I would get a beating whatever I said. Well, I told myself, I'd survived them before, and I would survive the one I'd earn by my answer.

"I've had enough to eat," said Misha, my timid protector. "May I go for a walk, mother? And may I take Anna with me?"

He spoke mildly, hesitantly, but it was enough to deflect the Countess's wrath away from me and on to her son.

"You've hardly eaten anything," she said. "Can't you do anything right, anything manly? Look at the body on your

61

father, and then look at your own. Have you seen yourself in a mirror? You're ten years old, but you have the frame of a child of seven."

It was cruel, and it wasn't true. There was nothing Misha could do about his slight frame, sensitive features and long, artistic hands. All the food in the world couldn't have made him grow to be like his father. But fairness had never been the Countess's forte, and over the time I'd lived in the Big House I'd seen her attitude to Misha change from tolerant affection to virtual loathing.

It was because of me, of course, and I knew it, even then. The more he tried to shield me, the more her dislike of him increased. Ah, Misha, what sacrifices you made for me. What a hero you made out of yourself, *for me*. What would have happened if I'd never met you? Would you still be alive now, an old man surrounded by the beautiful things he had spent his life lovingly collecting?

"I'm sorry, mother," Misha said. "But I *have* had enough. May I take Anna out?"

I watched the Countess's face twist as vindictiveness fought out an ugly, losing battle with disgust. "Get out of my sight," she said finally. "You make me sick, both of you."

We walked through the orchard, still muddy after the thaw. Misha stopped, suddenly, at the base of one of the cherry trees. "Look!"

He was pointing at the first violets of spring, purple against the brown mud, new life rising from among the dead leaves. He bent down, plucked one, and gave it to me. "This will be our last Easter together," he said as I held the delicate flower in the palm of my hand.

"Our last Easter?" I asked, panic in my voice. "Are they sending me away?"

"No," Misha said. "It is I who am going away. In the summer I'll join the Corps of Pages."

"The Corps of Pages? Like in a book?"

Misha laughed. He had a light, infectious laugh on the few occasions he found anything in this cruel, hard world to amuse him. "It's a military school. An exclusive one. I'm very lucky to be going there. And very happy."

He spoke almost as if he were delivering a speech he'd learned by heart in an effort to convince himself, and me, that it was a good idea. Poor Misha. If anyone was ever unsuited for army life, it was him.

"You look upset," he said, and though he sounded sorry that he'd distressed me, he was pleased, too, that I *cared* enough to be distressed.

"I'm more than upset," I told him. "I . . ."

I felt a sickness, an emptiness, which started in my stomach and slowly spread, like a cancer, until it gripped my whole body. Life without Misha was unthinkable. It wasn't that I'd miss his protection – his efforts to shield me from his mother often angered her so much that the final punishment was more severe than it would have been without his intervention. But I would miss *him*. Now that Sasha was gone, he was the only friend I had left in the world. He was a sweet, earnest boy who cared for me – so it seemed at the time – simply because I needed to be cared for.

I felt a sudden, deep urge to give him something – a present. Yet what could I, a poor *muhzik* girl dependent on his father's charity, offer him?

It was instinct which made me take his hand and lead him across the orchard towards the barn. "What are we going to do?" he asked.

I wasn't sure I knew myself. "I want us to be alone for a while," I said. "I just want us to spend some time together, so we can remember it when you're a soldier and I'm here all alone."

Or maybe I didn't say that at all. Perhaps it is just looking back at it with the eyes of an adult that I feel it is what I *should have* said.

We reached the barn. Inside, it was warm from the heat of the animals' bodies, and the oxen shifted slightly in their stalls as the door clicked closed. I led Misha down the aisle to the empty end stall. We climbed the bars and jumped down onto the prickly straw.

Was I trying to seduce him? I don't think so. I knew how

63

baby animals were made, knew that girls like Natulia did the same thing for their own pleasure. But that had nothing to do with Misha and me. I didn't want to make love, have sex, whatever you want to call it – I just wanted to be close to him.

We sat in silence, side by side, holding hands. The scent of the beasts and the sickly-sweet smell of the sweating straw enveloped us like a familiar, comfortable cloak. The sounds around us – the gentle lowing of the oxen, the muted crackling as they pawed the straw, a cockerel crowing in the distance – were the ones we had grown up with. And yet I felt that *something* had changed, that somehow I had disturbed the balance of things as they used to be, only five minutes before.

I looked at Misha, wearing his first frock coat. I imagined how I would look to him in my knee-length polka dot frock with a big red bow at the back and smaller ones on the shoulders. We were dressed like adults, but we were not really grown up, and we both felt lost in this strange new world I had forced upon us.

"Would you mind if I kissed you?" Misha said finally.

Poor Misha! As if he needed to ask!

Children in this silent land of my exile know all about kissing – and so much more – almost from the time they learn to walk. Television, that magic box which dominates their living rooms – and their lives – provides them with all the answers. Their own first kisses may be hesitant, but at least they've seen such things enacted a thousand times before in dramas, soap operas – even commercials. Misha and I had no such guidance. That first kiss was a step into virgin territory, and it frightened us.

Misha drew me awkwardly towards him. Then, placing a hand over each of my ears, tilted my head slightly to the side. Our lips touched. Our first kiss was softer than I'd imagined it would be, almost like the brushing of a feather. I could taste his breath, sweet from the Easter cakes. I could feel his heart, beating rapidly against me.

Suddenly, it was no longer a gentle brush of lips. Misha's

mouth was half open and he was pressing hard. My tongue, as if it had a will of its own, left my mouth and began to explore his.

Misha's hands stroked my back and then he gently pushed me away from him. I looked into his sensitive eyes and saw that he was crying. "I love you," he said.

"And I love you."

With tentative fingers, he reached forward and began to unfasten the front of my frock. When it was open to the waist he put his hands inside, fought his way through my undergarments and began to caress my young breasts.

"You're beautiful. Do you know that?"

I'd never even thought about it before. We peasant girls are valued for our ability to work hard and our strong, child-bearing hips. Beauty, as my comrades of later years would say endlessly, was a bourgeois concept.

"I want to take all your clothes off," Misha said uncertainly. "I want to see you totally naked. Will you let me?"

"Yes."

He stripped off my dress and my underwear, my white stockings and my shoes. Russians are not self-conscious about their bodies. Though groups of men and women bathe separately in the river, it's always within eyesight of each other. So why did I become so shy then, aware that my breasts had only just begun to bud, that my new pubic hair was a very inadequate thatch for what it was intended to cover? Perhaps it was the way he looked at me which made me feel so unsure. His gaze said that I was the most marvellous, wonderful, delicate thing he had ever seen. No body, no matter how perfect, could have lived up to the look in Misha's eyes that day.

"I . . . I want to get undressed too," he said, and I did not object.

He was clumsier with his own clothes than he'd been with mine, and I had to help him with his buttons. It wasn't until he was completely naked that I really looked at him – his slim chest, each and every rib clearly visible; his slender, young hips; his pubic hair, even fluffier and less substantial than mine. And there, between his legs, a boy's penis which had hardened as if it belonged to a man.

"Could we . . .?" he asked.

Could we make love? He seemed physically able, and I was willing – there's no doubt about that. I didn't know what it would be like, or why I wanted to do it with him, but now I realised that this had been what I'd been waiting for since I took his hand and led him towards the barn.

"You've picked the right place, Misha," a harsh voice said from out of nowhere. "If you're going to rut with that little sow, you might as well do it in a barn."

I looked up, my eyes wide with fear, my heart thumping furiously. Mariamna was leaning on the bars of the stall. The skin was tight across her cheeks, her mouth was twisted in a sneer of contempt. Her eyes blazed with disgust, but there was more in them than that. There was a sort of satisfaction – almost a perverted kind of happiness. She was nothing more nor less than a smaller version of her mother.

What we had been doing had seemed so natural, so right, I hadn't really thought about it. Mariamna's expression changed all that. I realized the way she saw it was the way other people, people who knew nothing about Misha and me, would see it too. I felt unclean and ashamed.

"Mariamna . . ." Misha mumbled.

"Just like animals," the girl spat. "What a pity you've only got two tits, Anna. However will you manage when you drop Misha's litter?"

She turned and was gone.

"She'll tell Mama," Misha said. "She'll tell her right away. What can we do? Where can we go? They'll send you back to the *mir*. They'll make me . . . make me . . . I don't know what they'll make me do."

As Misha's panic rose, my own started to ebb. "She won't tell your mother," I assured Misha.

"She will. She will. She hates you."

"I know, but she doesn't want me thrown out of the house. She wants me where she can keep on punishing me. So don't worry that she'll tell – worry about her price for keeping quiet."

*   *   *

66

We started paying the next day.

"If we have *borscht* for lunch, you're to leave half of it," Mariamna told me. "If it's anything else, you're to eat all you're given, and then ask for second helpings."

"But why?" I asked.

"Because I say so!"

She made demands on Misha, too. "You're to tell father that you don't feel well enough to ride today."

"What if he—"

"Just tell him you're sick. *Do you understand?*"

"Yes, Mariamna."

She decreed that we all went to the lake and made Misha take his clothes off. "Look at him!" she ordered me. "Do you like what you see?"

"I . . . I . . ."

I didn't know what to reply. How could explain to her that I did like Misha's body, not for it's own sake but simply because it was the body that belonged to Misha.

"Get into the lake, Misha."

Misha waded into the water, up his knees, up to his thighs. He crossed his arms over his chest and gasped.

"Further, Misha."

Up to his waist, up to his chest. He turned, as if expecting Mariamna to tell him that that was far enough.

"Further, Misha."

Up to his neck.

"You're to bend your knees until your head is completely under the water," Mariamna said. "When I want you to come up, I'll throw a stone into the lake. If you surface before that, I'm going straight to Mama. Do you understand?"

Misha's disembodied head bobbed for a second on the surface of the lake, and then was gone. I lowered my own head and began to count silently to myself. One hundred, two hundred, three hundred . . . I had reached nine thousand before I dared look at Mariamna. She smiled, triumphantly, as if that was what she'd been waiting for.

"Do you love him?" she asked me.

"Yes."

She snorted and turned her back on me.

67

Nine thousand one hundred, nine thousand two hundred, nine thousand three hundred . . .

"No!" I screamed. "No! I don't love him. I don't love him at all."

Mariamna turned her head again, maddeningly slowly this time, until she was looking me in the eye once more. "Do you really mean it?" she asked. "Or are you just saying it?"

I wondered how much longer Misha could stay under the water. Perhaps even now he was blacking out. "I really mean it," I promised her. "I hate him. I swear on my mother's life."

Mariamna hesitated, glancing first at the few bubbles which found their erratic way to the surface, and then at me. She bent down, picked up a pebble and threw it into the water. It landed very near where Misha had submerged himself. The water rippled, but he didn't appear. And the bubbles had stopped.

I ran into the water. My dress was slowing me down and I wished I had the time to take it off, but there was no time . . . no time.

I reached the spot where Misha had been standing and dove. Weed floated in front of my eyes and I brushed it away with the slow-motioned impatience which is all that is possible under water. I could see Misha, lying on the bed of the lake. I managed to get my hands under his armpits, and by a combination of swimming and purely desperate kicking tugged him into the shallow water. I pulled him onto the shore, gasping for breath myself. Once he was lying on his side, his mouth opened, and a mixture of water and slime poured out.

"I'll . . . be . . . all . . . right . . . in a . . . minute," he managed to gasp.

I looked up at Mariamna. She was standing as still as if she'd been carved out of rock. But statues do not cry – and tears were flooding down Mariamna's cheeks.

Summer came, Misha's last summer at home, but we drew no pleasure from it. Mariamna never again tried any trick as dangerous as the one she'd pulled by the lake, but she had a fertile mind, and it was easy for her to come up with a series of more minor torments. Worst of all was her strict order that Misha and I were never – never – to be alone together.

And then, the berries were ripening, and it was time for Misha to go. I stood in the driveway, one early autumn morning before the frost had melted away, and watched as the *drozhky* set off for the nearest railway station. Misha turned once and waved sadly back at me, but I hadn't the heart or the energy to return the wave. Even before the *drozhky* had disappeared, the Big House, despite Miss Eunice and all the servants, was already beginning to seem a cold and lonely place.

Mariamna continued to persecute me every way she could, but her petty tasks and impositions were easier to bear now that Misha was in Petersburg, now I knew that he was not suffering too. I prayed that the Corps of Pages was not being too hard on his sensitive soul, and ached for his return the next holiday.

He didn't come home for Christmas.

"The weather's rather hazardous for travelling, so he's staying with family in the capital," the Count said airily, as if he weren't actually announcing the most tragic news in the world.

His words had robbed Christmas of all its magic. I looked at the tree, gold-painted nuts tied to some branches, Crimean apples and tangerines weighing down others. I tried to admire the candles burning away and the bright paper crackers hanging so tantalizingly before me. It was no good. Without Misha, everything was pointless.

Chapter Seven

How my life had changed since I entered the Big House! The small girl who'd believed that the Tsar lived only a day's walk away now travelled by first class train to spend the Season in France. Twice!

On borrowed money, we stayed at the Hotel de Califone in Nice. While our motherland froze under feet of snow, we basked in the mild air of the Mediterranean. In the mornings, we walked in Chiplatz Park, high above the town, and looked down at the sea, the endless blue sea. In the afternoons, we took tea in the Palm Court. Yes, it was fine life we led, but even all that luxury – all that pampering – could never compensate me for the loneliness I felt, could never fill the gaping hole in a soul which yearned to be loved.

Countess Olga's hatred of me only grew as I went from triumph to triumph in the schoolroom, outstripping her daughter with effortless ease. Mariamna herself continued her campaign of making my life as unpleasant as possible

And the Count? To his wife and daughter's disgust he watched my progress with interest and discussed my lessons with me, often talking as if I were another adult. How desperately I wanted to love and respect him. But I couldn't. He had sold his soul to Countess Olga in return for her dowry, he had mortgaged it again to Peter and sent Sasha to Siberia. Try as I might, I couldn't make a god out of him.

Even with Miss Eunice, it was sometimes hard to find real affection. She knew as well as I did that any kindness she showed me would immediately be matched by a show of cruelty by the Countess, and though I was willing to pay the price, she was reluctant to do anything that would bring me pain.

Oh, Misha, I used to think as I sat at the dining table, surrounded by people but completely alone, why did you ever have to leave home?

After my day with the family, I would descend the stairs to spend the night on the ground floor with the servants, who had once been *my* people, but were not any longer. "The Mediterranean's so exciting," I told Natulia one evening. "You look out to sea and you know that on the other side of it are people completely different from both the French and the Russians. Arabs and black men. Camel drivers and ivory hunters."

As I spoke, I saw her eyes glaze over, and realized I'd lost her. If I'd been older, more experienced, I would've tried harder to re-establish a point of contact between us. But at the time I didn't understand what was going on. If Natulia couldn't follow me, I argued, it was because she was too lazy to. I didn't realize then that learning to read had done so much more than give me the ability to transform mysterious symbols into words. I didn't realize then how different from Natulia's view of the world mine had become.

And if I had difficulties with the servants, who at least lived on the fringes of my new life, how much harder it was to understand, and be understood by, the *muhziks* in the *mir*. It was like being in a foreign country where the language was the same, but the meaning attached to the words was so different that I could only hazard a guess at what they were saying. I became more and more discouraged, and after the summer of 1910 – when I was robbed of the one real reason left for those visits – I stopped going at all.

It was a peasant boy who brought the message which sent me on that last, frantic journey to the *mir*. I was sitting on the veranda when he arrived, red-faced and gasping for air.

"Your mother sent me," he said. "She's got the fever."

Alarm tingled through my body like an electric shock. "When did she catch it? Today?"

The boy shook his head. "Two Sundays ago."

How long was it since I'd been to the *mir*? Three weeks? Four? More than that? And if she'd been ill for so long . . .

"How sick is she?" I demanded.

The boy looked down at his bare feet. "I think she's dying."

I saw one the grooms crossing the cobbled yard in front of the stables. "Volodya," I shouted, "saddle my horse. Quickly, man, I'm in a hurry!"

He was a good groom, one of the best we had, and in no time at all my horse was saddled and I was galloping towards the village. "Please God, let me be in time," I prayed guiltily.

There were no anxious friends gathered around the door of my parents' *izbá*. The sick can't work, but everyone else can, and at harvest time they have to. I tethered my horse to the rail and pushed open the door. The *izbá* seemed small, dark and claustrophobic. I wondered how I could ever have lived there, how I could have stood the stench of animals and dung, of clothes which were washed, at best, once a week.

Mama was lying on the stove, a small, pathetic bundle wrapped in a rough blanket. She was perfectly still and her eyes were closed.

"Oh God," I whispered to myself. "Oh God, I'm too late."

I bent over her and could feel her faint, wispy breath against my cheek. I stepped back and stood in silence – just watching her. Her beauty, in full bloom a only few years earlier, had withered. She looked like an old hag, but so did every woman in the *mir* beyond the age of thirty-five.

While I had gone for horse rides or sat on the veranda reading a book, my mother had toiled, hour after back-breaking hour, in the fields. While I had eaten food so rich that it had once made me sick, my mother had survived on cucumbers and black bread.

The Soviet saw to it that everyone got equal shares whether they were *muhziks* or aristocrats, Sasha had told me. But the Soviet, like Sasha himself, was only a memory, and for women like my mother mere survival was as great a struggle as it had always been.

She stirred, and opened her eyes. "Anna?"

It was little more than a croak.

"I'm here, Mama."

"Come closer to me."

I reached over to her and took her work-roughened hand in my soft one. "How do you feel, Mama?"

"I'm dying, Anna."

A loud snoring sound made me turn my head. My father was lying on the floor next to the bench. Drunk!

"I can't see you properly, Anna," my mother wheezed. "It's too dark in here. Go into the light."

I stepped past my unconscious father and walked to the open door. Mama began to move slowly and agonizingly, and I realized that she was trying to sit up. I made a move to help her.

"Stay where you are!" Her voice was weak, yet so commanding that I froze. I watched as she struggled up onto one elbow, then stood self-consciously as she examined me like a fly under a microscope. "You look like one of the *dvorianstvo*," she said finally. "You won't grow old and ugly like me, Anna, there's too much of *him* in you."

"Mama, I—"

"How many women can say they've given birth to a lady?" my mother asked. "I can die happy. Enjoy *your* life, Anna. Live like the Empress herself. Enjoy it all – the clothes, the jewels – *everything*."

The clothes! The jewels! None of that mattered. It was in the schoolroom that the real treasure lay.

My mother's sacrifice had bought me knowledge. I wanted to explain that to her, to make her realize what a great gift she'd given me. And it broke my heart to know that however hard I tried, it would never make any sense to her.

I started to walk back across the room to the stove. If I couldn't make her understand, I could at least show her how much I loved her.

"Don't move," my mother ordered.

"I want to hold you, Mama."

"And I want to *look* at you. I sent your brothers to the fields, I let Papa get drunk. All of it so we could be alone. All of it so I'd be sure that the last thing I saw before I died would be you."

"Mama—"

"You're above me, Anna. I wasn't meant to hold you, I was meant to admire you from a distance."

"Mama, it's not true."

"Let a dying woman keep her dreams," my mother said. "Let her believe what she wants to believe."

I felt helpless and ashamed, but I did as she asked me – she was entitled to that.

For perhaps five minutes we were a frozen tableau; myself framed in the doorway, my mother weakly propped up on the stove, my father snoring drunkenly between us. Then my mother spoke once more. "Be a lady, Anna," she said. "Always be a lady."

Her eyes closed and her elbow gave way beneath her. The rattle in her throat seemed as loud as a cannon bombardment. By the time I had reached her, she was already dead.

I rode back to the Big House slowly. My horse sensed my mood and took heavy, mournful steps. *My* horse. The animal was mine, a gift from the Count.

"How many peasant girls have a horse of their own?" I could almost hear my dead mother say.

It had taken my mother's death to make me realize how much I'd changed. When I heard she was sick, my first reaction hadn't been to run to the *mir*, it'd been to order – order – one of the grooms to saddle my horse. How adaptable children are. And how quick to take things for granted.

The Count was standing by the stable door, almost as if he had been waiting for me. "I've just heard about your mother," he said. "Is it all over?"

"Yes."

Volodya the groom took my horse from me and led it away to be rubbed down.

"I'm very sorry," the Count said, and he sounded as if he really was. "When she was younger she was very—"

"I want to move," I interrupted him. "I want a bedroom on the second floor, like Misha and Mariamna."

The look that could almost have been grief disappeared from the Count's face, and was replaced by a troubled one.

74

"Is one of the girls in the dormitory annoying you?" he asked. "Tell me who she is, and I'll discipline her."

"It's not a question of servants annoying me," I told him. "I'm different from them. They feel uncomfortable in my presence. And I've earned a room of my own."

Concern had become panic. The Count took in a deep gulp of air to steady himself. "Walk with me," he said shakily.

We strolled through the orchard. The blossom had gone and the first fruit was ripening. Birds chirped in the trees and invisible insects buzzed in the lush, green grass. Everything was in perfect peace and harmony – except for the two of us.

The Count's hands wouldn't keep still. First, they kept clenching and unclenching. Then, they rose to his head and his fingers raked through his hair. Finally, they fastened on to his jacket, where they tugged so hard that one of the buttons came away. "You know why you're here, don't you, Anna?" he asked.

"Here? In the orchard?"

"Not in the orchard," he replied impatiently. "In the Big House."

"No. I don't know."

The Count stopped walking. He placed his hands on my shoulders and turned me round until I was facing him. He looked deep into my eyes. "You really don't know?" he asked, incredulously. "None of the servants has ever told you?"

"Told me what?"

He opened his mouth as if he were about to say something else, then snapped it tightly closed again. Why didn't I press him? Why didn't I make him tell me? Because, I suppose, I didn't want to know the answer. Because even the *thought* of an answer frightened me.

"But you do know that my wife hates you?" he said. "And you're too intelligent not to realize that every time I give you something, like your horse, she . . . she . . ."

"Finds a way to make you pay for it?" I suggested.

He laughed, bitterly. "Yes, finds a way to make me pay for it. As long as you live with the servants, my wife can persuade herself that you're one of them. If you move upstairs, she'll be forced to recognize the fact that

75

however much she dislikes it, you're part of the family."

"I know."

"At the very best, she'll make us both suffer for that. At the worst, she might be able to force me to send you away." He waved his arms in exasperation. "For God's sake, Anna, you already have all the other trappings of a privileged life. Does it really matter to you where you spend the few hours of the day when you're asleep?"

"It matters," I said. "I've been a good pupil, I've worked hard to master my studies and learn the ways of the house. I've become *what you wanted me to be*, haven't I?"

"Yes," he admitted. "Yes, you have."

"I've done so well that anyone who didn't know us would take me for your daughter rather than a peasant girl you had brought into your house. I deserve a room on the second floor."

"And if my wife simply won't allow it?"

"If she won't allow it, then she won't have to *throw* me out – because I'll leave."

"You'd do that?" the Count asked. "You'd leave the house? And where would you go? Back to the *mir*? Back to the life of a peasant?"

"If no one else will have me, then, yes, I'll go back to the *mir*," I told him.

It wasn't too late to change my mind, I thought. It wasn't too late to tell him, truthfully, that it didn't matter to me where I slept. But I couldn't bring myself to do it.

"Our duty to the past is a terrible thing, Anna," the Count said. "It's a burden we carry throughout our lives. Look at all this." He swung his arm round in an arc. "Do you think I'd have acted as I have done if hadn't been for the estate, for the responsibilities which were passed on to me by my illustrious ancestors? Without all this, I'd have been free. Without all this, I could've done what I really wanted to." He paused, and pulled another button free. "Was I betraying my family honour the day I took you in?" he asked in a rush. "Or was I at last proving that I could have some honour which was entirely my own?"

"I don't understand," I said.

"Of course you don't. How could you, when there seems to be a conspiracy to keep the truth from you, a conspiracy that even I daren't . . . Do you remember what you were doing the first time we met?"

"Could I ever forget it? I was arguing with Zossim over the price of my strawberries."

"I knew about you long before that day, and I did nothing. But once I'd seen you, I had no choice but to take you in. You had such a fine spirit. I couldn't let that be crushed by the poverty and ignorance of the *mir*." He laughed ironically. "So I can't really complain when that same spirit causes me a few difficulties with my wife, can I? You'll get your room, Anna. But whether you keep it or not is quite another question."

He turned and walked quickly away.

A feeling of faintness swept over me, and I clutched at the cherry tree for support. What a fool I was being, I thought. What a terrible gamble I was taking. I could lose the schoolroom, my Aladdin's cave where I spent my days soaking up knowledge as a dry plant gulps in water. And what did I stand to win? Only status, the outward trappings of rank – things which were totally unimportant to me.

But they *were* important to my dead mother.

"Are you happy, Mama?" I asked softly, looking up at the bright blue sky. "Are you proud of me?"

The room was mine, though I never learned what price the Count was forced to pay. When we had parties, I no longer dressed in the servants' quarters, squinting into a cracked mirror as I adjusted my frock. Instead, I stood before a full-length glass whilst the maids fussed with my gown.

"We'll never get it right unless you can learn to keep still, Miss Anna," they complained.

It was always *Miss* Anna now.

Once dressed, there was no climb from the dormitory to the first floor, but a regal progress *down* the stairs to the ballroom where the party was being held – just like Mama would have wanted.

What parties they were! Even the expensive dinners which

77

my great-granddaughters throw for the bosses of their yuppie husbands – and which they brag to me about incessantly – are as nothing compared to the parties at the Big House. Our guests didn't start to yawn at midnight and phone for a mini-cab at one – they stayed for days!

The parties varied in size and composition. Sometimes they'd include the Count's relatives from Petersburg, a bunch of time-servers and pensioners who, in their greed, would have put a pack of ravening wolves to shame. Sometimes, though never, of course, at the same time, Countess Olga's family descended on us. They were a stiff-necked, disapproving group of people who couldn't look at one of the Count's heirlooms without mentally pricing it. During the hunting season, neighbours – which in Russia can mean any one who lives within a hundred miles – often stayed with us and occasionally we were graced with the presence of a grand duke or government minister.

So many parties, so much extravagance, at a time when more and more of the Count's lands were being mortgaged or sold off. They all blur together in my mind, those grand affairs where pounds of jewels were worn and mountains of food consumed.

No, that isn't quite true. I remember one very clearly, the one the Americans were invited to. They were called Mr and Mrs Hiram T. Block, and they hailed from Cleveland, Ohio. Mr Block was a bulky man who wore his Savile Row three-piece suits as if they were overalls – but he looked no fool. Mrs Block was 'a faded blonde' whose conversation seemed limited to only two things – sables and Fabergé.

"They're very rich, Anna," the Count confided in me, "and probably," he sniffed, "very Jewish."

"Why are they here?"

"Block wants to buy my forest."

"You should be careful," I warned him. "You're no man of business, are you?"

"Of course not," the Count said, sounding slightly offended. "I'm a gentleman. But that may be to my advantage. The Americans have no aristocracy of their own, so they're like children in the presence of the foreign variety. Once we get down to business, I'll soon make him feel ashamed for wishing to haggle with a man from such a noble family as mine."

"You'll need help," I told him.

"And I'll have help. I've asked an old friend of mine, Prince Mayakovsky, to stay with us. He'll be arriving later today."

Prince Mayakovsky! How like the Count to choose another aristocrat as his advisor, and probably one who, like he himself, had frittered away most of his land.

"You'd be better off letting Peter negotiate the deal for a commission," I advised.

The Count was stung. "You're a very clever girl, Anna," he said, "but this time, you're wrong. Wait and see. They'll be so impressed that by the time Mayakovsky and I have finished with them, Block will be willing to sign anything."

Prince Mayakovsky – Konstantin – did indeed impress the Blocks of Cleveland, Ohio, and not only because of his title. He was an imposing figure, six feet four, with broad shoulders and a barrel chest. He'd just turned thirty-six, and his temples, which were beginning to grey, framed a face composed of deep, intelligent eyes, an aquiline nose which stopped short of being a beak and a wide, generous mouth. To cap it all, he was wearing the full-dress uniform of a Colonel in His Majesty's Hussar Guards.

The Clevelanders were lost. Mrs Block slipped into a half-curtsy, wondered if she was doing the right thing, decided she wasn't, and straightened up again awkwardly – like a mother hen getting off her nest. Mr Block gave a semi-bow as he shook hands, then said, "Pleased to make your acquaintance, Your Ma . . . uh . . . Royal . . . uh . . . Highness."

"My title is *knyaz*," Konstantin said easily. "In English, prince. You can call me that. We Russians tend to be informal about such matters."

"Uh . . . thanks, Prince."

Watching the scene, I found it hard to suppress a giggle at the Blocks, yet, I suppose, they were right to be impressed by Konstantin. He was what they would call 'the genuine article'. He was rich, had been educated at the Corps of Pages and was now an important officer in an important regiment. And if he chose to dazzle the Americans with a uniform he normally only wore on ceremonial occasions, it was not because he really needed it as a prop, but merely to exercise his sense of humour.

The Blocks found the Russian capacity for food and drink a strain to keep up with, and excused themselves from the dinner table early. The Prince followed their bloated progress to the door with his eyes, and I watched him, watching them. "We'll take them on a wolf hunt," he told the Count after they'd gone. "A good wolf hunt, and they won't be able to resist buying your forest at whatever price you care to name."

"A wolf hunt?" I said. "But it's summertime."

"Hunting in winter is no sport for a man," the Prince said, seeming to notice me for the first time. "Where's the skill in waiting while your beaters drive the wolves towards you and then blowing big holes in them before they even get close enough to be a real danger? I don't suppose you've read *War and Peace*, have you, child?"

Child! How dare he!

"Not yet," I replied. "I have a list of books I intend to read when my studies permit me the time. *War and Peace* is, I believe, the fourth one down."

I sounded priggish, but I didn't care. It had been a long time since the Count had spoken to me as if I were anything other than his intellectual equal, and I resented being patronized by this visitor. I'd recently turned fourteen and knew all the answers. I wish I could be as sure of *one* thing now as I was of *everything* then.

"Fourth on your list, is it?" the Prince asked. "It should be at the very top."

I was furious to see that he was amused, rather than justly chastened. "Indeed," I said coldly. "And why is that?"

"So that you can see Russia through Tolstoy's eyes – not as a mealy-mouthed land full of milksops, but vast, grand, magnificent – a land big enough for heroes to live in. Do you ride?"

"Yes," I admitted.

80

"As if she'd been born in the saddle," the Count said proudly.

"Then you'll ride with us on the hunt, and see me kill a wolf in a manner of which Tolstoy would have approved."

The Count kept no wolf hounds, but Prince Mayakovsky had brought his own dogs and whippers-in with him, and two days later, just after first light, we all assembled in front of the house, ready to start the hunt. Mr Block, uncomfortably perched on a borrowed horse, looked positively ill as he watched the Prince drain a silver goblet of mulled brandy and follow it with half a chicken washed down by a bottle of Bordeaux.

"This is the traditional way to start off a wolf hunt," the Prince shouted across to the American.

"Of course. Tradition," Block called back, though he seemed far from convinced. "We just love tradition back home."

The Prince leaned forward in his saddle so that his head was close to mine. "We just love tradition back home," he mimicked. "My family was faithfully serving the Romanovs a hundred and fifty years before his country ever came into existence. What can he know about tradition?"

Perhaps it was his arrogance which annoyed me, perhaps it was merely that my vanity was still stinging from the way he had spoken to me over dinner. Whatever the reason, I refused to nod my head like a good little girl should.

"Do you think I'm wrong?" the Prince asked.

"Yes, it's a very young country," I admitted. "And perhaps it does have no tradition. But still, it is they who are coming here to buy our forests, not we who are going to America to buy theirs."

The Prince threw back his head and laughed. "You may be impertinent, child," he said, "but at least you're never dull."

"Why are you here?" I asked, before I could stop myself.

"To help the Count sell his land."

"Yes, but—"

"But what?"

But he didn't seem the kind of man who would become

81

involved in dealings of this sort. He didn't even seem the kind of man who would choose the Count as a friend.

"I served with Feodor in the army," the Prince said. "And I make a point of always aiding old comrades. Besides, child, I find it amusing to impress these boring, stodgy people with my titles and my uniform. Things *I* know don't matter a fig. Don't you find it amusing?"

"I'm not sure."

"Where's your sense of sport?" the Prince demanded. He took a last gulp of wine and wheeled his horse round. "Come, little fire-tongue, let's go and kill a wolf."

"D'you think we'll find a wolf, Prince?" Mr Block asked as we trotted along.

"Yes," the Prince said. "A mother will never move far away from her cubs, and my men have already located the den. We'll find the wolf, all right. The interesting question is, what will happen then?"

I heard Block gulp. "Are they dangerous?" he asked.

"A wolf lopes along as though she's got all the time in the world," the Prince said. "But she's fast, very fast. She can even run down a horse which is galloping for its life."

The Prince's answer did not seem to have done much to reassure Mr Block. "Fast . . . yeah. But I mean, are they really fierce?"

"Look at the dogs," the Prince said, pointing to the pack of *borzois* at our heels. "How big would you say they were on average?"

Block squinted at the animals. "About two and half feet tall, maybe a little more," he hazarded.

"A good guess. And do *they* look fierce?"

"Sure do."

"In single combat with a wolf, the *borzoi* will *always* lose. Even if they attack as a pack, she'll probably kill one or two of them before they finish her off."

Block was looking distinctly green.

"A wolf is not just a bigger version of a fox," the Prince said. "A wolf is a powerful, totally ruthless, fighting machine."

We came to a halt where fields ended and forest began. The

Prince issued instructions to his whippers-in. Some plunged into the forest with their hounds, but others began to lead their animals along the perimeter.

"Why are you splitting up your pack?" I asked.

"Because I have a plan," the Prince told me. "It will be most interesting if it works out."

Half an hour passed quietly, then, suddenly, there was a cacophony of noises – "Ulyulyulyulyu" from the handlers as they urged their dogs on, the baying of the hounds themselves, the neighing of our horses as they sensed the presence of a wolf.

The barking in the woods got closer and closer, but we still could not see the dogs. Then there it was – out in the open – a huge grey she-wolf with a pointed muzzle and wicked, bright eyes. She was running straight at us, so intent on escaping her pursuers that she hadn't even noticed this new threat. My horse started to rear, and it took all my skill to keep the animal under control. Mr Block, no horseman, was not so lucky. From the corner of my eye I saw him flying off his mount. But I didn't see him land – I could not tear my gaze away from the huge, loping monster which was almost on us.

Seconds before she reached us, she veered to the left, as effortlessly as if that had always been her intention. Seconds more, and she was already a distance away, skirting the forest.

"Let's see how good you really are on a horse," the Prince said, spurring his own mount. "Follow me."

How we galloped. Jumping hedges and ditches. Fording three or four shallow streams. I was a good rider on a good horse, but the Prince was better, and it was only my pride which kept me in pursuit of him long after it was clear that I was losing the race. Yet if the Prince was losing me, the wolf was losing him, widening the gap between us with every stride.

In the distance, there was fresh barking, and as I bumped up and down in my saddle, I saw the second half of the Prince's pack of *borzois* appear.

Oh cunning Konstantin! As cunning as the quarry he was chasing.

From being free and clear, the wolf now found itself surrounded by a circle of snarling, yelping curs, who were slowly and steadily closing in. I felt a twinge of disappointment. Was this what the Prince meant by 'interesting'? Watching a pack of dogs tear a wolf apart? And we wouldn't even see that. By the time we reached them, it would all be over.

The Prince whistled, once, and the dogs – the whole pack of them – stopped in their tracks. I blinked, unable to believe my eyes.

Once a wolfhound has the scent of blood in its nostrils, it can only usually be controlled by the whip. There are men, it's true, who develop such a close relationship with one particular hound and can call it off by command, though they are few and far between. But to be able to call off a whole pack – impossible! I blinked again. The *borzois* had not moved.

The wolf had been preparing to fight for her life, and this unexpected development confused her. As she hesitated, weighing up the odds, the Prince reached the edge of the circle and reined his horse to a halt.

He did nothing more than watch the wolf until I had drawn level with him. "A magnificent animal," he told me. "Look at her, surrounded by her enemies. Most men in that situation would be too engulfed by fear to do anything, but there's a lot of fight left in *her* yet. Watch, little girl, and learn."

He eased his mount forward, nudging two dogs aside, and entered the arena. The wolf didn't move, but with her bright, cold eyes assessed the new foe.

"Trunila! Karay! Attack!" the Prince shouted.

Two dogs, from opposite sides of the circle, began to advance slowly. The wolf could not watch them both at once, and it didn't even try. Instead, the animal kept its gaze firmly on the man and the horse.

The dogs edged closer, the wolf remained fixed to the spot. "Trunila! Throat!" the Prince called.

The hound on the left sprang forward. The wolf twisted round and snapped its powerful jaws in the empty air. The dog retreated.

"Karay! Hind!"

Karay lunged from the right at the back legs, but the wolf

84

had already twisted back, and as the dog's teeth sank into her rear, she bit down on his shoulder. Karay released his grip, yelped, and fell back.

A lesser animal would have followed through its attack on Karay, but the wolf was too clever for that. She had turned once more, ready to fend off a fresh onslaught from Trunila.

The Prince spurred his mount and galloped into the centre of the ring. The horse passed within two feet of the wolf. The horse passed – but the man didn't. The riderless steed sped to the edge of the circle, scattering dogs. The Prince, hunting knife in hand, was sitting firmly on the wolf's back.

For the first time, I saw panic in the wolf's eyes. She tried to shake the man off, but his thighs were clamped firmly to her sides. She tried to turn and bite, but the Prince had his arm around her neck, pulling the head back, immobilizing the powerful jaws. She tried to run, but the Prince's feet were firmly anchored to the ground, and the muscles in his neck bulged as they took the strain of holding the animal.

The Prince's free hand swung, and his hunting knife flashed briefly in the sun before it disappeared under the wolf – into the wolf. Blood spurted onto the brown earth as steel penetrated the heart, the wolf's legs buckled, and it was all over.

The Prince climbed to his feet and stepped free of the still-twitching body. "So, little girl," he called to me, "what do you think of a truly Tolstoyan wolf hunt?"

What did I think? My cheeks were burning and my heart was pounding furiously against my ribs.

I took a deep breath. "Since this was all organized to impress Mr Block," I said, "it's a great pity that he wasn't here to see it."

The Prince smiled. "Why should I care about a fat American when my heroic deeds can be witnessed by the flower of young Russian womanhood?" he asked. "*You* are impressed my dear, are you not, and that's all that matters."

Of course I was impressed, and Prince Konstantin Mayakovsky knew that very well.

Damn you, Konstantin! Why were you always so right, and

how did you always succeed in making me feel such a idiot? If there is such a thing as heaven, you'll have talked your way into it somehow. You'll be there now, looking down at me – and still laughing at my foolishness.

Chapter Eight

Today is Thursday, the day my social worker sweeps down on me like a Cossack at a street demonstration. She's not my first, there have been a succession of them since I turned seventy. A succession – and a progression. The denim suits and earnest expressions are a thing of the past, the long scarves which hung down over the backs of padded Millets' anoraks have gone for ever. My newest social worker dresses in tweed skirts and sensible shoes. She represents the high point of the social services evolutionary scale, and she knows it. She stands, better than anyone else I know, as a symbol of the late 1980s. She is, in other words, a self-opinionated, hard-faced bitch.

Yet she has power over me. One word from her in the right place, and I will fall victim to the Knock on the Door. The men standing outside won't be wearing belted raincoats and felt hats pulled down over their eyes. They won't inform me in dull, flat voices that I'm wanted for questioning. They will make no mention of Comrade Stalin. Instead, they'll say that they have come from 'the Home'.

The Home! What they'll mean is that they have come from the death camp, the institution where the old are left to dribble and moan to themselves and slowly fade away. What they'll mean is that after all I've endured, I've finally been taken prisoner – and this time there is no escape. They'll tell me to pack my case, they may even offer to help. And I'll tell *them* that I'm quite happy where I am, and they can stuff the 'nice bed' and 'kind nurses' they have promised me.

My protest won't do any good. The old are not invisible – they're far *too* visible for some people's liking – but they are inaudible. My words will go as unheeded as if I'd spoken in my native Russian.

So . . . I have to be careful, I have to be polite. I must watch my social worker carefully, gauging what she considers to be normal behaviour – safe behaviour – and doing my best to conform to it.

She is here, scowling at me, as if annoyed that I've managed to survive another week. I smile, and offer her a chair. "A cup of tea, Mrs Forbes?"

See! I can remember her name! Could I do that if I'd gone ga-ga?

"No, thank you, Mrs Mackoksky," my angel of mercy replies.

She can't get *my* name right. Why don't they lock *her* up?

"It's no trouble," I tell her ingratiatingly. I want her on my side. I want to show her that I'm still capable of making tea.

"I really don't want a drink," she says firmly.

She never does. She never will. Because although my room *looks* clean, although I have spent hours preparing it for her, you can never tell with old people. Look at my hands, wrinkled and covered with liver spots. Isn't there something slightly unhygienic about them, however well scrubbed they are?

My social worker snaps open her briefcase and pulls out a buff-coloured file which *she* thinks contains everything worth knowing about me. "Your granddaughter Sonia phoned me up yesterday," she says.

"Great-granddaughter," I correct her. She frowns. Easy, old woman. Don't argue with your social worker.

"She's very keen for you to move to somewhere you can be properly looked after."

"I know, but I don't want to go."

My social worker glares at me. "Don't you think we're being just a teeny bit selfish, Mrs Mackoksky?"

"I don't want to be any trouble to anyone," I tell her. "Or any expense. I'd rather the girls spent their money on themselves."

Liar! I don't give a damn what they spend it on. They can burn it or flush it down the toilet for all I care. As long as they leave me my freedom. Not much of a life, is it – tottering up to the shops, drinking my daily bottle of Guinness in the Vulcan? But it's all I've got, and I want to hold on to it.

"Your granddaughters worry about you," my social worker says.

They worry about their friends finding out where I live. They worry that I might do something to embarrass them. But worry about *me*? Not a chance.

"And it's all very well to go on about not being a trouble to anyone," my social services saviour continues, "but you're troubling people just by being here. My caseload is heavy enough, heaven knows, without having to deal with people who've been offered a place in a perfectly beautiful Home, and are just too stubborn to take it."

I know why she's pushing. She doesn't fool me. She's found that Edward – Jennifer's husband – has some very important contacts in her department, and she'd do anything to ingratiate herself with him.

"Why can't I live out my last few days the way I want to?" I ask.

"Now, Mrs Mackovsky, we can't always do just we want. You should know that."

"I'm a person, you know," I tell her. "I have rights."

At last I've found some way to amuse her. A smile flickers briefly across her lips. "You have obligations, too," she informs me. "To your family, to your—"

Something snaps inside me. I don't mean it to, but it does. "Obligations!" I say. "I've given up my life to obligations."

"As we all have, Mrs—"

"Have you ever marched towards a line of soldiers, knowing they might open fire any second?" I demand. "Have you ever been willing to lay down your life for the rights of the workers?"

She looks horrified. She's not used to people using dirty words like 'workers' rights'. "I . . . er . . . understood that you were a political refugee," she says, glancing at her folder, her secret-welfare-police dossier. "From the Communists."

89

"No! It wasn't the Party I was running away from – only what Stalin had done to it."

"You're a Communist yourself!" she says accusingly.

Than which, there is no worse.

I'm suddenly filled with disgust – at myself, at her, at the whole situation. I lean forward until our faces are almost touching. "Of course I'm a Communist," I tell her. "Who wouldn't be? You get to rob the rich, eat dead babies and . . ." I deliberately lower my voice to throaty whisper, ". . . best of all, you can fuck as many men as you want to."

She shrinks back, as if she wishes the chair would swallow her up. She's frightened! Of me – for God's sake! I step clear.

"Get out of here, you complacent bourgeois bitch," I order her.

She rises shakily to her feet. Her briefcase is not properly closed and only by quick action on her part does she avoid spilling her precious files all over the floor.

It's not until she is safely in the doorway that she seems to find the power to speak. "I think you're going senile," she shouts. "I . . . I'm going to recommend that you be locked away and—"

I slam the door in her face and listen to her angry footsteps retreating down the hallway. I've done it now. If only I hadn't lost my temper with her.

If . . . if . . . if . . .

If the bullets hadn't missed me in Petrograd, I would already be long dead. If, that terrible winter in Murmansk, I'd given in to the cold and lain down on the snow with my child, there would have been no Sonia and Jennifer now. If Mariamna and her mother hadn't been on holiday in the Crimea in the summer of 1912, when Misha came home from the Corps of Pages . . .

If Mariamna and her mother hadn't been on holiday in the Crimea, things would never have developed as they did. Had Mariamna been there, the summer would have followed its normal pattern. She'd have ordered us to follow her petty dictates, and we'd have obeyed. Our clumsy attempt at love making in the barn was now five years past, but Countess

Olga, if she'd found out, would've treated it as if it had happened just yesterday. And she would have found out, if Mariamna had been there, if we'd not done exactly what our tormentor told us to. With Mariamna there, our relationship would have had no room to grow. But Mariamna was not there – and it did.

The Count made his announcement over dinner. Just the two of us were dining – Miss Eunice had rushed back to Scotland to visit her sick father – and we sat opposite each other at a table half the size of the average *izbá*.

"Misha's coming home for a while," he said.

"Is anything wrong?" I asked, alarmed more by the heaviness in his voice than the words themselves.

"No, no, nothing wrong, nothing wrong at all. He's just got some unexpected leave." He hesitated before speaking again. "Anna, I hope you are not *too* fond of him."

Too fond? My mother was dead, Sasha was in exile. Misha had been kind to me when I first came to the Big House, he'd taken a beating to protect me. Apart from Miss Eunice, he was the only person left I really cared for.

"*Why* should you hope that I am not too fond of him?" I asked.

The Count was bent over his plate, cutting his meat with the precision and concentration of a surgeon. Though he could not have failed to hear them, he seemed deaf to my words.

"Why?" I asked again.

The Count laid down his knife, but he didn't look up at me. "I've visited Misha in Petersburg," he said reluctantly, "but you haven't seen him in nearly two years. He's changed – and so have you. I . . . I wouldn't like to see you hurt. For your own protection, you should keep yourself distant from my son."

Misha changed? So changed by life in the capital that he had the power – perhaps even the will – to hurt me? I imagined him mixing with the cream of Petersburg society, speaking with scorn of the girl who used to be his playmate, and bringing that scorn back home to me. I imagined a sensitive boy suffering under the harsh regime of a military school,

91

gradually adapting to its ways until all his sensitivity had gone, until he become a ruffian, a brutalized solider. It didn't matter *how* he had changed, I realized, just the fact that he wouldn't be *my* Misha was enough to break my heart. For my own protection, I must steel myself for the changes.

"I won't do anything foolish," I promised.

"No," the Count said. "You've never been a fool. So why, in all these years, have you never guessed . . ."

He gagged, as though a morsel of food had become lodged in his windpipe. But his fork lay on the table, and his plate was untouched.

"What's the matter?" I asked.

He slammed his hands down on the table, and pushed himself violently to his feet. His chair rocked, then fell backwards, clattering onto the floor. He walked quickly – almost ran – around the table to the door.

"Tell me what's wrong," I pleaded.

He turned to look at me. His face was pale and his eyes were watery. "A chill," he said. "I'm going to lie down. But later, we must talk, Anna. *We have to.*" Then he flung the door open, and was gone.

Misha had become a stranger, I told myself, and I should be prepared to treat him as a stranger. I should expect nothing from him beyond the normal pleasantries I received from any other house guest. I shouldn't read into a kind word – if kind word there was – anything beyond politeness. I spent those days before his arrival in hardening my heart, and when I heard the clip-clop of his horse's hooves coming up the driveway, I didn't even rush out to greet him.

I was trying to fool myself, and I knew it. I was hoping all the time that despite the Count's warning, my new armour would not be necessary, that the Misha who had made my childhood bearable would come home to me.

I sat in the armchair, trying to read and yet all the time calculating. It would take him this long to give his horse to the groom, this long to walk into the house, this long to greet his father. I had told the servants to leave the drawing room door open – foolish little Anna, why pretend not to care? –

and I heard the sound of his footsteps as he mounted the stairs, walked down the corridor and finally entered the room. I laid down my book and looked up.

He was dressed in the field uniform of the Corps of Pages – plain blue – and wore his peaked cap at a rakish angle. He'd started to grow a pale, insubstantial moustache. He was taller than he'd been the last time I saw him, but though the military life had put some muscle on him, he was still slender.

"Misha!" I said warmly, despite all the promises I'd made to myself.

"It's good to see you, Anna," he replied, but his tone, flat and neutral, showed no sign of pleasure.

I rose to my feet and walked slowly across the room, slowly so that I could really look at him. I gazed into his eyes, searching for traces of my old love. The eyes were cold. No, not cold! They were blank, the eyes of a boy – of a man – who no longer feels anything.

He embraced me as if I were an old aunt he despised, but to whom he was forced to be pleasant. His arms felt as stiff and wooden as puppets, his lips touched my cheeks for the briefest of moments and then made their escape. He broke away from me as soon as he possibly could.

We stood two feet apart, looking at each other awkwardly.

"Hasn't he turned into a fine young man?" asked a new voice which seemed both proud and relieved, and I realized that the Count had entered the room.

A fine young man! The boy I had swum with, played games with, *lain down naked in the barn with*, was now standing as rigidly as if he were on parade, his eyes fixed on a point somewhere above my head. "Yes, he has," I said to the Count. "He looks every inch a soldier."

The summer was unreal. The flowers had no smell, the birds no song, the sun's pleasant warmth failed to thaw out the coldness in my flesh. Young people from the neighbouring estates came over to visit us, and we, in turn, visited them. We boated and played croquet. There were dances and moonlight picnics. Yet looking back on them, they might have been things I merely read about, rather than attended. I felt as if my life – my very soul – had been frozen.

When we were alone – and Misha avoided that, if at all possible – we went for rides or played vigorous games of tennis in which he showed an aggression I'd never seen in him before. We talked little. He answered my questions about Petersburg in the same dry, dull tone he had used when he first arrived, painting a picture of his life there which was as flat and one-dimensional as a badly taken photograph. Sometimes, in the middle of one of these conversations, he'd break off and abruptly leave the room – just as his father had done the night he told me Misha was coming – and, despite myself, I would feel the hot prickling of tears in my eyes. I began to long for the day he returned to the Corps of Pages, the day when I could slowly, painfully, start to rebuild my life.

The closer the departure date came, the longer and heavier the days seemed to be. Looking at Misha, I'd get the urge to scream, to shake him – to do something, anything, which might make him treat me, if not as the girl he had been so fond of, then at least as another human being. But I always held myself back. I couldn't force him to want me, couldn't compel him to feel about me as I felt about him.

Not much longer, I told myself, not much longer, and it would all be over.

There were only two days of his visit left when my horse cast a shoe on the way back from a neighbour's. We were in the middle of nowhere – the nearest estate was seven *versts* away, the nearest *mir* at least five. Misha inspected my horse's hoof, satisfied himself that there was nothing to be done and said, bad-temperedly, "I suppose you'd better ride with me."

I should have sat side-saddle – but I'm a natural rider, not a natural pillion, and as I climbed up behind Misha I instinctively straddled the horse.

It's impossible to share a horse and not to touch. And indeed, the idea never occurred to me. Yet as we trotted along, as an occasional jog flung us together, I started to feel vaguely uncomfortable. I became aware of my legs touching

94

Misha's, of my breasts pressing against his back. I began to experience a strange, new feeling which was exciting – but also frightening. I could sense that Misha was feeling something, too. His body went as rigid as it had done when he embraced me on his return home, then slowly, almost reluctantly, it began to relax.

He turned his head to speak to me. His eyes were more alive than they had been all summer. "Do you remember the spot by the river where we used to go swimming?" he asked.

Back to the good, old days, when we were still friends, and everything was wonderful! "Yes. Of course I remember it."

"Would you like to go there now?"

"If *you* want to," I said cautiously. When what I really meant was, "Yes, oh yes, let's go back to a place where we were happy. Let's try and snatch at least one good memory from this miserable summer. Give me warmth, Misha, just a little warmth, to keep me going through the long, bleak months ahead."

The copse of trees – our copse of trees – lay before us, the green leaves gleaming in the afternoon sun. The trees had grown taller in the years since we'd last visited them, yet they looked smaller than they had when viewed through the eyes of childhood.

Misha dismounted first, and though I didn't need any help, I liked the feel of his hands on me as he lifted me from the horse.

"Shall we swim now?" I asked, heading for the side of the copse where I would undress, and already starting to unbutton my riding coat.

"Yes, we . . . No! No! In the name of God, no!"

I turned sharply round to see what was wrong. Misha's face was flushed and his hands tugged nervously at the lapels of his jacket. "No," he said, a little more calmly. "I don't think it would be a good idea. Why don't we just sit here for a while."

We didn't sit. We lay on our stomachs as we had done when we were younger, chins resting on hands, eyes towards the river. We watched as fish jumped, gnats dived and butterflies

95

fluttered delicately by. We looked into the water and saw the sun, the clouds and the green leaves which hung over our heads.

"It was all so much easier then, wasn't it?" Misha asked.

"Then?"

"When we were children. Before we knew what a wicked world we were living in."

"Is the world really wicked?"

"The people who live in it are. My mother calls the *muhziks* animals, and she's right. We're all animals, every one of us, driven on by urges which have nothing to do with love or caring. And I'm one of the worst. Why can't I . . . why couldn't I just . . ."

"You're not like that at all," I told him. "You're kind. You've always protected me."

"I . . . want to protect you now, but I haven't got the strength any more."

I laughed. "Protect me from what?"

He didn't answer. Instead he picked up a stone and threw it into the water. Circles formed around the point where it had landed, and we watched them spread wider and wider, and then grow fainter, until they had finally disappeared.

"We're just like that stone," Misha said miserably.

"First we're animals, then we're stones," I joked. "You want to make up your mind which we are."

But Misha was not to be put off. "We are like that stone," he said. "We die, and it's as if we'd never been. There's no trace left of us. So does it really matter *what* we do on that short journey to death? Shouldn't we do what we want to do?"

"What do *you* want to do, Misha?" I asked, my mood now matching his.

"I want to make love to you," he said. "Will you let me?"

If he'd been my Misha all holiday, I might have expected it. Instead, he'd been a cold shell from which the boy I loved was only just emerging – and what he asked took me completely by surprise.

"Will you?" he pleaded.

A little warmth to keep me going through the long, bleak months ahead. "Do you really love me?" I asked.

"Of course I love you," he protested. "I've never loved anyone else."

We stripped off our clothes as quickly and sexlessly as if we were going from a swim, then turned and faced each other. We had both grown since the last time we had been naked together. My breasts, mere buds then, had burst into full flower. Misha's penis seemed twice the size it had been in the barn.

Misha gasped. "I used to lie awake at night in the barracks," he said, "thinking of you, imagining you without your clothes. But I never dreamed you could be as beautiful as this."

"What do I do now?" I asked awkwardly.

"Lie down," Misha said, his voice trembling with excitement. "Just lie down. Leave everything else to me."

I lay on my back and he knelt beside me. Our lips met, locking us together, uniting our souls. I felt his hand rest tentatively on my knee, then settle in the space between my legs.

"What are you going to do?" I asked.

But I already knew. Often, alone in my bed at night, I'd guiltily allowed my own hand to follow the path that Misha's was following now. I felt the familiar sensations of pleasure shoot through my body – familiar, yet deeper, more intense. Misha leant forward and cupped my right nipple with his lips. I closed my eyes as his tongue caressed me . . . back and forth, back and forth.

His mouth withdrew, his finger ceased its paralysing, ecstatic work. He lowered his body gently onto mine, and then he was inside me, thrusting and thrusting and thrusting, until he exploded, I exploded, the whole world exploded.

As I lay there, more relaxed, more at peace, than I'd ever been before, I felt Misha suddenly tense. What was the matter, I wondered. Had I done it wrong? Was there something else I was supposed to do? I'd thought he'd liked it as much as I had. Maybe it was different for a man.

He eased himself out of me, turning his head to one side so that he wasn't looking at me.

"Misha . . ."

He went over to his clothes, picked up his shirt, and began

to put it on. I wanted to get up and rush to him, but I was afraid to. If he brushed me aside, or laughed at me, I knew I'd die. So I stayed where I was, frozen in misery, while he put on his breeches, his boots and finally his jacket.

He began to walk towards the horses, then stopped, dead, in front of a thick oak tree. He stood for a few seconds just looking at it, as if would provide the answer to an unspoken question – and then he attacked it.

His nails sank into the bark, he butted the trunk. One, two, three times, his forehead struck the hard oak. I was on my feet and running to him when his legs buckled and he sank slowly down to the roots of the tree. By the time I reached him he was huddled in a ball, crying.

"Are you all right?" I cried. "Did you hurt yourself?"

He looked up at me. His face was wracked with pain, but it was not the tree which had caused the hurt. "It was wrong," he sobbed. "I should never . . . I had to come back and see you. I thought I could do that without it going . . . without me doing . . . what I've dreamed of night after night. But it *was* wrong, Anna, *terribly* wrong."

"How *can* it have been wrong?" I demanded angrily. "We love each other. Isn't it what people do when they love each other?"

"It wasn't wrong of *you*," Misha sobbed. "It was wrong of *me*. You didn't know."

Didn't know what?

"I should've told you. I should've given you the choice." Misha struggled to his feet and lurched towards the edge of the copse like a drunkard.

"Come back," I shouted. "Please come back. I love you!"

He ran past the horses and into the bright sunlight. He didn't look back – not even once.

Dressing for dinner was an ordeal, descending the stairs to the dining room drained me of most of my remaining courage. I hesitated on the threshold, not knowing how I could face Misha – what I would say to him.

"Are you all right, Miss Anna?" the butler asked.

I nodded, and forced my feet forward.

Misha was not there! The Count sat alone, a brooding figure looking almost lost in vastness of the dining table. "Misha came back on foot this afternoon," he said.

"Yes. My . . . my horse cast a shoe and he lent me his. Will he . . . is he coming down to dinner?"

The Count shook his head. "He doesn't feel well. He says he has a fever."

We didn't exchange more than a dozen words over the meal. It was a relief when it was over, and I could return to my lonely room.

After a sleepless night, I rose exhausted but with fresh resolve. I would *make* Misha tell me what was wrong. Whatever the problem was, we loved each other and we'd find a solution. I'd waited for years for him to come back, and I wasn't going to lose him now.

One look at the Count's trouble face and Misha's empty seat was enough to dash all my hopes.

"He's gone, hasn't he?" I asked.

"Yes. He told me he couldn't stay here any longer." The Count twisted his fork nervously in his hands "Do you know what's wrong with him, Anna? Did something happen yesterday afternoon?"

No. Nothing had happened, I'd only thought it had. Our passion on the riverbank, which had seemed to me to complete our love, to lock us together for ever, had only served to drive him away. He hadn't even said goodbye.

"Anna?"

"We went for a ride, we stopped by the river. That's all." Tears were streaming down my face. I stood up. "I'm glad he's gone. I hope he never comes back!"

I fled from the table and up to my room. I locked the door and wouldn't come out, even for the Count himself. I felt used. I felt betrayed. I would never trust a man again.

By the time Mariamna and the Countess returned from the Crimea a week later, I'd recovered sufficiently to put on a brave face. Misha's sister, at least, would never learn of my humiliation. But the hurt inside hadn't disappeared

99

– if anything, it had grown, until it seemed to be eating away at me.

I thought of killing Misha. I thought of killing myself. I had to do *something*. I couldn't go on like this, I just couldn't – it was driving me mad.

The last days of summer dragged by, and autumn was upon us. I'd still not decided what to do when the leaves began to turn brown and I had my first attack of morning sickness.

Chapter Nine

It was Mariamna, of course, who first noticed the change in me, Mariamna who watched me like a hawk until she was sure, Mariamna who chose the moment of maximum impact to break the news.

The dinner table. The Count, the Countess, Mariamna and Anna dining *en famille*. Anna is quiet and withdrawn, but she has been like that for several weeks and the Count is now used to it. Besides, she never says much in the presence of the Countess because she is far too intelligent to give Olga ammunition to fire back at her.

The atmosphere is not exactly pleasant, but it's as relaxed as it ever gets in the Big House. The Count, having for once spent a day as a conscientious landowner, is talking about his animals, in particular one sow which is expected to deliver its litter only with difficulty.

"You should send Anna down to look after it," Mariamna says. "They'd be company for one another."

"Mariamna!" the Count says sternly. He will allow his wife to insult the peasant girl with whom she is forced to share a table, but only in his moments of weakness can his daughter get away with it.

"I wasn't being rude, Papa," Mariamna continues innocently. "I only meant that since they're both pregnant . . ." She trails off, a smile playing on her lips.

The Count turns pale, already suspecting the terrible truth. The Countess, who was not there to see Misha's departure, is suddenly radiant. At last, after all these years, she has an excuse to banish this upstart girl from her home.

"Pregnant!" she says triumphantly, pointing her spoon accusingly at the transgressor. "And do you know the name

101

of the father? Or have you been rutting with every boy in the village?"

"Not with every boy," Anna says defiantly. "Only with one. Only with Misha."

"Misha!"

The Countess drops her spoon and screams hysterically. The Count is now so white that he seems on the point of fainting, and his hands, resting on the table, are shaking. Anna sees the violence of their reaction and wonders why it so disproportionate. It makes no sense to her at all, unless . . .

Anna, slowly realizing the truth, feels her heart start to beat against her ribs and wishes she were dead.

Only Mariamna is undisturbed. The knowing smirk on her face grows wider and wider.

We sat in the Count's study, he behind his great mahogany desk, me in a chair in front of it. The desk made him feel better, I think. It gave him back his air of authority. "I tried to warn you," he said. "I told you to be careful with Misha."

"You told me to keep away from him, but you didn't tell me he was my brother. Couldn't you see that I was in love with him?"

The Count nodded his head miserably.

"How could you keep it secret from me?" I demanded. "Didn't you think I had a right to know?"

He held out his hands in supplication. Did he expect me to rise to my feet and grasp those hands . . . to call him Papa? I stayed where I was.

"I thought you did know," he said. "I always assumed that someone must have told you. When I realized, in the cherry orchard, that nobody had, I tried to explain – but I couldn't."

"It shouldn't have been too difficult. You had only to open your mouth and say, 'I'm your father'."

"I love you more than either of my other children," the Count replied, his voice thick with shame and self-pity. "Perhaps because of you yourself, perhaps for your mother's sake. I wanted you to love me. What would you have said to me if I'd told you the truth that day?"

102

"I'd have asked how you could have allowed my mother, who you must also once have loved to live a life of poverty and die before her time!"

"Yes, you would have said exactly that," the Count responded sadly. "You wouldn't have seen the imposibility of my position then any more than you see it now. And I knew that. I thought . . . I hoped . . . that you might in time come to love me as your protector. But I was sure that if you learned the truth, you'd only despise me."

Weak! Weak! Weak! And weaker yet for hiding that weakness. When will men learn they'll never win our love by disguising their true selves, that their only chance is to offer themselves up as they are – blemishes and all. I *might* have understood if he'd told me. I might have come to love him despite his faults. But now it was too late. Now I was carrying my half-brother's child in my belly.

"We . . . er . . . still have to decide what to do about your problem," the Count said.

"My problem? *My* problem?"

"I believe that there are ways of . . . perhaps the doctor could give you some medicine or perform an operation—"

"None of this is the child's fault," I said angrily. "I will *not* have my baby aborted."

"It might be easier—"

"Easier! Where are your feelings?" I asked bitterly. "It's your grandchild we're talking about. You're the grandfather *on both sides.*"

The Count's hands twitched, and he shuffled some papers on his desk. "That's where the difficulty comes in, Anna. I'm not sure how much you know about these things but there's a good chance, given its parentage, that the child will be backward, or deformed – or both."

"I don't care if it's a cripple!" I told him. "If it's crippled it'll need me more than ever, and if I have to spend the rest of my life looking after it, I will do. I'll sell myself to the drunks of the *mir* for a few *kopeks* if necessary. I've already given myself to my own brother – what can I do that is worse than that?"

I don't mean to sound heroic – I certainly didn't feel it.

There was no bravery to facing the Count, not any more. He was a broken man. And I can claim no merit in defending my unborn child either. My mind and spirit were no longer in control of me – my body had taken over. I was in the grip of Nature, fighting for its own survival.

"You must go away then," the Count said. "Petersburg would be best. I have relatives there. You can stay with them."

Petersburg! How often have I seen provincial eyes light up at that magic word? Petersburg! The capital! It lit no fire in my eyes. This house, this estate, were my world. I could abide the Countess's hatred and Mariamna's contempt, just as long as I was allowed to stay.

I desperately, desperately, wanted my child to grow up in the Big House. If it was able, it could learn in the schoolroom, as I had done. If, as a result of my incestuous union, it had poor, fuddled brains, then at least it could sit in the park and be soothed by the birdsong and the smell of the blossom. "Don't send me away," I pleaded. "Let me stay. I'll move back to the servants' quarters. I'll scrub your floors for you. Punish me if you want to, but don't punish your grandchild."

"You can't stay," he said. "Not after what's happened. My wife would never allow it."

That was the Count – my father! – always knowing where love and duty lay, always sacrificing them on the altar of ease and expediency.

I was unclean – a social leper. It took over a week to make the arrangements for my move to Petersburg, and the whole time I was kept a virtual prisoner in my room.

It was a grey October morning when I left. Crows were cawing in the blackened trees of the park. Flowers were withering and dying in the beds in front of the Big House. I looked around, committing everything that was dear to me to memory, wishing my last view of it could have been at a time of life and growth, not now, when everything was decaying.

My luggage was piled onto the *drozhky* and the Count ordered the servants back into the house. Standing in the

104

driveway, he looked up at me. "I'll ride with you to the railway station," he said.

"I don't want you to."

"Anna—"

"No."

"I'll visit you in Petersburg soon," he promised.

"If you come, I'll refuse to see you."

"You are still my child," he said.

"Then let me stay!" I begged him.

He glanced back at the house. The curtain of the sitting room window moved. Mariamna and her mother were relishing their final triumph. "You know I can't let you stay," he said.

"You can do anything you want to," I told him. "Anything you *really* want to."

"I'm sorry, Anna . . ."

Overhead, the black clouds rolled ominously. In the distance, a sheet of lightning seared the sky, and the thunder followed seconds later, growling its displeasure at the state of the world.

"It's time to go," I said. "I want to get there before the storm breaks."

The coachman looked down at his master, and the Count nodded. The whip cracked, the horses broke into a gentle trot. For a moment, the Count stood completely still, then he started running. As he drew level with the *drozhky*, he held out his hand to me. "Anna—"

"Goodbye," I said, and turned my head away.

I didn't look back, not at him, not even at the house where I'd discovered the magic of learning.

He was dead before Christmas, shot through the head with his own pistol. It was an accident, they said, and maybe it was. I didn't cry when I heard the news. I had shed tears for my mother, I had wept over Misha, my reservoir of pity had run dry.

The Count's relatives had a small house in Voznesenki Prospekt, just on the edge of the fashionable district of Petersburg. The husband was a civil servant who swaggered

105

around the house in his uniform and rarely seemed to spend much time at his ministry. The wife – Madam – was a social climber who would have sold her soul for an invitation to the right salons. They didn't want me in their home, but they wanted the money the Count had paid them – no doubt behind Countess Olga's back. They treated me like a servant, but I didn't mind that – there is some honour and decency in honest service.

They were greedy, selfish people, the watered-down stock of the man who generations earlier, had secured their entry into the aristocracy. My brief stay in their house touched me not at all, and I wouldn't even have mentioned it had it not been for the fact that it was in their drawing room – their pretentious, over-furnished drawing room – that Konstantin first came to see me.

I was engaged in cleaning the cooking range when Madam burst through the door looking red-faced and twitchy. "Prince Mayakovsky is here," she said. "In the drawing room."

A catch indeed for her, I thought, and no doubt she'd be on the telephone to all her friends just as soon as he'd left. I wondered why she'd bothered to come and boast to me.

"It's you he wants to see," she continued breathlessly. "Don't just stand there, go and change into your best clothes. And for God's sake make sure you've wiped all the grease off your face and hands."

I started to walk towards the door.

"Wait!" Madam called. "You must tiptoe past the drawing room. You mustn't let him know . . . you . . . just make sure you're quiet."

I was tempted to go and meet the Prince as I was. It would embarrass Madam beyond endurance and shock the life out of Konstantin – both of which would have given me a great deal of pleasure. But I was living in Madam's house and would continue to do so at least until after the baby was born, so it was prudent to follow her instructions. I climbed the stairs up to my garret room as silently as I could.

It was twenty minutes before I was presentable enough to go down to the drawing room. The scene which met me when I entered almost made me laugh out loud. Konstantin was standing next to the fireplace, his elbow resting on the mantel shelf. Madam was sitting uncomfortably in one of the easy chairs. I sensed the conversation had been strained. That Madam had been doing her best to impress, and had failed miserably.

"Here you are at last," Madam said with a mock severity she'd never used with me before. "You're a very naughty girl to keep the Prince waiting so long."

Konstantin's generous mouth widened as he smiled. "It's understandable," he said. "Unless one is Cinderella, one cannot be transformed from a kitchen maid into a radiant beauty in much under half an hour."

Madam's mouth fell open. "How did you . . ." she managed to gasp.

"I make it my business to be well informed," Konstantin replied.

And I'd thought I'd shock him by coming in straight from the kitchen. Would I *ever* be able to do anything to shock the Prince?

"We . . . we have a servant problem at the moment," Madam explained, the words coming faster and faster as her desperation grew. "Anna offered to help out. She likes to keep busy."

"Oh, I think I understand the situation perfectly," Konstantin said. He looked pointedly at Madam. "Thank you. That will be all."

Dismissing her – in her own house! Yet she showed no sign of outrage – people who treat those they consider their inferiors as dirt are usually prepared to receive the same treatment themselves from those they regard as their *superiors*. Yet though Madam did not react to the insult, she still resisted leaving.

"Anna is still a young woman," she said. "It's not proper that she should be without a chaperone."

"The girl's pregnant, is she not?" the Prince asked.

Was there *anything* he didn't know?

"Y. . .yes, she's pregnant," Madam stuttered.

"Well then, I think it's probably a little late now to try and preserve her virginity. Unless, of course, Christ has chosen in his Second Visitation to be a Russian."

Madam gasped at both the blasphemy and his mention of virginity, but she dared not rebuke someone as important as the Prince.

"If you'll excuse us, Madam," Konstantin said patiently.

Madam rose to her feet and walked hesitantly towards the door. She twisted the handle, then turned to make one last, desperate try. "If there is anything you need . . . tea, vodka, we have some excellent Beluga caviar—"

"If we need anything, we'll ring for it," Konstantin said. *"Thank you*, Madam."

Defeated, Madam made her exit. The Prince walked across to me, took my hand, and kissed it.

"How did you know I was here?" I asked. "Oh, I forgot, you make it your business to be well informed. Do your spies watch *every* house in Petersburg?"

The Prince shook his head. "I wouldn't have known at all if Feodor had not written to me just before he died and asked me to keep an eye on you."

I knew what sort of eye he would keep, too – a *patronizing* eye. "Is being a nursemaid yet another of your accomplishments?" I asked.

The Prince refused to take the bait. "You've grown, Anna," he said. "How long is it since we killed the wolf?"

"It's well over a year since *you* killed the wolf," I told him. "You must have done many other heroic deeds and impressed many other 'flowers of young Russian womanhood' since then."

To my annoyance, Konstantin laughed. "I'm a soldier, and there's little chance of heroism in peace time. Tell me, Anna, what are your plans? Do you intend to stay in this house?"

"Only until the baby's born."

"And then where will you go?"

"I don't know," I admitted. "Somewhere there is a chance of making a new life. America, perhaps. If Mr Block could become rich, maybe I will, too."

"I'm rich already," the Prince said. "Perhaps even richer than our stodgy friend from Cleveland."

"Perhaps you are," I said cautiously

Konstantin walked back to the fireplace, so that he had a clear view of me, and I of him. "And I have only myself to spend my money on . . ." he continued.

"No," I said firmly. "I don't want a gift. I won't even accept a loan, not from a man I hardly know."

The Prince laughed again, and I felt once more that his mind was one move ahead of my own. "I'm not proposing a gift or a loan," he said. "I'm suggesting a partnership."

"A partnership?"

"Yes. You could marry me."

"I . . . could marry . . . you?" I gasped.

"Is the idea so preposterous? I'm considerably older than you, but I'm still in excellent physical condition. I'm very wealthy, I'm a nobleman, and," he smiled again, "though you probably won't admit it, even to yourself, you like me."

"But why would *you* want to marry *me*?"

"I ought to be married," he told me. "The Tsar remarked on it only the other day. And if I'm to marry, why not to you? You have many fine qualities." He began to count them off on his fingers. "You're young. You're beautiful. You're intelligent. You have a sense of humour. You ride well. There, I've used up all the fingers of one hand, and I've not even begun to list all your virtues."

"But I'm pregnant," I told him. "Do you even know whose child it is?"

"Your half-brother's – the weak son of an even weaker father. That doesn't matter." Konstantin walked back to me, put his hands gently on my shoulders, and looked deep into my eyes. "Your pregnancy is a bonus to me, Anna. I need an heir."

"And you'd settle for another man's child?"

"Yes."

"Can't you have any of your own?" I asked. "Are you impotent?"

Did I sound insensitive? Did I sound cruel? I didn't mean to be. It was simply inconceivable to me that the Prince, that towering symbol of virility, was incapable of having children.

"No," Konstantin said quietly. "No, I'm not impotent. I am homosexual."

I stepped back, astonished. I knew that homosexuality was fashionable among the aristocracy, but that was all it was – a fashion. Nor was I so naïve as to imagine that all homosexuals were slight, slack-wristed lispers. But – for God's sake! – I had seen this man kill a wolf!

"Have you . . . have you tried to make love to women?" I asked.

He nodded. "Many times. It doesn't work."

"What if the child dies?" I asked. "What if it's crippled or an idiot? Will you still want me then?"

"Yes. I shall still want you, and I shall still want the child."

"And your family name? How will that be carried on if the child I bear is not fit to be your heir?"

"There'll be other children."

"But if you're a homosexual, then I don't see how—"

"I have no intention of remaining celibate once we are married," Konstantin said. "Nor would I expect a young woman like you to condemn herself to the life of a nun. You'll have affairs . . . discreetly. It won't be long before you're pregnant again."

It was insane. It *had* to be insane. I pinched myself to make sure that the room, the gaudy over-ornamented room, was actually there, that Konstantin and I were really having this conversation.

"But the children I bear will not be yours," I protested.

"Are we what we are because of who we are born? Or is it because of the way we are brought up?"

I thought of the *muhziks* in my *mir*. I thought of myself, being shown a map and imagining it was an *icon*, being unable to see any sense in knowing the shapes of the different countries and their relationship to one another. "The way we are brought up is very important," I said seriously.

Konstantin smiled. "I'm so glad we agree," he said. "I will be a good father to your children. They may not be born mine, but they will *become* mine. You are willing, then, to become my wife?"

110

I nodded. What else could I do? What else could I say to a man like him?

Oh, wonderful, wonderful Konstantin. Well read, intelligent, strong, courageous, kind. My first father was a drunk who sold me. My second, a coward who could not find it in himself to protect me when I needed him most. Konstantin was my third father, and as far above the others as the sun is above the earth.

There are other ways to betray a man besides physical infidelity, and I started to betray Konstantin – I had no choice – almost as soon as we were married. Yet I loved him as much as any woman is capable of loving any man.

I still do.

Chapter Ten

Once it was settled, Konstantin moved events at a breathless, almost frightening speed. I would be leaving immediately, he told Madam. Until the wedding I would have a suite at the *Hotel Astoria*. Madam was not to worry about chaperoning, his cousin Lisa would be my constant companion.

"Such a lot of trouble," protested Madam. "She could just as easily stay here."

"We couldn't possibly trespass any further on your hospitality," Konstantin said stiffly, though the corner of his mouth twitched as he spoke, a sign I'd already come to recognize as meaning that he was laughing inside.

And Madam, realizing that by her previous treatment of me she'd thrown away her *entrée* into high society, bowed her head and accepted the inevitable.

I had hardly arrived at the *Astoria* when Konstantin's cousin, Lisa, descended on me. She was a brisk, bony woman in her mid-thirties, the sort destined from birth to be a maiden aunt.

"This is Vera," she said, pointing to the girl of about my age who she'd brought with her. "She'll be your maid. Vera, unpack Miss Anna's luggage. Anna, get changed. We've shopping to do."

My trousseau first. Dozens of slips and sets of underwear, countless pairs of black silk stockings and equal number of lisle ones, dresses, scarves, cloaks, bonnets, gloves, parasols – even sheets, pillowcases and table cloths.

"But surely Konstantin must already have plenty of table cloths!" I said.

"Where's your sense of tradition?" Lisa sniffed, selecting

112

another piece of expensive lace and handing it to the over-loaded shop assistant.

My wedding dress next, cunningly tailored to hide the growing bulge in my stomach.

"No veil," Lisa said, explaining, "we already have one. It belonged to the Empress Josephine."

Fabergé for jewels, a tiara of rock crystals and diamonds to go with the wedding dress. And other baubles that Lisa said I would need – *need* – for the season.

I welcomed the activity, the rushing from shop to shop with no time to think, no time to do anything but buy, buy and buy more. It was the evenings I dreaded, when I lay alone in my bed and waited for the blessed unconsciousness of sleep. I would picture the future, not the distant future, ten or twenty years hence, but the one which was just around the corner – the wedding and the ball which would follow it.

It would be a grand society affair attended by hundreds of people, but they would all be Konstantin's friends. Who would be there to give *me* support? My dear Miss Eunice was still in Scotland. My reluctant stepmother, Countess Olga, had written a curt note to say that she and her daughter were in mourning for her husband. True, my half-brother-lover Misha was in the capital, but clearly he could not be invited.

The feeling of loneliness, which at first sat in my stomach as small as an acorn, grew quickly into a mighty oak, spreading its branches throughout my whole body. For days I managed to build a wall between my feelings and the expression of them, but it was a very thin wall indeed, and it only took one probing, necessary question from Lisa to breach it.

"Who'll be your bridesmaid?" she asked.

My bridesmaid, my unmarried friend who would stand beside me just as Konstantin's unmarried friend would stand beside him. My bridesmaid, who would hold a gold crown over my head whilst our marriage was sanctified.

"Well?" Lisa said, a little snappishly. "What's her name? Give me her address so I can get in touch with her. Come on, Anna, there's still loads of arrangements to be made."

"There isn't anyone," I said, feeling a tear trickle from the corner of my eye.

Lisa was so busy organizing my life that she didn't notice I was upset. "There must be someone," she abstractly. "Everybody has someone they can ask."

"I don't," I sobbed. "I don't have anyone – in the whole world."

I ran into my bedroom, locking the door behind me, and flung myself onto the bed in a flood of tears.

"Anna! Anna!" Lisa called anxiously, tapping on the door. "Don't get upset. We can probably hire someone if we have to."

Hire someone? Buy me a friend? "Go away!" I sobbed

"Anna, listen to me—"

"Go away! I want to be alone!"

Wasn't that what I was anyway – completely alone?

I heard her footsteps retreating and then the sound of her picking up the telephone. She was doing what the Count and so many other people in difficulty had done before her – ringing Konstantin. As if he were a magician who could solve any problem by one wave of his magic wand. And the strange thing was – he often could.

From my tear-stained pillow, I heard the door open, and the sound of Lisa's voice as she poured out the whole story. I expected Konstantin to bang on my door and demand that I come out immediately – but I didn't know him then. It was half an hour before I felt brave enough to face him, and when I finally emerged, he was sitting on the sofa, waiting patiently.

He rose to his feet and I rushed over to him and flung my arms around his strong, reassuring body. It was the first time we'd ever been so close.

"I've no one to be my bridesmaid," I told him.

"I know, Annushka."

"But don't you see what that means? There's no one, in the whole world, who I can ask to hold my crown for me."

"The life you've led hasn't given you much opportunity to make close friends," Konstantin said. "But if you can't have

114

someone you care about to be your bridesmaid, then the next best thing is to choose someone important."

"Why?"

"To show how important *you* are. I think my best man's daughter would serve very well."

I pulled away from him. He'd laughed at me before, but he'd never mocked me like this. How could he be so cruel? His best man's daughter! The Church would never allow someone with children to be his best man.

Konstantin read my thoughts. "My best man has a special dispensation from the Holy Synod," he said.

"How is that possible?"

"They're wise enough to know which side their bread's buttered on."

"I still don't understand."

"They'd think very carefully before turning down a request from the man who pays their salaries."

"The Tsar!" I gasped. "The Tsar is going to be your best man?"

"And the Grand Duchess Tatyana will be your bridesmaid. I used to dandle her on my knee when she was smaller, I'm quite sure she'll do it if I ask her to."

The coach had the Mayakovsky family crest picked out on its side in mother-of-pearl and delicate gold and silver filigree. Between its shafts stood four of the purest white horses I have ever seen. In front and behind were mounted officers of Konstantin's regiment, in full dress uniform. Is it any wonder that as we progressed up Nevsky Prospekt, people stopped and stared?

Part of the Prospekt near Kazan Cathedral had been blocked off by soldiers. As my coach approached, they divided, and snapped smartly to attention as it passed through the gap. Ahead of me, I could see the metal dome of the cathedral, and below it, waiting under the Corinthian colonnade, a mass of people.

I felt a surge of panic. Who was I, a peasant girl, to be marrying a Prince? Why was I, a woman with normal appetites, marrying a homosexual? It was all a foolish, tragic,

115

mistake. I had only to open the carriage door and I'd be free. I could run and lose myself in the crowd of sightseers which was already beginning to build up.

Lose myself! In a silk and lace wedding dress? With a diamond tiara in my hair? I giggled, tried to stop, and found it impossible. The carriage came to a halt, and the door was opened from outside. The Archbishop of St Petersburg in flowing white robes and mitre, was standing there, waiting for me to descend. Next to him was Konstantin, in his Colonel's uniform. And behind them both was a small, dapper man, also in uniform, who was nervously stroking his beard. I had never met him before, but I knew who he was – Nicholas Alexovich Romanov, Emperor and Autocrat of all the Russias.

Even with the giggles, I couldn't keep all these important people waiting any longer. I took a deep breath, rearranged my veil, and allowed Konstantin to help me down.

Bride, groom and priest passed through the great bronze doors together, followed by the best man, bridesmaid and then the rest of the congregation. Into the great, hollow building we went, our footsteps, and those of the people behind us, echoing around the vast, vaulted ceiling.

We approached the *Iconostás* – the screen which shields the altar from the rest of the church. At the table in front of the *Iconostás'* middle door, we came to a halt. This was the table at which the ceremony was to take place. I was breathing easily and my pulse seemed to be beating at its normal rate. I congratulated myself on how well I was keeping my head.

I wasn't really, of course. At the storming of the Winter Palace, I was calm. Fleeing for my life across Soviet Central Asia, with Stalin's *OGPU* snapping at my heels, I was calm. After both those events I could remember every detail, every incident in its logical order. And what are my memories of my wedding? Nothing but a series of disjointed images. Calm? I was terrified.

Images. The candles and perpetual lamps burning before the sacred *icons* which hung from the *Iconostás*. The solid silver balustrade in front of the *Iconostás*. The choir singing, the bells pealing. The scores of banners and eagles captured from Napoleon which gave the church a military air and made it, I thought 'calmly', an appropriate place for my husband to be married in.

My husband?

My husband!

Not quite yet. There were still forms to be observed, rituals to be gone through.

The Archbishop fastened our wrists together with a cord and, so bound, we walked three times around the table. The knot had been tied, we were now as one.

We were handed a cup of wine, and we drank it as we were supposed to drink in life together, first Konstantin taking a sip and then me. As he handed me the cup, I looked up at him. Can we really do it? my eyes asked his. Can we actually we share our lives? Will the bond between us ever become really strong, or will it always be as easy to loosen as the cord which tied us just a few minutes ago?

And Konstantin's eyes said to me, You and I can do *anything* we set our minds to.

The Archbishop told us of our obligations and led us through our vows while the Tsar and the Grand Duchess Tatyana held our crowns over our heads. The Grand Duchess sighed several times, I remember. Perhaps she was wishing that it was she who was marrying Konstantin.

It was finally over. Konstantin led me from the cathedral and out into the open once more. The bright light made my eyes water, and the crisp winter air cleansed my nose of the smell of incense. I felt as if I had just woken up and, like many sleepers, tried to reconstruct the dream I'd just had.

The crowd had swollen, and was being held back by the soldiers. My eyes swept over the sea of faces – civil servants and shopkeepers, workers and bourgeois ladies. All craning their necks, like crowds always do, in order to miss none of the spectacle. Then suddenly my gaze was being drawn, as if by a magnetic force, to one particular spectator. Unlike everyone else in the mob, he was neither impressed nor envious. His eyes were hard and unforgiving. His face bore the signs of suffering – both in the past and at that very moment.

My mind was playing tricks on me, I told myself. It was impossible that *he*, of all people, could be . . .

I felt a gentle pressure on my arm. "What's the matter?" Konstantin asked. "You look as though you've seen a ghost."

A ghost! A phantom! Nothing more. It couldn't be any more.

"It's just the excitement," I told my husband, as he helped me into the fairy-tale coach which was to take me to my new home on the bank of the Neva.

"How much further?" I asked Konstantin as our coach approached a large building which had to be either a very rich bank or an important ministry.

"We're nearly there," my husband replied.

"And is your palace as impressive as this," I joked, pointing to the ministry/bank.

Konstantin smiled, and the coach turned. "It *is* this," he said.

The carriage passed under and archway and came to halt in the courtyard.

I looked around me, trying to absorb it all. The palace breathed elegance. The walls, so white that even the weak winter sun reflected dazzlingly off them. Tall windows with neo-classical mouldings above them. Pillars which led the eyes upwards towards heaven. It was a Renaissance palace fit for a Renaissance prince like Konstantin. But where did I fit in?

"Do you like it?"

"It's so . . . so . . ."

"So big?" Konstantin asked innocently.

"Yes – and so beautiful."

"It is one of Quarenghi's more impressive works," my new husband admitted.

"If I'd seen it before we got married," I confessed, "I wouldn't have dared go through with it."

Konstantin laughed. "Don't underestimate yourself, my little princess."

Little princess? Yes, I was, wasn't I?

118

An army of servants was lined up in the courtyard to greet us – footmen, coachmen, chauffeurs, grooms, carpenters, stone masons, blacksmiths, cooks, confectioners, valets, personal maids, upstairs maids, scullery maids, washerwomen, boot-boys, messengers, porters . . .

The women bobbed in curtsey to me, the men bowed. All of them looked up at Konstantin with adoration.

"You must change out of your wedding dress, and then I'll show you the house," Konstantin said.

"I want to see it *now*."

"You'd be much more comfortable if you—"

"Now," I insisted. "And I want to see it all."

"As you wish, my impatient princess," Konstantin said with mock resignation.

He was right, as usual. I should have changed, and if I'd known just how many miles of corridors there were, it would have been into my riding clothes!

For his own amusement, Konstantin took me at my word. I'd asked to see it all, and all I would see. Every bedroom, every salon.

"Just *how many* rooms are there?" I asked, after an hour had passed and we still far from completing our inspection.

"I couldn't really say," Konstantin admitted. "You'll have to ask my butler."

He showed me his library, which smelt of old leather and – despite being huge – was crammed to bursting point. "First Folios of Shakespeare," he said, pointing to one of the shelves. "They were extremely difficult to get hold of."

He took me into the theatre, big enough for a full-scale production, luxurious enough to satisfy even the choosiest sybarite. "I sometimes ask the Mariinsky Company to put on a private performance," he told me.

"And they agree?"

He nodded. "I pay well, and they prefer my stage to their own."

He led me around his art gallery, showing me the originals of pictures I recognized from books, pointing out the work of other artists I was totally ignorant of.

"That study in blue is by a young Spanish artist," he said.

"His name's Picasso. I think he's going to be very important. Certainly he deserves to be."

Do I make my husband sound boastful? Nothing could be further from the truth. In all the time we were married, I never saw Konstantin deliberately try to impress anyone else, though he rarely failed to do so. His books and paintings were for his own pleasure, and nothing more.

We finally arrived in the bigger of the two ballrooms, where the crystal chandeliers which had once belonged to Louis XVI hung majestically from the ceiling. "And now, my dear, you really *must* go and change," Konstantin said, "or you'll be late for your own ball."

Strictly speaking, there should have been no ball. By the rules of Petersburg society, they were only held in the season, and the season began with the Tsar's ceremonial appearance at the Winter Palace on New Year's Day.

"It's only out of respect for your great beauty that His Majesty has graciously consented to let me break with tradition," Konstantin continued. "If you don't appear, there'll be trouble."

He was making fun of me. The Tsar had consented out of respect for Konstantin, his old army comrade. And that consent mattered! My Konstantin was afraid of nothing living or dead – he would have faced the Devil himself with a smile on his face – but his devotion to the Tsar was absolute. Without his master's nod, there would have been no ball. Without his master's nod, there would have been no marriage.

What a ball it was! Konstantin had spared no expense and people said there'd been nothing like it since the fancy dress ball at the Winter Palace in 1903. If I close my eyes now, I can still see it. The soldiers' uniforms – white and scarlet. Their helmets of gold and silver, surmounted by the Russian eagle. The Court officials in their uniform, heavy with gold embroidery and tailing off into short breeches and white silk stockings. The ladies, in their low-cut court gowns, shoulders bare, walking carefully to avoid stepping on each other's trains.

And in the middle of it, me – little Anna – drenched in the diamonds that my husband had given me just that day. A diadem set with two rows in my hair. A *ferronière* with a single diamond crossing my forehead. A diamond necklace. Diamonds bordering the neck of my dress. A flower on the back of my gown made entirely of the precious stones. Two diamond chains leading to the front of the bodice and then to a buckle at my waist. If I had one quarter of the stones now, I could buy the whole of Matlock Road, and yet, had I worn any less, I would have been considered underdressed.

As I stood by my husband's side, I found myself searching the gathering for the face I'd seen outside the cathedral that morning, the hard, unforgiving eyes, the scarred face, the . . .

Ridiculous? Of course it was! Though there were hundreds of people at the ball, it was still a very exclusive affair. He, of all people, could not possibly be there. But I couldn't stop looking.

It was an hour before dawn when the last of the guests departed and we were finally left alone.

"You look tired, my dear," Konstantin said. "Shall we go to bed?"

To bed?

Yes!

But how?

Together?

This was my wedding night, but the marriage, though sanctified, was never to be consummated. I realized I had no idea what part Konstantin expected me to play in his life.

My husband took my arm and led me up the grand spiral staircase. Vera, my maid, followed at a discreet distance with Konstantin's valet.

Would we, at some point, part? Would Konstantin suddenly say, "This is your room," and disappear down the corridor? Did I want him to? Questions, questions, questions!

Perhaps Konstantin was wondering, too. Perhaps he didn't finally make up his mind until we stopped outside the exquisitely carved, heavy oak door.

"I prefer to sleep at the back of the house," he said. "It's away from the noise of the *prospekt* and has a view over the river."

I wasn't even aware that we'd reached the back. I was totally lost in the palace of which I was the supposed mistress.

Konstantin opened the door and ushered me through it. I'd grown used to splendour that day, but this room – which he'd not shown me on our tour – took my breath away. The Empire bed, with its canopy of shot silk, looked big enough to sail to America in. The Persian carpets which covered the floor were of a delicacy I'd never before seen.

And the paintings! There were three of them, abstracts. Though I was not very familiar with the form, I could still admire the sweep of them, the use of colour. They pumped out a feeling of energy. They were a triumph in themselves because they gave a sense of the triumph of life.

"Picasso again?"

Konstantin shook his head.

"Who then?" I asked.

"They're Konstantin Mayakovsky's. I keep them here as a constant rebuke. But one day, I'll devote the time to them that art demands. Then I may, perhaps, have something really worth displaying."

One day! Even wise Konstantin did not always realize that 'one day' may never come. Only the old, I think, carry the knowledge with them constantly, and then fate, like the cruel joker it is, surprises them with another morning.

Konstantin opened the door in the wall opposite the bed.

"Your dressing room," he said.

"Is it?" I asked, knowing I sounded stupid, yet unable to bring myself to ask any of the questions which sprang to my mind.

I sat down at my dressing table. It was a beautiful thing – Chippendale. Konstantin had sent his servants scouring all of Petersburg to find something special for me, and had paid well above the market price when they did. He never told me that himself – I discovered it later. I wondered then, and wonder now, how many other kind marvellous things he did for me that I never found out about.

While Vera unpinned my hair and Konstantin's valet struggled with his boots and breeches, we talked – in English – through the half-open door.

"How do you feel now, my little princess?" my husband asked, and though I was not looking in his direction, I knew he was smiling.

I felt *overwhelmed*, as I had that day he killed the wolf. I felt I had been on a merry-go-round which had only just stopped turning. But part of me – a large part of me – felt guilty. "Was all that ostentation really necessary?" I asked.

Konstantin laughed. "The Court expects it, if you can afford it. And I – we – can."

"But those crystal bowls with the uncut sapphires and emeralds in them – just lying around as if they were of no more value than chocolates. What purpose can they serve?"

Konstantin laughed again. "It's the fashion among the wealthy, to show just how rich they are. I do it mainly to annoy the people who *can't* afford it."

"But why?"

"Because I don't really like Petersburg society, Anna. Any of it. It's mean and nasty and greedy. Were it not the Tsar's explicit wish, I'd never entertain at all."

"The waste still seems wrong," I protested.

"So what would you have me do? Follow Jesus' teaching? Sell all I have and give it to the poor?"

"Why not?"

"I'm very rich, Anna, but not that rich. Were I to give every peasant and worker in Russia his share of my wealth, each one would receive very little indeed."

Looking into the mirror, I could see that I was frowning. "You could help some at least," I suggested.

"Very well, then. Your wish is my command. Tomorrow we'll sell the precious stones and distribute the profits."

"Where?"

"Why not in your *mir*?"

And what would happen then? The crops would rot in the fields. The *muhziks* would go on an incredible spree and

123

probably drink themselves to death – if they didn't kill each other in brawls first.

"Well, my little princess, shall we do it?"

"You're laughing at me," I accused him.

"Of course I am. I hope I'll always be able to laugh at you. But if that's what you want, we'll do it. Is it what you want?"

No, it wasn't. The muhziks were too ignorant and narrow to save themselves, as ignorant and narrow as I had been when I entered the Count's house for the first time. They needed education, they needed leading. They needed to be dragged to their salvation whether they wished it or not.

But where was the leadership to come from? Not the Little Father. Even my brief stay in Petersburg had shown me that he and his creaking government machine were not up to the task. Not from the aristocracy – they were as self-absorbed as the *muhziks*. There had to be another way.

My mind drifted back to a conversation I'd had long, long ago.

"The S. . .Soviet is rule by the workers. It sees to it that people get f. . .food, and that each person gets a f. . .fair share."

I'd been so absorbed in my thoughts that it came as a shock to me to realize I was fully undressed and in my night-gown. Her task completed, Vera wished me good-night, and left. I heard the click of the corridor door to the dressing room, and knew that Konstantin's valet had gone, too. There was only us now, with one thin wall keeping us apart – and the thought terrified me.

I told myself I was being irrational. Konstantin had no wish to make love to me – and I wouldn't have minded if he had. There was absolutely *nothing* to be frightened about. Except . . . except perhaps that how we behaved to each other that night, our first night together, would set the pattern for the rest of our married life.

Konstantin coughed to let me know he was there, standing in the doorway between dressing room and bedroom. He was wearing his night-shirt and, for once, he looked uncomfortable. "There's a bed in my dressing room," he said. "I'll sleep there if that is your wish."

"What do *you* want to do?" I asked the man who'd saved me from the gutter and given a name to my unborn child.

For a long time, he didn't speak, and though I tried to read his face, it gave away nothing. "We're an odd couple, you and I," he said finally. "We can never experience the love that most couples share, but I think . . . I think I could learn to love you in another way. Perhaps I already do. I'd like to share your bed, Anna."

And I wanted to share his.

We lay stiffly side by side for a while, and then Konstantin reached over and pulled me to him. As his firm muscles pressed against me, I felt passion rising in my belly and fought it back – though it was one of the hardest things I've ever done in my life.

The yearning for him became easier to suppress in time, but it never went away, and while millions of women throughout the world feigned sexual excitement, I was forced to lie there and pretend the opposite.

I wish, just once, my dear Konstantin, we could have broken down the barriers and I'd been able to show you how *much* I cared for you.

Konstantin was soon asleep, but my brain refused to rest.

The window, the small voice which lives inside my head nagged. *Go to the window!*

I gently disentangled myself from Konstantin's arms and climbed out of bed. The winter sun was rising, shedding its watery light over the Artillery School and the Finland Station. I looked down on the Liteiny Bridge and was not surprised when I saw the solitary figure standing there.

He was too far away for me to distinguish his face, but I was sure he was staring in my direction. Sure, too, that he'd been waiting in the freezing cold for most of the night. And though he looked little bigger than a matchstick or a toy soldier, I was convinced it was him I'd seen in the crowd outside the Kazan Cathedral.

Watching him, I felt a sudden chill, as if he had brought the icy winds of Siberia back in his pocket – and was hurling them at me.

"I know you hate me now," I said softly to the tiny shape against the railings, "but I'm glad you didn't die. I always hoped you'd escape. Honestly, Sasha."

Chapter Eleven

Tsarskoe Selo – which means *The Tsar's Village* – was only twenty-eight *versts* from Petersburg, but as I sat on the train and let Vera fuss over untangling the knots in my hair, I couldn't help wishing that the journey could be much longer because I had knots of my own – in my personal life – which needed to be untangled.

For reasons I did not then understand, I had been invited to tea with the Imperial family. I liked the Tsar, at least as much as anyone is ever allowed to *like* royalty. And I knew it was important to Konstantin that I bear myself well. But . . .

But the Tsar was the at pinnacle of the system which had driven my mother to a premature grave, the system which had allowed Sasha to be exiled to slavery in Siberia.

Poor Sasha. I wondered what had become of him after the night of my wedding, when he'd stood on the bridge in the freezing cold, looking up at the window which he knew instinctively to be mine. We'd been so close back in the *mir*, so very, very close . . .

I was avoiding my problem. The Tsar was at the pinnacle of a system which was unfair, and the stronger he became – the more men like my Konstantin could breathe fire into his soul – the more entrenched that system would become. My husband believed that the alternative to autocratic rule was no rule at all, but just this once, he was wrong. There was another option – the Soviet.

The Soviet! Would I always be haunted by the spectre of 1905? Would I always look back to a Golden Age which I'd been too young even to play a part in? How could I both be true to both my husband and pay off the debt I owed my mother?

"If you could just keep still for a minute, madam," my maid said, "we'd soon have all the knots unravelled."

Ah Vera, if only it had been as simple as that.

The track which had paralleled ours from Petersburg now peeled off, and looking down it I could see gendarmes, guarding the route to the Tsar's private station.

"We're nearly there," I said.

"Yes, madam," Vera complained. "And I'm not half finished."

"I'm sure it's perfect. Why must you always worry so much about me?"

"It's just that I like you to look nice, madam. I take a pride in your appearance."

"Doesn't it ever bother you that you're a servant?" I asked. "Don't you ever resent the fact that you do my hair and I never do yours?"

Vera looked puzzled. "No, madam. Why should it? You're a princess and I'm not."

I sighed. Changing Russia, and the Russians, was not going to be an easy task at all.

I was led through the huge domed entrance hall of the Palace and into the antechamber of the Imperial apartments. Here, generations of painted tsars surrounded me, majestic and fierce, their lacquered eyes glaring both at me and at the bicycles which the Grand Duchesses had propped up against their gilt frames.

My escort was a gigantic Abyssinian, dressed in a white turban, baggy red breeches, a black jacket embroidered with gold – and yellow shoes turned up at the toes. The room he led me to was, by contrast, as mundane as could be. It was filled with ugly Victorian furniture which, even at a glance, I could see was machine made. It wasn't there by accident. The Tsar, one of the richest men in the world, liked it – and bought it by the roomful from Maples of London.

The family were already seated and waiting to take tea. I curtsied to each of them in turn. Nicholas, who was wearing a tweed suit, nodded diffidently, as if he were embarrassed.

128

The Empress's pretty face was strained and so pale that it was almost the colour of her white tea gown, but her eyes blazed with a fire which almost bordered on madness. The Grand Duchesses, all wearing identical polka dot dresses despite the difference in their ages, looked first at me and then at each other, and giggled. The Tsarevitch, clad in a sailor suit, scowled.

How very bourgeois – how very *English* – they all looked. 'The Romanov family of Peckham – circa. 1913.'

The Tsar rose awkwardly to his feet and pulled out a chair. "Princess Mayakovsky," he said, "Anna – if I might call you that – do please take a seat."

Poor man, compelled by his coronation oath to rule an empire which stretched from the Prussian border to the Pacific Ocean – a sixth of the world's land mass – and contained over a hundred million people. He *would* have been much happier living in Peckham, catching the trolley-bus to the bank in the morning, putting in eight hours conscientious – if uninspired – work and returning home as darkness fell for an evening of cosy domesticity. To this day, I hate him as a symbol, but though his incompetence caused the death of thousands, I could never bring myself to hate the man.

I sat, as instructed.

"We are very fond of your husband," the Tsar said stiffly. "He served with us in the army. He's a good soldier and a loyal comrade."

"He will be greatly honoured when I tell him what you've said, Your Majesty," I replied, "which, with your permission, I will."

The Tsar nodded his head in assent. "Could you pour the tea, please, Wifey?" the absolute autocrat of all the Russias asked his Empress.

Countess Olga would have been outraged if anyone had suggested that *she* pour the tea. The act was below her. That was what servants were for. The Empress Alexandra simply smiled at her husband and reached for the silver teapot.

Sandwiches, scones and cakes were passed around the table with the proper show of genteel manners, and the Tsar finally began to unbend a little. "And what have my Sweet Chickens been up to all day?" he asked his daughters.

The four Grand Duchesses outlined their doings in voices which should have belonged to much younger children. Annoying as it was, I suppose their emotional backwardness wasn't really their fault. The family led a very private life. The only people the girls ever saw were close relatives.

So why was I there? Especially at tea, the only time in the Tsar's long day when he had a real opportunity to see his children? Out of respect for my husband? Konstantin hadn't thought so when I'd asked him. It was a mystery.

I caught the Empress staring at me, as if she wanted to say something, but was afraid to. She was painfully shy, poor woman. Each year she attended fewer and fewer social functions, much to the annoyance of court officers and high ranking civil servants who would have gained *cachet* from meeting her. And when travelling on the Imperial train, she'd pull the blind down at stations, thus enraging the local aristocracy who'd waited for hours to catch a glimpse of her. It was a vicious circle. The less she appeared in public, the more unpopular she became. And as her unpopularity grew, so did her reluctance to go out and be seen.

"You . . . you come from peasant stock, do you not, Anna?" the Empress said in a rush, finally finding her courage.

"Yes, Your Majesty."

"And how do they feel about my husband in the country-side?"

I was lost for an answer. How could I tell her that the only thing a *muhzik* felt anything for was his earth, and any loyalty he had for his Tsar was based on mystical self-interest?

They were waiting for me to speak – all of them. I thought back to my days in the *izbá*, sitting by the stove and listening to Papa describe how he would travel to Petersburg and, with typical peasant cunning, talk the Tsar into giving him more land.

"My father often mentioned His Majesty," I said. "He saw the Little Father as both a friend and a protector."

Clever Anna! What a fox you were then! Why couldn't you

130

have handled your social worker this morning with even half the cunning you used before the Empress?

Alexandra let out an audible sigh of relief.

"Yes, the common people love their Tsar," she said. "They know that he has been placed on the throne by God, *by God*, to rule them. That's why the bureaucrats, the aristocracy, the so-called intelligentsia, all conspire to set up a wall between him and his people."

She really believed that – they all did. Everything the government wanted to do, every action taken by the parliament, was part of re-enforcing a wall – a *strednostenie* we call it in Russian – which kept the Tsar away from his true subjects. If only the Tsar could find a way to breach that wall and make contact with the peasantry, Alexandra thought, he would receive the adoration he deserved.

How easy it is to be romantic about *muhziks* when you don't know any! Perhaps that's why Nicholas never followed in the footsteps of his illustrious ancestor, Catherine the Great, and made a grand tour round the country – there's a comfort in romance which is rarely to be found in reality.

"Could I have another cup of tea please, Wifey?" the Tsar asked.

Wifey dutifully poured. "*You* see the truth, Anna," she said, as she handed her husband his drink. "Coming from the country, you can see it in a way that none of the court officials possibly could."

I was beginning to see *something* – the reason I'd been invited. I was their chink in the wall, a nicely sanitized peasant who would tell them what they wanted to hear.

"And do you know our dear friend Grigorii?" the Tsar asked.

"Grigorii?"

"Grigorii Rasputin. He's a *starets* – a holy man – from Siberia. You must have heard of him."

As a matter of fact, I *had* heard a great deal about Rasputin. He had no table manners, it was said – his way of eating his favourite food, fish soup, was to plunge his fingers into the liquid, pull out the solid pieces of flesh and then, when he'd eaten them all, to suck his fingers clean. He was known to

131

have a voracious sexual appetite, and to take any woman to his bed – from the grandest countess to the commonest prostitutes – with equal gusto. He frequented the gypsy camps on the outskirts of the city, where he often drank to the point of collapse. There were new stories about his excesses every week, each one more outrageous than the last – and most of them were true.

"You must *surely* have heard of the wonderful work he's done," the Empress said, impatient to hear me sing his praises.

"I'm told he's a great healer," I said cautiously.

"Indeed he is," she replied warmly. "He's the only one who can relieve our poor son's pain."

Alexei, the poor son, had already been diagnosed as a haemophiliac, an illness transmitted only through the female line, and his condition had contributed both to the Empress's sense of guilt and her unpopularity in the city.

I was surprised to hear the door click open behind me. The servants had strict instructions not to disturb the family during tea. I was surprised, too, at the instant change in the Empress. The tension drained from her face, her smile was almost saintly. I turned, and saw *him* standing there.

He was dressed like a peasant in baggy trousers, blouse and boots, but the boots were highly polished leather and the blouse pure silk. The man who was to contribute so much to the fall of the Romanov dynasty was then around forty-eight. He was about medium height and had powerful shoulders. His hair was parted in the middle, his skin had the weather-beaten complexion of a Siberian peasant. But it was his eyes which were most striking. As he turned his attention on me, they seemed to grow larger and larger. It was said that he could expand his pupils at will, though perhaps this was just illusory – like so many other things about him.

He'd been a *real* peasant when he first arrived in Petersburg, said people who'd know him at the time. His beard had been filthy, his skin mottled with dirt. Yet even then there'd been something about him which had made society ladies take him up and teach him him to use expensive pomades on his beard, to look after his hands and fingernails, to wash

132

in water rather just relying on steam in the bathhouse to cleanse him.

"Grigorii! Dear Friend!" the Empress sighed.

The *starets* rushed across the room, flung his arms around the Tsar, and kissed him. It was no great coincidence that he had arrived just as we were discussing him. The Empress was *always* talking about him. And Rasputin, himself, with greater access to the royal family than any court official, was a constant visitor.

Breaking away from the Nicholas, Rasputin kissed the Empress, and all the children. It was only when he finally relinquished his hold on pasty-faced Alexei that he spoke.

"Mama, Papa, I am come to guide you . . . the sins of the world I take upon myself . . . for has not the holiest man . . . for as the eagle shall fly to the top of the mountain, so shall the worm sink below the earth."

It was all gibberish, of course, but Rasputin's reputation was never built on his words – it rested solely on the impression he made.

The royal couple trusted him completely, and not just in the matter of their son's health. Two years earlier, the Tsar dispatched him to Nizhny Novgorod to 'look into the soul' of its governor and decide whether or not he would make a good Minister of the Interior. Later on, in the war, he grew so powerful that he could force a change of government almost at will.

Were Nicholas and Alexandra fools to have so much faith in him? Perhaps, but they were not the only ones. He had a large following amongst the society ladies of Petersburg and the support of several eminent churchmen.

Nor was the *starets* a complete charlatan. Drunkard, lecher and bribe-taker that he was – as any *muhzik* would have been in his position – he was convinced of his own holiness.

Even I, at that first meeting, could feel his power, and though I didn't believe for a second it came from God, it still terrified me.

"Who are you?" Rasputin asked, and I realized that he was talking to *me*.

I was suddenly incapable of speech. It was the Empress who supplied my title.

"The Prince's new wife!" Rasputin exclaimed. "Beautiful, beautiful."

He leant forward and kissed me. His lips brushed against my cheeks in the Russian way – once, twice, three times. My nose was filled with the smell of the strong, cheap soap which he would always insist on using, despite his society disciples' protests.

I suppose I was lucky he didn't fondle me then and there. He often caressed women in public, saying he was tempering them against passion, telling them there was no harm in *him* touching them intimately, because they were all his sisters. I suppose I was lucky – but the kiss was bad enough.

"Anna," he murmured. "Little sister . . . only through weakness shalt thou find strength . . . only through temptation shalt thou discover redemption."

I was smothered by his presence, flooded with a mixture of fascination and horror. I felt as if his lips were sucking my essence from me. The moment he stood back I rose hurriedly, but shakily, to my feet.

"If Your Majesty will excuse me . . ." I said.

The Tsar nodded absently. The 'dear friend' had arrived and the family wanted him to themselves. I would still have gone anyway, with or without permission. I couldn't have stayed in the room with Rasputin a second longer.

He spoke to me once more as I was opening the door. "You must come to my house," he said. "63–65 Gorokhavaya Street . . . come and eat with my beloved sisters . . . and the Lord said, 'Yea, to the pure all things are pure' . . . You must come."

It wasn't until I was back in my own palace that I felt safe, until I had the arms of my kind, strong husband around me that I finally stopped shaking.

There is too much of the Russian fatalist in me to deny that some things are *meant* to happen – that there is a guiding force which plots at least part of our destiny. And this guiding force, this 'god' if that's what you want to

134

call it, has both a sense of humour and a flair for the dramatic.

I understand him very well, this puppet master in the sky. Know the way he thinks, the way he works. Know, with absolute certainty, that he can rarely resist the temptation to show us the contrasts and contradictions which exist in all our lives. Which is why, on the night after I'd visited the Alexander Palace, I drew back the curtains of my bedroom window and looked down on Liteiny Bridge. Which is why, when I saw the solitary figure standing there and looking up in my direction, I wasn't surprised. I'd been to the bastion of autocracy and tradition. Why should it now seem strange that the other end of the scale should be trying to suck me towards it?

I closed the curtains, opened them again and closed them a second time. It was not a prearranged signal – how could it be when we hadn't even talked to each other since I was a child? But it said, "I'm ready!" and I was sure Sasha would understand.

I waited ten minutes before opening the curtains once more, and when I looked down onto the bridge it was deserted.

Chapter Twelve

When three days had passed, and nothing had happened, I began to question my instincts. Had it really been Sasha on the bridge on the night of my wedding? Him I'd signalled to from my window? Or had the tiny figure I'd looked down on been a stranger – a drunk or a tramp – who'd stopped on the bridge simply because he had nowhere else to go?

We'd been so close, Sasha and I. When we'd sat by the well and talked, the words we'd spoken had been important, but more important still had been the understanding which lay behind them. Or so I'd thought. Perhaps I'd been wrong all along – romanticizing my childhood, imagining an empathy where none had existed.

If it *was* you, Sasha, why won't you contact me, I thought worriedly.

Like so many things we wait anxiously for, the message, when it came, took me by surprise. I was shopping on Nevsky Prospekt – buying baby clothes – when the note was thrust into my hand.

"Who . . . what . . . ?" I asked, but the messenger boy had already dashed off, without even waiting for a tip.

I opened the folded piece of cheap paper and looked down at the careful, self-taught writing. 'I will be in the *Café de Paris* until noon,' I read. 'If you don't come by then, you'll never see me again.'

The note was unsigned.

I looked at my watch. It was nearly eleven-thirty. I started to walk briskly – almost to run – down the street.

"Is something wrong, Madam?" my chauffeur called after me.

"Take the parcels back to the palace," I shouted over my shoulder. "I'll get a cab."

He was sitting at an isolated corner table, dressed in an English tweed suit. It was a poor disguise. Sasha was a peasant through and through, and would never look like anything else until the day he died.

His long, thin face bore marks of suffering which were new since our days in the *mir*. A scar ran across his left cheek, another cut deep into his forehead. His jaw was lopsided, as if it had been broken and not properly reset.

Why was he sitting there, still as a statue? Why wasn't he rushing across the room to meet me, to throw his arms around me in a loving bear hug? Closer and closer I got, until I was standing right by the table. And still he hadn't moved.

"Hello Sasha," I said weakly.

He pointed to the empty chair opposite him. Feeling a weight of disappointment which almost crushed me, I sat down.

It's absurd what details I can remember. The potted palm which brushed against my shoulder as I lowered myself gingerly, heavy with child, on to the chair. The clink as my wedding ring connected with a mock-Empire teacup on the table. The sound of the string quartet filling the half-empty room with – I'm nearly certain – the latest dance tune to come out of Vienna.

Our eyes met. Mine pleaded for a sign of our old friendship. His were as cold as the deep Russian winter. Had the prison camps done that to him? Was that what it took to survive?

To show him I cared – to show him I understood, I said, "It must have been terrible for you in Siberia."

"Si. . .Siberia was bad," he stuttered, "but the escape was w. . .worse. Do you know what a Si. . .Siberian sandwich is?"

I didn't *want* to know! But I knew he wanted to tell me. "What is it?" I asked.

"In a Si. . .Siberian sandwich, there are three men. Two strong and one weak. Th. . .they all escape together. Can

137

you guess why the st. . .strong men take the weak man with them?"

"No," I said, already fearful of the answer.

"Be. . .because they know he's not going to make it. He'll die out there in the fr. . .frozen waste. And when he does die, the others will eat him."

"That's horrible."

"The w. . .weak man always knows why the others want him to go with them – I did – but he goes anyway. Be. . .because there's just a chance that he *won't* die, there's just a f. . .faint glimmer of hope burning inside him that he'll survive. And there's no hope in the camps, n. . .no hope at all."

"I'm sorry, Sasha," I said.

"I went back to the *mir*. My wife and ch. . .children have gone, nobody knows where they are. You'd gone, too. I c. . .came to Petersburg to rescue you. But you didn't need rescuing, did you?" he asked bitterly.

He'd come to be my knight in shining armour, only to find I'd married the dragon.

"You've joined the enemy, Anna," he continued. "You dress like them, you talk like them – you don't even speak good Ru. . .Russian any more."

I was becoming as angry as he was. What right had he to speak to me like this? What did he know about my life? All right – I'd confirm his prejudices! What did I care? "Russian is a language I use very little these days," I said, "except with my servants."

"Your s. . .servants! How easily you say that. As if you were born to it. Have you fo. . .forgotten where you come from, Anna? Where your duty lies?"

"No, damn you! I haven't forgotten. Why are you here Sasha? To insult me? Or to ask for my help? Because if it's my help you want, you'd better tell me now."

But he didn't want to talk about that. Not yet. "How could you ma. . .marry a prince?" he demanded. "How could you ma. . .marry a blood-sucking leech?"

"He's a good man," I said hotly. "He's built a school on his estate. And a hospital. He's brought in a German to teach

138

the *muhziks* how to farm more scientifically. Nobody who was once his father's serf goes hungry. No widows and children are ever left to starve."

Sasha wasn't listening. "Wh. . .what about this child you are carrying?" he demanded. "Is it his? Or does it be. . .belong to one of his friends. How m. . .many of the aristocratic bastards have you given yourself to, Anna? Ten? Twenty?"

It could have been Countess Olga talking! I would have slapped any other man immediately, but there was a desperation in Sasha's voice which made me hold back. He didn't *want* to hurt me, he *had* to – he just couldn't help himself.

"You're drawing attention to us," I hissed. "You're a fugitive – remember? Do you *want* to be sent back to Siberia – for good, this time?"

He took a deep breath and I saw Sasha the man recede and Sasha the revolutionary take control once more. "We want your h. . .help," he said.

"Who is we?"

"The Bolsheviks."

Of course it would be the Bolsheviks. Sasha would never have joined anyone else but the extremists. Yet in a country where the problems, too, were extreme, wasn't that really the only sensible course of action?

"What do you want me to do?" I asked.

"Three days ago, you vi. . .visited Nicholas Romanov in Tsarskoe Selo."

"You want me to spy on the Tsar! That's why you stood on the bridge, watching my home!"

"Your *palace*, you mean!" Sasha sneered. The revolutionary's shell was starting to crack and the Sasha who now seemed to despise me was coming to the surface.

"All right. My palace," I agreed wearily.

"Do you make love to Nicholas as well?" Sasha demanded. "Do you sp. . .spread your legs for your monarch?"

"Why were you on the bridge the night of my wedding?" I asked, wanting to hurt him as he was hurting me. "Was it because I'd seen the Tsar *that* day, too – in the cathedral? Or were you just interested in seeing for yourself how many

139

of my husband's aristocratic friends I'd be willing to fuck on my marriage bed?"

"Anna, I . . ."

He looked down at the table, as if he were ashamed. Was there a third Sasha hiding beneath the revolutionary and the man who hated me, I wondered. Was my old, dear Sasha in there somewhere, waiting for me to coax him out?

"I will *not* spy on the Tsar," I told him.

"Because he has done you the gr. . .great honour of entertaining you in his palace?"

I thought back to that 'entertainment'. The Tsar, shy and nervous except when he was listening to his children. The Empress, strained almost to breaking point until the 'dear friend' arrived. "No," I said. "Not because he's honoured me, but because he's trusted me."

"And you'd ne. . .never betray that trust," Sasha sneered.

"Yes, I would, but not just to give you family gossip and tittle-tattle. There's a price for which I'd sell my conscience – but it's not as low as that."

"What fine terms you talk in now you are rich and educated. So you w. . .won't help us."

"I didn't say that. If you want money, I can provide it. And perhaps when my Russian is a little better," I added sarcastically, "I can be of some use to you in organizing the workers."

The waiter brought me tea and I drank it the peasant way, holding the sugar between my teeth and letting the liquid wash over it. "You see," I challenged Sasha, half joking, half serious, "I haven't forgotten how to be a *muhzik*."

For some time he said nothing, but stared moodily down at his cup, stirring it occasionally and watching intently until the turbulence had settled. "Sp. . .Spying on the Tsar is safe. Any other work could be dangerous," he said finally, and there was a new tone to his voice which could almost have belonged to the old Sasha.

"I accept the danger," I told him.

I had no choice. I'd a duty to pay to my dear, dead Mama. I only wished I could have paid it in a way she'd have hated less.

Sasha took a *rouble* of his pocket to pay the bill. "Look at this," he said, holding it out to me.

I did as I'd been told. It seemed like a perfectly ordinary note to me.

"D. . .do you see the blood on it?"

I shook my head. "There isn't any blood on it, Sasha."

"Yes, th. . .there is. It's from a bank raid one of the fi. . .fighting squads carried out in the Ukraine. They used bombs, Anna. Five people were ki. . .killed. One of them was a child. Do you w. . .want to be a part of that?"

He was trying to scare me off, but it wasn't working. "I'd be a part of it whether I worked with the underground or spied on the Tsar," I told him. "Innocent people are bound to die before it's over. Maybe we will, too. But if we don't do something to change the system, there'll be even more deaths – from disease, famine, or just from over-work."

Sasha nodded his head. He knew all that as well as I did. He paid for our drinks, and taking my arm, led me to the door. "I w. . .want you to see something," he said.

"What?"

"One of the f. . .factories in the Narva District."

"Why?"

"Because if you're g. . .going to risk your life, you sh. . .should at least see what you're risking it for."

We took the No. 14 tram which ran down Sadovya Street, past the Haymarket and across the Kalinkinski Bridge. Its terminus was the Narva Triumphal Arch – a memorial to Russia's victory over Napoleon. "We can walk from here," Sasha said.

It didn't take us long to reach the Narva Cotton Mill, a long brick building with small windows and smoking chimneys. I tried to imagine what it would be like to work inside it for ten or eleven hours a day. Hellish! At least the *muhziks* laboured out in the open.

"That's where they work their guts out," Sasha said. "Now let's go and s. . .see how they live."

The barrack block looked more like a factory than the mill itself, the thick walls more forbidding, the windows even

141

tinier. There was a guard on the door, an old Cossack. He winked at Sasha, and stepped aside and let us pass.

"A Party member?" I asked.

"A sympathizer. We have fr. . .friends everywhere."

Except perhaps in the Alexander Palace – which was why he'd been sent to me.

The dormitories were long, narrow and dark. The rows of beds were so tightly packed that there was not a *vershók* of space between them. The air was thick with the smell of cabbage and sweat.

"The worst *izbá* is better than this," I said.

"Much better," Sasha agreed. "This d. . .dormitory was built for migrant workers who had only to stick it for a few months and then could go back to their *mirs*. Now all the workers are p. . .p. . .permanent – and they have their families with them."

"Whole families live in here?" I gasped.

"Whole families. One b. . .bed per family. There's rats everywhere. S. . .sometimes they attack the babies. When there's sickness, they all g. . .get it. They're b. . .burying children nearly every week."

"But how can they – how could *any* man allowed his children to live in a place like this?"

"There's no ch. . .choice for them. Their land in the *mir* has either been sold or is t. . .too little to live off."

"In the *mir*, they'd at least have their own vegetable plots," I mused. "What do they eat here?"

"Black bread and cabbage. Meat *you* wouldn't feed your la. . .lap-dog is an unheard of luxury to them."

"You've shown me the worst," I said accusingly.

For the first time since we'd met again, Sasha smiled. "Of course I've sh. . .shown you the worst. There wouldn't have been much point in sh. . .showing you the best."

"I want to help those people," I said, when we were once more outside where the air, if not clean, was at least breathable.

Sasha glanced nervously over his shoulder. "The *Okhrana* have sp. . .spies everywhere," he told me. "We c. . .could be arrested at any moment. It would be much safer for you to do what I asked and r. . .report on the Tsar and his—"

"No," I said angrily. "I'll be a proper revolutionary, or I'll be nothing."

"Then perhaps it's b. . .better that you're nothing."

"If you won't put my name forward, I'll find someone else who will," I threatened.

Sasha bowed his head. "I'll put your name f. . .forward," he mumbled. "And you'll be accepted. The P. . .Party can make good use of you."

"When should I be able to start work?"

"Not yet. Not until a. . .after your baby's born. The fa. . .father is a class enemy, but it's still your child, and I wou. . .wouldn't want to see it come to any harm."

It was the kindest thing he'd said all day. And it made sense. I had so many duties – to the workers, my husband, my dead mother – but my first obligation was to my baby.

"If you're going to w. . .work with us, it's best we're not seen together more than is absolutely necessary," Sasha said. "You take the f. . .first tram back to the Central District and I'll wait the se. . .second."

"You take the first," I said. "I want to stay and look at the dormitory block a little longer."

"I don't think you sh. . .should."

"Well I'm going to, whether you like it or not. First get me into the Party, and *then* you can start ordering me around."

Without another word, he turned and walked away. I watched his retreating back. He seemed so thin and vulnerable. But he was much tougher than he looked, I reminded myself. When the Dragoons had taken him away, I'd thought it would be the last time I'd ever see him. The men he'd escaped with from Siberia had chosen him because they'd expected him to die on the way back. Yet here he was in Petersburg.

It didn't occur to me to ask myself why Sasha didn't want me to stay in front of the dormitory block. Even if it had, I'd never have guessed the reason. *He was afraid I'd be seen by the owner.*

I imagined at the time that the mill belonged to one of the *Old Believers*, a white-haired, white-bearded gentleman in a frock coat and top hat. Or else it was the property of foreign investors, who employed bully-boy local managers. I imagined wrongly.

If the mill owner had walked past at that very moment, I would have recognized him, and he me. The man who kept his workers in such desperate conditions was the same one who was directly responsible for Sasha's exile to Siberia.

The mill was owned by Peter.

Chapter Thirteen

I hear the pregnant women talking about it in the Vulcan. I sit in the corner, a silent old lady, and don't miss a thing.

I can usually tell when it's happened from the way they walk. They still waddle, of course, but somehow there's extra care to it now that the lumps in their stomachs have become more – so much more – than just a discomfort.

I love watching them, these women who are as graceful as hippos, as touching as a teardrop.

Aching backs resting against the bar, they scan the room for a friend – or at least a sympathetic listener. Sometimes, if no one else is available, that listener is me.

The mother-to-be eases her swollen body down on the seat next to mine. "Nice day again," she'll say.

The remark is only a conversational gambit. She doesn't care about the weather. It could be pouring down outside, and it would still me a nice day for her.

"Ask me about the baby!" she screams silently. "Ask me! Ask me!"

I could tease her – "The man on the radio this morning said we can expect rain soon" – but I don't. "How's the baby?" I say.

"He kicked me today."

"Was it the first time, dear?" I ask, knowing full well that it was.

"Yes, the first time."

"You must be very happy."

"I am. I really am."

And proud. Oh, so proud. They act as if they alone, in the whole world, were doing something unique and wonderful – which, of course, they are.

*   *   *

It wasn't happiness which swept over me when I first felt my baby move on the tram back from Peter's mill – it was fear. A tidal wave of fear. An ocean of fear. Though I'd never been pregnant before, I was sure, with the instinct inherited from a thousand generations of child-bearers, that something was very wrong.

I looked out of the tram window. Life on the street was proceeding as normal. Shoppers were shopping, traders were trading. It wasn't right! There should have been fire and brimstone, earthquakes, plagues of locusts. The whole world should have been turned upside down – because my baby wasn't perfect.

The Count had advised me to have an abortion, and I'd rejected the idea out of hand. I didn't mind if my baby was crippled, I'd told him. If it was, it would need me more than ever. Ah, but that was back then, when the baby was little larger than a pin head, as abstract and far away as Australia. Now it was real. Now I had to face the prospect of bringing into the world a small life which was, in some way, incomplete.

Abortion was illegal at the time, but for the rich anything is possible. I'd have more children after this one, Konstantin had said. And I would. I knew I would. So why run the risk of giving birth to a child for whom life would be nothing but misery?

The tram turned onto Nevsky Prospect. It suddenly became very important to me that I should reach a decision about the baby before we reached Palace Square. I'd decide by the time we reached Kazan Cathedral, I told myself, but we rattled past it, and I still didn't know what to do. I'd make up my mind before we reached the Singer Building, I promised, but we were there and I was still at a loss.

And then, like a sudden summer rainstorm, certainty poured down on me, soaking me through. Other women, before and since, have terminated pregnancies, and who am I to say whether they were right or wrong? I can only say that as I sat in that tram, rocked by its motions and my own tears, I knew that I could never have my baby aborted, that all practical, spiritual and moral considerations were as nothing.

I was in the power of the life force, and I was helpless to resist it.

In April the snow melted on the Neva, the roads were once more reasonably passable and it was time for the Royal Progress to begin. It was not to be a progress like that undertaken by Catherine the Great, a meeting of monarch and subjects, a voyage of discovery right into the heart of the country. Rather it was to be stiff and formal, like the Tsar himself, a ritualistic celebration of three hundred years of the Romanov dynasty.

The Imperial family was to visit towns of historical importance, retracing Tsar Michael's steps. First they would go to Michael's birthplace, then on to Kostroma, where he was offered the crown, and finally to Moscow, the scene of his coronation.

"His Majesty has ordered me to go with him," Konstantin said.

Of course he had. The shy, diffident Tsar was probably dreading the Progress. It was only to be expected that he'd want Konstantin, who was both his friend and his crutch, to accompany him. But what about me? My fears for the baby were growing daily. Wasn't it equally natural that I, too, should want Konstantin by my side?

"Ze child's 'artbeats are perfectly normal," the French doctor my husband had brought from Paris told me. "All zis worrying you are doing – it is nozzing but neurosis."

What did he know, this serious, grey-haired man? He was a doctor – but had he ever been pregnant? Did he really understand the biological link which binds mother and baby – a link which told me, with absolute certainty, that something was wrong?

And yet even as fear held its ever tightening grip on my swelling belly, I kept silent. It was right that Konstantin should accompany the Tsar. Right that he should witness for himself the ceremonial triumph of a dynasty to which he'd dedicated his life. The child wasn't his responsibility, and though I desperately wanted him beside me when it was born, I knew I *could* manage alone if I had to.

The closer Konstantin's departure date drew, the more unbearable it became to have him around. If I was to swim through the cold waters of loneliness, I wanted to plunge straight in, not dip a tentative toe and freeze by degrees. If he was going, then why, for God's sake, didn't he just go!

How the minutes stretched, how the hours dragged. Four days left, then three, two, and finally, finally, one. Only twenty-four hours more, I told myself on that last morning. Twenty-four short hours. And for most of that time he'll be occupied with official business. You can stand that, Annushka.

I looked in the mirror, forced my face into a neutral mask, and went down to breakfast.

Konstantin was already at the table. A smile played on his lips, as if something pleasant were about to happen. "I've arranged to keep this day free, my little princess," he said. "How would you like to spend the time? We could go for a ride in the car or perhaps visit the museum. Whatever you desire. I'm completely at your orders."

I wanted him to leave right at that minute, to take his coach to Alexander Palace and not to return until the Progress was over. I was terrified that if he didn't go soon, I'd break down and beg him to stay.

"Anna?" Konstantin said.

"I . . . I'm not free," I stuttered. "I have household duties to attend to."

I glanced up at my husband. The expression on his face was one of hurt, but the second he saw me looking at him, it was gone. And so we sat there, facing each other across the breakfast table, both wearing masks.

"Perhaps I should've given you notice I'd be here," Konstantin said finally, "but I wanted to surprise you. Very well, if you're not free, I only have myself to blame. I'm sure I can find something to keep me occupied."

"You'll be going into the city, then?"

148

"No. I can work just well here. It will be pleasant to be around you – even if you are busy."

I knew that if I touched him then, if I even stayed in his presence any longer, I'd crack. "I have a headache," I said, getting out of my chair. "I'm going to lie down."

A look of concern crossed Konstantin's face, and he rose to his feet. "Would you like me to . . . ?" he began.

In a second, he'd have me in his arms, and I'd be lost. "I don't want you to do anything," I shouted as I rushed to the door. "I just want to be left alone."

I locked myself in our bedroom and spent the rest of the morning pacing the floor and sobbing softly.

Konstantin himself came to tell me that lunch was about to be served. "I'm not hungry!" I told him through the bolted door. "Go away!"

It was half-past three before Vera knocked. "You must eat something, madam," she said. "If not for your sake, then for the baby."

"Later. I'll eat later."

"The master told me before he went out to make sure that you ate something," my maid persisted.

I felt as if a great weight had been lifted off me. "You say he's gone out?"

"Yes, madam. About half an hour ago. He said not to expect him back until after dark."

"Have a tray made up for me. Something light. Perhaps a chicken salad. I'll eat it in my sitting room."

I was safe – at least for a while. I unlocked the door.

In the bedroom, hiding from Konstantin, I'd told myself I wasn't hungry, but once the salad was put before me, I discovered a ravenous appetite. I felt stronger when I'd eaten – and I needed to. My problem had not gone away. It was already dark outside, and Konstantin would be returning soon.

I stood up and examined myself in the mirror. Eyes puffy from crying, complexion blotchy, but a little make-up and a short rest would repair most of the damage. You've been acting like a coward, I told my reflection. Konstantin planned

149

a free day to please you, and all you've done in return is to make him unhappy. I'm ashamed of you.

I'd make it up to him, I promised. There were only a few more hours until the Progress began, and for that brief period I would be the girl he had married, the girl – I believed – he had become fond of.

I was still in our cosy sitting room when Konstantin returned. Smile, I ordered myself as I heard his unmistakably masterful footsteps in the corridor. Smile and pretend that everything's all right.

I had a speech prepared but the sight of him temporarily robbed me of words. He was in full-dress uniform – and he looked grim. "I have been to see the Tsar," he told me.

"I'm sorry about this morning Konstantin," I said, recovering. "Pregnant women get irrational and . . ."

Wait! What was that he'd said? He'd been to see the *Tsar*?

"I didn't understand what was upsetting you at first," Konstantin continued, "but when I realized, I knew what I had to do."

"I don't—"

"You need me here. I've asked His Majesty to excuse me from the Progress."

"And he said yes?" I gasped.

Konstantin nodded gravely, as if he were acknowledging a death in the family. How miserable he must have been feeling! For three hundred years the Mayakovskys had served the Crown, and never once in all that time had one of them questioned or tried to avoid a direct order from the Tsar. And now Konstantin had – because I'd been weak. I thought my heart would break.

"It's my place to feel guilty, not yours," my husband said sternly. "I could have saved you a great deal of suffering if only I'd been a little more thoughtful. I should have known where my duty lay long ago."

But what about his duty to the Tsar? And what if Nicholas was so angry that he banished Konstantin from his favour? If my husband wasn't allowed to serve his monarch, he would die.

150

"What exactly did the Tsar say to you?" I asked urgently. "How did he behave?"

A new wave of misery swept over Konstantin's face as he relived the interview, and then, miracle of miracles, a smile came to his lips, his wolf-hunt smile, as if in trying to find the right words for me he had amused himself. What a fighter that man was!

"I can't remember his exact words," Konstantin lied. "Let's just say he was gracious – but displeased."

I ran across the room, threw my arms around his neck and buried my head in his chest. "Do you hate me?" I sobbed. "Do you hate me for what I've made you do?"

Konstantin stroked my hair. "Of course not, little princess."

"But you'll miss the Progress, and I know how much you wanted—"

"Hush now," Konstantin said soothingly. "The Progress will be a great spectacle, but in this very house something even more wonderful is going to happen. A baby will be born – a baby who will bear my name. I want to be there when it happens."

May came, and the ice floes from Lake Ladoga sailed gracefully through Petersburg on their way to the sea. The trees were in bud, the birds were building their nests. All of nature seemed to be following its proper timetable – except for my baby. Though it was now a huge lump in my stomach, though it had caused my feet, ankles, hands and face to swell, and even my vision to become blurred, it refused to come out.

My husband was in constant attendance, as were the French doctor and the two Russian ones who had been brought in to assist him. They fussed over me and checked the baby's heartbeat. They held whispered conversations in corners. It was all to no avail. The baby was not ready to face the world yet, and that was that.

My wilful child gave in to nature suddenly, in the middle of May. The contractions, once they came, were rapid and painful.

"It eez going to be a very queek birth," the French doctor said as I bit down on the rope.

His Russian colleagues agreed. "Perhaps we should give her chloroform."

I shook my head violently.

"It eez perfectly normal," the Frenchman assured me. "Queen Victoria 'erself took it at two of her confinements."

My body was burning up, needles of pain were being driven into me from all sides, but I desired no drug. I wanted to see my baby as soon as possible – to find out the awful truth. With all my remaining strength, I wrenched the cord from my mouth. "Bugger Queen Victoria!" I screamed.

The French doctor gasped, as if scandalized. "Madam, I am not suggesting it merely because it eez fashionable," he said, in a maddeningly logical tone. "What we are talking about 'ere . . ." He looked between my legs, and his voice changed. "Poosh," he urged me. "Poosh!"

I 'pooshed' with all my might. Each muscular contraction set my lungs on fire, and I gulped in the new air like I was drowning.

"Poosh 'arder!" the French doctor said. "'arder!"

I saw the head, round and pink, and could not believe that it had ever been inside me. I saw the trunk, looking so small, so insubstantial for such a large skull. And finally, as the Frenchman moved backwards, I could see the legs.

"Is it all right?" I asked. "Is my baby all right?"

And then I blacked out.

I was alive, I was sure I was alive, yet I was floating in a sea of darkness. As a first, cautious experiment, I flexed the muscles in my hand. They seemed to be performing satisfactorily. A second step. I moved my arm and felt the sheets caress my knuckles. I placed my hand on my leg – both registered the pressure. I appeared to be bodily intact.

My eyelids were glued together, but I forced them open and saw a blurry ceiling. Not infinite space, then. Not black nothingness.

The ceiling became sharper. I could make out the carvings. And more – I recognized them. The ceiling of my bedroom.

Therefore, I was lying in my bed, the bed where, sometime in the past – who knew when – I'd given birth to my baby.

I turned my head painfully to one side and saw Konstantin, my marvellous husband, holding the baby in his arms! A warmness – a deep love I'd never known before – welled up in me.

Yet the small voice in my head would still not be silent. "Look at the baby," it whispered. "Is there anything wrong with it?"

The infant was wrapped in the white lace shawl which had once held Konstantin, and his father before him. Its head was as red and as wrinkled as a blood orange, but that's how new-born babies are, and it was beautiful to me.

The eyes! I gazed at the eyes, looking for the signs of slowness which mark the in-bred village idiot. They were as clear and understanding as any eyes could be expected to be after the adventure of ejection into a strange, incomprehensible world.

"It's a boy," Konstantin said. "We'll call him Nicholas after my father and in honour of the Tsar."

Just as if it were his own child! My love filled the room, encompassing both Konstantin and the baby in a blanket of devotion, drawing them closer to me. Whatever the circumstances of the baby's conception, however unusual the nature of my marriage, we belonged together. We were a family – a little universe of three.

I would have thought it impossible that anything could destroy my happiness at that moment, that anything could douse the flames burning inside me. But Konstantin knew of something which could. And he, my kind loving husband, who would have suffered agonies himself rather than see me receive the slightest hurt, had no choice but to deliver the blow.

"You must try to be brave, Anna," he said.

"What's wrong?" I asked fearfully. "What's the matter with Nicky?"

"The doctors say that nothing *appears* to be wrong. All the muscles are perfectly functional – but a message from the brain doesn't seem to be getting through."

"Tell me!" I screamed. "For God's sake, tell me!"

Konstantin drew back the shawl and revealed the child's legs. They looked wonderful, those perfectly formed, chubby little limbs. My husband took a fold of flesh between his thumb and forefinger and gently twisted. When he released his grip, I could see a red mark on the soft, new skin.

"You understand?" Konstantin asked.

I understood. Oh God, I understood. What Konstantin had done wouldn't have hurt any infant, but it would have surprised it. It would have made the child squirm or kick and cry out. My baby had shown no reaction at all. My baby could feel nothing – nothing – in his legs.

Chapter Fourteen

Time can't be measured only by the clock and the calendar. A few minutes spent nervously waiting for a contact on a dark street corner can seem like a day. An hour's lovemaking is often over in a second. And the first few months of my little son's life were the longest I can ever remember.

How happy he made me in some ways, this bright, cheerful child who I held close to me, whose tiny heart beat against my cheek. But what sadness I felt at the same time, knowing that if he did not start to move his perfect little legs soon, they'd wither away until they were nothing but dried-up stalks.

Konstantin was driven to distraction. A succession of doctors from Petersburg and Moscow – and later Prague and Budapest – paraded through the palace, examined young Nicky, and then shook their eminent heads.

"There looks to be nothing physically wrong with the child."

"Then why can't he move his legs?"

"Perhaps a brain malfunction. It may correct itself soon."

"Or it may never correct itself?"

"That is a possibility we must be prepared for."

After the doctors came the faith healers and divines, holy men who were said to have performed miracles in some obscure corner of the Empire.

"Put your faith in God," said a wandering seer from the Ukraine. "In time, God will cure him."

"We must wait until there is a full moon," explained a turbaned Easterner. "Then, precisely at midnight, we must kill a frog and while its legs are still twitching, we must cut them off and place them on your son's."

And Konstantin, the most logical, the most rational of

men, submitted to the ritual – because he was utterly desperate.

Konstantin spent hours by the crib, the baby's ankles in his big strong hands, moving the legs up and down as if Nicky were pedalling a bicycle, and all the time crooning in a soft, pleading voice, "Come on Nicky. You can do it."

The baby would look at him and gurgle, but without the help of his adoring father, the legs would not move.

The time I could spare from my baby, I gave willingly to the Revolution. Work among the urban poor was a new life to me, and for it I assumed a new persona.

When I left the palace it was as Princess Anna, dressed in all the finery that Konstantin had lavished on me, but near the Litovsky Barracks, I'd check quickly over my shoulder and disappear down an alley which led to the back door of the bakery. There, amid the steam and the flour dust, I changed into a *muhzik* dress, headscarf and felt *valenki* and became Lyudmila, one of the dispossessed.

The bakers were Bolshevik sympathizers, but aside from knowing they were helping the cause, they were kept in ignorance of what I was doing. They were not even sure whether I was a lady pretending to be a peasant, or a peasant pretending to be a lady. And neither was I.

The meetings of the Narva Mill Bolshevik Cell were held in a series of dingy rooms in dilapidated boarding houses on the edge of the industrial district. Aside from Sasha and myself, there were four other members of the cell – an old man with grizzled grey hair whose job it was to sweep up at the mill, two young mechanics and a woman loom operator. For the first few months, the cell seemed to do nothing but talk about the golden future which lay ahead, and the treacheries of the Mensheviks who were attempting to undermine it. Talk, talk, talk – I thought we would be still be talking on our way to our graves.

And then the miners in the Lena gold field changed everything.

The miners put in a modest pay claim – and they'd have settled for less – but the management refused to negotiate.

156

During the demonstration which followed, the police opened fire and scores of the workers were killed. News of the massacre spread rapidly round Russia.

"They'll never listen to us," workers whispered to each other. "If we want something, we have to take it."

And in that, at least, they were right.

New waves of strikes broke out all over the country and inevitably, in the late Autumn of 1913, a spark flew and ignited the discontent which, like so much cotton waste, had been lying around the Narva Mill.

On the 11th of November a group of women reported late for work at the mill. "Our children are sick," one of them said.

"What do you expect me to do about it?" asked the foreman harshly.

"Nothing, but we'd . . . we'd like to go and see them in the middle of the shift."

"You're paid to weave cotton, and that's what you'll do."

"If just one of us could go—"

"No!"

The women bowed their heads and accepted the foreman's ruling. Perhaps one or more of the children would die during the day, but that was only a possibility. Without their mothers' wages, they would *certainly* starve to death.

"One more thing," the foreman said. "You were forty-five minutes late."

"The kids are sick!"

"You'll be fined half a day's pay."

Like autocrats throughout history, the foreman had failed to learn one vital lesson: you can push people – but only so far. Within an hour the entire workforce, six hundred men and women, were out on the street.

On the 12th of November, Sasha called an emergency meeting of our cell. "The st. . .strike is a fact," he told us. "If we don't take the lead, the Mensheviks will." He turned to the grizzle-haired sweeper. "W. . .What are the workers demanding?"

"That the women be given back their half-day's pay and

157

that nobody loses any money for the time they've been on strike."

"Not enough!" Sasha said, banging on the table with his fist. "D. . .double the wages, halve the hours! That has a good ring about it."

"There are other things more important," I said. "Pete . . . the owner of the mill is in breach of the law. He's required to provide free health, sickness benefit and pensions. He doesn't do any of those things. If we could harness the strikers' energy to press—"

"D. . .Double the wages, halve the hours," Sasha repeated, as if he had found a magic formula.

I suddenly realized what he was doing – applying the two basic laws of revolutionary activity – 'Things cannot get better until they have been made to get worse' and 'Never ask for the possible for fear that it will be granted'.

He was right, I could see that. We'd never really improve conditions by concession and gradual reform. We needed sweeping change. It was because I believed this that I was a Bolshevik. Even so, I couldn't wipe from my mind the image of the dormitory blocks, the sight of hollow-eyed, thin-chested children trudging grimly to work.

I wasn't a good revolutionary, I told myself. Sasha was being true to the cause, I was being weak and short-sighted. What I'd forgotten in the heat of debate was that Sasha wasn't fighting just *any* capitalist. He was locked in a struggle with his old enemy Peter, and would do whatever it took to defeat him. A heart filled with hatred is easier to harden, and unlike Sasha, I didn't have a personal hatred for Peter. Not then. *That* was a lesson I was to learn later.

The Mensheviks called for moderation, but the workers were angry, and it was to us they turned for leadership. I played my part as Sasha's lieutenant and had one small triumph of my own. By using Lenin's technique of talking until I was blue in the face – and then carrying on talking – I had made the social programme part of the conditions of returning to work.

The strikers blockaded the mill, stopping scabs and raw materials from entering. Deputations were sent to other local factories and to those in the Vyborg District, to encourage the workers there to walk out too. Though the weather turned bitter, the picket line held firm. The strike stretched into one week, and then into two.

I addressed rallies and argued my way through meetings. I had no fear that anyone would recognize me as a princess. Dressed as I was, acting as I was, even I forgot that I belonged to the aristocracy. I was Lyudmila, a fiery peasant revolutionary, and only when I dragged my exhausted body home to snatch a few hours with my child did my other life exist.

There was one link between my two lives – money. The workers ate better during the strike than they had ever done before, and if my husband had cared enough about possessions to put his hand into one of the crystal bowls of uncut gems, he would have found the bottom filled with pebbles.

Konstantin never commented on my frequent absences. He had his own duties to attend to, and when he was at home, he became totally absorbed with Nicky. Besides, he was not the kind of man who thinks he can only retain his wife's affection by keeping her a virtual prisoner. If it crossed his mind to wonder what I was doing, he probably concluded that I was having an affair. And I was.

It was inevitable, I suppose. I was a child-bride, an almost-virgin mother, with, furthermore, my husband's explicit permission to sleep with other men. I'd worshipped Sasha in the *mir*, and now we were working closely together, under great pressure, on something which really mattered to both of us. Moonlight, heavenly strings and chilled champagne were not necessary. As with the strike, it only needed the smallest of sparks to ignite us.

It happened during the first week of the strike. Another meeting, another depressing boarding house room, the six of us sitting around a battered dining table.

"The C. . .Central Committee is very pleased with the way things are going," Sasha told the cell.

"The Central Committee!" said one of the mechanics, with awe.

"Lenin himself is following the st. . .strike with interest," Sasha lied.

The workers, simple souls that they were, broke into spontaneous, excited applause. Sasha let them run on for a while, then lifted his hands to call for silence. "W. . .Workers of the world unite!" he proclaimed. "The international pr. . .proletariat *will have* their revolution."

". . . will have their revolution," the faithful chimed

"Get back to the picket lines," Sasha continued, his voice quieter and more businesslike now. "Make sure they stand f . . . firm."

The strikers left, and Sasha and I were alone.

"We've got the c. . .capitalist on the run," Sasha said gleefully. "The spectre of a w. . .workers' dictatorship hangs over him like the shadow of death."

It annoyed me to hear him still speaking jargon now that there were just the two of us in the room. "Remember the boycott in the *mir*?" I asked. "You thought you were going to win that time, too. Didn't you? Then Peter blamed the barn-burning on you, you were sent to Siberia, and the *muhziks* were back in the Count's fields that very day. So what makes you think Peter will give in so easily now? I know him. He'll find another barn to burn."

Except for the pale scars on his cheek and forehead, the whole of Sasha's face flushed bright red. "Peter! Peter!" he shouted. "You think he's so clever, don't you? You think he can beat me every time?"

Men! Was there ever a man – apart from my Konstantin – whose ego wasn't always teetering on the edge in my presence? They don't care how they look in the eyes of an old crone like I am now, but stand them next to a pretty woman and they instantly feel an overpowering urge to appear strong, to seem right.

"You're clever too," I said soothingly. "And *we* can win. All I meant was that we can't afford to be be overconfident."

Sasha was not to be mollified. He sprang to his feet, sending his chair crashing against the wall. He grabbed me

160

by the shoulders and swung me round to face him. My chair screeched its protest as it turned, my body cried out in pain as Sasha's fingers dug into me. "I'll r. . .ruin Peter," he said, shaking me. "I'll de. . .destroy him. Just you see!"

The violence left him as quickly as it had entered. He stopped shaking me and though he didn't relinquish his hold, it no longer hurt. His breath blew on my cheek, his face came closer and closer, and we were kissing.

His hands roved over me, worming their way under my clothes to play on my ribs, to caress my breasts. I was burning up – as I'd been on the river bank with Misha, as I had been on my wedding night with Konstantin.

Sasha eased me to my feet and lent me back against the table edge. I felt his hand lift my rough peasant skirt and climb my thigh until it reached my silk drawers. His finger probed, and his breath quickened as he realized that I was already wet, already waiting for him.

I heard the rustle of clothing and he was between my legs, entering me, moving slowly in and out, in and out. My knees rested on his hips. My ankles locked tight around his naked buttocks. He was moving faster and faster, penetrating deeper and deeper, until I thought I'd die.

And then it was all over. The passion drained from my body leaving in its place a wonderful contentment.

"It was you I escaped for," Sasha said softly. "I t. . .told myself it was for my wife and ch. . .children, but it wasn't. All the time I was on the run, walking through blizzards, f. . .falling down in the snow and f. . .forcing myself to get up again, it was your face that kept me going."

"Sasha, we—"

"I hated you when I f. . .found out you were getting married. I st. . .stood on the bridge that night, imagining you in bed with him, and I wanted to kill him."

"We don't make love," I said. "Konstantin is a homosexual."

"A homosexual! Then you can c. . .come and live with me."

"We don't make love, but I do love him," I said as gently as I could.

161

"And you d. . .don't love me?"

"I like you very much. I admire and respect you. And I want to make love to you again. Can't that be enough?"

"Of c. . .course it can't," Sasha said. "I want you to feel about me the way I feel about you."

"I'm sorry, Sasha, but I can't. I have a husband and a child. We're a family. There's no room in my life for any other person."

The arrogance of youth! To imagine that love was so mean-spirited an emotion as to limit itself. To see sex as uncomplicated and manageable, even though, all the time we'd been making love, part of my mind – part of my soul – had been back at the river bank.

Chapter Fifteen

It was in the third week of the strike that the rumours started.

"He's closing down the mill for good, and opening a new one in Moscow," one of the workers told me.

"He can't do that," I argued. "It would be far too expensive.

"They're going to arrest the leaders of the strike committee," the worried sweeper confided in me.

"How can they? They don't even know who the leaders are."

"Do you think it's true the army's had orders to fire on us?" the younger of two mechanics asked. "They say the government wants to make an example of somebody."

"If that was their plan, don't you think they'd have done it already?"

Still the rumours grew, each more more extreme than the one it followed.

"Can't you see that it's the owner's agents who are spreading these stories?" I demanded exasperatedly. "He wants to break your spirits."

And it was working. I found myself spending time on the picket line, breathing fire into the souls of the waverers, coming out into the open far more than a member of the underground ever should.

It was on Thursday afternoon that Peter decided to burn his barn, Thursday afternoon when those of us on the picket line first heard the dreadful sound.

Clip-clop-clip. Clip-clop-clip.

A murmur ran through the crowd. The strikers began to shift their feet and look nervously around them.

"Stand firm!" I shouted at the top of my voice.

Clip-clop-clip. Clip-clop-clip. Getting closer now.

Necks craned, breaths were held. From round the corner emerged a score of mounted Cossacks, their whips already drawn. The crowd let out a groan. They all knew, as I did, that a Cossack can do more damage with his whip than an average soldier with a sabre.

"Link arms!" I shouted, and the cry was taken up in other parts of the crowd – "Link arms. Link arms!"

The Cossacks' shaggy ponies trotted slowly towards us, their ears pricked up, their eyes alert. They had done this kind of thing before. They knew that at any moment the Cossacks might order them to charge the crowd, to weave in and out between the panicking people as their masters slashed with whips, to trample those who had fallen without losing their own footing. They knew all that – and they were ready.

"Stand firm!" one of my neighbours called out.

But how firm would *he* stand, I wondered, when he felt a Cossack whip across his cheek? How firm would *I* stand?

The Cossacks were twenty yards from us, then ten. The pale winter sun shone on their fur hats and reflected off their polished, spurless riding boots. It would have been easier to face rifles and the possibility of death than the certainty of the damage these incredible fighting men would inflict. Yet the line still held.

Five yards from us, without any visible signal passing between them, the Cossacks wheeled to the left and rode around the edge of the crowd. A great cheer went up, followed by cries of, "We've beaten them!" and, "They're in retreat!"

Fools! Did they really imagine the Cossacks would be deterred by a few hundred people? Did they know so little of their employer that they could think he'd let them snatch victory without a bloody battle?

The hoofbeats grew distant, the Cossacks disappeared from sight. The crowd became restive again. After all the excitement, it seemed pointless just to stand there. They actually *wanted* something to happen.

They didn't have to wait long. A female mill worker

appeared, running through the snow, carrying her small baby in her arms. "They've locked us out," she screamed. "The Cossacks! They came to the dormitories and threw us all out onto the street. Then they nailed up the doors."

There were some initial cries of anger, but it didn't take long for an air of despondency to settle over the crowd like a winter fog. It was November now, and cold – well below freezing at night – but it would get colder yet. They could have survived without wages, even if I'd stopped helping them. A little bread could have been scrounged from somewhere, and man does not live by bread alone. But without shelter in the Petersburg winter, man does not live at all.

More horses hooves in the distance. The Cossacks returning? If it was, they would meet with little resistance this time.

It was Cossacks, but only four of them, riding escort to an open cart. And on the back of the cart stood a man in a Savile Row suit which, despite his peasant bulk, he wore with a flair Sasha could never hope to emulate.

The cart pulled up in front of the growling mob and Peter, hands on hips, looked calmly down at us. "Go back to your villages," he said. "Go back and farm your land."

Silence. Sullen silence. Peter clicked his fingers at a man to my left.

"You – Yuri Andreiovich! Why d'you stand here wasting time? Return to your *izbá*."

"I have no *izbá* any more, master," the man muttered. He pointed in the direction of the barracks. "That's my home now."

"No!" Peter retorted. "The building's mine, and you live in it just as long as I let you."

Heads bent, acknowledging that what he said was true.

"I've lost three weeks' production because of this strike," Peter continued. "That'll have to be made up. By you – or by other workers. *If* I let you work for me again when I reopen my mill, I'll expect longer hours for no more money."

"Until we've made up for the lost production, master?" a defeated voice asked.

"Until I say otherwise," Peter snarled.

"What about medical care!" I called out desperately. "What about sickness benefit?"

Peter turned his burning gaze on me. "I was wondering when you'd open your mouth, Lyudmila," he said.

He *knows* me, I thought with rising panic. Or at least, he knew my *nom de guerre* and could fit the name to my face! I wondered what else he knew.

"What about medical care?" I persisted, keeping my voice as steady as I could.

"I pay my workers well," Peter said. "How they spend their money is up to them." He lost interest in me, and turned his attention to the strikers as a whole. "The dormitory will be closed until six o'clock tomorrow morning," he told them. "At that time, any of you that still wants to work for me can go back into it. Work at the mill starts at six-thirty. Sharp!"

They were all to have a night out on the streets as punishment. It would be miserable, but they would not die from a few hours exposure – at least, not many of them.

Peter whistled, his driver flicked the reins and his harnessed horse set off at a trot. The crowd stood in stunned silence for a moment, then began to disperse, a great beast of socialist unity fragmenting into powerless individual cells.

Cunning Peter. He could have locked them out of the dormitories at the start of the strike, but the weather hadn't been so cold then. Now, they were beaten and demoralized, and would agree to whatever demands he made on them – at least as long as the winter lasted.

I saw Sasha at the edge of the ever-decreasing crowd, grabbing workers by the sleeve, trying desperately to make them stay. "We're not f. . .finished yet," I heard him say. "We can break into the d. . .dormitory. We can expropriate it for the p. . .p. . .people."

He was wasting his time and even he knew it. Peter had beaten him again.

As the clanking tram made its way back to the city, my thoughts shifted from the strike to my other failure – my poor crippled son.

He's *not* crippled, I told myself. All the doctors agreed that

166

there was no apparent physical reason why he couldn't move his legs.

On Suvorovski Prospect, the tram came to a sudden, unscheduled halt. The Police? Stopping the vehicle so they could arrest Lyudmila the Bolshevik for her part in the cotton mill strike?

I looked out of the window, and relaxed. Workers dressed in heavy shoobas and thick mittens were repairing the tramlines in front of us. The No. 14 was merely being diverted onto another track.

I watched the men toil with their long iron tools. That was the problem with Nicky, I thought. The tramline from his brain to his legs was in need of repair, and all that was necessary was to find the right workman. A name from out of nowhere flashed into my mind. There was one man in Petersburg who might be able to help Nicky – a man so famed for his healing powers that he had the confidence of the Tsar himself. Though even the idea made my skin crawl, I knew I had no choice but to go and see Rasputin.

"The master's eating," the mousey servant told me.

"I'll . . . I'll wait until he's finished."

The girl looked me up and down as if she were inspecting a side of meat at the market. "There's no need to wait," she said. "He likes people joining him at meal times – and he'll like you, right enough."

He was not alone. Round his table sat seven women, most of them young. They were all dressed smartly, in tailored costumes and blouses. Three were wearing hats with feathers sticking out from them. The *rasputinki*, their detractors called them – members of the prosperous bourgeoisie who had become the *starets'* disciples. None of them looked up as I entered the room, their gazes were firmly fixed on Rasputin.

The *starets* noticed me, though, and his eyes burned with lust. Lust – but not recognition. Then realization came, and he smiled. "You look different, sister," he said.

I was still wearing my peasant disguise! Such had been my desire to see him before my courage left me, that I'd forgotten to go back to the bakery and change. It was as Lyudmila, not Anna, that I was appearing before him.

"I . . . I was born a peasant," I stuttered, "and I have come to you as a peasant. It's an act of humility."

"Humility. Yes," Rasputin said. "Rejoice in simplicity. We are the rebellious and wicked. Lord, work miracles, humble us . . . Sit down, and we will eat."

The servant brought me a chair, and I sat at the end of the table, among the *rasputinki*.

Eating with the *starets* had as much ritual to it as an Orthodox divine service. Rasputin piled spoonful upon spoonful of sugar into his disciples' teacups, and the ladies drank the sickly-sweet liquid with a smile, since they considered it a form of grace. He bit into a pickled cucumber and offered the remains to one of his disciples, which she ate as though it were the body of Christ. He distributed hard-boiled eggs, which the women solemnly peeled, preserving the shells carefully in their handkerchiefs as holy relics – I was told that women honoured enough to be allowed to cut his toenails did the same with the clippings.

All the time he ate, Rasputin talked. "We are thine, Lord . . . Great is thy love for us . . . only through sin can there be forgiveness . . . the sins of my sisters here I take on me."

As he spoke, he spat pieces of bread and cucumber rind from his mouth. He wore no napkin, and blobs of half-masticated food were soon caught in the long black hairs growing from his chin. If his followers noticed it, they took it as yet another sign of holiness.

Though I felt a growing sense of revulsion as the meal progressed, only once did I get the urge to stand up and run from the room – and that was just after Rasputin had dipped his fingers into the dish of jam.

He lifted his hand up for all to see. His fingers were covered to the knuckles with the sticky red substance, as if he had bathed in blood. He held out his hand to the woman closest to him. "Humble yourself," he said.

The disciple stretched forward and took a thick, peasant finger in her mouth. The finger stayed immobile, so it was her head which was forced to move back and forward during

168

the holy cleansing. Rasputin sat back in his chair and let a smile of perfect contentment play on his lips, a smile which acknowledged – and revelled in – the power he had over this woman.

When all the fingers were licked clean, Rasputin finally fixed his gaze on me. "Come," he said. "We'll go to my bedroom."

I rose to my feet and followed him meekly. The humiliation of the other woman had been just a taster – an hors-d'oeuvre – I was to be the main course.

The bedroom was straight off the dining room. As Rasputin closed the door behind us the *rasputinki*, now out of their master's presence, began to talk excitedly amongst themselves. Did they know what was about to happen? Probably. And did it bother them? No! Whatever the *starets* did was taken as a further sign of his holiness.

"Months have passed since I saw you at Papa's palace," Rasputin said to me. "I asked you to visit me."

"I wanted to see you," I lied. "I haven't been able to. My husband wouldn't allow—"

"The Lord will not wait forever. Yea, and he will smite the unrighteous with his sword and cleave them in two."

"I . . . I have a favour to ask of you," I said.

"A favour?" Rasputin smiled the smile of a cunning peasant who knows he holds all the cards.

"My son has no movement in his legs."

Slowly and deliberately, the *starets* placed his hands on my shoulders and pulled me towards him. My body screamed at me to resist, but my will held me firm – for the moment.

Rasputin lowered his head to mine. His lips were sticky and cold. It was as if a slug had fastened itself to me. The smell of him filled my nostrils – the cheap soap, the perfume, the decaying food in his beard. His tongue forced my teeth open and entered my mouth – exploring, violating. His hand moved to my left breast and began to paw it, pressing and squeezing, pressing and squeezing.

A second's weakness – I broke away.

"*Can* you cure my son?" I asked.

"Perhaps," the *starets* answered. "Love can cure many

169

things. And my love is great . . . great is my love. But love is a reservoir . . . it must be filled by the rain of more love. Do you love me?"

"Yes," I said.

"Then fill my tank . . . pour your love into me."

I could taste bile in my mouth, and felt I was going to vomit. I think Rasputin would have liked it if I had been sick. It would have added pleasure to my submission to him if he'd realized just how much I loathed him.

I swallowed hard. "Shall I undress?"

"Disrobe me first," he said. "Take the staff of my love in your mouth . . . yield righteousness from it . . . your sins I take upon me . . . you are my sister and no harm can come . . ."

I knelt down in front of him. The floor was hard against my knees. Rasputin's trousers bulged as his stiff penis strained against the cloth.

The *staret's* hands were on my head, his fingers tugging at my hair, raking my skull. "See, oh Lord, see!" he said loudly. "See how our little sister gives her love."

Trembling, I reached for for the top of his trousers – and felt his hand on my head, pushing me away. What had I done wrong? How had I displeased him?

"Store up your treasures," Rasputin told me.

"You want me to go?"

"Go! Go as the Canaanites and wander in the wilderness."

Did he want me to beg? Was that what would make him happy – to see me grovelling at his feet, begging him to let me take his foul prick in my mouth? Very well. "Please," I said. "I need your love. I need to be purified."

"Store up your treasures," the *starets* said again. "For if a gift be worth the giving, so it is worth the waiting."

I looked up at him, at the lust which still burned in his eyes, and suddenly understood. He wanted me very badly, but his desire for the flesh was not as great as his love of the power he had over me. Once I had performed the act, he would never be able to humiliate me quite as much again, whatever he made me do. He wanted me, oh yes, and he'd have me, but for just a little while longer he wanted to hold

170

on to the feeling of my submissiveness, my helplessness –
my shame.

"Tomorrow," he said again. "Tomorrow you will come
back and show me that you love me. Then I will cure
your son."

I took the stairs up to the nursery two at a time. I had to
see Nicky! I desperately needed the strength I could draw
from him – the strength I needed to go back to Rasputin's
apartment the next day.

I flung the nursery door open. Konstantin was there, leaning
over the crib, pedalling the baby's legs. I threw my arms
around my husband and sobbed. I knew it was weak, but I
couldn't help myself.

"What's wrong?" Konstantin asked worriedly.

I didn't dare tell him for fear that he might try to stop me.
"I . . . it's . . . it doesn't matter," I said. "I'll be all right in
a second."

"There must be something wrong," Konstantin persisted.

How tempting it was to spill it all out, to let Konstantin
take the responsibility for my visiting – or not visiting –
Rasputin again.

"I'm . . . I'm just upset about Nicky," I sobbed. "The poor
little mite."

Konstantin prised me gently away from him and turned
me so I was facing the crib.

"Look at him," he said. "Look at our child."

The tears streamed down my face, and it was as if I
were watching my baby through a window on a very rainy
day. But I could still see that he was the most beautiful,
wonderful child in the world. No sacrifice was too great to
make, I thought. What did my life matter when weighed
against his?

Konstantin leant forward again and ran his finger lightly
along the sole of the baby's left foot. Nicky gurgled with
happiness. And then he kicked his leg.

Nicky would always limp slightly, but it became hardly
noticeable. It didn't stop his having as normal a childhood

171

as was possible in those times. It didn't prevent him fighting by my side in Spain.

Perhaps whatever was wrong with him had been remedied by nature. Or perhaps Rasputin had been right, and he was cured by the power of love. But if that was true, then the love had not come from a healer who abused his blessed gift by bartering it for sexual favours – the love had come unselfishly from a man who'd have laid down his life for a child who wasn't even his own.

Chapter Sixteen

At one o'clock, having eaten my thrifty lunch, I set out for the Vulcan, as I do every day, come rain or shine. Why every day? Because there is something in me which fears that if I miss, even once, I will never be able to force myself to make the effort again.

Perhaps whatever happens, this will be my last visit. The armies ranged against me are formidable – my great-granddaughters and their husbands, the social service department, a whole society which believes that the old have outlived their usefulness, even to themselves. Yes, my foes are formidable indeed – and I am not the fighter I once was.

As I make my way carefully along Matlock Road, a feeling of gloom and despondency weighs down heavily on my thin shoulders. It is a feeling I have experienced before. In the spring of 1914, the whole of the city of St Petersburg was suffering from it.

Petersburg was drifting. Boredom, or gloom – or possibly a combination of the two – hung over the city like a black, sticky cloud. Suicide was almost an epidemic. Government was at a standstill as the Duma became embroiled in any number of petty squabbles with the Tsar's ministers. A wave of strikes and demonstrations – in which an underground revolutionary called Lyudmila was heavily involved – shook the capital. Things could not go on as they had been. Everybody knew it – though not many people could bring themselves to care. Something *had* to happen.

Konstantin was one of the few men in the city who seemed

to have any energy left – but his, as always, was that of three ordinary men. He had been posted to the General Staff, and was furious about it. "They don't take the job seriously," he complained. "There are fifteen religious holidays in May. Fifteen! And they intend to celebrate every one of them. When what they should really be doing is preparing for the war!"

"Are you sure it'll come?" I asked anxiously.

"Yes, I'm sure."

"But who wants it? Who's looking for it?"

Konstantin shrugged. "A few generals, perhaps. The odd ambitious politician. The arms manufacturers. A minority of the people in power, certainly."

"Then *why* will it happen?"

"Simply because it must. You can put a lot of wolf-hound puppies in one cage, but what happens when they start to grow?"

"They each need more space."

"Exactly. And unless the rest are prepared to defer to one leader, or one group of leaders, they'll fight for it. Fight for more territory, fight for the strategic position near the door, so they can get at the food first. Does that mean they're naturally bad-tempered or vicious?"

"No. It's just the situation they're in."

"And that's what it's like in Europe – we've all grown up and now the cage is too small."

Konstantin worked like a madman during those first few months of 1914, bullying men who outranked him, pushing through reforms against entrenched opposition – and all in aid of a war he was almost certain we couldn't win. Courage in the face of hopelessness is, I think, the greatest courage of all. I only wish that in all my defeats I had shown half the spirit which came as naturally as breathing to my husband.

Yet it was not all work, Konstantin made sure of that. He found time to take me to the Mariinsky theatre to see Pavlova in *Petrouchka* and to the Musical Drama Theatre to hear the great Chaliapine sing.

"A man who says he can't find the time to relax either has

174

too many decisions to make or is taking too long to decide," my husband told me. "In either case, he's performing his duties badly."

I don't think he even realized that he was indirectly criticizing his lord and master, the Tsar.

Though there was still some time before a formal declaration of hostilities, the slide into the Great War began on the 28th of June 1914, with the assassination of Grand Duke Ferdinand of Austria by a Serbian nationalist.

In early July, President Poincaré paid an official visit to Petersburg to reassure us of France's solidarity with Russia – but it only served to convince people that the outbreak of war was imminent. The Empress came out of seclusion to attend a banquet in his honour, and after it, she summoned me to her private apartments in the Winter Palace.

She looked terrible. Her face was flushed, veins stood out on her cheeks. She was only forty-two, but she looked like a woman preparing to die. "You haven't visited us for quite some time," she said reproachfully.

"Your Majesty has not invited me."

"I have not had the strength to put pen to paper," the Empress said wearily, "but you, coming from where you do, should have been able to sense that I needed you." Her face softened until it was almost pleading. "*Do* come and see me, Anna."

"I will, Your Majesty," I promised.

It would be comforting, now that I am nothing but a powerless, old woman, to ascribe statesman-like motives to that promise. Little Anna influencing the Empress, helping steer the ship of state through troubled waters. Or Lyudmila the Revolutionary, pretending to be Anna, giving the Empress false advice, hastening the fall of the Romanovs and the triumph of the proletariat. It would be comforting, but it wouldn't be true. Looking at that small, ill woman, the wife of the most absolute ruler in Europe but as lonely as the humblest pensioner in Matlock Road, my heart stirred. I promised to go and see her because I felt sorry for her.

*　　*　　*

On the 29th of July, Austrian gunboats bombarded Belgrade, the Serbian capital.

"The Austrians are fools," Konstantin told me over dinner. "Not only are they hell-bent on plunging us into a general conflict, but they've attacked before they're even ready themselves."

"I thought they mobilized their army four days ago," I said.

"They *ordered* the mobilization, yes, but that's not the same thing. Imagine it, Anna. After the soldiers have been called up, they have to travel to their units. The transport system, which works perfectly adequately in peace time, is suddenly swamped by millions of men and huge amounts of *matériel*. There are delays – inevitably. Men report for duty when they can, they're issued with equipment when it arrives. Eventually, all the units are up to fighting strength – but it takes time. I'd estimate they won't be fully ready for another eleven or twelve days."

I thought of Russia – its vastness and its inefficiency. "And it would take *us* even longer than that," I said.

"Much, much longer," Konstantin agreed gloomily.

The next afternoon, our weak, vacillating Tsar put his signature to a document declaring complete the mobilization of the army. Germany responded with frightening speed, sending an ultimatum to the Foreign Ministry demanding that Russia suspend all war preparations or face the consequences.

It had started – the armed struggle which would dissolve the Europe we'd known, the war which would turn the whole continent into a charnel house.

Chapter Seventeen

It's impossible to adequately describe the fever which swept through Petersburg. Gloom and despair became things of the past. Patriotism and loyalty to the Tsar were the new virtues. The German Embassy was attacked, and the two bronze horses on its roof were hurled down into the street, while the crowd, carrying flags and *icons*, cheered wildly. The Duma, from being at daggers drawn with the Government, voted almost unanimously to support it in its war effort. Strikes were called off, demonstrations were now *in favour* of the Tsar's ministers. The name of the city was changed from the Germanic sounding 'St Petersburg' to the thoroughly Russian 'Petrograd'. All over the country, peasants and workers responded willingly to the call-up and younger sons of the aristocracy put in rapid applications for commissions.

And then the war started to go badly. The border with our enemies was five hundred and fifty miles long. The army was poorly equipped, and poorly supplied. Only a fool would have considered taking the offensive – but that was exactly what Grand Duke Nicholas, the Tsar's uncle, did. Before even a third of his army was deployed, he attacked on three fronts. The defeats which followed were so bloody that even the German commander, Hindenburg, admitted to being sickened by the sight of the mounds of Russian dead who had to be moved in order to get a clear field of fire at the next, suicidal onslaught.

And all the time Konstantin fumed about being confined to General Staff Headquarters, while I offered up a silent prayer of thanks to whichever army bureaucrat kept him there – despite his countless requests for an active commission.

*   *   *

"Another Guinness, please," I say to Terry the barman.

He looks at me through narrowed eyes. "You sure about that, Princess? You usually only have one."

"Yes, I'm sure," I tell him.

And as I watch him walk back to the bar, I wonder why life should be so capricious. When I woke up this morning, I imagined it would be a day like any other – uncomfortable, slow and boring. Now here I sit in the Vulcan, anguishing over my last great battle against the state – a battle I'm sure to lose.

I should have felt like this in Petrograd, in the winter of 1914 and the early spring of 1915. The situation seemed hopeless then. The army was still suffering terrible losses. The government was collapsing around us. And yet those few months were some of the happiest of my entire life.

What is happiness? Freedom from responsibility! The joyful realization that whilst you can see where your duty lies, the path is blocked. Because the simple fact was that in the early stages of the war there was very little revolutionary enthusiasm to channel, and though I attended a few meetings, Lyudmila, like so many actresses, spent most of her time 'resting'.

For a brief period I was able to throw off the yoke of the Party, lay down the heavy load which my mother's life and death had placed on my shoulders, and be nothing but myself – a wife and a mother. I adored it.

I devoted much of my day to thinking of ways to please or amuse Konstantin when he came home, tired and frustrated, from the General Staff Headquarters.

I played with Nicky. He was walking now – dragging his left leg a little behind him, but without any sense of awkwardness or inhibition. He was talking, too, a few words of Russian, a few of English, a little French when his other languages failed him.

And I met Sasha regularly for long afternoons of passion. I'd told him love between us was impossible, but as the weeks passed my feelings grew, whether I willed it or not. I never loved him as deeply as I did Konstantin – yet come to love him I did.

I used to fantasize that things would go on as they were for ever, with Konstantin, Nicky and Sasha, the three males in my life, giving me everything a woman could ever ask for. Like most ideals, it would probably not have worked out – but it never had a chance even to try. Spring came, the mood in Petrograd changed, and Lyudmila forced herself back into my consciousness once more.

In May, a new Austro-German offensive smashed through the Russian front line. The army was in retreat, Russian Poland was to be abandoned. The scale of the disaster was unimaginable. Over *one million* refugees were making their way eastwards. *Two million* soldiers had deserted and were wandering in armed bands behind the lines. Over *four million* of our men had been killed in less than a year of war.

In the wake of defeat came the need for scapegoats – and one was readily found in the shape of Russia's Germanic population. In June, the mob in Moscow went on the rampage, burning and looting German shops, banks and factories, lynching people with German sounding names. Everything German was to be despised, they shouted. Everything German had to be destroyed.

"And the German Woman's the worst of the lot!" they yelled at the tops of their voices. "She's sending secret messages to the enemy at this very minute. The Teutonic bitch!"

They were talking, of course, about their Empress.

Alexandra was no traitor – far from it. As the war progressed, she became more and more patriotic, ever more deeply in the grip of a religion which united God and Nicholas.

"It is my husband's sacred duty to drive the invaders from our soil," she told me on one of my visits to the Alexander Palace. "God has placed this mission in his hands, and He has sent our dear friend, Grigorii, to guide him. Why must the Duma oppose him? Doesn't it realize that it's heresy to go against his wishes?"

Yet her hatred of the Duma was nothing compared to

179

what she felt towards anyone who dared attack her beloved Grigorii.

"He is so wise," she told me. "He is my teacher, my redeemer, my mentor. My heart longs for him when he's not here, and when he does come, when I can kiss his blessed hands, I know a peace that you could never imagine. You're lucky, Anna. You are so much freer than I. You can go to his house whenever you wish. Do you see him often?"

I shuddered. "I've been to his house once, Your Majesty."

"You shouldn't be afraid of him," she said, noticing my expression. "You shouldn't listen to stories. People accuse him of kissing women," she looked down at floor, "and of . . . er . . . other things too. They should read their Bibles before they dare to criticize him. Did not the apostles kiss women? It's just a form of greeting."

Should I have told her about his excesses? What would have been the point? She'd never have believed a word of it.

"He knows so much," the Empress rhapsodized. "Sandro – Grand Duke Alexander Mikhailovich – says he's desperate for aeroplane engines, but Grigorii tells me there are heaps of things he could use instead of them."

Like what? I wondered. But I said nothing.

"And he's helping me in other ways, too," the Empress continued, dropping her voice conspiratorially, even though we were alone. "He tells me which Ministers are loyal to my husband and which are not. He can see right into their souls. Some of the disloyal ones have already been replaced."

And despite the bizarre, often disastrous advice Rasputin was to give her, the Empress never once doubted his judgement. Even after his death she continued to follow his instructions which were received via nightly seances and conveyed to her by telephone the next morning.

I was alone in my small sitting room when Andrei, my butler, announced I had a visitor called Nechaev.

The name meant nothing to me. I walked over to the window and looked down at the courtyard. It was the White Nights – when twilight never lasts for more than half an hour and darkness is unknown – so though it was past ten o'clock, I could clearly see the Rolls-Royce sitting in front of the stables.

"Is that his car?"

"Yes, madam."

"What does he look like?"

"He's tall and solidly built. In his late thirties. I'd say he's . . . er . . . not always been as prosperous as he appears to be now."

Nechaev?

Peter!

"Did he ask to see the Prince?" I asked.

"No, madam. He asked specifically for you."

It was nearly two years since I'd stood outside the factory and watched him address his workers from a cart. What could he want now? What possible reason could he have for calling on me?

My instinct prompted me to say that I was not at home, but my reason overruled it. "Show him in," I said, and noticed that my hands were shaking.

I arranged myself nonchalantly in my chair. How should I react? How would anyone react to a person they were not supposed to have seen since childhood? Andrei ushered the visitor into the room and withdrew.

Peter was dressed formally, in a smart frock coat. He bowed, then raised his head again. A real gentleman couldn't have done it better. Why then did I get the feeling he was mocking me?

My eyes were drawn reluctantly to his face, just as they had been when I sat in the dirt and watched him arguing with Sasha at meetings of the *mir*. Still the same strong, almost sculptured nose. Still the same deep eyes and thick, sensuous lips.

Neither of us had spoken yet, but Peter seemed perfectly at ease with the silence. "What brings you here, Mr Nechaev?" I asked finally.

"I thought it only proper for one villager to pay his respects to another, Princess – even if that other is now so high that she can hardly see the ground."

181

Again, he was mocking me, I was sure of it. Did he think that his money put us on an equal footing? No, money alone wasn't enough – and he was too clever not to know that.

I motioned him to sit down and offered him the vodka tray. He poured himself a large shot and knocked it straight back.

"I knew you'd left the *mir*, but I wasn't aware you were in Petrograd," I lied. "I'm surprised you're not in the army."

"I'm too valuable for that," Peter said, though not boastfully. "My mill's making uniforms for the soldiers and I've just opened an armaments factory."

"A mill?" I said. "I didn't know you had a mill."

"Oh yes," he assured me. "Oh yes, I've got a mill. It's a model factory – a fine example of worker-management co-operation."

Every word was measured. Every word, as it fell, seemed to force a little more air out of the room. I rose to my feet. "It was very kind of you to call on me, but now, if you will excuse me—"

"Anna," he interrupted, "I need a favour."

"What kind of favour?"

"I'm getting married soon."

So that was what this was all about. The tension drained from me, and I laughed. "I never thought you'd marry. Who's the bride to be? Natulia? Tassaya? No, not them. I'd guess she'll be young, and probably a city girl."

"She's young, all right, but she's from the country. I'm going to marry Mariamna."

"Mariamna!"

This time, it was his turn to laugh. "D'you think you're the only one who can marry into the aristocracy? I own the land, I own the house – why shouldn't I own the woman?"

Why not indeed? The Count had married below him, his daughter was only following suit. It couldn't be cheap keeping Misha in the Corps of Pages.

"I hope you will be very happy together—" I began.

"Happiness hasn't got anything to do with it," Peter sneered.

"But you must understand that my relationship with that particular family is rather strained."

182

"Oh, I understand," Peter said. "It's only natural after the son tupped you and then ran away, leaving you to look after his bastard."

I was outraged. How dare he call my beautiful son a bastard? "Get out of here!" I screamed.

Peter's thick lips twisted into a broad smile. He made no move to get up.

The bell-push was above the fire place. I reached towards it. Now Peter moved, jumping out of his seat, clamping his huge work-hardened hand over mine.

People do not do that kind of thing to princesses. I wondered if he had gone insane.

Yet when he spoke again, his voice seemed perfectly calm. "It's a step up, marrying Mariamna, but it's not enough. I need your patronage."

"Patronage! What big words you use now that you're a mill owner."

"I want you to come to the wedding," Peter continued, as if he'd not heard me, "and I want you to throw a ball for us, right here in this palace."

"Never!" I shouted, struggling to pull my hand free. "I'll *never* do that."

"I think you will . . . Lyudmila."

Peter's hand released its grip, and he looked challengingly at the bell-push. I raised my arm, and then let it drop to my side again. "What are you talking about?" I asked.

"Did you really think that your disguise would fool me? Take the paint, the jewels and fancy hairstyle away from a princess, and most people won't even *see* her, but I remember you long ago, Anna, when being a peasant *wasn't* a disguise."

"This is ridiculous," I said. "You see someone at a strike who you think resembles me—"

"Strike?" Peter asked craftily. "Did I mention a strike?"

"You've confused me with some peasant girl . . . Lyudmila was it?" I asked, trying to brazen my way out.

"You know it was."

"And now you're trying to blackmail me. Well, go ahead. My husband will be home soon. Tell him your suspicions.

Tell the Tsar himself – if, of course, you can get an audience."

Peter chuckled. "I don't move in high enough circles to meet the Tsar," he said. "Not yet. And if a bit of a suspicion was *all* I had, I wouldn't try to blackmail a tough woman like you. But there's more. My strike was only your apprenticeship. You've gone on to bigger and better things now. You've infiltrated the army—"

"I never knew you had an imagination, Peter. You should be writing cheap romances instead of running a mill."

". . . The Litovsky Regiment to be exact – not ten minutes walk from here."

He was right. Ever since the retreat from Poland I had been building up a network in the Litovsky Barracks.

"You're crazy," I told him. "No one would believe that I, a princess, the wife of one of the Tsar's most trusted—"

"Your contact's a Ukrainian, Codename – Georgi," Peter said.

The room began to swim before my eyes. I grasped for the arm of my chair and sat down.

"And it's not just the soldiers," Peter said. "You've also been working closely with the bakers' union. Why bakers, Anna? What good can they do you?"

There was no point in pretending any longer. "Bakers are very important in times of revolution," I confessed. "Control the bread and you control the masses."

"You'll do what I want, won't you?"

I nodded, wearily.

"Good," Peter said.

Good? He didn't sound like a man who'd just won a victory – who'd got everything he wanted. "Let me know the rest now," I said.

"The rest?"

For the first time since he'd walked into the room, Peter looked uncomfortable. Stage by stage, that was how he worked. Burn the barn first, to get the Count in his power, then use it against Sasha. Let the workers strike until the weather got cold, *then* lock them out of their dormitories. Get me to hold a ball on his wedding day, then . . .

"Are you really asking me to believe that all you want in return for keeping me out of gaol is one ball? You're a businessman, Peter, you understand the value of things. And this time, the price you're asking is too low. So come on, tell me what you really want!"

His brow furrowed, his eyes flashed with calculation. "How do you think a peasant, even a rich one, manages to raise the money to buy two factories?" he asked finally.

And how did I think he came to know so much about me? Who'd given him the name my contact in the Litovsky Regiment? Who'd told him about my work with the bakers' union? To come by information like that, wouldn't he have needed the backing of some vast organization?

My stomach heaved. There was only one possible answer to my questions – and it couldn't be a worse one. His source had to be the secret police!

"You work for the *Okhrana*," I said.

"Yes."

But what had that to do with me? How did I fit into his plans? With a sudden, horrifying insight, I saw it all. "No!" I said. "I won't do it!"

"Yes you will," Peter told me. "You'll work for the *Okhrana* too – because you don't have any choice."

Chapter Eighteen

"I don't understand why you want to give a ball for that repugnant young woman," Konstantin said.

Want! It wasn't a question of wanting. As Peter had said, I'd no choice. "They took me into their house and—"

"The Count took you in. If it had been left to mother and daughter, you'd still be living in the *mir*."

I had no logical argument with which to oppose his, so I stooped to trickery and burst into tears.

"Why are you so upset?" Konstantin asked gently. "Is it guilt? There's no need for it. You don't owe that family a thing."

I was still crying, I couldn't stop – I was so ashamed to be manipulating my husband.

Konstantin sighed. "I suppose weak, self-centred people like them can always find a way to make others feel in their debt," he admitted, "especially someone as forgiving and kind-hearted as you. Very well then. Against my better judgement, we'll give them their ball, but after that the account will be considered paid, and we'll be free of them forever."

It was all my fault. If I'd kept out of politics, I wouldn't have had to put my husband in this difficult position. Yet I knew that if I had to make the decisions again, I wouldn't change any of them.

Or perhaps one. When Konstantin asked me to marry him, I'd turn him down – I'd spare him the anguish which my revolutionary activities might bring to him in the future.

"Misha will have to come," I said meekly.

Konstantin put his arm over my shoulder and pulled me

closer to him. "And why shouldn't he? He is the bride's brother."

I said nothing, but we both knew what I was thinking.

"He *isn't* Nicky's father," Konstantin said softly. "He gave up that right when he rode off and left you."

"But what if . . . what if coming to the palace awakens a desire in him to ask for his son and—"

"From what I've heard, he's turned into a very wild young man," Konstantin said. "He spends all his free time in low dives consorting with cheap prostitutes. Peasant girls just up from the country – very young ones. He'll not be interested in the responsibilities of fatherhood, even if his new brother-in-law gives him the money to support a child. Besides, if he did try to take Nicky away, I'd challenge him to a duel and kill him."

"Maybe he would kill you," I said anxiously.

"Do you think that's likely?"

No, I didn't. My Konstantin was a superman. My Konstantin was invulnerable.

"I'm not a very good wife to you," I said. "I'm more trouble than I'm worth."

I felt Konstantin's hand squeeze my shoulder. "No amount of trouble could be a true measure of your value," he said.

I wondered if he would still have thought that if he knew about my political activities at the Litovsky Barracks.

The ball was held at the end of August. Once Konstantin had made his mind up to accept something, he liked to see it carried through to perfection, and this occasion was no exception.

There was a magnificent sit-down feast, big enough to satisfy even Russian appetites – grey, black and deep orange caviar, marinated herring, smoked salmon, ham, paté, lobster and cheese. And after these appetisers came the main meal – consommé with mushroom *pirozhkies*, sturgeon in wine, partridge breasts in cream, thick steaks of meat. Ice-cream in an almost infinite number of flavours was served for desert, as well as pineapples, papaya and mangoes, all fruits which were supposedly unobtainable in Petrograd at the time.

The orchestra was the Mariinsky's own. I don't think they'd have slummed it for anyone but Konstantin.

All in all, it was the most splendid ball held in the city since my own wedding. Only the guests were a failure.

Mariamna, predictably, was petulant about it.

"There were *far* more important people at your ball," she said.

"Yes, but that was in peace time," I told her, "and just before the start of the season. Many of the fashionable families aren't even in Petrograd now."

I didn't add that even those who were in the capital had needed to be persuaded to come. This was not, after all, the wedding of a prince, merely the union of the daughter of an obscure provincial nobleman and a common tradesman.

It was not only the guest list which annoyed Mariamna.

"Your gown looks so much better than mine," she complained as we were dressing.

"We're about the same size. Take it."

"But then you'll only find another one, even better. You have thousands to choose from." She dropped her head into her hands. "Oh, why am I marrying this thick, coarse, peasant? Why, why, why?"

But she knew very well why she was marrying him. Common prostitutes like the ones Misha visited are not the only women who are forced to sell their bodies.

Mariamna cheered up once the ball begun. It might not be as grand an affair as mine had been, but at least this time she was the centre of attention. And there were *some* important people around – Prince Yusupov and a smattering of grand dukes.

"She's not as pretty as you," Konstantin commented as we watched her waltz across the floor, "but you can tell that she's your sister."

Looking at her, I could see that Konstantin was right. Her lips were more inclined to pout, her eyes were a little further apart, there was something of Countess Olga's sharpness about her, but we were undoubtedly sisters.

Even though I had invited him myself, it was a shock to see Misha leaning against the wall, talking to some of his friends from the Corps of Pages. It was almost as if his presence let my past into the room. I remembered the day he'd taken a beating for me, the afternoon by the river bank when he'd introduced me to lovemaking. There were suddenly butterflies in my stomach and my skin prickled. I didn't want to talk to him – I never wanted to talk to him again – but we Mayakovskys do not run away from our duty. I forced myself to thread my way around the edge of the dancers to where he was standing.

The young men with him bowed, and at Misha's signal discreetly withdrew. There seemed to be some truth in the stories Konstantin had heard about him. He was still a young man, scarcely more than a boy, but his face showed all the signs of hard living. I think he was drunk even at that moment.

"It's good to see you, Anna," he said.

"It's good to see you, too," I replied, not knowing whether I meant it or not.

He reached across and took my hand. "I was a fool to run away from you."

The baby! He wanted the baby! "You made your choice," I said shakily, "and now it's too late. Nicky is legally Konstantin's son and heir."

He gazed at me with glassy-eyed incomprehension. "Nicky? Nicky?" He shook his head as if to clear his brain. "Oh, your child! What's he got to do with anything?"

"I thought you meant . . . when you said you were a fool to run away—"

"A fool! A complete bloody fool! We'd loved each other so very much, for so long."

"Yes," I admitted. "We did."

"And then I lost my head."

"I was to blame, too," I said. I hadn't known he was my half-brother, that was true, but I'd wanted to make love just as much as he had.

"No, no, you weren't to blame," he protested. "You were perfect. It was me. I was trapped by bourgeois morality, and because of that, we've wasted years." He lowered his voice. "I have this room. No one knows about

189

it. We could go there. What marvellous times we could have, Anna."

I shrank back from him. As I turned to escape, I felt the touch of his hand on my shoulder. And felt something else too – an emotion I thought I'd buried a long time ago.

The hand was still there, pressing down, sapping my strength. I knocked his arm aside and rushed into a gap left by the dancers.

Ashamed and humiliated, I made my way across the ballroom floor, hardly noticing the couples who waltzed gracefully past me. How could I ever let such thoughts enter my mind? How could I have so desperately wanted to say, "Yes, oh yes, let's go to your secret room! I'll do anything to recapture that wonderful moment on the river bank – the moment before it all turned sour."

I was scared. Scared of Misha. Scared of myself. I wanted my husband. I wanted my Konstantin.

He was standing alone, looking so blissfully happy that he didn't even notice my distress.

"I've been talking to the General," he said. "The orders have come through."

"Orders? What orders?"

"I've been posted to the Front."

Konstantin at the Front – where thousands were being slaughtered every day! I wanted to beg him not to go – but I knew my man and knew, too, that though he would do almost anything to make me happy, he would not do that.

"Don't worry, my darling," he said, noticing the distress I was trying so hard to hide. "I'll be careful."

Liar, Konstantin! Bloody, bloody liar!

It was two days after the ball that I met Vyacheslav Molotov in a seedy boarding house in the Vyborg district and told him all about my meeting with Peter.

"So we have a problem," Molotov said when I'd finished. "What are we going to do about it?"

"I don't know," I confessed.

He had a bright future in front of him, this man. In another few years he would be a very important person in the Party, second only to Stalin. But that was all to come. In 1915 he was still a young man of twenty-five who was just starting to climb.

"We could have this man Peter Nechaev killed," Molotov continued, "but as there's probably already a file on you in *Okhrana* headquarters, that wouldn't do us a lot of good." He lit a cigarette and inhaled deeply. "So what I suggest," blowing out smoke through his nose, "is that you agree to do what he wants, and work for the secret police."

"Work for them!"

Molotov laughed. "It's not as outlandish as it sounds. The *Okhrana* does occasionally arrest our people, but its main concern is to keep tabs on us and to encourage factionalism. And do you know *how* they try and keep us at each other's throats?"

"No," I admitted, feeling like a political infant.

"They infiltrate *agents provocateurs* into our ranks – we know this for a fact. However, what the *Okhrana* doesn't know is that some the agents who they think are working for *them* against *us*, are in fact working for *us* against *them*."

"If I'm pretending to spy for them, I'll have to give them information," I pointed out.

"Of course."

"But when they find out it's false, they'll know I'm really working for you."

"Some of it will be false, and some merely misleading – but a great deal of it will be genuine."

"Why should some of it be genuine?"

"Because they'll give you intelligence in return, to feed to us. That, too, will be a mixture of the false, the misleading and the genuine. What I'm betting on is that the material they give us will be better than the stuff we give them."

"Why should it be?"

"They know the higher you rise in the Party ranks, the more access you'll have to secrets. And what better way to ensure your promotion than to give you genuine information on their own activities."

But the reverse of what Molotov said was also true. To get better intelligence from the police, I'd have to prove I was

191

worth it, and I could only do that by passing on better pieces of information about the Bolsheviks. The higher I got in each organization, it seemed to me, the more I would betray them both. I was still very new at this, and my head swam.

"I don't like it," I said. "How can I be sure that I'm being of more use to the Revolution than I am to the *Okhrana*?"

Molotov smiled. "You can't," he admitted. "But what you can do is to minimize to your contact the importance of the material he's handing you, and inflate the value of what you're passing to him. It's like a conjuring trick. You must convince him you've given him a diamond, when all he really has is a ruby – or perhaps even a glass bead."

What a talent we Russians have for double-dealing. Is it any wonder we continue to run rings around the Western intelligence services when we can make even a schizophrenic seem single-minded?

"This Nechaev," Molotov said, "is he, like so many of the decadent people who hold the reins of power, a homosexual?"

I shook my head. "Definitely not."

"Then perhaps we might exploit that. When the opportunity arises, seduce him."

"What!"

"Love is blind, Lyudmila – and so is lust. You're a very beautiful woman. If you can get Nechaev emotionally involved with you, he'll be more likely to take the information you bring him at face value."

I was cursed then – I am still cursed – with the ability to imagine things vividly, to see an incident in my mind's eye as if it were actually happening. Molotov's words triggered off such a scene at that very moment. Me, lying on a bed. Peter, the muscles in his naked body as hard as the knots on a tree trunk. The heaviness as flesh and bone pressed down on me. His breath on my cheek. His organ, thick and unyielding, ploughing into me.

I could feel pain and anguish, but not my own. Another face drifted into the picture, a face which was thinner, more intense, less primeval, than Peter's. The face was Sasha's. A single salt tear escaped from his eye and ran down his cheek, leaving a trail of sadness in its wake.

192

"I couldn't do it," I said.

Molotov stabbed his cigarette angrily into the lid of a tin which served as his ashtray. "Why not?" he demanded. "Has he got the clap? Are you a part-time nun?"

"No."

"Then there's nothing stopping you, is there?"

"There are other factors – other people – involved."

"Other factors! Other people! We're revolutionaries, Comrade Lyudmila. And we'll do *whatever* is necessary for the cause. Some of the information you hand over to the *Okhrana* will result in men being arrested, imprisoned – even executed. It's the price they must pay, a sacrifice they must be willing to make. And what am I asking you to do for the Revolution? To die? No! Merely to spread your legs."

"All right!" I shouted. "All right, you've made your point and I'll do what you ask!"

I bowed my head, ashamed that I had refused his order, ashamed that I was agreeing to carry it out.

Peter stood by the window, a silk dressing gown covering his powerful frame. His body was just the way I had imagined it to be, and he'd taken me in exactly the way I'd known he would – forcefully and masterfully.

He smiled, a crafty, watchful smile, like a wild bear which is happy to have eaten the honey, but now wonders if the bees will fight back. "Why?" he asked me.

"Why what?"

"Why did you let me fuck you? That wasn't part of the deal."

I wanted to tell him the truth – wanted him to know that I would never have slept with him if I hadn't been acting under orders. But then my sacrifice would have been for nothing.

"Does there have to be a reason?" I asked.

"There's a reason for everything in this life."

"And what was yours?"

He shrugged. "I never look a gift-horse in the mouth."

"Couldn't that be true of me, too?"

"You mean *you* wanted to fuck *me*? I wouldn't have thought I was your type."

193

"Didn't you ever notice how I watched you speaking at the *mir*?" I asked, working on the principle that the most successful lie is the truth. "I was only a child, but I was drawn to you even then."

Peter walked over to the bed. He grasped the sheet which was covering me to my chin and slowly pulled it down, revealing first my throat, then my breasts, my stomach, my pubic mound, my legs. His gaze never left me for a second, and I felt more naked than I would ever have thought possible.

"So you really just wanted to fuck me?" he said. "No other reason?"

"Yes," I replied, gritting my teeth. "I really just wanted to fuck you."

Peter slipped off the dressing gown and I watched with fascinated horror as his limp penis began to swell. "Well then," he said, "shall we do it again? Would you like that?"

I nodded.

I felt the bed sag as it took his massive weight, and braced myself. He was my third lover. The first had been Misha, taking me blindly after so many years of waiting. Next came Sasha, passionate and yearning, yet tender and sensitive. And now, finally, there was Peter, who had the morals of a wild beast and a cruel streak which far exceeded anything to found in the animal kingdom.

Of all my lovers until then, he was the least worthy. I would never – never – have chosen him of my own free will. Why then, I asked myself as I gazed at the ceiling, why, oh why, was the brute capable of arousing me to heights of ecstasy I'd never even approached with Sasha or Misha?

Chapter Nineteen

Terry the barman appears in front of me, a bottle of Guinness in one hand, a glass in the other.

"There yer go, me old Princess," he says. "Get that down you'll be able to bend girders, won'ja?"

"Mistake!" I tell him.

I've already had two, twice my normal quota, and it's beginning to have an effect.

"What'd ya say, Princess?"

"Mistake. Didn't order it."

"I know you didn't, Princess. Feller in the Public, Jock McBride, bought it for you. Says you used to know his grandad."

"Would he mean Davy McBride?" I ask.

"Search me, love. Not from round here, is he? Him being Scottish an' that. There's the feller."

He points across the counter to the other bar, where a broad, sandy-faced man is holding up his glass in salute. I raise my glass in return. He looks like Davy, all right – looks like the man I smuggled guns into Spain with. Davy McBride! Another dead lover!

"And listen, love," Terry says before going back to the bar, "I know you like to take your time, what with being old and everything, but we're closing soon."

He indicates the clock on the wall.

"Clock," my drink-fuddled mind makes me say.

"It never stops ticking, does it, Princess?"

No, it doesn't. Whether we're asleep or awake, it never stops, and the years go by. I can't be over ninety years old – I must only be dreaming that I've lived that long.

But I know it's no dream. The clock's finger sweeps round,

swallowing up the last hours before the men from the Gulag come for me. How much of my time I've used up already! How little I have left!

Time was running out for the Romanovs, too, though I am sure they never suspected it. On the 3rd of September, the Tsar and Empress made an appearance in Petrograd to pray for guidance. They visited three different churches and spent several hours on their knees, while I stood a discreet distance away, emanating the soothing, peasant presence which Alexandra imagined I had.

"With God's help, we have come to a decision," the Empress told me when they had finished. "Hubby himself will go to the Front and take over as Commander-in-chief."

"Is that wise, Your Majesty?" I asked, alarmed, because I didn't want weak, indecisive Nicholas in charge of any army *my* husband was serving in!

"Why shouldn't it be wise?" the Empress demanded, sensing criticism.

"He's . . . he's our leader, not a professional soldier."

"He will not plan campaigns. He will simply serve as an inspiration to his people.

"I'm sure he will," I said.

As long as Nicholas wasn't issuing orders which could put Konstantin in danger, he could inspire whoever he liked.

The Empress's face relaxed into a smile. "Ah, Anna, if only everyone had your solid peasant sense. If only the government ministers thought like you."

"They're against His Majesty going?"

"They say he's needed here. What rubbish! I am perfectly capable of ruling in his place. As long as I have our Dear Friend to guide me, why should they worry?"

She had answered her own question, though she didn't realize it. The ministers were worried precisely *because* she had her Dear Friend to guide her.

No sooner had the Tsar set up his headquarters in Mogilev, than Rasputin began his work of dismantling the Government. The Minister of the Interior was a personal enemy and very vocal critic of the *starets* – he would have to go. The Prime Minister fell next, rapidly followed by the Minister of War and the Foreign Minister. By the time the regime collapsed, eighteen months later, there had been twenty-one changes in Government, and most of the new appointees were Rasputin's creatures.

"Have you heard about the secret apartment where one of the Minister of the Interior's flunkeys has meetings with Rasputin?" Peter asked from the other side of the bed.

I rolled over so that I could see him. Massive torso, chest hair almost as thick as a bear's fur, tight, hard muscles. A body which he treated as a machine to give me a sensual pleasure I had never experienced before, pleasure which I fought – because I hated to receive it from *him* – but to which I always finally surrendered.

"No, I hadn't heard," I said. "What kind of meetings are they?"

"Very profitable ones – for Rasputin. The flunkey hands over a shitload of money and a list of things the Minister would like to do. Rasputin takes the list home and thinks about it over half a dozen bottles of Madeira. Then next morning, he phones and tells Alexandra which of the requests he approves of."

And the Empress, after due consideration and bearing in mind all the facts as conveyed to her by a half-literate holy man, would make her decision. In this way the largest empire in the world, fighting the greatest war ever known, conducted its business.

"Can I pass that on?" I asked.

"Oh yes," Peter said. "Pass it on to your mates in the Party, and tell the tight buggers I want something good in return."

He knew, without me having told him, that I informed on him to the Central Committee. He knew, too, that they were making use of him just as he was making use of them. And I was in the middle – an instrument both of them were playing, each hoping to get a better tune out of me than the other. And who *did* I play the better tune for? I tried to do it for the Party, but to this day I have no idea if I succeeded.

The cunning left Peter's face and was replaced by lust. I watched his spade-like hands moving towards me, and felt simultaneously sickened and excited. "That's the business out the way," he said. "Now let's get back to the screwing."

"If Rasputin didn't have so much power to do harm, the thing would be laughable," I told Sasha, as we stood by the Neva, looking up at the empty Winter Palace. "Do you know that the Ministry of the Interior has *thirty* policemen watching Rasputin's house – only they can't follow him when he goes out, because he has a car and they don't."

Sasha nodded his head abstractly. He'd seemed preoccupied all morning, and I was doing my best to snap him out of it.

"And after Rasputin's had his night on the town, it's the Ministry's job to clean up the mess," I continued, "and that's getting harder all the time. Rasputin just used to get drunk and make a lot of noise, but now he's taken to exposing himself. The restaurant owners have to be bribed not to make a fuss."

"H. . .how do you know so much about Rasputin?" Sasha asked.

I cursed myself for the fool that I was. In my efforts to cheer him up, I'd said too much. "The way Rasputin behaves is common knowledge," I said lightly.

"It's not common kn. . .knowledge how many policemen are guarding him."

"I found out through my contact," I admitted.

"And who *is* your c. . .contact?"

"You know I can't tell you that," I said.

Sasha's eyes went wild. He grabbed me by the shoulders and started to shake me violently. I tried to break free, but he had the strength of a madman. "It's P. . .Peter, isn't it?" he demanded.

"Why should it be?"

"Isn't it?"

"Yes!"

"And d. . .do you let him make love to you? Do you?"

"No," I lied. "But what if I did? Isn't anything justified if it helps the Revolution?"

Sasha's grip relaxed. "Yes, anything is j. . .justified for the Revolution," he said. "But if I thought Peter was so much as laying a finger on you, I'd k. . .kill him."

The winter came and went. The snow melted away, the ice was soon gone. Flowers bloomed in the Alexander Park, trees started to grow sticky, shiny buds.

On June 4th, 1916, a new offensive was launched by General Brusilav in the south-west. Konstantin – the bastard! the wonderful, wonderful bastard! – had anticipated just such a move, and had already managed to get himself transferred to the southern sector.

At first the army made rapid advances, but by the 20th September, a stalemate had been reached.

'When will they learn to co-ordinate?' Konstantin wrote bitterly. *'If the supply lines had been only even adequate, this campaign could have really shifted the balance. As it is, we've lost a million lives and nearly all our equipment!'*

I didn't care about the million men. My Konstantin, who seemed to have been involved in every single battle, was alive and unharmed! And with the bad weather setting in, there would be no more fighting that year. I hoped I could persuade my husband to come home – at least for a little while.

And then Romania declared war on the Central Powers and Germany invaded it. The weather was milder down there and a winter campaign was still a possibility. A Russian expeditionary force was sent to support the Romanians, and Konstantin, of course, went with it.

Petrograd was a desperate place in that last winter of Tsardom. Life for the workers was especially hard – wages had doubled since 1914, but prices had quadrupled. Not that there was much to buy, anyway. The common people had to queue for up to thirteen hours for black bread, often to be told when they finally reached the front of the line that there was none left. There was no butter or meat to be had, either, and most people subsisted on a diet of buckwheat porridge.

Naturally, there was a succession of strikes, and naturally, we Bolsheviks encouraged them. The governor called out the troops, but they refused to fire on the crowd. One hundred and fifty of the mutinous soldiers were executed, and support for the Party in military barracks increased so fast that it was hard to keep track of it. From then on, the governor would use regular soldiers as little as possible – security in the capital would be in the hands of the Cossacks.

Even among the privileged, the mood had changed. Members of the royal family said openly that the Tsar should abdicate in favour of his son. One of the grand dukes could act as regent and run the country, they argued – whoever was chosen, he couldn't possibly make a worse job out of it than Nicholas had.

The winter bit harder. It was so cold that at one point twelve hundred locomotives burst their frozen pipes, disrupting the whole railway system and adding to the already acute food shortages in the capital.

Feelings of doom and despair – from which we Russians seem to draw a morbid satisfaction – grew every day more widespread.

Rumour abounded. The Prime Minister was in the pay of the Germans and had offered to give them Petrograd. His cabinet colleagues had been bribed a million roubles to starve as many peasants as possible.

Morale was as low – and mistrust as high – in the barracks. "It's bad luck to be awarded a medal by the Empress," a private in the Litovsky Regiment explained to me.

"Why?"

"Get a medal pinned on you by her, and sure as I'll be rolling drunk at Easter, you'll have caught a bullet within the week."

It was hardly surprising that the man who drew most hatred was the one who had made himself most conspicuous – the man who had bragged loudly of his powerful influence at court. Subversive cartoons began to appear on the streets. They showed a simple-looking Tsar and his devious wife sitting in the hands of a huge, black-bearded figure – Grigorii Rasputin.

Sooner or later, someone was bound to come up with the idea of killing the *starets*. The leaders of the plot were Prince

Yusupov and Grand Duke Demetri, the Tsar's nephew. They lured Rasputin to Yusupov's palace, fed him enough poison to kill an elephant, shot him three times, and finally beat him around the head with a blackjack. And still he was not dead – when he was fished out of the river a few days later, the doctors found water in his lungs!

The Empress was destroyed by the news. She had issued muddled and contradictory decrees before, but now she issued no decrees at all. The head of the government had abdicated her responsibilities, and there was no one to take her place.

Chapter Twenty

Whose hands are these resting on the table in front of me? I look up and see a face. I know it should have a nose, a mouth, eyes, yet to me it seems as featureless as a big, pink balloon.

"What did you say?" I ask.

"I said you're going to have to go home now, Princess. We're closing up, aren't we? Told you that when I brought you the last bottle."

"What about all-day opening?" My voice sounds slurred, and I realize that for the first time in years, I'm drunk.

"Don't have all-day opening round here, Princess. Isn't really the call for it, is there?"

He laughs – *Terry* laughs. Having identified him, I can now, with effort, make my eyes focus his face back into something recognizable.

"We used to drink vodka by the bottle," I say, and instantly curse myself for falling into the trap of the aged, the random serving up of slices of the past. I should not have had that third Guinness.

"Let me help you up, my old love," Terry says.

He takes my arm and starts to lift. "There we go. Gently does it, my old love."

Feet touching the ground, legs, not backside, now supporting me, I take a ten-tententave – *tentative* – step forward. It works. The old machine might creak, but after a few complaints it will still do what I want it to.

"Will you be all right, Princess?" Terry asks. "If you like, you can wait until I've closed up. Then I'll walk you home, won't I?"

"I'll be perfectly all right," I tell him.

202

Ah, the foolish pride of the old! But is it foolish? What have we got left without it? Possessions? Achievements? Children? These are all the products of something we did when we were younger, different people. Memories? Memories are simply that – things of the past. Knowledge? No one is interested in our acquired wisdom. So all we have left is pride, pride that we can still function. It's the only way we can exist, the only way we can define ourselves independently of others who, unlike us, still have a contribution to make to the world. And when we lose that pride, we die.

I stop in the doorway of the Vulcan, and wait for my body to speak to me. Will it let me get back to my room without further interruption? Will my aged, wrinkled bladder store the Guinness until I am safely back in Matlock Road? I don't want to be caught short. I don't want to be like other old drunks I've seen – having to piss in the street.

If the legs aren't any slower than usual, I can hold out, my bladder promises me.

I take its word, and step onto the pavement. I must sober up before Jennifer and Sonia arrive. Eccentric, drunken great-grandmothers are perfectly acceptable to the aristocracy and the proletariat – they are a laugh, a conversation piece – but in Sonia and Jennifer's circle, they're a social embarrassment.

Where do the girls get it from – this smug, unimaginative, bourgeois self-righteousness? Not from me! And not from their grandfather, my son Nicky. From their father probably, named Konstantin, but never half the man my husband was. No heroic life and death for this watered-down Konstantin. He expired on the golf course – only fifty – from a massive, stockbroker's coronary.

The fresh air and the walking have helped to clear my head a little, but the rest of me is starting to feel worse. It's not just my bladder I should've questioned. I should have spoken to my heart, which is now beating too fast, and my lungs, which are having difficulty taking in air.

Thinking about it only makes it worse. Turn your mind to something else, old woman, and let your body take care of itself. I was remembering the death of Rasputin, the fact that when they fished him out of the river . . .

No, no, no! Why is it that every time I relive this narrative in my head, I seem to get stuck on Rasputin, as if he were a barrier in the road which the wheels of my mind cannot coast over? I know why. It's because of what's on the other side of that barrier. But painful journeys must be endured – there's no other way.

By Christmas 1916, the Germans had occupied most of Romania. On January 7th 1917, they decided that what was left was not worth the effort of taking, and suspended operations. On the 6th of January – the day before the end of the fighting – my husband Konstantin was wounded during an enemy artillery bombardment.

Thousands of desperate people swarmed fearfully along the platform. Scores of the walking wounded were trying to fight against the flow and reach the safety of the street – one-armed soldiers, one-legged soldiers, soldiers with eye patches, soldiers so swathed in bandages that it was impossible to know what was wrong with them.

The train's escort did its best to keep back the mob, but it was an almost impossible task. Row after row of parents pushed for all they were worth, hoping to see their sons – and sometimes wishing they hadn't.

"My God . . . it's . . . I don't . . . you haven't got a nose any more."

"Serge! It's me – your mother. Can't you see me?"

"Make a space! Make a space! Don't jostle my boy – he has no legs."

Others, recognizing familiar faces, demanded news. "Ivan Petrovich! Have you seen my Vyacheslav? Is he all right."

"I don't know. I . . . I heard someone say that he was killed just outside Bucharest."

Happy fathers, sad fathers. Mothers who wept, one who kept banging her head against a pillar until her husband dragged her away. Anguish, relief, disbelief – that was how it was at the Nicholas Station that January morning.

Nicky sat on my shoulders above the crush and sur-
veyed the mad scene. "Where's Papa?" he asked. "I can't
see Papa."

"He'll be at the other end of the train," I said.

In a proper carriage, not a converted cattle truck.

"You men on the left, form a phalanx and hold the line,"
called out a loud, authoritative voice – a voice I recognized
as my Konstantin's. "You men on the right, link up. We
need a passageway."

"Can you see Papa?" I asked Nicky.

"No, I . . . Yes! There he is. He's on a bed, but they've
pro . . . pro . . ."

"Propped it up?"

"Yes, on the side of the train. It's like he's standing up,
only he isn't really."

The crowd, including me, was slowly pushed back until
a corridor had been created for the injured soldiers to
walk down.

"Wave to Papa," I suggested.

"He won't see me. He's looking at the soldiers."

An hour passed. My face turned numb with the cold, my
shoulders ached from carrying Nicky, but the crowd began
to get a little thinner and by elbowing and manoeuvring I
managed to catch a glimpse of Konstantin.

He was as Nicky had described him, his stretcher leaning
against the train, his eyes watchful, his hands directing the
bearers of other stretchers and the soldiers who were keeping
order. Occasionally, he'd speak to one of the wounded men,
but mostly he said nothing as the procession of mutilated
young bodies was carried past him.

He seemed thinner, and I could tell the position he was
in was causing him pain. I wanted to shout, "Konstantin,
Konstantin!" but I knew my husband too well for that. Much
as he wanted to see me, he wouldn't thank me for disturbing
him at such an important task.

The stream of wounded finally dried up. "That's it!" one
of the guards shouted over the loud murmuring of the mob.
"Train's empty!"

The crowd let out a low moan of disappointment and

began, lethargically, to disperse. Who knew when the next train would arrive? Who knew if there'd *ever* be another one?

I pushed and shoved my way to the edge of the platform, put Nicky on the ground and threw my arms around my husband.

Konstantin winced with pain, and I released my grip. "Where is it?" I cried. "Where are you hurt?"

Konstantin grinned. "Just about everywhere below the neck. Shell fragments. They've taken some out, but I've still got enough metal in me to make a pair of skis."

"But you . . . you are going to be all right?"

"I'll never be able to kill a wolf for you again but with a little luck, I should make some sort of recovery."

I put my arms around him, more gently this time. "I never wanted you to kill wolves for me. I only wanted you back alive."

Our Hispano-Suiza had been used as a military ambulance since the start of the war, but this was the first time we'd needed it ourselves. I sat next to Konstantin's stretcher – feeling pain myself every time we hit a bump – while Nicky jabbered excited questions.

"What's war like, Papa?"

"War is a very bad thing, Nicky."

"Then why are we fighting one?"

"Because we have to."

"Did you kill many Germans, Papa?"

"Yes."

"Did you like it?"

"No, I didn't."

"Then why did you do it?"

"Because I had to."

"What's the fun in being a man if you're always *having to do* things?"

Konstantin smiled. "Would you like to answer that, my princess?" he asked.

"I've never been able to find satisfactory answers to your

questions," I said. "Why should I do any better with your son's?"

I had my family back together again. I was very, very happy.

The doctor slowly unwound the dressing which covered most of Konstantin. I wanted to cry, or be sick – or do *something* – but I stood there silently, looking down at the body which seemed to have been put through a meat grinder.

The doctor examined one of the wounds more closely. He frowned, and shifted his attention to a second one. Then a third! "There's been recent bleeding," he said, "and some of the stitches have burst. How did that happen?"

"They stood his stretcher on end so he could supervise the unloading of the wounded," I said, ignoring my husband's reproachful glance.

"They did what? Good God! Weren't you told that even the lightest jolt could damage you? You're only flesh and blood, you know."

"The crowd was getting out of control," Konstantin said matter-of-factly. "In another five minutes it would have become completely unmanageable and then who knows how many people might have been trampled to death? There was no one else to deal with the problem – I had to take charge."

"Had to take charge!" the doctor snorted.

"I'll watch you change the dressings," I told him. "I want to be able to do it myself."

"That's not necessary. The nurse will— "

"I want to change them myself," I said firmly.

I'd be Konstantin's nurse, and give him more care and attention than any paid attendant could. With deep regret, but without a second's hesitation, I'd abandon my revolutionary work – bury Lyudmila for ever. I'd almost lost my husband, and now he'd been returned to me, I'd devote all my time to looking after him.

Let Molotov warn me of Party discipline. Let Peter threaten to expose me to the *Okhrana* if I refused to continuing supplying him with information. I didn't care. If we had to run away and live in a Mongolian herder's *yurt*, what did it matter as long as we were together? Only my family counted.

With the death of Rasputin, the Empress fell into a mystical trance and spent hours every day kneeling by the *staret's* grave, praying for the destruction of her enemies. The Tsar himself was becoming increasingly isolated. After Rasputin's funeral – which only the Imperial Family attended – he didn't return to military headquarters, but went into seclusion behind the walls of Tsarskoe Selo.

Buchanan, the British Ambassador, went to the Palace to express the anxiety of the Allies and to urge him to do something to regain his people's confidence. "Do you mean that *I* am to regain the confidence of my people," Nicholas asked, "or that they are to regain *my* confidence?"

While the Tsar walked gloomily around his palace grounds or played games with his children – puzzles were their latest craze – Petrograd deteriorated further. The bakeries needed 90,000 *poods* of flour a day for even minimal production, but were receiving only 35,000 *poods*. Of the sixty-three blast furnaces in the Donbas, only twenty-eight were still operating. Lack of raw material was causing everything to grind to a halt.

The city buzzed with talk of revolution. In the aristocratic salons disloyal toasts were drunk and plans to force the Tsar to abdicate were openly debated – even in the presence of members of the royal family.

And still nothing really happened. Life went on much in the same way as it had for the last three years – except that it became a little harder every day.

Konstantin's wounds were not healing as they should, and though he tried to hide it from me, I could tell the pain was getting worse.

"A temporary set-back," he assured me.

"I'm going to ring the doctor anyway."

"Yes," Konstantin agreed, wincing as he spoke. "I think that would probably be a good idea."

*   *   *

"Gangrene," the doctor pronounced.

Gangrene! It couldn't be!

"Yes, that's it," the doctor continued. "Must have set in at the railway station. Split the wounds, you know. Always dicey, that."

"Will he . . . will he have to lose his legs?" I stammered.

"We often do amputate with gangrene, but I'm afraid it wouldn't do much good in this case. Most of the poison's in the trunk, you see."

"So what *can* we do?"

"Give him painkillers, keep the wounds aseptic and dry, and wait and see what happens. It's a question of blood. Sometimes the body can purify itself, sometimes it can't. Only time will tell."

"You knew even before he told you," I said accusingly, after the doctor had left.

Konstantin smiled at me. How, how, could he always manage to smile? "I guessed," he admitted.

"And you knew the chance you were taking on the Nicholas Station. Didn't you?"

"Yes."

"How could you run that risk?" I demanded furiously. "How dare you act like that when you have a family to consider?"

"I didn't have any choice," Konstantin answered softly. "There are things we must do even if they hurt our loved ones."

"Fine talk!" I said.

"It's more than just talk. And you should know that better than most people."

"Me?"

"You didn't really want to join the revolutionaries, did you? But you felt compelled."

"I . . . how did you . . . ?"

I looked at my husband's face, and saw that he was laughing at me. "What else could have explained your long absences from the palace, my dear?" he asked. "No affair however passionate, could have taken up *so* much if your time."

209

"You knew," I gasped, "and yet you didn't try to stop me."

"If you believed in the revolution as much as I believed in autocracy, then I had no right to stop you . . . though I might have had to fight you some day."

"You *will* have to fight me," I said passionately. "You *will*! But first, we have to make you better."

The wounds continued to suppurate poisonous gangrene pus and . . . I have seen worse . . . I've seen much worse . . . in Spain . . . men who had been human torches . . . who had scarcely an inch of unburnt flesh on them . . . and in the Bolshevik war against the Whites, I . . . why, after so long, can't I think about it without . . . he was strong . . . he could stand pain more easily than most men . . . I've seen worse . . . much worse.

Konstantin . . .

Konstantin was delirious for much of the time. And I tended his wounds, soothed his brow, and tried to force a little nourishment down him.

Nicky came to see him every morning, as soon as he'd woken up from his troubled sleep. "Why doesn't Papa get up?" he'd ask, his eyes barely open, a troubled expression filling his young face.

"He's still sick."

"When will you be better, Papa?"

"He's sleeping now, Nicky. Being ill makes you very tired."

Occasionally, the fever would abate itself and Konstantin became lucid. I loved these times – and I hated them. Loved them because for a short period I had my own dear Konstantin back with me. Hated them because of the things he said. "It's time for me to go. I'm glad I won't live to see my Tsar fall."

There was no self-pity in his voice, just a simple acceptance of the logic of his own situation – and of Russia's.

"You *won't* die!" I said angrily. "Damn you, I won't *let* you!"

"Have I done nothing to stifle the irrational side of your nature, my dear? How can you ever expect to fulfil your destiny as a revolutionary if you cling to a symbol of the old regime – a social dinosaur – like me?"

He was laughing at me. The facial muscles were weak, but the true force of his smile – the gentle, mocking amusement – was as powerful as it had ever been.

"Would you have me any other way?" I asked. "Would you change me if you could?"

He shook his head feebly. He scarcely made a dent in the pillow. "No. I've had a very good life in many ways, but the last few years, with you, have been the best of all."

"They've been wonderful for me, too."

"I'm sorry that I could never love you as a man should love his woman."

"Do you think I care about that?" I asked him fiercely, as Peter's face flashed across my mind. "Any man can give me that kind of love. But what you've given me, no other man in the world could. That's why you *can't* die."

Not all gangrene cases die, I said to myself over and over again. And Konstantin's a very strong man.

He *couldn't* die. He was the centre of my universe and God simply couldn't take him. How I prayed for a cure! Kneeling before the Virgin of Kazan until my whole body ached, gazing at the blessed icon until my eyes watered and the Madonna herself seemed to be shedding tears of pity.

"Grant me this one request," I implored, "and I'll give up everything I believe in. Grant me this, and I'll devote my life to Your work."

Miracles do happen! Jesus raised the dead. Rasputin, whose very existence mocked the Lord, still managed to bring the Tsarevitch back from the verge. And Nicky, our dear son, was born a cripple, yet learned how to walk.

But miracles, to be miraculous, must also be rare. On a cold, frosty, morning, just as the winter sun was rising over the Neva, Konstantin died.

He was buried in the family vault on his estate outside

Novgorod. The Tsar was not there – he was now so far gone that he couldn't make the effort even for his oldest friend – but the officers from the Regiment turned out in force.

Troopers mounted on jet-black horses met the casket at the railway station, and solemnly escorted it back to the house. Cannons had been placed on the terrace, and a salute was fired. Four Captains who'd served under him carried the coffin to its final resting place. It was a magnificent ceremony.

"What are *they* all doing here?" my dead husband said in my head, as the soldiers marched past. "Don't they know there's a war going on? Their place is at the Front, leading their men, fighting for the Motherland."

"Not everyone has your sense of duty," I told him in my thoughts.

"What about you, my little princess? How are you managing without me?"

"It's hard. I loved you so much."

"Will you become a revolutionary again, now that I'm gone?"

"I expect so . . . I don't know . . . nothing seems very important any more."

"Don't give in, Annushka! Fight for what you believe in – like I did."

"I will," I promised. "I will."

I looked at the row upon row of *muhziks* who had come to pay him their last respects. Who could have guessed then – seeing them openly weeping for Konstantin – what they would do only a few weeks later? *I* should have guessed. A peasant myself, I should have been able to get into their minds. But my brain was clouded with grief, and it was of some comfort that others were sharing that grief with me.

When the pomp and circumstance was finally over, I took Nicky into the library. He was wearing a uniform which was an exact replica of Konstantin's, and throughout the whole ceremony, he had been a brave little soldier.

"I'm going back to the city," I told him, "but I want you to stay here with Vera."

"Why Mama?"

212

"Petrograd's going to be very dangerous soon. You'll be safer here."

"You would be, too."

"I've got work to do. But I promise to very careful."

His lip quivered slightly, but he refused to cry. "All right," he said.

"You like it here, don't you?" I asked guiltily.

"I'll like being close to Papa," he replied.

Oh, the poor child! "He's not going to suddenly appear at breakfast one morning, like he used to do when he'd been away," I said. "He really is dead."

"Oh, I know that!" Nicky said, almost contemptuously.

Like his father, he was no fool.

Two disembodied voices echo in my ears. One is flat and reasoned, the other is lighter, the rhythms flitting like a butterfly from word to word.

"Is she going to be all right, do you think?"

"Don't know. You hear me, Princess? Wha's happenin'?"

I can see oranges and bananas, tins of curry powder and bags of rice. I am in Ali's corner shop, sitting on a rickety chair, though I have no recollection of even entering the store.

"Wha' say we call a doctor?" Winston asks.

"Or an ambulance," Ali suggests.

"No ambulance," I croak.

"Say wha'?"

"No ambulance . . ." firmer this time.

Ambulances mean hospital. Hospital means that I'll not be at my 'residence' when Sonia and Jennifer call. And I know how they'll react when they learn where I've been taken. First, they'll shake their heads, implying they expected this all along. Then their busy little bourgeois hands will begin to pack up my things – because when I'm released from hospital it won't be to Matlock Road they take me, but to the Gulag.

I must protect my mind. I – must – protect – my – mind. As long as that is clear, as long as I can see him as he was, Konstantin is not dead. But let me once get into that home, let one of the spores of geriatric woolliness which float around once settle on my head and begin to grow, and the picture will fade, the memories will decay. And it will be as if my wonderful, wonderful husband had never existed.

Chapter Twenty-One

I was in my bedroom when the nausea hit me. First came the taste of bile in my throat, then the room began to swim before my eyes. And with the nausea came the fear, a river of ice which rushed through my veins, chilling my whole body.

I clutched the dressing table for support. Sofia, my new maid, hovered uncertainly. "Is anything the matter, Madam?"

"It's nothing," I managed to gasp. "You can go."

"Are you sure . . . ?"

"Get out!" I screamed.

Sofia gathered her skirts and scuttled out of the room, leaving me alone. Alone with my thoughts. Alone with my problems.

I made my way shakily over to the window and gulped in a breath of crisp winter air. How would my two lovers react when they found out about my pregnancy? I wondered. Sasha would definitely want the baby. But perhaps Peter would, too – he seemed incapable of love, but he knew all about possessions. I imagined confessing to them that I did not know which was the father, and trembled at the thought of what they might do to me – and to each other.

It was three days after my first attack of morning sickness that I took part in the demonstration which – though we didn't know it at the time – was the beginning of the end of the Romanov dynasty. The march started in the Vyborg District, a grimy industrial area on the other side of the Neva from the smart Nevsky Prospekt. The crowd which gathered was composed largely of women textile workers from the Lesnoy factory.

215

We paraded around Vyborg. Other women – thousands of them – joined us from the other textile factories. Steelworkers from the Putilov plant swelled our ranks, and then men from the Anchar and Obukhov works.

As the numbers grew, so did the confidence of the marchers. They were not little people any more, at the mercy of the Government, the *Okhrana* and their bosses – they were a mighty force, and they were unstoppable.

"Bread," they chanted, "We want bread!"

I surreptitiously slipped a candied fruit into my mouth. What right did I have to be indulging in such luxury when these women were half starved? I thought guiltily. Yet I couldn't help myself. My body had developed a craving for sweet things, and I was a slave to its demands.

"Down with the war," the marchers proclaimed. "Down with the Tsarist monarchy."

Yes, down with the Tsar! I thought. Down with privilege! Candied fruit for everyone!

I had started out at front of the march and intended to stay there, but new people joined us from side streets, and by the time the column reached the Liteiny Bridge, I was perhaps twelve or fifteen rows back.

I looked down at the river. It was still iced over, yet there was a spring-like feel to the air. I looked across the water at the palace which belonged to Princess Anna. I gazed at her boudoir window and thought of the luxury the room contained. How I hated her at that moment.

An excited buzz ran through the crowd. "Police! Police!"

They were on the other side of the bridge, trying to stop us from entering the central district. We marched on, crossing the bridge, getting closer and closer. Then, suddenly, the column came to a jerky halt. Messages passed down the line as those at the front became the eyes for the rest of us.

"The police have taken out their truncheons!"

"Somebody's down!"

I was a Party member. It was my duty to lead – to be the first to take whatever punishment was being meted out. And yet a part of me was relieved that I was not there, being battered by the police. I didn't mind getting hurt myself – what was mere physical pain after the agony of Konstantin's death? – but now I was no longer a free agent who could choose whether to live or die. Now I had the responsibility for the child I was carrying.

We were in retreat! Yet though we gave ground to the police, though we returned to the Vyborg bank, we did not turn round – we walked backwards, never once taking our eyes off the splendid buildings on the other side of the river.

"We can cross the ice!" somebody shouted.

The words spread through the crowd like a breeze rippling through long grass. "The ice! We can cross on the ice."

People rushed to the steps or scrambled down the embankment and soon there were thousands of us edging our way over the slippery surface. The police on the bridge started to move towards the far embankment, but they must have known they faced a hopeless task. On the bridge we had all been crammed between two parapets. Here on the ice, we spread out, no longer a column, but a tidal wave.

We climbed the embankment and marched along the riverside. We met with no opposition. We invaded Nevsky Prospect, perhaps a hundred abreast, bringing trams and cars to a stop. We looked up, at windows from which middle class office workers looked down, and chanted, "Bread. We want bread!"

We were showing these complacent people who had never even been inside a factory that we had power. They would realize now that the world as they had known it was finished. They must be trembling in their boots.

Life is not slow to mock the overconfident. I returned home to find an invitation to a grand ball at Princess Leon Radziwill's palace the following Sunday. It should have arrived earlier in the day, my butler informed me, but the messenger had been delayed by 'some slight disturbance' on Nevsky Prospekt!

Only hours earlier I had been marching down Nevsky Prospekt with my comrades, and now I sat in my parlour, watching Peter sip his vodka. It was hard to believe it was still the same day.

"I didn't hear your Rolls-Royce drive up," I said.

"I walked."

"Yes, I suppose even someone who likes flaunting his wealth as much as you wouldn't be foolish enough to drive so ostentatious a car through the streets tonight."

Our meetings were always like this – each of us trying to get the advantage, each trying to hurt the other. The antagonism existed even in bed, but there it served only to intensify the passion to a degree which was frightening.

"They've been arresting people all over the city," Peter said casually. "Most of your Central Committee is in clink."

"And you came all the way here just to let me know? How kind."

"When the Government had the whip hand, it was happy just to keep tabs on you. But now it's like a cornered rat – it's attacking because it's desperate."

I was tired of playing games with him. "Why are you here?" I asked.

Peter sat down and stretched out his great, muscular legs. "If the Government's going to fall, then it's time to change sides."

"You – a revolutionary!"

"The air always smells sweeter at the top of the dung heap. I'll back whoever's in charge."

"You still haven't said why you came," I told him, and I realized that could only be one reason why – one reason he'd confided his plans to me. "You . . . you want *me* to help you come over to the Party!"

"You *will* help me."

I laughed contemptuously. "If the Government falls, your power over me is gone."

"I could still denounce you."

"Denounce me! Who to? If the Tsar goes, the *Okhrana* goes with him. Do you think it'll bother me if people find out that I've been working for the Revolution? Now that my husband's dead, I don't care who knows."

Peter chuckled. "Your husband! What a idiot he was to

218

marry you when he could see from the swell in your belly that you were used goods."

How dare he say that? When he could never know. When he could never understand. I wanted to hurl myself at him and claw his eyes out – but that wasn't the way to hurt Peter.

"*Konstantin* was a fool?" I asked. "What about you? You married a woman who despises you – for the sake of her aristocratic connections. Tomorrow there may not even be an aristocracy any more, and you'll still be saddled with a shrew. Tell me, Peter, have you ever bedded her?"

From his face, I could see he had. Of course! He might not care about her, but he wanted children with blue blood in their veins.

"What's she like in bed?" I taunted.

"She's a fucking cold bitch," he growled.

"Perhaps you're too rough for her," I suggested. "Perhaps she's taken an aristocratic lover."

He leapt from his chair and advanced towards me – a big, angry beast. I stood my ground. I wanted him to hit me, however much it hurt, because to hit me would be to admit defeat.

He stopped, suddenly, and his body relaxed. He grinned. "Shall I tell you why you'll help me, Annushka?"

"You can tell me why you *think* I'll help," I said, trying to sound more confident than I felt.

"I've lifted your dossier from the *Okhrana* files. It proves you've been working for the police."

"Molotov knows—"

"Molotov knows you've been working as a double agent. The dossier says you were the *Okhrana's* double agent, not the Party's."

"It's a pack of lies."

"So is that crap you preach about a workers' paradise. But enough people believe it. And enough people will believe what your dossier says. It'll ruin you with the Bolsheviks. They might even have you shot."

"They may have you shot as well," I reminded him.

He shook his head. "I've got another dossier – mine. You should read the last entry. It's good – I dictated it myself."

"What does it say?" I asked, my feeling of dread growing by the second.

"Says *my* first loyalty's to the Revolution. It even orders my arrest."

"So why do you need me?"

"I'm offering you a chance to help me, Anna, because it'll be easier that way. Shit sticks, and I don't want even a hint of suspicion hanging over my head. But I'll make it, with or without you."

"I'll fight you all the way," I promised him.

"No you won't – and I'll give you two good reasons *why* you won't. If you try, I'll hand over your *Okhrana* dossier, and whatever happens to me after that, you'll be out of the Party. You won't like that, Anna. You want to be at the centre – making things happen."

He was right. Apart from my child – my children! – the Party was the only life I'd got left.

"And your second reason?" I asked belligerently.

"Once we're both in the Party, we'll be fighting on common ground, and you'll have more chance of beating me."

"But you don't think I could, do you?" I demanded.

Konstantin, in Peter's place would have said, "I don't know, my dear, but it will certainly be interesting finding out. Without you, life would be very dull indeed."

Peter was no Konstantin. There was no amused smile on his face, only a self-satisfied smirk. "Course I don't think you can beat me," he said. "If I did, I'd never give you the chance in the first place. But I know you, and *you* think you can do it. So you'll bide your time. And you'll keep your trap shut, if and when I decide to join the Party. Won't you?"

"Yes," I agreed.

Because he was right again. One day, I'd consign him to hell, but at that moment he held too many high cards.

"Shall we go to your bedroom?" he asked.

Oh God, I wanted to. Our arguments always increased my physical need for him, and in any other place, I wouldn't have been able to resist. But not there! I couldn't make love to him in the home Konstantin and I had shared.

220

"Get out," I said, as angry with myself as I was with him. "Get out before I have you thrown out."

He was chuckling as he walked to the door, and on the threshold he turned round and looked back at me.

"In an hour, I'll be screwing some whore," he said. "And what will you be doing? Sitting here, wishing we'd gone to bed after all."

He stepped out into the corridor and closed the door behind him.

I wouldn't give him the satisfaction of being right, I told myself as I heard his footsteps retreating down the hall. I'd never sleep with him again. But I knew that it wasn't true. The best I could do was to hold out against him for as long as possible – hold out until my body betrayed me.

The next day was a repeat of the one before. Workers swarmed over the bridges from Vyborg, Vasilovsky Island and Nerva – all heading for the centre of the city. No trams ran, no cabs moved. The shops were closed, the factories on the other side of the river were idle. The whole of Petrograd was out on the streets.

The Government called out the Cossacks, but though their officers ordered them to charge us, the tough Siberian warriors refused. All day we paraded the streets – demonstrating our power – then night fell, and with the cold setting in, people began to drift away to their dormitories and lodgings.

The uprising was coming to the end of its second day. Cobblestones and lumps of ice had been thrown, sticks had been waved, but no one had been seriously hurt. That was about to change. Two days later – on sunday – there would be a massacre – and I'd be part of it.

"The Empress," my butler said, holding out the phone. "She's called six times."

I picked up the receiver. "Your Majesty?"

"You've been out!" Alexandra said accusingly.

"Yes."

"It's not safe to go out. I've written to Hubby and told him all about the hooligans who shout about there being no

221

bread simply because they want to cause a disturbance. And about the strikers who are too lazy to work themselves and stop other, more willing hands from doing an honest day's labour. They need whipping – all of them!"

I was suddenly weary of it all and could pretend no longer. "Have you seen the people on the streets yourself? They're shouting for bread because they're slowly starving to death."

"And whose fault is that? My husband's, I suppose."

"He must take part of the blame."

There was a pause before she spoke again, and when she did her her voice was so low it was impossible to tell whether she was angry, or merely sad. "You've forgotten where you come from, Anna. You think like the aristocracy now. You don't remember how much the *muhziks* love their Tsar."

"They don't love their Tsar," I told her, exasperatedly. "They don't even really love their own families. All they care about is their land!"

"I never want to see you again," the Empress said shakily. "I never even want to hear your name mentioned in my presence."

The line went dead.

Did I convince her? Did I manage to plant even the tiniest seed of doubt in her mind? No. Even in her dying moments, she probably believed that though there were some very bad people in charge of Russia now, the *muhziks* still loved their Tsar.

My break with her had to come sooner or later, and I suppose I should have been glad when it did. I hadn't chosen her as a friend – she'd chosen me. She was a foolish, insensitive woman who could see no further than the needs of her own family. In many ways she, as much as her husband, had the blood of the Russian people on her hands. Why then, when I heard of her execution, did I find myself crying? I really don't know.

After three days of comparatively peaceful demonstrations, the Government decided to fight back. The attack came on Sunday afternoon, when we were occupying Nevsky

Prospekt again – and it was as sudden as it was deadly.

I felt the panic long before the first shot was fired. Now, I know it must have been started by the people close to the intersection of Nevsky and Sadovaya, who could actually see the soldiers being deployed. At the time, I only knew that fear was spreading through the crowd like a deadly virus.

And then the firing started.

Women screamed, men shouted, children began to cry. We were all moving frantically, our footfalls and panting breaths mingling with the reports of the rifles. People fell, some hit by bullets, others merely tripping or being pushed. Everyone searched desperately for shelter – in doorways, behind the ludicrously skeletal poles which carried the streetcar cables – anywhere there might be a chance to escape.

A bullet flew just past my head, buzzing like an angry, metal wasp. I hurled myself to the ground, trying to let my arms, not my stomach, take the impact.

More shots followed, and more, and more, filling my ears until I thought the sound would never, ever, go away.

A dead worker was on the ground a few yards from me. I crawled up to him and huddled against his back. There were bullets everywhere – whining overhead, thudding into brickwork, pinging against streetcar poles, ricocheting from walls, smashing windows.

And then, as suddenly as it had started, the firing ended. I raised my head cautiously, over the worker's corpse. The soldiers rose to their feet and retreated in an orderly fashion down Sadovaya. What had made them cease the attack then? That was as unfathomable as what had made them open fire in the first place.

I climbed groggily to my feet. Many people remained crouched in doorways and the ones who were actually moving seemed to be in a trance. Some were still on the ground, too afraid to get up. And there were others who would never get up again.

I saw a woman soaked in blood. I saw a man with half his face blasted away. But it was the little girl who affected me most. She was perhaps six, with long black hair tied in plaits.

223

I picked her up and hugged her to me. Her skin was already turning cold, and where there should have been a heartbeat, there was only a terrifying stillness.

I noticed a medallion around her neck and read the inscription – Tania. Knowing her name only seemed to make the tragedy greater.

"This can't go on!" I screamed across the confusion of the square.

It *couldn't* go on. The army had to be turned before more little Tanias died. My legs trembling, my heart thudding furiously, I walked away from the carnage and towards the Pavlovsky barracks.

Chapter Twenty-Two

"I tek you home, Princess," Winston offers as I stand on the threshold of Ali's general store.

"Let him go with you, Princess," the gap-toothed Pakistani urges.

I shake my head. Much as I could use Winston's strong arm, I daren't accept. I know that Sonia and Jennifer might already be waiting, and to see me being supported by a man, worse yet, a *black* man – a *Rastafarian* with dreadlocks – would be all the proof they needed that I'm no longer capable of looking after myself.

But they are not here when I arrive, and now I have time to prepare a little. I need a plan of campaign, a strategy. Like I had in my days as a Bolshevik agitator. I knew then how to act – knew all the weaknesses and fears of my factory workers, my bakers, my soldiers, and played on them ruthlessly. All in a good cause, of course, everything we Bolsheviks did was always in a good cause, Joe Stalin was a kind man who murdered forty million people in a good cause . . .

Enough! You're wandering, old woman. There must be something I can offer my great-granddaughters. There has to be a price – a price I can afford to pay – which will allow me to keep my freedom.

Footsteps in the hallway. The sound of a key being turned in the lock. They know I'm here and all they have to do is knock, but they don't bother. It would be troubling an old woman too much to expect her to get off her chair and admit the guests herself. Besides, why should she *want* to do that? What need has she for privacy – at her age?

The door swings open, and they are standing there. Jennifer, the elder of the two, is dressed in smart suit which, if not exactly severe, is at least crisp and efficient. Sonia, in contrast, is wearing a dress which, while neither frilly or fluffy, manages to give the impression of being both.

"Hello, great-grandmother," Jennifer says. "It's Thursday again."

"Yes," I agree. "Thursday again."

I try to fight back my dislike. I shouldn't be too hard on them, I tell myself. My great-granddaughters are just as much prisoners of their safe, complacent, bourgeois world as my father was of the *mir*. They are as incapable as the Empress of seeing life through any other perspective but their own.

And what do they see when they look through their perspective at me? An old woman with whom they have nothing in common, but who, nevertheless, they feel obliged to visit. An aged relative whose living conditions are a social embarrassment – and yet who steadfastly refuses to move. A time bomb ticking away, ancient but not yet defused, a withered radical with still enough strength left in her to get arrested at some demonstration and humiliate them in the press. Yes, I can see their point – I only wish they could see mine.

My great-granddaughters consider they live in great style. They have servants! And if these servants are not loyal family retainers but Filipinos on two-year contracts (return flight included), well, these days that's what you have to settle for. They throw lavish dinner parties – these granddaughters of my Nicky – at the end of which the ladies actually withdraw and the gentlemen pass around the port . . .

I know about these parties for a fact. I attended one – and only one – of Sonia's.

An invitation to my great-grandaughter's house. I needed a new dress, Sonia fussed, something classic. And I must visit the hairdresser's just before the party. Did I have any of my old jewellery left? What, none? Not even in the bank? It didn't matter, some could be hired. I wasn't to worry, Charles would pay for everything.

Imagine it – a group of people around a long rosewood table, people who would have loved to attend one of the banquets we used to have in Petersburg – but who would never have been invited.

"Great-grandmother is a princess of old Russia," Sonia said to the merchant banker on my left.

He was a heavy man, though not exactly fat, with a smooth pink skin. Sonia's words made him raise one pale eyebrow in appreciation. "And if my understanding of the Russia hereditary process is correct," he said pompously, "that makes you a princess too, doesn't it?"

Sonia giggled. "I suppose it does, though I never use the title."

But she would if she thought she could carry it off!

"Terrible thing that happened to your country," the banker told me. "The greatest tragedy of the Twentieth Century."

"Do you mean Lenin?" I asked carefully. "Or Stalin?"

"Whole pack of them," he replied. "The Tsar might not have been perfect, but at least there was some sort of order in the country."

Some sort of order in the country! The bread lines. The millions of young men walking into battle without even a rifle. "No, Nicholas wasn't perfect," I agreed.

"That's where you slipped up and we didn't," the banker explained patronizingly, pink skin gleaming in the candle light. "Certainly our ruling class is not as evident as it was fifty or sixty years ago, but it's there, behind the scenes, still ruling."

"We made mistakes in Russia," I admitted, "but we meant well."

"I'm sure you did, and then the Bolsheviks came along and—"

"I'm talking about the Bolsheviks," I told him. "I was a Bolshevik myself."

It was one of those moments which sometimes occur at dinner parties when all other conversations have temporarily stopped and your words, intended only for the person next to you, carry to everyone else. Mouths around the table dropped open, people forgot what they'd been just about to say. The banker didn't know how to react. The silence continued.

"Better dead than Red," he said finally. "Trouble was, with

Stalin in power, being the latter often meant ending up being the former."

He laughed as though he'd said the cleverest thing in the world, and the others joined in.

He was right. Stalin killed a lot of good men. But they hadn't given up their lives merely to be the butt of this man's humour, the source of an amusing quip which would break the tension. He shouldn't have joked – not about that.

I'd promised myself I'd behave, but now he'd made it impossible. I wanted to hurt him and I knew exactly how to do it – I've not lived so many lives without learning how to spot a fake when I see one.

"I should have thought a man with your background would have sympathized with a working class movement," I said to the banker.

His face froze for a second, and I knew I'd hit a sore point. "What background?" he asked, recovering slightly. "My father was a *Queen's Counsel*."

"But what about your grandfather? What was he? A miner? Or a cotton mill worker?"

Beads of sweat were forming on the smooth skin. The eye under the pale brow fluttered as a nervous tic set in. No one else was saying a word. "He . . . he served LMS Railway in an administrative capacity," the banker managed to splutter.

"Ah," I said, "a ticket clerk."

Suddenly, everyone was talking at once.

The inquest took place after all the guests had gone, me sitting in a chair, Sonia pacing the room.

"We went to a great deal of effort to prepare you for this party, great-grandmother."

"I know."

"Charles was very willing to do it because he thought you might . . . er . . ."

"Be a social asset?"

"Because he thought that you might enjoy meeting other people, and other people might enjoy meeting you."

"I did enjoy meeting other people," I said, thinking of

228

the look on the banker's face when he realized I'd seen
through him.

"There were so many things you *could* have talked about.
The Empress. The balls. Our guests would have found that
interesting."

"That wasn't my life, not my *real* one."

"Well, anyway, there was no reason to insult Roger."

"Did I insult him? What did I say that was so terribly
rude?"

"If he doesn't want people to know his grandfather was a
clerk, then I think we should respect his wishes."

"He's sold out his class," I told her. "It doesn't do him any
harm to be reminded of that now and again."

"You insulted him," Sonia persisted, "and he'll never
forgive you for that."

Nor will you, Sonia.

They both give me a dry peck on the cheek, then sit side by
side on the bed. They look uncomfortable there, as though
expecting it to collapse at any moment.

"Your social worker rang me today, great-grandmother,"
Jennifer says.

"I thought she would."

"She . . . she feels you're finding it difficult to cope on
your own."

"She's wrong. I'm doing fine."

Jennifer laughs, and the laugh says, "Aren't old people
funny – the way they pretend!"

"Be honest, great-grandmother," Sonia tells me. "It can't
be easy. You are over ninety, you know."

"I led the march from the Volynsky Barracks which toppled
the Romanovs," I say.

Both my great-granddaughters look embarrassed, and for
once, I can't blame them. I am doing what I promised myself
I'd never do. I am *talking* like an old woman, attempting to
defend my present with my memories of the past.

"That was all a long time ago, great-grandmother," Sonia
says.

Ah, but that's the problem, you see. It isn't a long time ago.

It's as clear as this afternoon, as fresh as if I'd only stopped in at the Vulcan for a bottle of Guinness on my way to the Volynsky Barracks.

Perhaps it is an exaggeration – the false pride of an old woman – to say that I led the march the day after the massacre on Nevsky Prospekt. But I was there. Right at the front. And it was my work, and the work of my fellow agitators – carried on throughout the long night – which had persuaded the Volynskys to mutiny.

They put on a magnificent show, marching in strict military order with the regimental brass band playing them on their way. Soon, our ranks were swollen by thousands of cheering workers, and by the time we reached the centre it would have been obvious even to the Empress – had she been there to see it – that hubby's reign was all but over.

What sights I saw that day! Men with rifles firing round after meaningless round at the carved heads on public buildings. Workers leaning from the windows of the *Okhrana* headquarters, throwing out secret files – and people catching the files in midair and tearing them to shreds. Women and children gleefully smashing the windows of police stations and then grinding the broken glass with the heels of their boots until it was little more than powder.

There were other sights, too, sights to chill the blood. I remember the policeman being dragged by an angry mob down to the Fontanka Canal. I think he was a young man, but his face was too much of a mess to know for sure.

"Don't drown me!" he screamed, blood and terror bubbling on his lips. "I swear to God I did nothing wrong. I didn't hurt nobody."

It was hard to condemn his persecutors. They'd suffered under police repression for years, and now they were striking back. Whatever the scared young policeman had screamed in his desperate defence, it was more than possible he'd been involved in incidents in which workers – or their families – had been killed. But guilty or not, it was no way to die.

After my work at the Volynsky Barracks that morning, I knew I was as responsible for the policeman's death as any

230

of the mob. People always die in revolutions – it's the price you have to pay for things getting better – and I know that better than most people. But does that mean I am to feel no personal guilt for what happened to that policeman? I'm no Joe Stalin – I can still feel his blood sticking to my hands.

By Monday night the Military Governor of Petrograd had only enough troops left under his command to control the Mariinsky Palace – where the Council of Ministers was meeting – and the telephone exchange. He was almost on the point of collapse, people said later, hands trembling, eyes full of the glazed indifference which comes with true hopelessness.

The Council of Ministers declared a state of siege in his name. A thousand copies of the proclamation were printed, but no one could find either brushes or paste, and in the end they were simply spiked on the iron railings around the Admiralty Building. By morning, they were all lying in the Alexander Gardens, waiting to be trampled under foot. The proclamation, like the Government which had issued it, had no substance behind it to make it stick, and needed only the slightest breeze to become dislodged.

That evening, in his private railway carriage which was stuck in the middle of the countryside by order of the railworkers' union, the Tsar abdicated. A provisional government was set up, headed by Prince Lvov – though he would soon be replaced by a fiery lawyer called Kerensky – and overnight three hundred years of tradition were discarded. I thought of my Konstantin when I heard the news and for one moment – one brief, mad moment – I was glad that he was dead.

Chapter Twenty-Three

The letter had taken three weeks to reach me, but I supposed I was lucky to receive it at all. I tore open the envelope, my hands trembling, and pulled out the piece of paper inside. It was a drawing of a group of grey, stick-men, walking through the snow towards an *izbá*.

'SOLDIERS COMING HOME FROM THE WAR,' Nicky had written in neat block capitals underneath.

I turned the page over, hoping desperately he'd written something else. He had! There it was, in the corner of paper, almost as if he'd been reluctant to burden me with it.

'I GO TO PAPAS TOOM EVERY DAY. I MISS YOU MAMA. CAN I COME HOME.'

I felt tears running down my face. But how could he come home, when the situation in the city was so uncertain? And how could I leave Petrograd at that moment? The fall of the Tsar hadn't solved anything – the war continued, more factories were closing, the bread queues had got no shorter. The liberal Provisional Government argued with the Menshevik-dominated Soviet about who was in control, but in reality, no one was. And we Bolsheviks were doing nothing, just sitting there and waiting for our leaders-in-exile to return. I loved my child deeply, but I couldn't desert my country.

I picked up my pen, chewed the end of it, and frowned. It is so difficult to communicate to a child with words. How much easier it is to tell him with a hug that you love him, to show him with a smile that he makes the whole world worthwhile.

'I AM FINE,' I wrote. 'I HOPE YOU ARE BEING A GOOD BOY AND DOING AS VERA TELLS YOU. I

LOVE YOU, TOO, AND I HOPE TO SEE YOU SOON.'
I hesitated. Should I write more? I scribbled the next line
quickly, before I lost my courage. 'IN THE AUTUMN, YOU
WILL HAVE A NEW BABY BROTHER OR SISTER, BUT
YOU MUSTN'T TELL ANYONE. IT'S A SECRET.'

I was crying again, because I'd miss seeing the expression
on his face when he read my news. I pictured him in my mind,
folding the letter carefully, hiding it in his secret place. And
I knew what he'd do next, too. 'You mustn't tell anyone,'
I'd written, but there was one person he'd have to confide
in. He'd rather die than reveal my secret to another living
soul, but he would go straight down the steps to the family
vault and talk it over with his father.

Yelaginski Park was as quiet and peaceful as if the Revolution had never happened. I walked by Peter's side, enjoying
the sun, trying not to think about the hold – the holds! – he
had over me, knowing that sooner or later I would have to
tell him about the baby.

"Lenin will be back within a week," he said confidently.

"Within a week?" I gasped. "*We* haven't been told that."

Peter chuckled. "*You* haven't got my contacts in Germany
and Switzerland, have you?"

"Is that why you told me to come here? Because you've
decided it's time to join us?"

He shook his head. "You should win in the end. You're
the only party with enough guts to be real bastards. But the
bull's not mounted the cow until he's got his prick right
inside her. So I think I'll wait a while, just to be sure."

What a planner he was! Still making a fortune from the
factories – somehow, whatever the shortages, raw materials
got to *him* – but constantly scanning the future, calculating
what changes could occur, assessing how he could make a
profit out of each and every one of them. And yet I don't
think it was the money he lusted after – the game was more
important than the gain. He *liked* being in a situation where
not even his survival was guaranteed.

"How long've you been wearing that pistol?" he asked
casually, though nothing he ever did was casual.

"Ever since the Tsar abdicated."

"And can you use it? Or is it just there for decoration?"

"Yes, I can use it. The Count taught me how to shoot."

"Show me," he said.

"Why?"

"Because it excites me."

Ashamed as I am of it, the thought of Peter being excited, excited *me*.

I looked around the park and saw that it was almost deserted. I unstrapped my holster and took out the pistol.

Peter had moved away from me. I raised the gun and pointed it at him. I sighted it on his head, then lowered it until it was aimed at his heart. The man responsible for Sasha's exile to Siberia, the man who held a threatening *Okhrana* document over me, was completely in my power.

I felt the trigger against my finger. It would only take a gentle squeeze. At this range, I could not miss.

A move, just one move, and he would have been dead. He didn't move. Instead, he smiled his broad, confident smile.

I lowered the gun, I can't explain my reason – I just did it. "What would you like me to shoot?"

He glanced around. "There's a squirrel in that tree—"

"No! He hasn't hurt me, I won't shoot him."

Peter shrugged his shoulders as if he hadn't understood. And probably he hadn't. How could any man who'd turned his workers' children out onto the street in the middle of November be expected to feel anything for a squirrel?

"What about that branch there?" I suggested, and Peter nodded.

I raised my pistol and took aim. I pulled the trigger, felt the recoil, re-sighted and fired again. When I lowered my weapon, I could see two pale gashes, almost touching, cut into the blackness of the branch. As I watched, the branch swayed, creaked and finally broke in two.

"You *are* good," Peter said admiringly. "Bloody good. Let's go into the bushes."

"You want to . . . ? Here? It's too cold."

"We don't have to take off all our clothes. I want to screw you, not give you a bath."

I hesitated.

"You know you want it as much as I do," Peter urged.

He took my hands and pulled me towards the bushes. I didn't even try to resist.

Later, when we had both quenched our lust and I hated him again, we walked slowly back to the Rolls-Royce.

"You don't carry a gun, do you?" I asked.

"No."

"Because you're too arrogant to think that you might ever need to use it?"

"When you can see the wolves' eyes, it's too late to go running for your *izbá*."

"Meaning?"

"Meaning, if found myself in a position where I needed a gun to defend myself, I'd be as good as fucking dead already," Peter said. "And if I wanted someone killed, I wouldn't do it myself."

"You mean you'd hire an assassin?"

"Maybe," Peter replied. "Or maybe I could get it done for free."

The laughter started as a gurgle in his throat, then built up into a fit which gripped him so hard that he had to stop walking.

"Why don't you let me in on the joke?" I said angrily. "Then I could have a good laugh, too.

"Oh, I'll let you in on it," Peter managed to gasp. "I'll let you in on it, but not yct – not until the time's right."

Lenin was coming! Lenin was coming and the streets around the Finland Station that early April evening were crammed with workers and soldiers, waving red banners and shouting out excitedly. Armoured cars moved slowly through the crowd, trams were reduced to a crawl. Lenin, who had not set foot on Russian soil for over ten years, was finally returning from exile.

On the platform, we members of the Bolshevik Welcoming Committee drank in the mob's enthusiasm until we were almost intoxicated by it. A cheer went up! The train was coming. It chugged into the station, a huge metal monster snorting steam, its single eye bathing the platform in dazzling light. The band struck up the *Marseillaise*, the monster drew to a halt, a door opened – and there he was!

So many statues of Vladimir Ilyich have been carved since, so many pictures painted, that it is tempting to think of him as huge, a colossus towering above us all. The truth is very different. Standing in the doorway, dressed in an ill-fitting suit, was a dumpy, unprepossessing man with a balding head. Yet he had a determination and dedication that none of the rest of us could match. He was hard, he was ruthless, totally devoted, totally convinced that he – and only he – was right. I don't think that Konstantin could ever have liked him, but he wouldn't have been able to prevent himself admiring the man.

The captain of the Honour Guard of Khronstadt sailors saluted. Lenin looked surprised, almost lost, then he raised his own arm and returned the salute. I'm sure it was the first time he'd made such a gesture in his life!

The Bolshevik Welcoming Committee stepped forward to greet him. "This is Lyudmila," the man next to him said.

"I've heard of you," Lenin told me. "You've done good work."

You've done good work! I used to have a whole drawer full of medals, but none of them ever meant as much to me as those few words. As I stepped aside to allow other party faithful to meet our leader, I was bursting with pride.

The introductions over, Lenin made a speech. The Provisional Government told nothing but lies, he said. What the people wanted was bread, peace and land. Only the Bolsheviks could give these things to them.

He was carried on the shoulders of cheering workers to the armoured car which was to take him to our headquarters. The car made slow progress down Simbirsk Street. Several times, the pressure of the mob forced it to stop altogether, and every time it did, Lenin thundered out his speech again, hammered home his simple message.

Bread-peace-land. Bread-peace-land.

It's strange, remembering that scene, to think that only a

236

few weeks later the same people who cheered him would be baying for his execution. But that's the way with revolutions. They rarely move in a straight line, rather they swing back and forth, favouring first one faction then another. And the trick is to hold on, to wait until the pendulum has slowed down and then to plant your feet firmly on the ground and make a grab at it. Which is what Lenin – despite his moments of weakness and self-doubt – finally managed to do.

What giants men were in those days. Not just Lenin, but Trotsky, Konstantin . . . even Peter. It is hard to believe that they could ever have died, but they did, all of them.

"Dead . . . all of them dead . . ."

I'm rambling. I look anxiously across at Sonia and Jennifer, but they're far too absorbed in their own conversation to have heard me.

". . . she thinks that because her father's a baronet, she can act like God Almighty. But she's only a prep school teacher – and I told her so!"

"Good for you! And *I* made it quite clear to her that after all the effort I'd put into the Mothers' Committee I expected to see Justin play in the Inter-Schools Football Cup – especially if Royalty's going to be there."

Ignoring me is nothing new. These visits to their great-grandmother are an opportunity to catch up on gossip and exchange grievances. Besides, their chat helps fill up the awkward silences.

They sense my eyes on them, stop talking to each other and turn their attention to me. "Well, great-grandmother, have you thought about it?" Sonia asks.

"Thought about what?"

"The Home," Sonia says, pronouncing each syllable slowly, 'Th-e Ho-me', as if that will make everything clearer.

"The men in the white coats," I say, before I can stop myself.

Sonia laughs, condescendingly.

"Whenever we mention the home, you always talk about the men in white coats. Why is that?"

"I'm thinking of hospital orderlies," I tell her. But I'm not. I'm thinking of the men in white coats who used to stalk the streets of Moscow when all was quiet, all was still. The men whose knock on the door sent fear rushing to the bravest heart.

"What have hospital orderlies got to do with it?" Jennifer asks.

"Taking me to the home," I say, knowing I'm putting on a poor show, wishing I could do better.

"You're confused," Jennifer says. *"We'll* take you. In the *car.*"

"Why do you want to shut me away?" I ask.

Jennifer sighs. "I'd hardly call it shutting you away," she says. "It's one of the best private retirement homes in London. A lot of old ladies would think themselves very lucky to get in."

But not me! My life is out there – on the streets – like it always has been. Once inside a Gulag, even a carpeted one, I'll go to pieces.

"You certainly can't continue living here," Sonia says. "I mean, we're not actually rich, but what would our friends think if they knew we let one of the family exist in such squalor. You haven't even got your own bathroom, for goodness sake!"

How easy life would be for them if I were to submit to the Gulag. Then they could brag to their smart friends about their great-grandmother who was a Russian princess, knowing that the embarrassing reality was safely locked up.

"Your friends won't find out," I promise. "If you leave me alone, I won't bother *anybody*. I'll live out my last few days quietly here. I won't go beyond the end of the street if you don't want me to."

It's not enough! The price I'm willing to pay is not enough. But what else do I have to offer them?

Yet on the verge of defeat, I pluck at a fresh straw of hope, just as my husband would have done. I've heard all their arguments before, but there's something new behind them today. A fresh edge. An urgency. Why are they in such a hurry? If I can find that out, I may have something to fight with.

"I could just stay here," I repeat, but now I am studying their faces, searching for clues.

"If only it were as simple as that," Sonia says exasperatedly.

"Why shouldn't it be?"

"Because there are people who still remember what you used to be. Like the man the other day . . ." Sonia says, then sees Jennifer shooting her a sharp glance, and dries up.

"The man the other day?" I ask.

"It's nothing to do with you," Jennifer says hurriedly.

But it is! I know it is!

"We'd like you to go voluntarily," Jennifer continues. "That would be better all round. But . . . you remember the doctor, don't you?"

Oh yes, the doctor. A senior medical officer for the area – and an old chum of Edward's. "I remember him," I say.

"He was ready to sign the committal order right away. Only I said we should wait – to give you time to get used to the idea."

"I'll fight you every inch of the way."

How many times have I said that in the past? But then I had something to fight with. Maybe I still do. Maybe . . .

"Isn't it better if you go willingly?" Jennifer asks. "I know you'll love it once you're there."

"You seem in a great hurry," I say. "Is that anything to do with The Man The Other Day?"

That is what he has become – a man in capital letters, a shadowy figure who I sense is my salvation.

"He's a journalist," Jennifer says, now that it's clear I've got my teeth locked on the bone and will not let go. "He wanted to do an article on you."

And they want me behind bars before he has a chance to talk to me! "When's he supposed to be coming?" I ask.

"He's not. He wanted your address, but we wouldn't give it to him."

In my younger days, I would have leapt up out of my chair. Now, I struggle to my feet, my joints screaming out in protest, and stand over the two of them – a towering shrunkeness. "How *dare* you?" I demand. "How dare you take that sort of decision for me?"

"We . . . we thought . . ." Sonia splutters.

There must be some power left in my cracked old voice – for once, I have got them on the defensive.

"What would have been the point of it?" asks Jennifer, who's always been the stronger of the two. "Why rake up the past again? It wouldn't do you any good, and it would only be embarrassment to us. Edward's standing for Parliament, and Charles certainly doesn't want it known that anyone in my family was actually on speaking terms with Lenin."

"I should have thought there was some cachet in that," I say. "He was a world leader, after all."

Jennifer shakes her head. "It's not just Russia, is it?" she asks, and I can tell from the expression on her face that she thinks she's being very fair and understanding. "I mean, if it was, we could explain it all away as youthful high spirits. But you've never stopped, have you? First there were all those hunger marches in the Thirties, then the Spanish Civil War, and finally the CND. After you were arrested at Aldermaston, Daddy didn't dare show his face at the club for weeks."

I laugh, in spite of myself. My Konstantin didn't give a hang what anyone thought, but his grandson-by-adoption rarely considered anything else. And these, his daughters, have inherited the trait.

"You've always been so wilful, so unreasonable," Jennifer says accusingly. "If you could only have brought yourself to behave, it might have been different."

Behave! As if I were a child. Well, I suppose I'm as helpless as a child. "I will behave in future," I say meekly, my bubbling anger subsumed by my need to survive.

Jennifer shakes her head. "You can't. You never could. I suppose that's how you got mixed up in the Revolution in the first place. I'm sorry, great-grandmother, but we're just going to have to be firm on this one."

My anger spills over. "Get out!" I tell them.

"Really, great-grandmother!"

"Get out, you complacent little bitches!"

Sonia lets out a gasp of shock.

"We make a lot of allowances for you – because of your age," says the more unflappable Jennifer, "but there has to be a limit. I think you owe us an apology."

As if they had been practising it together, they both fold their arms and jut out their chins determinedly.

"We're not leaving until you apologize," Jennifer threatens.

Oh you aren't, aren't you? I am old and weak, they are young and strong, but I will *not* be pushed around any more. I look for a weapon I can use. Not the chair, I'd never lift that. The vase – the vase is not too heavy.

I pick it up and hold it like a club. Pain shoots from my elbow to my shoulder. I advance towards them.

"Be careful with that," Jennifer warns.

"Out!"

"You don't want to hurt yourself!"

"Out!"

They rise to their feet and edge their way towards the door. Jennifer glares, but Sonia is not even looking at me. The door is open, they are standing in the corridor. "It seems to me it's not an old people's home you need to go to," Jennifer says angrily, "it's a lunatic asylum."

I hurl the vase as hard as I can. It falls two feet from the door and smashes into a hundred pieces.

I have to sit down . . . have to . . . catch my breath. I think about The Man The Other Day. A journalist, Jennifer said, wanting to write an article and what good did I think that would do me? What good indeed? And yet, it gave me hope.

What is it you expect, foolish old woman? A piece in the newspapers which attacks your wicked great-granddaughters? A national outcry about the way they treat you? Nobody *really* cares about the old. Any piece the journalist wrote would merely be for its curiosity value. There is no hope. It's over. It would be best to end it now.

Knife! Gas! Sleeping Pills! They are all available to me. Why is it that this frail, pain-wracked body of mine is so reluctant to let go? I look up at the ceiling, at the yellow, cracked paint and the battered lamp shade.

"Tell me what to do, Konstantin," I plead. "Tell me what to do."

Chapter Twenty-Four

It was late one afternoon when Vera arrived at the palace with my sweet little Nicky.

"Why did you leave the estate?" I asked her, when I had finally finished hugging my son. "You were safe enough there, weren't you?"

Vera shook her head. "The peasants, madam . . ."

"What about them?"

"They . . . they went wild. They killed all the chickens, and then they slaughtered the cattle and smashed the greenhouses. After that, they came up to the house. They told us to go. They said as soon as they'd emptied the wine cellar, they were going to burn the house down."

They could have had eggs and milk all the year round, calves the next spring, tropical vegetables and fruit in the early summer. They could have used the house, perhaps as a school, perhaps as a hospital. Instead they'd indulged in an orgy of mindless destruction and were probably still drunk – while the cattle they had slaughtered for their feast lay rotting in the fields.

The same could happen to the palace, I realized. There were bands of drunken deserters all over Petrograd – how long would it be before one of them had the idea of breaking in. For Nicky's safety, we would have to move to somewhere less conspicuous. Besides, I was no longer Anna, I was Lyudmila, and perhaps the time had finally come to let my past go.

Nicky, Vera and I moved into cheap lodgings in the Vyborg District. I had the palace reopened as a hospital during the Civil War – but I never lived there again.

They surrounded Bolshevik headquarters, an army of the

walking wounded. One-legged soldiers hobbling on make-shift crutches. Sailors with stumps hanging where strong arms had once been. They should have been a pathetic sight, but they were not – their blazing rage transformed them into the wrath of God.

Some carried placards: 'Lenin and Company – Back to Germany'. 'Death to the Enemies of Russia'.

As I eased my way through the mob towards the front door, men spat and cursed at me. If I hadn't been a woman, I think they'd have attacked me – striking me with their crutches until I was nothing but a bloody pulp on the ground.

And it was not just these poor men who were angry. The sailors who'd been Lenin's Honour Guard had passed a resolution against him. The Volynsky Regiment – whom I had led out of their barracks – said that if the Government didn't arrest Lenin, they would.

The Red Guards at the entrance parted to let me pass, and I entered our headquarters. The building was almost empty, and a feeling of black despondency hung in the air. It was hard to believe that only weeks earlier, we – especially Lenin – had been heroes. I made my way upstairs to our leader's office.

He was sitting at his desk with his head in his hands. When he looked up at me, I saw sheer exhaustion in his eyes.

"Is it true?" I asked.

"You too, Lyudmila? And I thought you were one of the few people in the Party I could rely on to trust me."

"You must tell me whether it's true," I insisted.

Ilyich ran his hand over his bald head. "When the Tsar fell, I was in Switzerland and it was imperative that I return to Russia as soon as possible. The Germans offered me safe conduct. I travelled in a sealed train, I spoke to no one from the German Government."

"They were using you," I said. "Don't you see that?"

"Of course they were using me," he snapped back angrily. "They wanted me to undermine the war effort. But that was what I would have done anyway – so what difference did it make?"

I said nothing.

"I have never been a German spy," Ilyich told me.

"Everything I have ever done has been for the workers and peasants."

What power that man had to convince. I never met anyone who didn't leave mesmerized after a conversation with him – even though we all knew he would lie whenever the truth became inconvenient.

"I believe you," I said.

"They don't believe me," Lenin replied, pointing out of the window. "Nor do many of the Party. And even those who accept that I'm not a spy, are losing faith in me as a leader. I'm not gradualist enough for them."

He began pacing the room slowly, tiredness showing in every step.

"Is there anything I can do?" I asked.

"If only I could get it all out of my mind," Lenin said. "Even for a while. I feel as if my head were bursting." He stopped talking, and tugged hard at his beard and ran his eyes up and down my body. "Lyudmila," he continued, and it was the only time I ever heard him sound hesitant, "Lyudmila . . . could you . . . could we . . . ?"

"If it will help."

"There's a bed in the other room." He began walking towards the door, then stopped dead in his tracks. "No!" he said miserably. "No! I've failed in so much else. If I were to fail in that—"

"You're thinking of giving up!" I said, horrified.

"What's the point—"

"Think of the peasants toiling eighteen hours a day," I said. "Think of the workers slaving away in hell-holes. You're the only man in Russia who can save them."

Ilyich banged his fist on the table.

"You're right," he agreed. "I must fight on. Leave me now."

"If you're sure . . ."

"As long as I have loyal comrades like you, I'll never give up."

But did he mean it? I asked myself as I made my way heavily down the stairs. Could he really hold out against such contempt – such hatred? Those were black days for Lenin.

And for me. Days when all hope seemed to have gone. They were as black as the days which face me now.

The fire crackled brightly. Nicky and I knelt in front of it, our hands spread out to get the full benefit of the warmth while the black market logs lasted.

"I watched the bulls and cows on the farm, Mama," Nicky said shyly.

"And?"

"I know how they get babies."

I had been dreading the possibility of this moment, almost as much as I feared telling Peter and Sasha that I was pregnant. My mouth was suddenly dry, and I felt my heart pounding.

"How long does it take to make a baby?" Nicky asked.

I put my hands on my hips in mock-exasperation. "Enough of your foolish questions!" I said.

But Nicky stood his ground. "How long?"

I had never lied to him, not even about Konstantin's illness, but I was tempted to lie now. I wanted to say a year, or two years, but Nicky would sense I was not telling the truth, and ask someone else. There was no running away – the problem had to be faced now.

"A baby takes about nine months to grow," I said.

"How long's that?"

"Our baby will be born in September, so it started growing just after Christmas." I reached out my arm and pulled his hand towards me, in an effort to distract him. "Rub Mama's tummy. See if you can feel anything."

I should have known than to try a trick like that on Nicky. He pulled his hand away again. "Papa was at the Front then," he said.

"I know."

A tear trickled down Nicky's cheek. "That means that the new baby . . . isn't Papa's."

I stared into the fire as if, in the glowing shapes the splinters of wood formed, I would find an answer to my dilemma. I was terrified that Nicky would hate the baby. Or me.

My child had started to cry. And he had turned his back on me. I reached over to him, put my hands on his shoulders, and twisted him round. His head was bowed, and he was gazing down at the floor.

"Look at me, Nicky," I said.

He did not move.

"Look at me!"

Slowly, reluctantly, he lifted his head. I felt my arms trembling. I could lose him now, lose him for ever. And if I lost him, I would lose all I had left of Konstantin, too.

That was it!

"Why are you Papa's boy?" I asked, my voice quavering. Careful, Anna! I told myself. Get it right! Make him understand, because you only have this one chance. "Are you Papa's boy because you think Papa did to Mama what the bull did to the cow?"

Nicky shook his head.

"Why then? What makes you Papa's boy?"

"Because Papa loved me."

"And he'd have loved the new baby, too. It would have been his, just as much as you are."

Nicky frowned. It was an almost adult expression. "But Papa's dead."

I wanted to reach across and touch him, but I didn't dare in case he repulsed me. "Papa lives on in us," I told him. "You because you're his son, and me because I am the woman he made me. No baby I ever had could be anything but your father's. Do you understand what I'm saying?"

Nicky wiped a tear from the corner of his eye and squared his shoulders. "Yes," he said.

I don't think he did. But he did understand that when I said the baby would be Konstantin's, I really meant it. And that was good enough for him.

I reached across to him and stroked his silky hair, now grown so long that it was almost touching the collar of his sailor suit. He did not resist.

"You'll have to be both father and brother to the new baby," I said. "Do you think you're brave and strong enough for that?"

Nicky nodded earnestly. "If it's a boy, we'll call it Konstantin."

247

"And if it's a girl?"

"If it's a girl, you can make up a name for it," my son told me.

"But you'll love it just as much?" I asked anxiously.

"Yes," Nicky said. "But if Papa hadn't died, he'd have wanted you to choose."

I held out my arms to him. "I love you, Nicky."

Nicky moved closer to me and put his small arms around my neck. "I love you, Mama."

And then we cried and cried for what seemed like hours.

A knocking on my door. "Princess! Princess! Are you in there?"

How long have I been sitting here? It was light when I last looked outside, but now darkness has almost fallen. I rise creakily to my feet and hobble across the room, carefully avoiding the pieces of the vase I threw at my great-granddaughters.

I *must* get that cleaned up later.

I open the door to find Mandy, the woman from the room across the corridor. Her hair is long and straggly and she's barefoot. She's dressed, as always, in a kaftan and flowery choker, as if the Sixties had never gone away. Who can blame her? We all hark back to our Golden Age. That's what I have been doing all day.

"There's a man at the front door to see you, Princess," she says.

So why has Mandy, the most hospitable of women, left him standing outside? "Is there something wrong with him?" I ask.

"Well, no. But I . . . er . . . heard your argument with your granddaughters this afternoon. Well, I mean, I couldn't help it, and I thought they might have sent him."

She's a good girl, but she needn't have worried.

"Edward and I will come for you ourselves," Jennifer told me.

They wouldn't entrust my incarceration to anyone else. They'll want to be sure there isn't any last minute dash for the wire.

"Thank you, Mandy," I tell my flower-child neighbour. "I can handle it from here."

I walk stiffly to the end of the corridor. The door's open, but the chain is on. I peer through the six inch gap. I see him – and his white coat! He's wearing a heavy, belted raincoat just like the men who used to pay late-night visits in Moscow.

Get a grip, old woman! I order myself. It isn't the Nineteen Thirties, and we're in England.

I raise my eyes from the mackintosh to his face. He's quite a young man, with blunt features but lively, opportunistic eyes. Though I can't remember where, I know I've seen him before.

"Princess Anna Mayakovsky?" he asks.

I suddenly remember why his face is familiar. "You were at Gregory Lovosky's funeral."

That freezing day in Highgate Cemetery four years ago, when I buried my last old friend. Yes, this young man was there, looking at me – staring at me – then turning and walking away. Leaving me trembling.

"I was there," he admits readily. "I was doing a story on it. That's when I first noticed you."

Doing a *story*? So that's who he is! The Man the Other Day – the journalist, my saviour. He looks too ordinary to be a saviour.

"And you want to do a story on me," I say.

"That's right."

"So why did you wait four years?"

"I . . . er . . . couldn't see the angle of the story before."

"And now you can?"

He shrugs. "Times change, conditions change."

He's been carrying me around in his head for four years, and only now has he decided to confront me. The fear which gripped me in the cemetery returns. I want to close the door in his face, but I force myself not to. When our only hope is the Devil, it's to the Devil we must turn.

"What do you mean? Conditions change?" I ask.

"Frankly, Princess, you're more important than you were four years ago."

"How can that be?"

"It's a little difficult to explain on the step. Would you mind if I came in?"

Reluctantly, I unfasten the safety chain. He follows me down the corridor to my room. I gesture him to go inside.

"Mind the bits of china on the floor."

"An accident?"

"In a way. Sit down."

He looks around and sees there's only one chair. "I don't mind standing. You take the chair."

"You'll need to write. You do want to write something about me, don't you?

"Well, not exactly write, but I do want to—"

"It'll be easier for you to write if you're sitting down," I tell him firmly.

I lower myself onto the bed, unsure of whether the creaking is the old springs or me. The reporter has no pad and pencil. Instead, he produces a small black tape recorder. "I want you to tell me your history," he says.

"All of it?"

"Certainly, all of it. But perhaps we could start with your life during the last months of the Provisional Government. Say . . . the days before the July Uprising."

He seems very well informed. I like that.

"Which paper do you represent?" I ask. "The *Sun*? The *Daily Mail*?"

He looks at me blankly. Apart from his eyes, he really is a very nondescript young man. So why does he make me feel so uneasy?

"Or do you work for a local paper?" I continue.

Although I try to hide it from him, my voice is tinged with disappointment. The *Kilburn Courier* has no power to save me.

He's still not spoken.

"Well," I demand, irritation overcoming my misgivings, "which paper *do* you work for?"

"Several," he says, sounding puzzled.

Why does he sound puzzled?

"And also for our national television," he continues. "Are you all right, Princess?"

No, I'm not all right. I am suspended half-way between shock and anger with myself.

Stupid old woman! Ever since this man entered the house we've been speaking to each other *in Russian*.

Chapter Twenty-Five

It's my personal history in the Revolution that he wants to hear, not a history of the Revolution itself, says the journalist. Well, if it's my history he wants, that's what he'll get – all of it. Anyone I could harm with my stories is long dead, and personal shame is a luxury I abandoned years ago.

"When did you first really begin to believe that the Bolsheviks were destined for power?" he asks.

I know what he expects me to say – he expects to pick some significant historical event – but I don't.

"When Peter Nechaev first came to our Party head-quarters," I tell him.

"Oh, yes."

I wait for him to ask me who Peter Nechaev was, but he doesn't. "Have you heard of him?" I say.

He nods.

I'm surprised. Peter played a big part in my life, and a significant role – for a while – in the Party, but in the grand sweep of history he's not a great name. I am right to fear this man. He's no ordinary journalist and this is no ordinary interview. He wants something which has nothing to do with his story. But what can it be? And how can I turn it to my advantage?

"When Peter Nechaev turned up at Bolshevik headquarters . . ." the journalist prompts.

There was no mob outside that day, condemning Lenin and demanding his execution. The scandal had died down, and new ones blown up to take its place. We were even beginning to regain some of our support.

Peter had chosen to wear a suit for the occasion – a

good one, but fairly well worn. He looked no better dressed than most of the Bolshevik intellectuals who inhabited the building. "I have a meeting with Comrade Stalin," he told me. "You're to come too."

Stalin was sitting behind a paper-strewn desk, the pipe in his mouth belching out clouds of thick, grey smoke. He gestured us to sit down, and turned immediately to Peter.

"The weapons," he said, without preamble.

"Stored in my textile factory," Peter replied. "Under bales of cotton. Both rifles and machine guns."

Stalin nodded coldly. He did everything coldly. I have often seen him smile, but never with real pleasure. "Mr Nechaev tells me you worked with him in the Petrograd underground before the fall of the Romanovs, Lyudmila," he said.

"Yes."

"He tells me that between you, you managed to extract valuable information from the *Okhrana* and to feed them misinformation in return."

"That's correct."

I wasn't doing a very good job, and I knew it. I didn't want lying, scheming, ruthless Peter in the Party. But if I opposed him now, I'd lose. The time to fight was later, when I had a better arsenal at my command.

Stalin stroked his bushy moustache reflectively. "Would you say that Mr Nechaev would make a good Party member?"

"I would say he's already proved himself worthy of membership," I replied, trying to pull back a little ground. "He's a businessman, but businessmen – millionaires, even – have helped us in the past. He's done excellent work in the underground, and is deeply committed to the triumph of the workers' revolution."

It sounded wooden, but it was the best I could do.

"Thank you, Lyudmila," Stalin said, to signify that the interview was over.

I looked into his cold, hard eyes, and saw that he hadn't believed a single word I'd said. But I saw also that it didn't matter a damn. Stalin had found in Peter both a kindred spirit and a man he could use. He would see to it that

253

Peter encountered no difficulties in making the transition from industrialist to *Comrade* Nechaev.

Perhaps Peter hadn't read our future leader's eyes as well as I had. The moment there was a door between us and Stalin, he grabbed me by the arm – hard – and began to drag me down the corridor. The first three or four rooms we passed were occupied, but we finally found one which was empty. Peter pulled me inside. He was still keeping a tight grip on my arm. He leant over me so that our faces were almost touching.

"You little bitch!" he said.

"I . . . I did what I promised."

"A guard dog that only whimpers is worse than no dog at all."

"You're hurting me," I told him through clenched teeth. "Let . . . go of . . . my arm."

"You know Lenin," Peter said. "You can get me to him. At a time like this, there's a fortune to be made if you have the right contacts. But I won't get them unless you play your part properly."

"I'll do better next time, you bastard!" I promised. "Now let go of my bloody arm."

"The threat of getting you kicked out of the Party isn't enough, is it?" Peter asked. "I need something else." He thought for a second. "We need to talk, but not here. Be at the apartment at three o'clock."

He meant the apartment we'd so often met at before – the apartment in which I'd always felt so ashamed – and yet so excited.

"What if I don't come?" I asked.

"You'd better," he threatened, "or I'll see that Stalin gets that *Okhrana* dossier on you – whatever it costs me."

He released my arm at last, and stormed away.

It was still early enough in the day for Sasha and I to be able to find a secluded corner in the Bolshevik canteen. We sat down opposite each other, and as Sasha began to eat his meal – boiled beef, liberally covered with cabbage soup – I

254

steeled myself to speak. Because there was no way around it – Sasha had to be told.

"Peter's joining the Party," I said, as calmly as I could.

Sasha's spoon fell from his hand and landed with a plop in his bowl. Cabbage soup spattered onto his jacket. "He's j. . .joining the Party?" he asked incredulously.

"Yes."

"But he's the very enemy we're f. . .fighting."

"He knows which way the wind's blowing," I said, leaning across and drying Sasha's lapel with my handkerchief. "He knows we're going to win."

"I'll d. . .denounce him," Sasha said.

After all those years, how little he still knew about the way Peter worked. "It won't do any good," I told him. "Peter will only find a way to discredit you instead."

"Then I'll k. . .kill him."

He was ready to murder Peter at that very moment. He had a gun and the other man didn't. But Peter needed no weapon – he had me. He'd known exactly how Sasha would react, I suddenly realized, and how I would, too. He could almost have written this conversation for us. I felt a grudging admiration for the big peasant who'd built up a business empire from nothing. If only he'd been *really* on our side. If only he'd had some basic humanity.

"If you killed Peter, you'd be dead yourself within an hour," I said. "Do you think Peter hasn't got plans to cover that? Peter has plans for everything."

Sasha looked down at his bowl. "It d. . .doesn't matter if I die."

"It does," I assured him, reaching across the table and taking his hand in mine. "What good can you do for the cause if you're dead?"

"Getting rid of Peter will d. . .do the cause some good."

"Peter doesn't want to destroy the Revolution," I argued desperately. "Just to make money out of it. The Party will be better off with both of you in it than with neither."

Sasha raised his head again and looked at me. His eyes burned with loathing, but also, I thought, with sorrow. "He t. . .took my land".

"He what?"

"When I was sent to S. . .Siberia, I had debts. What *muhzik* hadn't? And my f. . .family couldn't pay them off, so Peter did – and he took my land in exchange."

Ah, his land. Even Sasha, who would have been prepared to give up everything for the Revolution, still felt the earth tugging at his soul. Is it any wonder then that lesser men than Sasha killed millions of their own animals rather than have them collectivized under Stalin?

"That's when I became a r. . .revolutionary," Sasha continued, "a *real* revolutionary. I hate everything he st. . .stands for. I'd rather die than see him prosper."

"He won't," I said soothingly. "Not in the end. Once he's in the Party, where we have some influence, we'll be fighting on more equal terms. We'll find a way to destroy him."

"When?" Sasha demanded.

"It may take a while," I admitted. "You'll just have to try and be patient. Will you try?"

He nodded. "I'll be p. . .patient."

"There's something else I have to tell you," I said. "I'm pregnant."

He looked shocked at first, then the widest smile I'd ever seen spread across his face. "That's w. . .wonderful. We'll g. . .get married right away."

"You already have a wife and children," I reminded him.

"I h. . .haven't seen them for over ten years. They c. . .could all be dead by now, and even if they're not, they'll have f. . .forgotten me. I love you, Anna. M. . .marry me."

I was tempted. I didn't love him in the way I'd once loved Misha, nor in the way I'd always love Konstantin – but there are many kinds of love. I respected him more than any man alive. He was kind, he was caring. But . . .

But I couldn't do it to Nicky – couldn't let Nicky see another man take his father's place, couldn't break my promise to my son that he'd be both father and brother to the new baby. Besides, what if the baby was not Sasha's, but Peter's? Despite his best intentions, Sasha would come to hate it, as he hated everything which came from his old rival.

"Anna?"

256

"I . . . I . . . Sasha, I just can't."

I was breaking his heart and there was nothing I could do about it. "You d. . .don't have to make up your mind now," he said miserably. "W. . .will you think it over?"

"I'll think it over," I lied.

Should I have told him then that though he assumed he was the father, I had no way of being sure? I couldn't bear to hurt him any more at that moment. And though I'd talked him out of killing Peter for joining the Party, I knew there was nothing I could have said to prevent him if he'd realized there was even the slightest chance that the baby might be Peter's.

I reached Peter's secret apartment just after three and let myself in with my own key. Peter invariably got there first. Sometimes he'd be waiting for me in the sitting room, a glass of vodka in his hand and a self-satisfied smirk on his face. At other times, he'd be in the bedroom – already naked.

He wasn't in the sitting room that day. For a moment, I actually thought of turning around and leaving. Then I remembered his threats that morning. And – yes damn it – if I'm honest, I wanted him. Cursing my own weakness, I walked over to the bedroom and opened the door.

It was the pile of clothes I saw first. They lay at the foot of the bed, the man's mingled haphazardly with the woman's. They told a tale of burning passion – of being stripped off hurriedly and cast aside without a second's thought, so that desire could be satisfied.

The man and the woman were on top of the bedclothes, she lying on her back with her legs locked tight around his behind, he ploughing away with a relentless ferocity. I saw the woman's face at the same time as she saw mine – and wondered if I was going mad!

Innumerable times, I'd lain on this bed and let Peter do to me just what was being done to her. But I wasn't there now – I was standing by the door. Watching, not taking part. I was all one, not split into two. And yet the face looking up *belonged to me.*

I raised my arm and grasped the door to steady myself. The

257

woman on the bed smiled – widely, triumphantly, maliciously
– and the spell was broken.

Gripped by passion, her face *had* been mine, but the smile
had transformed it back into its old, familiar expression. Now,
though she still looked similar, very similar, anyone seeing
us together would soon have noticed the difference. There
was a certain tightness about her skin which was so like
her mother, a certain sulkiness about the eyes, even at a
moment like this. It would have been obvious to any impartial
observer that though we might have been twins, we were far
from identical.

The man was still thrusting, unaware of the change that
had come over his partner, unaware there was a third person
in the room. His back was muscular, but it was a young back,
without the massive strength of Peter's. A delicate back it was
– an aristocratic back.

The man realized that something was wrong, sensed my
presence in the doorway. His body slackened and he turned
to look over his shoulder. When he saw me, his mouth fell
open and his eyes became huge with horror.

"Hello Mariamna," I said, thinking as I spoke how foolish
it was to go through the normal social niceties in a situation
like this. "Hello Misha."

Misha rolled off his sister. Flat on his back, he became
aware of his nakedness and his hand shot down to cover his
genitals. I don't think that he was shy, it was just that he felt
so unprotected, so . . . vulnerable.

Mariamna raised herself on one elbow. The smile was still
in place. "So you finally know," she said. "I'm glad you
found out."

Misha's mouth was opening and closing, and like a landed
fish, he made no sound.

"This . . . this is nothing to do with me," I said. "I'll
go. But you'd better be careful, Peter's supposed to be
coming here."

Mariamna laughed harshly. "Do you think I'm afraid of
that brute? Do you think that he's been as ignorant about all
this as you've been? He doesn't care what I do, as long as it
doesn't interfere with his own filthy games."

258

"He might feel differently if he were to actually catch you together."

"He won't come here," Mariamna insisted.

"We arranged to meet at—"

"Misha was all I ever wanted," Mariamna said. "Even when I was a little girl. Now I've got him. And it's me *he* wants – not you. It's me he loves."

Why, why, why, did Misha find the strength to speak at last? Why couldn't he have acted true to character a little longer, just until I had left?

"I . . . I only went with her because you wouldn't have me," Misha told me. "She . . . she's your sister, and if I close my eyes I can pretend I'm with you."

Mariamna's face flooded with despair. That was how she must have looked when she found us naked in the barn, when she finally realized she'd lost Misha. Despair hadn't lasted, that day long ago. By the time she leant over the side of the stall to taunt us, she'd channelled her anguish into hatred, into her thirst for vengeance. And that was what she did now!

She leapt from the bed and reached for her purse.

I knew what she was going to do next! "No, Mariamna!" I pleaded. But my own hand was already reaching for my holster.

Mariamna flicked the catch of her purse and pulled out a gun. It was a small, pearl-handled piece, a lady's weapon. Hand shaking with rage, she raised it and pointed it at me.

"Stop her, Misha!" I shouted.

He was lying on the bed, as still as if he were a statue, as rigid as a corpse.

I looked into my half-sister's eyes, searching for the brief flicker which would tell me she was about to pull the trigger. Do it first, I told myself. You owe her nothing! Do it first!

The eyes were quite mad. Was any of this really her fault? Was it any more than the work of the puppet-master in the sky, who had caused her to be born as she was, and now was pulling the string which raised her arm?

"It doesn't have to be! It doesn't have to end like this!" I screamed.

The eyes flickered and she fired. The bullet whizzed past

259

my cheek and buried itself in the doorpost. I had my own gun raised, but I couldn't bring myself to pull the trigger.

Mariamna fired again and I felt as if I'd been hit by a giant hammer. I staggered back against the wall, my left shoulder burning. Mariamna was ready to shoot a third time. She was getting the range. Her next bullet would do more than wing me. I pulled the trigger of my pistol.

I wanted merely to disable her. I was a good shot, I should have been able to do it, but my wound was aching and the room was starting to swim before my eyes. My bullet struck her forehead, gouging open a third, obscene, red eye. Her lifeless body collapsed onto the bed, her head striking the chest of a terrified Misha, her long black hair cascading so it brushed both his chin and his stomach.

I was lying on the floor, my back pressed against the wall, and Misha was leaning over me. "Are you all right?" he asked. "Oh, my sweet darling, are you all right?"

"Help me to my feet," I told him.

He put his hands under my armpits and lifted me up. God, it hurt! I looked around the room – at the window, the bed, dead Mariamna. Waves of pain rippled through my body. The floor and walls wouldn't stay still.

"We have to get out of here!" Misha said urgently.

"We . . . we can't just . . . leave her," I managed to gasp.

"We'll be arrested," Misha said hysterically. "We have to go."

"And if . . . the police find her body . . . here?" I said with difficulty. "How long do you . . . think it would take them . . . to trace it to us?"

"I've got to go," Misha sobbed. "I can't stay."

"Then go, for God's sake!"

It wouldn't be the first time he'd deserted me, wouldn't be the first time he'd left me lying there – wounded, bleeding. My hazy mind drifted back to the river bank.

"Will you . . . will you be all right?" Misha asked.

"Yes," I said, making no effort to hide my contempt. "It's only a scratch. Get out while you can."

He struggled awkwardly into his uniform, not bothering to

fasten it properly or even lace up his boots. "Are you sure . . . ?" he asked.

"Go!" I said wearily.

And he was gone.

I walked stiffly over to a chair, and sat down. I looked at my half-sister, still lying there. Poor Mariamna. I'd outstripped her in the schoolroom, I'd defeated her in love – though, God knows, I'd never wanted to. I'd even made better use of our shooting lessons with the Count.

It was ten minutes before I heard the sound I'd been expecting – the key turning in the lock and the heavy footsteps crossing the sitting room. The bedroom door swung open, and Peter walked in. He looked across at his dead wife and smiled, but when he turned and saw me, his jaw dropped and his eyes turned wild.

He rushed to my side, and knelt down. "You've been shot!" he gasped. "How the fuck did you . . . I never thought . . . You're more than a match for her." He saw my injury was little more than a flesh wound, and relaxed. The sardonic smile was back on his lips. "You tried to bloody-well talk her out of it," he said.

"Yes," I agreed.

Peter shook his head in wonder.

"Never give your enemy a fair chance," he said. "Especially when she's a hard little bitch like Mariamna."

"You couldn't have known she'd try to kill me," I said.

Peter laughed. "I'm a gambler," he explained. "But I've always got a pretty good idea which shell the pea's under. Put the three of you together and the odds were for things turning out like they did. And of my dear brother-in-law abandoning you when it was all over. Running away like a shit-scared rabbit."

"Why?" I asked.

"Because that's the way the little arsehole is."

"I didn't mean that."

He feigned surprise. "Oh, you mean why did I get you to kill Mariamna?"

"Yes."

261

"To tighten my grip on you, so you don't go screwing me up like you did this morning. You're a murderess now – and I can get you arrested any time I want to. How long do you think Misha will be able to stand up to questioning from the *Okhrana* – or whatever you call the secret police after you take power?"

"And why did you want her dead?"

"Because with the Tsar gone, she'd become more of a liability than an asset. And in my game, you get rid of your liabilities as soon as you possibly can."

I was sure that everything he'd said was true, but there was more to it than that – there always was with Peter. And in a sudden flash of insight, I knew what that 'more' was.

"You wanted her killed because you couldn't satisfy her in bed," I said, "but Misha, that scared little rabbit, could."

"Hah!" Peter replied, but there was unease beneath his contemptuous dismissal.

"And you wanted me here when it happened," I pressed on, "so that I could see for myself how weak Misha was. You weren't just worried he could keep Mariamna happier than you could – you were frightened that it might be true with me as well!"

It hit home. I could see it had hit home. But I hadn't finished with him yet.

"You put my child in danger," I said.

For a moment, he didn't understand. "Your child? But Nicky's not . . . You're pregnant!"

"Yes, you bastard," I said. "I'm pregnant."

Sasha had been entranced by the news, Peter merely became brisk and businesslike. "You'll have to move," he said. "I'll get you an apartment on this side of the river. When's it due? Not yet, by the look of you, but we'd better get planning. It's not as easy to find a good doctor as it used to be."

My wound was throbbing, my judgement gone. I wanted to hurt him, and I didn't give a damn about the consequences. "The baby may not be yours," I said.

"Not mine?" he asked, thunderstruck. "Who else is there?"

"Think about it," I goaded. "Think back to the days in

262

the *mir*. We were all there. You, me, Mariamna, Misha and . . . ?"

"Sasha!"

"S . . . Sasha! Poor, earnest Sasha. You broke his Union of Peasants, you defeated again when he organized a strike at your mill. But maybe he's beaten you, this time."

His huge hands locked around my throat and began to squeeze. Black spots floated before my eyes, and I gasped for breath. He'd always been powerful, but now his strength was almost superhuman. I couldn't take much more of this. Soon, I would pass out. There had to be something I could say to make him stop.

"The baby . . . don't . . ." I managed to croak.

His hands relaxed. I gulped in air greedily, then retched. When I looked up again, he had moved away from me.

"One job at a time," he said, as though he hadn't been on the point of murdering me. "First we get rid of my 'dear' wife. Then I'll deal with Sasha."

"If you kill him, I'll kill you," I threatened hoarsely, cursing myself for putting Sasha at risk.

Peter laughed. "I won't kill him," he said. "That's too easy. That's for people who are just an inconvenience – like Mariamna."

He approached me again, and I shrank back.

"I'm not going to hurt you," he assured me. "I'm just going to look at your wound."

He swabbed the wound, bandaged it, and made me a rough sling. The hands which had almost strangled me were now remarkably gentle. "You'll need a doctor later," he said, "but that should do for now. Can you walk?"

"Yes."

"Then we'd better get the hell out of here."

He went into the sitting room room, and when he came back he was carrying a flour sack in his hands. He opened the sack and bundled Mariamna roughly inside. "She's as much fucking trouble dead as she was when she was alive," he complained.

He lifted me to my feet and helped me on with my *shooba*.

263

"Where are we talking her?" I asked.

"You'll see," he said, flinging the sack over his shoulder.

He loaded the body into his Rolls-Royce and we drove out of Petrograd to the marshes near Tsarskoe Selo. As we pulled off the road, the sun was just setting, its dying rays casting a red glow over the water.

Peter pulled the bundle from the car, then wrapped some heavy chains around it. He tested the weight of his load, heaved it above his head and hurled it into the marsh. It hit the water with a tremendous splash, and sank.

"Goodbye for ever, you stuck-up bitch," he said, as the ripples of water spread out and began to disperse.

"What if they find her?" I asked.

"They won't, not for a few days, anyway. And by then, even her own mother wouldn't recognize her."

"What will you tell her friends? That she's run away from you?"

"That I've sent her away," Peter said hotly.

What wondrous creatures men are! It bothered him not at all to arrange for his wife to be killed, but he bristled at the idea that people should think she'd left him.

The last of the sun's rays had disappeared, and darkness was beginning to fall. I shivered.

"Come on," Peter said. "Let's go and find you a quack who knows how to keep his mouth shut."

He reached out his hand. To touch me? To offer me support? I don't know. I brushed it angrily aside.

He had a weapon now – a real weapon – to use against me. Killing someone, even at that time, was not an act which could be lightly overlooked. Even if I escaped jail, I'd be branded as an aristocratic murderess – the Bloody Princess. The Party would disown me – it would have no choice – and I couldn't bear the thought of that, not when there was finally a chance of victory. So I'd see to it that Peter met Lenin and I'd work for his success within the Party, though every fibre of Bolshevik feeling in me would cry out against it.

But in some ways, he'd *lost* his hold over me. Never again would I pant for him like a bitch on heat, never again would

I long to be in his arms. In killing Mariamna, I'd killed my yearning for him – and now only my hatred remained. I knew now exactly how Sasha must have felt when he learned Peter had taken his land, had robbed him of something of himself. And one day – one day – Peter would pay for what he'd made me do.

Chapter Twenty-Six

The trees put out sticky fingers, and finding the air to their liking, the fingers opened to clothe the trees in green. Spring had come to Petrograd once more, ending the desperate search for fuel, making standing in the bread queues just a little more bearable.

I remembered the last time I was pregnant. How different life had been then. I was a princess living in a palace. And I had a husband.

"And what am I offering *you*, Baby?" I asked the swelling in my stomach.

Nicky had been born to a loving father. The new infant had a possibility of two – one I could not love as a wife should and another whom I hated.

"It'll be all right, Baby," I assured the tiny life inside me, sending it messages of love in much the same way as my body sent it oxygen. "Nicky and I will look after you."

I saw little of Peter during those days. Even when he came to Party headquarters, he would immediately disappear into Stalin's office, where the two men would spend hours closeted together. But still I worried. Peter had said he'd make Sasha suffer, and Peter always kept his word.

"Watch out for him," I warned Sasha. "He'll destroy you if he can."

"W. . .why?"

"Because he hates you."

"He's always h. . .hated me. W. . .why should he want to destroy me more now?"

I couldn't bring myself to tell him – couldn't stand the thought of the hurt in his eyes. "Just be careful," I said.

Yet I knew that he was never careful. Sasha, the only

muhzik who had ever been brave enough to openly defy the Count, saw the world as straightforward, black and white, and had the simple faith that good would always triumph in the end. He had no idea of the shadows and shades which existed in Peter's mind, of the twists and turns Peter's intellect was capable of. No, Sasha would never be able to defeat his rival. If anyone was to protect him, it would have to be me.

Spring turned into early summer. The baby grew bigger and bigger.

"Put your ear to my tummy," I told Nicky.

He lowered his head gently onto my swollen stomach.

"Do you hear anything?" I asked.

"Yes. A 'boom, boom'. Like a drum. What is it?"

I took his hand and placed it against his own small chest.

"It's a heart," he said excitedly. "It's our baby's heart."

I wanted the baby – whoever its father was – so much. I wanted the Bolsheviks to take power and solve all the country's problems. And I wanted Peter to fail in his attempt to get revenge on Sasha. I wanted a lot!

It was July 4th – American Independence Day – and as I gazed out of the window of Lenin's office, I could not help but think about the time, only a few weeks earlier, when I'd seen an angry mob demanding our leader's arrest. There was a mob there now – Khronstadt sailors, soldiers from the 1st Machine Gun Regiment, workers from the Putilov munitions factory – but the pendulum had swung back again, and once more they were on our side.

"They've surrounded the Provisional Government building," Lenin said. "They want us to stage a coup now."

"It's too soon," I argued. "We're not strong enough yet."

Lenin began to pace the room, as he always did when he was agitated. "I know it's too soon," he said. "But do we have a choice? Will we keep their support if we don't lead them when they demand it?"

There was a sound of running footsteps down the corridor, and a great deal of shouting. Outside, the mob suddenly

267

seemed very angry. The door burst open and a messenger boy rushed into the room.

"The . . . the army's fired on some demonstrators," he gasped. "Fighting's starting all over Petrograd."

Lenin smacked his open left palm with his right fist. "The coup goes ahead," he said decisively. "By tomorrow, the city will be ours."

He may have said more – knowing Ilyich, he probably did – but I was no longer listening. Instead, I clutched at his desk. "I have to go home," I said.

"Now?" Lenin asked. "Just when I need your support?"

How awkward my children were, I thought. One had refused to come until long after his time was due, the other was insisting on arriving early. "The baby," I explained to Lenin. "I'm going to have the baby."

A car was commandeered, and I was bundled into the back. We could not go straight home. Some streets were completely empty, as still as if they'd never been walked by a human soul, but others were blocked off and we had to find a diversion round them. The air was filled with rifle fire, some close, some distant, but never entirely absent. The breeze carried with it the smell of cordite.

The journey was a nightmare for me, but it was not the wider world which filled me with dread – it was what was going on inside me. Was it possible, I asked myself, that I'd got my dates wrong? No! The baby was going to be born prematurely. What did that mean? How would that affect it? I didn't know! I just didn't know!

At last we reached my lodgings. I fumbled with the key. Shots rang out, somewhere close, perhaps not more than half a *verst* away. I pushed open the door and my driver helped me up the stairs.

Nicky and Vera were sitting on the floor – well away from the window – playing cards. My entrance startled them.

"Contractions!" I gasped. "Every five minutes."

Vera – my good, reliable, little maid – allowed herself a second's shock, then took control. "Have your waters broken, madam?"

"In the car."

"See if you can find a doctor," she told my driver. "Although, God knows, anybody with any sense'll be keeping well out of the way today."

She led me towards the bedroom. "Don't worry, madam," she told me. "I've had brothers and sisters enough of my own. I've seen how it's done."

She stripped off my clothes and laid me gently on the bed. I heard a nervous cough, and realized that Nicky had followed us in.

"Out of here, Prince Nicky," Vera said briskly. "This is woman's work."

"I want to stay," Nicky said firmly.

"Well you can't," Vera retorted.

"Please, Mama, let me stay. Let me hold your hand."

If anything was wrong with this baby, born so much before it's time, there would be no Konstantin to calm me, to tell me that everything would be all right. I needed Nicky by my side.

"Let him stay," I said.

"Huh!" Vera exclaimed. "The very idea!"

But she had learned long ago that there was little point in arguing with any of the Mayakovskys.

"It'll soon be over, madam," Vera assured me.

"How . . . how long has it been so far?"

"About twelve hours."

Twelve hours! It seemed as if I'd *always* been lying on this bed, writhing in agony, fretting about what premature birth might do to my baby, wishing a doctor would arrive.

Nicky sat next to me on a little stool. Occasionally his eyes would droop and his hand would fall from mine, but the shock would awaken him immediately, and he'd reach for me once more.

"It has to come soon," I screamed, as another spasm of pain shot through my body.

I felt Nicky's hand squeezing encouragingly. "Don't worry, Mama," he told me, "we're going to have a beautiful baby."

What courage he gave me.

269

Outside, the gunfire continued unabated. Where were Peter and Sasha, the two possible fathers of my baby? Sasha would be in the thick of the fighting, a pistol in his hand, taking risks most men would consider insane. And Peter? Probably selling bullets to both sides, or else taking the opportunity to plunder the houses of the rich.

The shooting intensified. Out on the streets, my comrades were fighting for their lives and for the Revolution, but I could spare no more thought for them then. I was fighting too, for the small life inside me which had decided it was time to come out and face the world.

"The head!" Vera said. "I can see the head. Push harder, madam."

It was the eighteenth hour. I didn't know how I could summon up the energy to push any more. Yet somehow I did.

"There she is," my maid said.

She! A girl! Nicky left my side and rushed around the bed. I tried to raise myself on one elbow, but I was too weak.

"What's that coming from her tummy?" I heard Nicky ask, the exhaustion in his voice now tinged with excitement.

"Back in the *mir*, we call it the rope of life," Vera said.

"Is my baby all right?" I croaked, but so faintly that I don't think either of them heard me.

A cry!

"You hit her!" Nicky said accusingly.

"Just waking her up."

"Is she all right?" Tell me she's all right," I pleaded.

"Why are you cutting the rope?" Nicky asked anxiously. "It won't hurt her, will it?"

"Not even a little bit," Vera replied briskly. "Now get from underfoot while I'm washing her head."

Vera was suddenly standing over me, holding the baby in the shawl which had once been Nicky's – and Konstantin's. I looked anxiously at the baby's big black eyes, her tiny nose, the wonderful little mouth through which she was screaming her protest at her rude awakening.

"She's a bit underweight," my maid said, "that's only to be expected, but otherwise she looks fine. And she's very noisy and demanding, Prince Nicky, just like her big brother."

"What will you call her, Mama?" Nicky asked, looking down at the sleeping baby.

I thought of the massacre on Nevsky Prospekt, of the dead child I'd held in my arms. "I'm going to call her after a little girl who was killed before she ever had a chance to grow up," I said. "I'm going to call her Tania."

From outside came the sound of machine guns, spitting death.

Whatever my feelings of duty towards the Party, the birth had left me too weak to be of much use, and I was forced to stay in bed, listening to the fighting going on outside, wishing I could take part in it, but glad I could not. On the third day, when the sounds of battle had all but disappeared, Sasha came to see me. He looked as haggard as I had ever seen him – but at least he was still alive.

"I only j. . .just heard," he said, leaning over the crib and looking down at the baby. "What's her name?"

"Tania."

"Tania," he repeated softly. "I th. . .think she's got my eyes."

"What's been happening on the streets?" I asked.

"It was t. . .terrible," he replied, his joy at seeing the baby now battling for control of him with his painful memories. "W. . .we must have lost hundreds of men. It's all over."

"What is?"

"Our ch. . .chance. Most of the C. . .Central Committee have been arrested."

"Lenin?"

"He's run away. He's h. . .hiding in the forest."

Our leader, hiding in the forest! Like a common criminal. "Is there anybody left to run the Party?"

"St. . .Stalin. The Government doesn't seem to th. . .think he was involved."

Of course they'd think that. How like Joe to sit in the wings while our more charismatic leaders occupied the centre

271

stage, and then, when they were vanquished, take over the whole theatre.

Sasha bent forward and gently tickled Tania under the chin. She gurgled happily. "The new offensive on the Western Front has f. . .failed," Sasha continued mournfully. "People are saying that Lenin led the rising on the orders of the German H. . .High Command."

"That's absurd!" I said, but I could see how it might seem that way.

"L. . .let's leave here now," Sasha suggested. "Let's take the ch. . .children and make a new life somewhere else. I want to be with you and my little d. . .daughter."

"Your daughter!" said a scoffing voice from the doorway. "What makes you think she's *your* daughter?"

The tone, rather than the voice, carried me back to my days in the *mir*. Big Sasha and little me, sitting by the well, perfectly happy, perfectly relaxed in each other's company. Peter appearing from nowhere, and spoiling those meetings for ever.

And here he was again, standing in the doorway of my cramped bedroom, an evil grin on his face. I felt the hatred flow between the two men like an electric current. It was years since they'd met, but time had only increased their mutual loathing.

"I said, what makes you think she's your daughter?" Peter asked again.

"Anna and I are l. . .lovers," Sasha said proudly.

Oh, my poor Sasha!

Peter shrugged his massive shoulders. "I mount her now and again myself," he replied.

Sasha turned to me, a look of horror on his face. "Is that t. . .true, Anna?" he demanded.

"I was carrying out Molotov's instructions."

"And is the b. . .baby mine?"

"I don't know," I admitted. "I want it to be."

Sasha turned again, ready to fling himself at Peter.

"The baby!" I screamed. "Think of the baby!"

Sasha's hands fell to his sides, though rage still filled his scarred face. "She's r. . .right," he said to the man in the

272

doorway. "This isn't the p. . .place to settle things between us. But they w. . .will be settled, Peter. One way or the other."

He walked quickly to the door. Peter stood aside to let him pass, and I just lay there, miserable, wishing I'd told Sasha the truth long ago. Peter walked over to the crib, examined the infant and then, to my astonishment, tickled her under the chin just as Sasha had done.

"You've robbed him of one family already," I said bitterly. "Why must you try and take this one from him?"

"If something's mine, I never *give* it away," Peter replied.

"I will *not* have Tania used as a weapon," I told him.

Peter picked the baby and rocked her in his cradled arms.

"Did you hear me?" I demanded, but he didn't seem to be listening.

I watched with stunned fascination as Peter – the man who had thrown his workers' small children out onto the street in midwinter – played with my baby. Finally, and reluctantly, he placed her gently back in the crib.

"If you need anything, let me know," he said. "I can lay my hands on most things."

"And how will I pay you? In bed? Those days are gone forever."

"There'll be no charge," Peter replied, walking towards the door.

"It's not like you to give something for nothing, Peter," I mocked. "Are you turning soft?"

He wheeled round, and though there was a smile on his face, I could tell he was angry. "It's not something for nothing," he said. "It's an investment."

"Was one of those men the one you made Tania with?" Nicky asked when Peter finally left.

"Yes."

"Which one? The big bear or the beanpole?"

"It could be either."

Nicky nodded his head, as though he'd suspected that was the case.

"I like the beanpole," he said. "I don't mind if he comes and plays with Tania sometimes."

273

But would Sasha ever come again – or had I hurt him too deeply? So much of our lives seemed to have been interwoven that I couldn't stand the thought of losing him completely. And now the Bolshevik grab for power had failed, now it seemed like I had lost, forever, the chance to help build a better world for my children to grow up in, I needed his friendship more than ever.

Chapter Twenty-Seven

For days I lived in dread of hearing that Sasha had killed Peter and been arrested – or that he'd tried and been killed himself. But our worst fears are rarely realized and tragedy, when it comes, sneaks up unexpectedly and taps us on the back with its icy finger.

Peter was no longer in Petrograd. He left the city almost as soon as he'd made his ominous farewell to me. Did I think he had run away? Not for a minute. Whatever else he was, he was no coward. And in my relief that he'd gone, I never really stopped to ask myself *why* he'd gone. Party business, I blandly assumed. So it was, but I should have remembered that Peter's actions never had a single purpose. I should have used my influence to find out exactly what he was doing – I should have started trying to protect Sasha earlier.

Not that Sasha wanted my protection – he wanted *nothing* from me. If we met accidentally, he would turn away. He had requested, and been granted, the right to be excused any duties which would involve him working with me. We had once been friends and lovers, now he would not even accept me as a comrade.

He visited Tania when I was not in the house – "Beanpole came again today," Nicky told me. I could have forbidden the visits as a way of putting pressure on him to at least *talk* to me, at least let me *explain*. But I didn't. I'd told Peter I would not allow him to use Tania as a weapon – I was not about to use her myself.

And then, early in August, Sasha disappeared completely. "He's working on a special project. Something for Comrade Stalin," a Party worker whispered to me in the ladies' washroom of the Smolyn Institute, which had once been a posh girls' school and was now our new headquarters.

Stalin! But Stalin was as thick as thieves with Peter. And Sasha had neither the ability nor the patience for 'special projects'. He was a street fighter like me, not a revolutionary bureaucrat of Stalin's ilk.

I worried about him, my brave, naïve Sasha, but there was nothing I could do. How could I make sure he didn't fall into any of Peter's traps when I didn't even know where he was?

It was about three weeks after Sasha's disappearance that the rumours started to fly.

"General Kornilov's going to stage a coup."

"You can't be serious!"

"He's marching towards Petrograd. He could be here any day."

The Provisional Government was thrown into a panic. It could not rely on the soldiers stationed in the capital, so to whom could it turn? To the workers, of course! Posters went up everywhere calling on all citizens of Petrograd to come to its defence. Weapons were issued to everyone who asked for them – including twenty-five thousand Bolshevik Red Guards.

For three hectic days we toiled to transform the city into a fortress, building barricades across all the prospekts, uprooting railway tracks to prevent troop movements. How I wished, as I laboured, that I had my oldest comrade by my side – Sasha, the man who'd guided me when I was a small child, turning my instincts into beliefs. But for him, I might not have been on the barricades at all. But for him, I might just have grown into Countess Olga.

Nicky likes him, I thought, pushing a timber almost my own weight into the barrier we were building around the Warsaw Station.

And perhaps Nicky's liking would grow into love. Perhaps, one day, my son would be prepared to admit him into the family. If Sasha could find it in his heart to forgive me and if – after General Kornilov's onslaught – I was alive to be forgiven.

The onslaught never came. There was a swing against Kornilov, even among his own men and he was arrested before he ever reached Petrograd. Bolshevik stock began to rise again. We were not traitors selling out to Germany after all. We had been there with the best of them, ready and willing to die to defend the city. Lenin was still in hiding, but other members of the Central Committee were released from jail and we were gaining new recruits to the Party every day.

Imagine the situation in Petrograd in the early autumn of 1917. Army units refusing point blank to go to the Front. Thousands of deserters wandering the streets in open defiance of the authorities. Food scarcer than it had ever been. Unemployment soaring as more and more factories closed down.

Imagine the situation at the Front. *Muhziks* deserting in large numbers and returning to their *mirs* to grab their share of the aristocracy's land. Soldiers who would not serve in the trenches, but quite happily organized football matches against the enemy. Renegade units robbing the trains carrying supplies to their comrades. The Germans could have defeated us easily, but they didn't choose to. Russia was no longer any threat – there was no point in wasting good men on her when they were needed on the Western Front.

It was obvious to everyone that Prime Minister Kerensky's government had lost control. But what would replace it? There was only the Soviet, and the Soviet was now dominated by the Bolsheviks. Talk of a *coup* started in late September, and by the middle of October the question was no longer *if* but *when*.

Lenin, finally back in Petrograd, should have been elated. Yet he fretted. "I don't trust the rest of the Central Committee," he confided to me.

"But they've agreed that the *coup* should go ahead."

"Agreed! Yes! But they can still call it off. Or worse, they might start the insurrection, lose their nerve and go into retreat. That's why I need people like you, people I can rely on, to keep me informed. When it starts, I want you to travel around the city and see what's going on. You'll be my eyes and ears."

The eyes and ears of the man soon to change the face of Russia. I've had worse roles.

The journalist is still here, sitting in the chair opposite me. His tape continues to whirr and record every word I say. He doesn't switch it off even when I pause, as I'm doing now. Yet he's no passive listener like his tape recorder. He's weighing what I say – I can read it in his eyes. And he's not weighing it for truthfulness or accuracy, rather it's something else which balances on the other side of the scale. *And I don't know what that something else is.*

I can hear the clock on the wall ticking away remorselessly. Tick, tick, tick.

Each second which strikes and is gone brings me closer the moment when I lose my freedom for ever, when I feel once more the terror I felt when I heard the midnight knock at the door . . .

A freezing January night in 1931. Two men in the doorway, their pale, belted raincoats almost ghostly in the dim light burning in the corridor lamp of that shoddy Moscow apartment block.

"Does Lyudmila live here?" one of them asked.

"Lyudmila?"

I could think of nothing else to say. My mind was as frozen as my body would feel once it was exposed to the icy winds of the Gulag.

"Lyudmila," the *OGPU* man repeated. "Also known as Princess Anna Mayakovsky."

I thought of trying to bluff it out, of saying, "You've come to the wrong house," or "Lyudmila does live here, but she's away on Party business."

It would have been pointless. They knew I was Lyudmila. They were just going through the motions, playing their tragical farce as they always did.

The spokesman took a crumpled piece of paper out of his pocket and smoothed it against the wall. "I have here a warrant for your arrest," he said, squinting to read it in the poor light.

278

"You are charged under the following articles of the Soviet Penal Code . . ."

So many articles. So many crimes I seemed to have committed. And all the time he was reading in his flat, judicial voice, one thought kept flying round my head. What can I give them? What can I say that will save me?

But I'd known, even before I opened the door and saw them – known from the moment I heard the knock – that Stalin had put a black mark against my name and I was doomed . . .

Forget the arrest, old woman. That can come later. It's the Revolution this journalist wants to hear about, not your fall from grace. And what do I want? I want to discover what has suddenly made me important, so that I can turn it around, use it in my defence against Jennifer and Sonia.

"Is all this of any use to you?" I ask, looking for a reaction – a clue.

He smiles for the first time, as if he is amused by me, amused by the whole situation. "It would certainly be a revelation to my fellow countrymen," he says.

What can I give him? What can I do that will save me?

"Sasha's back," said my washroom informant.

Relief flooded through me. My old friend and lover had returned. How foolish I'd been to worry.

"Where is he?" I asked excitedly.

"Well, he was here. He went to see Comrade Stalin, and then left."

I set out straightaway for his lodgings, hope bubbling up inside me. It was nearly three months since he'd first seen Tania – since he'd learned about Peter and me. Perhaps time had blunted his hurt and he would be able to forgive me.

I was on the corner of his street when I realized that something was terribly wrong. Small groups of people stood tightly bunched together, talking animatedly but falling silent when I approached. Bedroom curtains twitched as I walked past. The air was filled with the atmosphere of fear and excitement which always settles after an act of violence.

I started to run, and by the time I reached Sasha's house, I was gasping for breath. I took the stairs two at a time, one hand held out to steady me in case I fell, the other clutching my pistol. One look at the door to Sasha's room told me I was too late. It had been battered in, and now hung at a crazy, twisted angle, only holding onto the jamb by one hinge. What few sticks of furniture Sasha possessed lay smashed on the floor, as if they themselves had engaged in a bloody battle.

Sasha wasn't there. Of course he wasn't there!

I knocked frantically on the door next to Sasha's.

"Go away!" a fearful voice called from within.

"Please let me in!" I begged. "I have to know what's happened to Sasha."

"Go away!" the man said again.

I turned the handle, but the door was locked. I put my pistol against the lock, pulled the trigger, and kicked the door open with my boot. The man who wouldn't help me was cowering on his bed. I waved my pistol in his face. "Where is he?" I screamed.

"They . . . they came and took him away," he moaned.

"*Who* came and took him away? The soldiers?"

"Not soldiers. Just men. Men with guns."

Men with guns. I didn't know who they were, or where they'd taken him, but I was sure that Peter was behind it.

The march of history is not halted, even for a second, by personal tragedies. I might have lost Sasha, but the Revolution was going ahead. On the evening of the 23rd of October, only hours after my one real friend had disappeared, Trotsky sent Political Commissars to every garrison in Petrograd.

"We're from the Soviet," they told the soldiers. "We're your new commanders."

A few regiments rejected them, but most were prepared to follow their orders – at least as far as they were prepared to follow *anyone's* orders.

Now we controlled the army, the theory went, and therefore we must control the city, and hence the country. A Bolshevik delegation was sent to see the Military Governor of Petrograd, to demand that he recognize the Political Commissars as the legitimate source of authority in the army.

"Get out of here before I hang the lot of you," the Governor told them.

We should have sent in the Red Guards to arrest him. Instead, we did nothing. Lenin was right to distrust the rest of the Central Committee – they didn't have the will to carry it off properly. They didn't even begin to fortify our headquarters until after Governor had sent the delegation away with a flea in its ear.

Nor was the Governor any more decisive. He didn't have many loyal troops still at his command, but he had enough. If Konstantin had been in charge, he'd have marched them to our headquarters then and there, and bagged the almost entire Bolshevik leadership, but the Governor just sat and waited.

I was Lenin's eyes and ears. However much I ached to be with Nicky and Tania, however desperate I was to find Sasha, I had other responsibilities. On this, the second day of our grab for power, it was my duty to report to our leader on the Revolution's progress.

What progress? What revolution? The shops were open as usual, the streets as crowded as ever. Tramcars ran as they did every other day. The cinemas were selling tickets for their evening performances. Trotsky had sent out an impressive proclamation to all military units and to the factories on the Vyborg side, but many citizens in the central district had no idea that this was anything other than a normal day.

Only outside the Winter Palace, to which Prime Minister Kerensky had moved his government, was the Bolshevik threat being treated at all seriously. Guard posts had been set up round the palace approaches. Six armoured cars stood in front of the Palace itself. Soldiers, mainly Cadets, were marching up and down. Both the Revolution and the Government were digging in. Neither of them seemed prepared to launch an offensive.

The more I walked around the city, the more depressed I became. We weren't *in* power, we were only pretenders to it. We were acting like some ousted Central European monarch who sits in London or Paris and issues impressive documents bearing the royal seal which are ignored by everyone.

281

It's not enough to *say* we're in control, I thought angrily. We have to prove it.

And soon – before Kerensky could bring in loyal troops from Moscow or the Front.

It was early evening by the time I reached the Smolny Institute and heard the awful news that Sasha had been arrested.

"Who arrested him?" I demanded.

"The Party. Us," said my informant.

"But what for? What's he supposed to have done?"

"Friend of yours, is he?" the man asked.

"Just tell me what you know, you bloody fool!"

"All right, all right, keep your hair on. The way I heard it, Comrade Stalin's been using him as a fighting fund collector. He's been all over Russia collecting money."

"And?"

"And then he stole it."

The money had gone missing, I was sure of that, but it wasn't Sasha who had taken it. Now I knew what Peter had been doing since he left Petrograd. Visiting the same cities Sasha would be going to. Laying his trap. How like Peter to accomplish two things with one action – frame Sasha and enrich himself. How like Peter to use the Party Sasha had given his life to as his instrument of destruction.

"Where are they keeping him?" I demanded.

"Don't know," my informant admitted. "But I'll tell you something for nothing. As soon as anybody can find the time, they're going to try him. And then they'll shoot the bastard."

Chapter Twenty-Eight

Only Lenin could help me save Sasha, and Lenin had disappeared again. I spent a long night searching, questioning everyone who might know where he was. Every second counted. Every minute which passed increased Sasha's danger. Where the hell was Lenin?

It was not until early the next morning – the third day of the Revolution – that I tracked him down to the Smolny Institute, our headquarters.

There were guards outside what had once been Ladies' Classroom Number Seven, and was now the meeting room of the Bolshevik Central Committee.

"Can't go in," one of them told me. "Nobody can. Lenin's orders."

I stood by the door, waiting and worrying. They were too busy with other problems to think about Sasha. They wouldn't do anything to him until the Provisional Government had really fallen. Unless Peter decided that a dead Sasha was a safe Sasha, and arranged for his execution.

Around me, everything was confusion and excitement. Peasant and worker delegates rushed to meetings, tramping the mud from their boots all over the floors of the long, vaulted corridors. Girls with short skirts and bobbed hair staggered under the weight of piles of newspapers, proclamations and propaganda leaflets. Red Guards boasted loudly of their exploits and slapped each other on the back.

Inside the Committee Room, they were arguing so loudly that the sound carried beyond the door.

"We're letting it slip through our fingers," Lenin complained bitterly.

"We've got the power station," someone shouted back, "and the telephone exchange and the state bank."

"Yes, yes," dismissively from Lenin.

"And the Baltic, Nicholas and Warsaw Stations, so now Kerensky can't get any troops by rail."

"I know all that."

"We're in control of almost the entire city except the General Staff Headquarters, the Admiralty and the Winter Palace."

There was a thud, and I pictured Lenin banging his fist on the table as I'd seen him do so often in the past. "Exactly!" he said. "We don't control the Winter Palace! It's more than a building, it's a symbol of the old order. As long as it remains untaken, the Provisional Government still exists. As long as it remains free it will serve as a rallying point for the soldiers who Kerensky's called in and who are marching on the city *at this very minute*."

He was right. We'd never convince the people we really were in charge until the Winter Palace had fallen.

The meeting broke up, a chastened Central Committee left, and Lenin was alone in the room. I knocked and walked in. He was sitting at a battered table, his head in his hands. He looked up at me, and smiled. "Ah, Lyudmila, my eyes and ears. How—"

"I need a favour," I interrupted.

"What sort of favour?"

"I want Sasha Krasnov to be granted a free pardon."

Lenin frowned, as if trying to remember the name.

"He's charged with stealing Party funds," I explained, "but I know he didn't do it."

"I can grant no pardons," Lenin said firmly. "He will be given a fair trial by a revolutionary court and subjected to revolutionary justice."

A trial, fair or not, was of no good to Sasha. He had been tried before, back in the *mir*, and found guilty. And he would be found guilty again, because once more, Peter had stacked the evidence against him.

"Ilyich—" I began.

"This is neither the time nor the place to discuss such trivial matters."

There had to be something I could offer which would buy Sasha's freedom. I could not stand by and watch him dragged away in chains once more – this time for ever. But *what* could I offer? Back at the Big House, I'd threatened to return to the *mir* if Sasha wasn't freed, and the Count had called my bluff. I was older now, and had more resources at my command, but I felt as helpless, as powerless, as I had back then.

"If I could speed up the fall of the Winter Palace, would you give Sasha a pardon?" I asked.

"Speed up the fall . . . ? If the Military Revolutionary Committee can't do it, how do you expect to?"

"Let me try," I pleaded. "What have you got to lose?"

Lenin nodded, sombrely. "What, indeed?"

He picked up a piece of paper and scribbled a hasty note on it. He looked at what he'd written, frowned and scrawled his signature at the bottom. I think he would have liked to have added an official stamp, but he didn't have one. We weren't that organized yet . . . and we were nowhere near official.

He handed the paper to me. "This says you are my personal representative," he said. "Go the Winter Palace. See what you can do."

That I had made the offer shows the extent of my desperation, that he had accepted it shows the depth of his.

I have rarely known such despair as I experienced on that journey between the Smolny Institute and the Winter Palace. In my bid to free Sasha, I had set myself an almost impossible task, and I would fail him, just as I had failed him when I was a little girl.

Nor was Sasha the only cause of my misery. During the heady days before the Tsar fell, the air had buzzed with danger – but also with excitement. When we'd marched down Nevsky, there'd been a general feeling we mattered. That we were making history. And this feeling was absent on the second day of the Bolshevik takeover.

There'd been no real fighting, no heroic struggle to grapple the power from the hands of entrenched interests. Not a shot had been fired. Shops were open. Citizens moved freely. It was business as usual. If there was so little enthusiasm now, I thought, how would we ever persuade the masses to follow us as we embarked on the gigantic task which lay ahead of us?

I reached Palace Square – that great, open space between the Winter Palace and the mighty River Neva. The barricades around some of the palace's larger arched entrances had been strengthened since the previous day – if no one else was taking us seriously, at least the Provisional Government was.

Not that there seemed to be anything to take seriously. The big square should have been packed with Bolshevik shock troops, ready to storm the barricades. Instead, apart from one military vehicle at the end furthest from the palace, it was completely deserted.

Podvoisky – the Bolshevik Military Revolutionary Committee's second-in command – stood by his staff car, examining the palace through a pair of field glasses. I gave him Lenin's letter. He read it, and sniffed.

"He's been on at me all day," he said. "Threatened to have the whole MRC shot. Who's he going to get to shoot us, that's what I'd like to know. We're the only ones with guns. Is he going to get us to shoot ourselves?"

"You promised him you'd take the palace by noon," I said, "and it's nearly two o'clock now. What's the new estimate?"

"Three o'clock," he said decisively.

I looked around at the empty square. "Doesn't seem to me as if you'll be ready, even by then."

"Listen," Podvoisky exploded, "I've taken the Mariinsky Palace. Why isn't Lenin happy with that?"

"The Mariinsky wasn't guarded, and there was no one important in it anyway. It's Kerensky you've got to worry about, and he and his ministers are in the *Winter* Palace."

"The ministers might be, but Kerensky left just after dawn," Podvoisky said. "Borrowed a car from the American Embassy. Nobody knows where he's gone to."

It was obvious where he'd gone. To rally troops outside the city! "You must attack immediately!" I said.

286

"Can't do it without the men," Podvoisky sniffed, "and I haven't got enough of them yet. Maybe when the sailors from Khronstadt get here . . ."

"And when will that be?"

He shrugged his shoulders. "Should be some time today."

I could have killed him for his complacency. He was losing us the Revolution. And yet . . . and yet at the same time, I wanted to kiss him. His inactivity meant there was still a chance to play a part in the fall of the palace and save Sasha. But what part *could* I play, one woman alone?

"What's the geography of the palace?" I asked.

"The Provisional Government occupies the rooms on the second floor looking out on the Admiralty and the Neva," Podvoisky replied, glad to get off the subject of Lenin and stormings.

"And what's the rest of the building used for?"

"Mainly a hospital for war invalids."

"How strong is the defence force?"

"Hard to say, exactly. There's some Cadets, some Don Cossacks and a company from the Women's Battalion. Maybe . . . round about two thousand all together?"

Two thousand. To defend a building of fifteen hundred rooms which covered four and a half acres. Pathetic!

"What about the entrances?" I asked. "Are they well guarded?

He pointed to the barricade. "You can see for yourself."

"I mean the ones around the side and the back?"

Podvoisky rubbed his forehead with his hand. "Hadn't thought of them," he admitted.

There were scores of unguarded entrances along the side of the Winter Canal. Too easy, I told myself as I stepped inside the palace.

Far too easy. It had to be a trap. There had to be an ambush waiting for me at the top of the narrow flight of servants' stairs. I climbed the stairs and froze, waiting for the inevitable and hoping it would be over quickly. Nothing happened. No ambush – no tell-tale click, followed by burning agony and leading to an all-encompassing blackness.

Corridors, miles of corridors stretched before me, corridors which had once been trodden by hundreds of servants carrying trays weighed down with delicacies. I strained my ear for the sound of an approaching patrol and heard only silence. Taking my courage in both hands I set off in search of someone to corrupt.

The sound of female voices drifting through an open door told me that I'd reached my destination. I stopped, and looked inside the room. Most of the furniture had been removed – probably sent to Moscow to save it from the Germans – and the rest was covered with dust sheets. The ten young women were sitting on the floor. They were dressed in khaki uniforms, and speaking in heavy working class accents.

Don't ever let anyone tell you that women don't make good soldiers, Mr Journalist. Those girls might not have had the strength of most men, but they looked tougher – and much more ruthless. For a moment, my courage almost failed, then I took a deep breath and walked into the room.

God, they moved quickly. One second their rifles were on the floor, the next the stocks were against their shoulders and the barrels pointing at me. "Who are you?" said their Corporal, a thin, pointy-faced woman. "What do you want?"

"I want you to leave before it's too late," I told her. "When the attack comes, you'll be outnumbered. And the attackers will mostly be from Khronstadt."

A couple of the girls shivered at the mention of the savage sailors, but the Corporal merely glared at me. "You're a Bolshevik agitator, aren't you?"

I nodded. There was no point in denying it.

"Then you're as good as dead," she said.

"Please, I'm a mother—"

"That won't save you."

"You don't understand. It's *because* I'm a mother that I've come to see you."

The women looked puzzled, as I'd hoped they would. "What're you talking about?" the Corporal said. "You're not making no sense."

"I know how wonderful it is to give birth," I told her, "to hold a new-born baby in my arms. Do you?"

Some of the girls shook their heads, others looked away for a second – but their rifles were still pointing squarely at me. "Get on with it!" the Corporal barked.

"It's every woman's right to have children. Don't give up that right. Don't die before you've really begun to live."

I was deliberately manipulating them, playing on their emotions – and I believed every word I was saying.

"I joined the army to fight Germans, not Russians," one of the girls said, lowering her weapon.

"An' they never told us we'd have to defend the palace anyway," another chipped in. "They said we was coming here for a parade."

Now the crack in the dam had appeared and water was trickling through for all to see, most of the women nodded their heads in agreement. The Corporal gave in to the inevitable. "How do we do it?" she asked.

"Go through any of the doors which open onto the Winter Canal. There's no one to stop you."

The Corporal thought about it. "All right," she agreed.

"And before you leave, try to persuade your comrades to go with you," I implored her. "They have the right to be mothers too."

The journalist nods his head. I have to find out what he's looking for. I have to discover why, after four years, I'm suddenly worth visiting. He says he only wants the truth – but that's what the interrogators used to say.

"We only want the truth, Comrade Lyudmila. Tell us how long you've been spying for the enemy. Tell us about your meetings with German agents."

"I never—"

Slap!

"Tell us the truth, comrade. We only want the truth."

I've been telling the truth to this journalist, but perhaps it's not the right truth for him. I'm willing to lie. I'll tell him anything he wants if it will keep me out of the Gulag. But like the interrogators of old, he has to communicate to me *what* truth he wants. He has to help me define what truth is.

"Does what I'm saying square with what you learned in school?" I ask.

He has only to say, "You're memory is defective, old woman. You've forgotten how heroic it was," or, "You haven't mentioned the fact that Lenin himself was there," and I'll know what he's after.

"Don't worry about what the official histories say," the journalist tells me, his voice flat, expressionless. "Just go on telling the story in your own way."

Bolshevik agitators – some recruited by me, others acting independently – swarmed all over the building like leeches, slowly sucking the blood out of the palace defences. A squad of Cadets left under their urging, a unit of Cossacks decided to pull out. The palace was slowly dying, the MRC now had troops concentrated in some force at the other end of the square – and still the attack hadn't come. Didn't the MRC realize that at any moment they might hear a new noise, the sound made by the tramping boots of troops still loyal to the Provisional Government?

And what about Sasha? Peter could even at that moment be orchestrating a trial in some grimy cellar – although he would keep well away from it himself.

"Sasha Krasnov, you stand accused of stealing funds meant for our glorious Revolution. How do you plead?"

Sasha would shake his head in bewilderment. "I'd. . .didn't do it."

"Then where's the money?"

"I d. . .don't know."

They would shoot him then and there. I could see him, lying against a blood-stained wall, a reproachful look in his dead eyes, a look which, though not intended me for me, cut deep into my soul.

I looked across the square at the massed Bolshevik troops. "Attack, you idiots," I urged them across the still air. "Storm the Palace, you bastards."

* * *

290

The shooting started at nine-thirty in the evening. It was mainly machine guns and light cannon at first, their shells streaking through the night like demented fire flies. Then the armoured cars joined in, adding their own peculiar growl to the cacophony of explosions. The noise of battle – finally! – should have cheered me, but it didn't. Both the defenders and attackers were safely behind barricades. It was all only sound and fury, and it wouldn't advance the palace's fall one jot.

At ten o'clock the firing stopped, as suddenly as it had started, though the explosions continued to echo in my ears.

Was that it? I wondered desperately. I thought of ringing Lenin and begging him to write the letter which would get Sasha released, but I knew that until I could report the Winter Palace had fallen, he would be deaf to my pleas.

It was after midnight when I found the small, sharp-faced man. He was dressed incongruously in a pea-green sailor's jacket and a wide-brimmed, white hat – the sort a painter or poet might wear. Antonov-Ovseyenko, the man in charge of the assault on the Winter Palace, was wandering its corridors like a little, lost boy.

"Hello, Lyudmila," he said, as if we were meeting each other unexpectedly in the park. "Where is everybody?"

"What are you doing here?" I demanded.

"I'm here to negotiate a surrender," he told me. "But I can't find anyone to negotiate with."

"They're mostly gone," I said, trying to hide my contempt.

"Then we could just walk in and take over?"

Bloody fool! Bloody, bloody fool!

"You might meet some resistance," I said, "but not much."

Antonov-Ovseyenko thought for a moment. "It'll probably be best to bring the troops in through the Winter Canal entrances, the same way as I came," he said. "Then the opposition'll be taken by surprise, and we'll have the defenders at the barricades sandwiched between two forces."

Yes, that would be the logical way to do it, but I didn't think it would be the *right* way. I thought back to the scene in

291

the streets that morning. Unexcited. Uninspring. A revolution by default. I remembered Lenin's words—

"It's more than a building. It's a symbol of the old order."

Just as the Bastille had been in the French Revolution.

"If you want History to love you, comrade," I told Antonov-Ovseyenko, "you'll go in from the front."

I stood at the gates of the Litovsky Barracks, grateful for a chance to catch my breath, yet knowing every second mattered.

"Seems to be in order," the sentry conceded, handing back my Bolshevik pass. "All right, Lyudmila, you can come in."

"Executions?" I gasped. "Where do they hold executions?"

"Parade ground," the soldier said. "Beyond the main barracks. At dawn."

The darkness was already fading. I glanced over my shoulder and saw the beginnings of a crimson glow.

I ran furiously along the narrow passageway between the barrack blocks, avoiding sleepy soldiers who had just risen and were heading for the ablutions.

Parade ground . . . beyond the main barracks . . . at dawn . . . went my thoughts, matched in their urgency and jerkiness by my pounding feet.

I reached the parade ground and saw the execution party at the far end, six men with rifles, an officer and the condemned man with his hands tied behind his back, all bathed in the blood-red light of the relentlessly rising sun.

I would never make it! "Stop! Stop!" I shouted, but my words came out as no more than a strangled croak.

The officer walked over to the wall, and held out a strip of white cloth. The prisoner shook his head. Sasha didn't want a blindfold. Even back in the *mir*, he had always looked fearlessly into the face of death.

My lungs were burning, my heart was at bursting point.

Would they give the condemned man one last request? "Ask for a cigarette, Sasha!" the voice in my head pleaded.

But I knew he didn't smoke.

The officer stepped clear of the line of fire and unsheathed his sabre. He raised it high in the air, and in response the soldiers brought their rifles up to their shoulders.

"Wait!" I screamed.

The squad turned their heads to look at me. I was close enough now to see the expression of annoyance on the officer's face. He barked an order, and the soldier at the end of the line detached himself, placed his rifle on the ground, and turned to me, arms outstretched.

Sasha had seen me, too. "K. . .keep back, Anna," he shouted. "Keep back, it's t. . .too late."

I had been unable to prevent Konstantin's death – I would not let them shoot Sasha.

"Stay of execution," I yelled, waving the document in my hand.

The soldier waiting to catch me shook his head disbelievingly. Hysterical girlfriend, his look said. Try any trick in the book to stop us shooting her sweetheart.

I weaved to left and so did he, then to the right and he followed. I felt his arms grasp my hands.

"Easy, love," he said. "There's nothing you can do."

"Take aim," the officer called out.

I lunged out with my knee and felt it make contact with my captor's groin. Air whooshed from his mouth, he released his grip, doubled over and staggered backwards. I ran around his crumpling body. I was heading for Sasha, but I was looking at the man with the sabre.

The officer's face was almost purple with rage. "Get out of the way, or you'll be shot, too!" he yelled.

I didn't doubt it. Officers like him had ordered their men to fire on crowds of women and children – he would not lose any sleep over me. But nothing would stop me now.

"No, Anna, no!" Sasha, moving awkwardly because of his bound hands, was rushing towards me.

We met half-way between the firing squad and the wall. I was trying to throw my arms around Sasha, to lock him to me. He was doing his best to shoulder me out of the way. We were both shouting madly, though I've no idea what.

"Fire!" the officer commanded.

My fingers gripped Sasha's jacket. I leant backwards and pulled with all my might. We hit the ground at the same moment as I heard the shots.

It was difficult to say, sprawled there, whether I'd been shot or not. Difficult to know for sure if I was even still alive. Perhaps my body was already dead and my soul merely lingering. Then four rough hands pulled me to my feet.

"Get the bitch away from here," the officer said furiously. "I'll deal with her when we've finished with the prisoner. You two, get him back against the fucking wall."

I looked down at the piece of paper Ilyich had so hurriedly scribbled. I looked up again, and saw that the officer had noticed it, too. "You'd better read that first, you bastard," I said. "It's a free pardon signed by Lenin himself. If you shoot Sasha, you could find yourself the next one standing against that wall."

"I w. . .wish I'd been with you to watch the storming of the W. . .Winter Palace," Sasha said later.

"You didn't miss much," I told him.

"D. . .didn't miss much?" Sasha protested, half joking, half serious. "It was o. . .only the most important thing that's ever happened."

He thought it was like the pictures, you see, Mr Journalist. You know the ones I mean. The workers and soldiers are charging forward. It's obvious this is no easy attack, but they're not to be deterred. In the foreground, a soldier with a red flag attached to the barrel of his rifle is urging his firm-jawed, resolute companions on. Some are already firing their weapons and one is even bayoneting a fallen enemy.

I gave up trying to tell Sasha the truth. What would have been the point – he'd *wanted* to believe it had been an inspiring sight, and nothing I could have said would have persuaded him otherwise. But I'll tell you, Mr Journalist, what I really saw as I stood at one of the windows overlooking Palace Square and watched it all.

At one-twenty on the morning of the 26th of October, Antonov-Ovseyenko launched his assault. A whole day later than Lenin had expected it! It didn't look very military, or even very threatening. A telephonist who saw the start of the action phoned through to the Ministers, we discovered later, to tell them that a delegation of three or four hundred was approaching.

A delegation! Not the armed vanguard of the Proletarian Revolution, at the very thought of which, the capitalist lackeys tremble in their boots. A delegation.

The 'delegation' didn't even attack the barricades in front of the main door. Instead, they went in through two other entrances, which were not guarded at all. Once inside, it was easy to overwhelm the remaining Cadets. It took longer to arrest the Ministers – but only because the Red Guard didn't know exactly where, in that vast palace, to look.

The popular story of the storming was a lie, but it was a necessary one. Every revolution needs its mythology, and Antonov-Ovseyenko and I had created ours.

"A g. . .glorious event," Sasha said.

I ran my finger tenderly along the scar on his forehead. "Yes, my dear," I agreed. "A glorious event."

"And now I've got my f. . .free pardon, I can start to work for the Party again."

It was almost as if he'd never been through his terrible ordeal, almost as if he'd not missed death by inches. But that was Sasha, a passionate idealist, never stopping to think about how he'd got into trouble in the first place, never considering that Peter, having once been thwarted, would redouble his efforts to destroy his old enemy.

"The W. . .Winter Palace has fallen," Sasha said again, as if it were a magic spell. "The revolutionary struggle is over."

The revolutionary struggle was *not* over – it had only just begun. The ousted Prime Minister, Kerensky, was advancing on Petrograd with a small army. Moscow was proving difficult to subdue, and there were several days of bitter fighting when victory could have gone either way. All the other political parties combined with the most important unions – railway, telegraph and postal – to bring us down.

We sent messages to distant cities informing them that we had taken power, but if they refused to accept our authority we had no way of enforcing it. We were a party of less than two hundred and fifty thousand members trying to control a vast empire of over one hundred and seventy-five million souls.

Lenin waited desperately for the revolutions in the more developed countries of Europe – France, Britain and Germany – which would save his own. They never came.

Yet we survived – survived to fight a bloody civil war. Admiral Kolchak's White Army attacked us from the east and General Denikin's from the south. And we did not only have to battle our fellow Russians – the whole world seemed to be against us. The British invaded, and the French, the Romanians, Poles, Baltic Germans, Letts, Finns, Canadians, Italians, Serbs and Czechs.

We survived that too, but at what a cost. Whites massacred Reds, Reds massacred Whites. Bolshevik Commissars, sent to requisition food from the peasants to feed the towns, were killed in horrible – indescribable – ways. New Commissars, appointed to fill their places, retaliated by taking the crops by force, often expropriating so much that the *muhziks* starved to death.

Tears are streaming down my face now, just at the thought of it. Some terrible, terrible things were done . . . terrible, terrible things . . .

Chapter Twenty-Nine

"They dug up my husband, you know," I tell the journalist, who says his name is Yuri.

Great salt tears pour down my face. Pull yourself together, old woman! This is not the way to get what you want.

"Dug him up?" Yuri asks.

"The local soviet. They opened his tomb and burned the body. I didn't find out until much later. My comrades in Moscow kept it from me. I . . . I don't even have his ashes."

"These things happen in a revolution," Yuri says.

How many times have I used just those words myself?

Yuri clicks the recorder and slips it back into his pocket.

"Is that all?" I ask, alarmed.

Is he leaving? I can't let him leave!

"It's only a start," Yuri says, shifting to a more comfortable position in my hard chair.

He's not going, he's merely stopped recording. Why has he stopped recording? I've pinned so much hope on this man, and yet it's hard to see a way in which he can help me. Money? Journalists often pay for their material, but how much will a newspaper – a Russian newspaper – give me for my story? Not enough to save me from the clutches of Sonia and Jennifer. And if not money, what *can* he offer me, this saviour to whom I speak in my native language?

"Do you remember La Pasionaria, the great Spanish Communist?" Yuri asks.

"Of course I remember her. Do you ever forget your enemies? She and her people used the Spanish socialists I was working with, and then they sold them down the river."

"In other words, you lost!" Yuri says.

His tone is not aggressive, yet there's an edge to it. It's as if he's testing me. In fact, this whole meeting has seemed more like a test than an interview. But *what* is he testing, old woman? And why does he want this part of the test off the record? Before you can turn the game to your advantage, you must first discover what the rules are.

"You did lose, didn't you?" he prods.

"Not in the end," I say. "Where's Joe Stalin's monolith now? I wish . . . I wish I could bring him back to life, so I could take him round his Empire and show him what's happened to it."

Yuri smiles, as if I have passed the preliminaries and can now compete for the major prize. "La Pasionaria lived in exile for over forty years," he says.

"I know."

"But in the end," and he is annunciating his words very slowly and deliberately, "in the end, they allowed her to go home."

Home! The idea had never occurred to me. "You . . . you want me to go back to Russia?" I ask.

"Initially, just for a visit. We have the idea of producing a new television history of the early Soviet period, and you are in an almost unique position to tell us about it. We'd take you round the old sites, the Winter Palace, the Eastern Front, and you could talk about your experiences and how things have changed." He pauses. "It would be just like bringing Joe Stalin back to life and showing him his crumbling empire."

"Are you really a journalist?" I ask.

His eyes flicker, as if he is about to lie, then he sees I have noticed, and changes his mind. "I am a journalist," he says carefully, "but I'm also a Party member – a progressive."

"Who in the Party ever thought they were not progressive?" I ask. "Who in the Party would ever concede that there was any other way to the Marxist utopia but their own?"

He laughs – but uncomfortably. "If you prefer it," he says, "we can substitute the word 'liberal' for 'progressive'."

"And you want to *use* me, don't you?" I demand. "I am a walking witness to a discredited revolution, and you want to use me as Gorbachev's stick to beat the conservatives with."

"Yes, we want to use you," he admits, "but the reactionaries will try to use you too, to support their own case. History is no longer as objective as we once believed it to be – that's one of the things Stalin did manage to teach us."

Of course they'd all try to use me. The Party always did. What was I doing when I addressed the women textile workers in the Vyborg District? When I persuaded the soldiers to leave their barracks? Using them! And in this, at least, the Party does not stand alone in its guilt. Everyone, everywhere, uses everyone else. Very well, then, I'll use Yuri for my own particular ends.

But what are my ends? An hour ago, I had only one aim in mind – to keep out of the death camp. And now this journalist, The Man the Other Day, is offering me something I'd never imagined possible.

Do I want it? Am I brave enough to leave the silent land of my exile and return to the greater silence of Russia? Could I . . .?

Don't lie to yourself, Annushka! Not now! Not now! It's not silence you fear – there can be no silence for you in Russia.

I could stand alone on vast steppes, without another living thing to be seen from one horizon to the other, and there would be no silence. The land would speak to me, as it has spoken to a hundred generations of Russians before me.

"Beat us, steal from us, sleep with our wives and daughters," the serfs used to say to the men from the big houses. "We are yours, do with us what you will – *but the land is ours.*"

I've seen much, I've done much, since I left the *mir*, but I can't escape from that line of ancestors, stretching into the mists of time, who planted and sowed, sweated and slaved. I am in the land – the land is in me.

I, too, have planted and sowed, and though my crops, my few personal seeds, have long since been harvested – or died before they ever bloomed – I'm not sure I still have the courage to go and see where they once lay.

"Your daughter would like to see you again," Yuri says.

I start to tremble. "T . . . Tania? Is she still alive?"

Yuri laughs again, this time because *he* has scored a point. "Very much so, Princess. She's as tough as her mother."

There has been a silence between us for nearly half a century, ever since the day she decided to return to Russia and work for – instead of against – the butcher who called himself our General Secretary. The silence is of her making, not mine – but who am I to complain? I taught my children to put their duty, as they saw it, above all else. Perhaps if Konstantin had lived longer, I would have felt it necessary to cut myself off from him, just as she has cut herself off from me.

"The Mayakovsky Palace?" I ask. "Is it still there?"

"It's still there, Princess."

"What is it now?"

He shrugs, as if it doesn't matter. Well, it matters to me.

"Don't you know?" I ask.

"I . . . er . . . believe it houses a number of enterprises – a co-operative press, a workshop, even a small museum."

And Konstantin. He'll still be there, I'd be able to feel his presence in every room. I'm too old to be hurt again!

Going home would bring back other memories, too, of friends and comrades lost, of lives wasted, of that terrible night in the Crimea which even now I find it hard to think about, which even now I . . . I . . .

The Advance of the Red Army in the Southern Campaign of 1919. I was a political commissar by then, Trotsky's watch-dog over the 'military specialists' who had once been Tsarist officers. No order could be issued without my counter-signature on it, no decision could be taken without my being consulted. I was not quite twenty-three, and I had more power than a General.

The White armies had been routed and we were liberating as much territory each day as we could cover in that day's march. The chaos was indescribable. Partisan bands who'd fought behind enemy lines now offered their services to the regular army or else set up small, temporary states of their own. Columns of refugees, either fleeing from the Whites or following them, begged and scavenged as best they could. Freed Bolsheviks pleaded for transport to their homes, often

300

hundreds of miles away. Captured Whites milled around listlessly in hastily constructed prison camps and pondered on their fate.

There were streams of requests to be granted or refused, thousands of decisions to be taken and orders to be issued. It seemed never ending. I hadn't seen my children for months. Tania would have grown out of recognition by the time I returned home, Nicky would have scores of new triumphs to relate to me.

I worked eighteen or twenty hours at a stretch. Sometimes I got no sleep at all. I worked while I ate, as I travelled in the staff car, even when recurring attacks of diarrhoea forced me to spend hours on the toilet. My eyes prickled with tiredness and my body felt as if it would never stop aching again.

Perhaps if I'd not been so exhausted, I'd have acted differently that night in the small Crimean town whose name I've forgotten. But I don't think so. What else could I have done?

We'd reached the Black Sea that day, and I'd set up my headquarters in the house of a local priest who'd fled with the White Army. I was in the dining room, in conference with some senior officers, when my aide entered.

"There's a local partisan leader outside, Comrade Commissar. He wants to see you."

I slammed down my pen in irritation. "Isn't there anyone else who could deal with him?"

"It has to be you. He says it's important."

Not all the partisans were pro-Bolshevik. Some hated us as much as they hated the Whites. It wouldn't be wise to offend a guerrilla leader at this point in the campaign. "Show him in," I said wearily.

He was a formidable man with a thick, black beard and flashing, angry eyes. On his head, he wore the close-fitting cap of a Crimean Tartar. He was not alone. A frightened-looking, dark-haired girl, perhaps fourteen or fifteen, was by his side. Despite her slightly Asiatic features, she reminded me very much of myself at her age.

"How may we help you, *Aga*?" I asked.

301

"I want justice for my daughter," he said in strongly-accented Russian.

"How was she wronged?"

"Tell her," the Tartar demanded.

"I was walking back from my grandmother's village," the girl said, gazing down at the floor. "This . . . this officer came along on his horse. I was quite frightened at first, but when he spoke, he seemed so nice. He asked me if I wanted a ride. I was tired, and so I said yes. He . . . he took me into the woods. We stopped by a stream and he told me to undress. When I wouldn't, he beat me, and then he ripped my clothes off and then he . . . and then he . . ."

"Raped you?"

The girl nodded mutely.

"And when did this happen?"

"Yesterday," the Tartar said.

"We only arrived today."

"It wasn't one of your lot, it was one of the others," the Tartar said dismissively, as if all Russians were the same.

"Then I don't see what I can do. The White Army is in retreat."

"Not this bastard. He was taken prisoner. They're holding him in the cattle pens. They won't let me get near him."

I turned to my aide. "Go with the girl," I told him. "If she can identify the man who raped her, have him brought here."

"What will you do with him?" the Tartar snorted. "Slap his wrist?"

And have him and his partisans go on the rampage? Risk the lives of my own men for the sake of one brutal enemy soldier? Oh no!

"If I'm satisfied that he is the one who raped her, I'll have him shot," I said.

The Tartar nodded his head. He would obviously have preferred a slow, painful death for the violator of his daughter's innocence, but he was prepared to settle for a bullet.

An escort returned with the accused man ten minutes later. They marched him to the centre of the room and called a halt.

Standing there, with a soldier either side of him, he looked very vulnerable, and the crimson scratchmarks on his cheek served only to emphasize his paleness. The girl's father, now being restrained by two of my bodyguards, shouted abuse at him, but he refused to look in the Tartar's direction. He was guilty, there could be no possible doubt about that.

"Take the *Aga* outside," I said, aware of the tremble in my voice. "The escort can leave as well." I turned to the officers sitting around the table. "You, too, comrades, if you wouldn't mind."

"But he's a dangerous enemy, Comrade Commissar," one of them objected.

Dangerous? Not now. Not with me.

"And I am armed," I told them, holding up my pistol in a shaking hand. "If he makes a wrong move, I'll shoot him."

"But Comrade Commissar—"

"Go! For God's sake, go!"

I was silent while the others reluctantly left the room. The prisoner stepped forward and clutched at the top of a chair for support. Finally, the door closed behind the last officer, and we were alone.

"Why, Misha?" I asked.

"I don't know," he said. "I suppose it was because they all reminded me of you."

"All?"

"She wasn't the first, not by a long way. I always started out just wanting to hold them, to be nice to them, but then, I don't know, I'd feel this rage building up inside me, and I'd have to hurt them. It's as if . . . it's as if I wanted to punish them for not being you."

Or to punish me *for* being me.

"If only you hadn't been my sister!" he blurted out.

Ah yes, if only I hadn't been your sister. You were weak, Misha, you ran away when I really needed you. But you could also be brave, like the time you took the beating to save me. Perhaps with you I'd have found the tenderness I had with Sasha and felt the passion which Peter aroused in me. Perhaps, too, with me to guide you, you could have been a better man, more like my dear Konstantin.

If only I hadn't been your sister.

"I'm going to have to order your execution," I told him. He gasped. "You can't . . . you just can't!"

"I don't have any choice. It's your life against dozens of others. And do you really think that even if I spared you, those Tartars out there would just let you walk away?"

He nodded his head solemnly, as if he accepted the point. "But not by firing squad," he pleaded. "I couldn't take that. I'd break down, I know I would. Let me at least die with a little dignity."

I slid my pistol across the table. "Take it," I said.

He picked up the gun. His hand was trembling as much as mine. He cocked the hammer, placed the barrel against his forehead, and closed his eyes. I wanted to turn away, but I forced myself to watch – I owed him that at least. It was not warm in the room, but droplets of sweat were forming on his forehead.

My eyes became transfixed by his trigger finger, which seemed to grow and grow until it filled my whole field of vision. The seconds ticked by. One . . . two . . . three . . . four . . . five . . . Misha lowered the gun.

"I can't," he said miserably.

"You have to!"

He slid the weapon back to me. "Couldn't you do it?"

"Me! You want me to kill my own brother?"

"It's because I am your brother – and your lover – that I can ask you. You do still love me, don't you?"

"Yes," I admittedly heavily, "I still love you." I picked up my gun and raised it until it was level with his chest.

"No, not from the front," he said. "I know I've got to die, but I don't want to see it coming."

He walked to the centre of the room and turned his back on me. "Do it when you're ready," he said. "Only don't speak. Don't say a word. Shall I tell you what I'm thinking about? I'm thinking about that day in the woods, by the riverbank."

I cocked my pistol again and rose from my chair as quietly as I could.

"I hadn't planned it," Misha continued. "If your horse hadn't cast its shoe, it would never have happened."

I edged my way around the table, being careful not to bang against any of the chairs.

"I've never stopped thinking about it. Never. Not just when I was with Mariamna or any of the other girls – I think about it all the time!"

I stepped silently across the floor until I was standing right behind him.

"It was a warm, sunny day. Do you remember? The sun has never felt half so kind since."

Shooting deserters and spies in the back of the head was a standard method of execution then. I'd seen it done many times. I lifted the pistol so slowly, so carefully, that not even a rustling of clothes gave my movements away.

"I never imagined that anyone could be as beautiful as you were that day. Your face, your breasts . . ."

Pistols have been known to jam. If this one jammed on me now, I told myself, I'd take it as a sign that God, or Fate – or something – didn't want me to shoot Misha, and I'd do my best to help his escape, whatever it cost me – or anyone else.

"It was the happiest moment of my life," Misha said. "It was my only really happy moment. Perhaps I should have died then and there."

I squeezed the trigger. The pistol did not jam.

How *can* I go back to Russia? How can I visit the palace my husband died in? The town where I killed my brother? How can I face the daughter who, to preserve her ideological purity, banished me from her life for so long – the daughter who was hardly more than a girl the last time I saw her, and is now a pensioner?

I can't. I can't. I'm old. I'm weak. There's no fight left in me.

"I'm sorry, Yuri," I say to the journalist-politician. "I'll help you in any way I can, but returning to Russia—"

"What's this! What the hell are you doing here?"

Jennifer has, as usual, neglected to knock, and her angry words are directed not at me, but at my visitor. She's not come alone. Sonia is standing beside her in the doorway, and in the corridor I can see Charles and Edward.

"I said, what are you doing here?"

"It is a free country," Yuri replies, speaking for the first time in English, "or so you Britons always claim."

Jennifer advances into the room, crunching broken pottery under her heel. She stops for a moment to inspect it. "You see," she says to her sister. "She's not even swept up the vase she threw at us. She's totally incapable of looking after herself."

"I know, I know," Sonia chimes from the hallway.

Jennifer is bending over me now. Her face is white with rage. "You had no right to talk to him!" she says through tight lips. "No right at all!" She turns on Yuri. "What has she been telling you?"

"She talked about the Revolution. Lenin and the storming of the Winter Palace."

"You should never have bothered her," my great-granddaughter says. "Can't you see she's easily confused?"

"She seems lucid enough to me," Yuri replies mildly.

She seems lucid enough to me. Is that all the support I can hope for from my only ally? Well, what did I expect? That he would spring to my defence like a knight in shining armour? He's a journalist – and a political fixer. He's just doing his job. He doesn't give a damn about me.

You're on your own, old woman. You have been since your husband died.

"I can't stop you saying what you like in Russia," Jennifer says, pointing her finger at the journalist, "but if you print one word of your lies in a *British* paper, I'll sue you for every penny you've got."

Ah, Jennifer, so like your father. So worried about what your fancy friends will say.

Sonia has moved into the room now, and is opening the chest of drawers.

"What are you doing?" I ask.

"Packing your things." Brisk, efficient. "All the arrangements have been made."

I am sitting here and letting it happen. I am giving in to the inevitable. Perhaps I knew all along that I would in the end, and was only fooling myself. All I can hope for now is a quick death.

"Arrangements?" Yuri asks. "What arrangements?"

"Great-grandmother is going into a home," Jennifer says. "Somewhere she'll be protected from people like you."

I've been staring at the wall straight ahead of me – practising to be an imbecile – but something in Jennifer's voice makes me turn towards her.

The expression on her face shocks me. I thought I'd seen them all – her sulks, her looks of reproach and disdain, of contempt and exasperation. I've even seen her smile before – ingratiating smiles offered up to her husband's superiors, regal smiles bestowed on the servants. But I've never seen her smile like this.

It's a look of triumph, of pure bourgeois complacency. It's a look that could only play on the lips of a woman absolute convinced she's one of the chosen few. She is *so sure* she's right.

Thank you, great-granddaughter. Thank you for giving me the strength to fight back. "I don't want to go into a home," I say. "I want to return to Russia."

"Return to Russia," giggles Sonia, who's still putting my clothes into my battered suitcase. "How could you afford that? You haven't got two pennies to rub together."

"He'll pay for me," I say, pointing a bony finger at the journalist who is still sitting in my only chair.

Jennifer swings round on him like a wildcat. "Is that true? Have you told her you'll pay her fare back to Russia?"

"Not me personally, but Soviet television is certainly willing to do so."

For a second, it almost looks as if Jennifer will accept the situation. To a mind like hers, bounded by the better areas of London, Russia is indeed a long way away, a convenient dumping ground for an old woman who has outlived both her friends and her usefulness. Then her face clouds over. She squares her shoulders and shakes her head. "I can't allow it," she says. "We're still responsible for her."

And once in Russia, there's no telling who I might talk to

307

or what I might say, is there, Jennifer? Once in Russia, you'd have no control over me.

"You can't stop me if I want to," I say, like a defiant child.

"I'm sorry, great-grandmother, but I can," Jennifer says firmly. "You've forgotten already, haven't you?"

No great-granddaughter, I haven't forgotten, but still I watch with horrified fascination as she snaps open her handbag. So Charles has got his doctor friend – his club-friend – to sign the appropriate order. And with so much haste! Yuri must really have worried them. Jennifer pulls an official-looking piece of paper out of the handbag, and holds it up.

"Do you know what this is?" she asks Yuri.

"It's a Gulag *billet-doux*," I tell him.

He nods his head, understanding immediately, but Jennifer merely looks puzzled. Of course she does. She never lived through it. Wasn't brought up, as Yuri was, in a country where it was a recent, painful memory.

"It's a committal order," she tells the journalist, and then turns back to me. "I told you before it would be better for everyone if you went voluntarily, but you never listen, do you? Well, here it is, all signed and sealed."

All signed and sealed. Like the orders which used to come out of Stalin's Secretariat.

"Twenty years' hard labour. No appeal."

And there's no appeal now. Who would side with an old woman against an army of doctors, social workers and concerned relatives? But I *won't* give up yet.

I look across at Yuri. He shrugs his shoulders as if to say he doesn't think there's anything he can do to help – but that he'll try anyway. "Why don't you let the Princess come back to Russia?" he asks. "It's her life."

The two husbands have been standing in the corridor like the useless appendages they are, but now Edward, our budding politician, steps just inside the room. "Look here, old chap," he says, "I'm not sure how you handle things in your country, but what my wife's holding in her hand is a legal document, and we British are brought up to respect the law."

308

We British! Oh Edward, you pompous windbag, I almost love you!

I rise stiffly to my feet. Edward and Charles move closer together, blocking the door. Do they expect me to make a run for it? At my age! I step round Sonia and open the top drawer of my chest, the one which contains my pension book, bits of string and money-saving coupons.

"What's she doing now?" Sonia says.

Why don't you ask *me*, Sonia?

My hands are trembling with excitement, but also with fear. Is it here? It should be. Where else would I have put it? Leaflet on saving electricity, pair of scissors, magnifying glass – it has to be here somewhere. My fingers brush against stiff cardboard and I know I've found what I am looking for.

I pull it out of the drawer and wave it triumphantly at Jennifer. "Russian passport!" I say.

Jennifer snatches it from me. Clumsily, for she still clutches her precious piece of paper in one hand, she flicks through my passport, a part of my history. She swoops down on the page containing my personal details. The words are mumbo-jumbo to her, but the numbers are the same.

"What's this mean?" she demands, holding out the page for me to read.

A younger Anna, a pretty Anna, stares up at me from my photograph.

"Don't you know?" Jennifer asks. "Have you forgotten your Russian?"

No, I haven't forgotten. "It says, 'Expires'," I tell her.

"Then it's over sixty years out of date!" Jennifer scoffs. She hands the passport back to me, now that she no longer considers it a danger. "And surely, you took out British citizenship."

No, I never did. I may have been an exile with no hope of returning home, yet somehow I could never bring myself to cut that last link. "Can I get my passport renewed?" I ask Yuri.

"There should be no trouble about that, Princess," the Russian says, smiling broadly now.

Jennifer has clenched her fists. She's scrunching up her

neat, white legal paper. "This is ridiculous!" she explodes. "What does it matter whether she's British or Russian. We've got a *committal order* here."

"I'm . . . er . . . not so sure it applies any more," Edward says cautiously. "We could still put great-grandma in a retirement home, of course, but if the Russian Government made a request for her return to her own country, we'd have to comply. And the whole incident might . . . er . . ."

Might leave a nasty taste in the mouths of the electors who Edward hopes will vote him into a nice, easy living at the Palace of Westminster?

"Oh really, this is impossible!" Jennifer says – almost screams.

But it isn't, my girl. Just once in a while things happen differently from the way they should in the World According to Jennifer.

Sonia, with the compulsiveness common to her type, has never stopped packing during the whole argument. Now that she's finished, she's at a loss.

"Close the case, Sonia," I order her.

And that's exactly what she does.

"Great-grandmother," Jennifer says wheedlingly, "you don't really want to go back to Russia. It'll be like a foreign country to you."

I don't even bother to answer her.

"Can you find somewhere to put me up until it's time to leave?" I ask Yuri.

"I think my budget could stand a modest hotel," he says cheerfully.

"Then if you wouldn't mind giving me a hand with my suitcase . . ."

He stands up and takes the case from an unprotesting Sonia.

"My coat!" I say to Edward.

I speak to him as if I were Countess Olga, and he one of the servants at the Big House. And he acts like a servant, mutely reaching for my coat and holding it while I put it on.

Charles stands out of the way so that I can pass. Corridor, front door, and we are in the street. It's cold here, but it will be colder still in Russia.

Yuri's car is parked in front of the house. He helps me in. My relatives, the survivors of the once great house of Mayakovsky, stand on the front doorstep, rigid as statues. They are still standing there when the car reaches the corner of Matlock Road.

"Stop, please," I tell Yuri. "Stop right now."

"Have you forgotten something, Princess?" he asks, pulling up to the curb and glancing nervously over his shoulder at Jennifer and company.

"I've never forgotten anything," I say, half-jokingly. "That's my curse."

My aged arm winds down the window, and the three men standing in front of the shop – Ali, Winston and Terry the barman – turn around to look at me.

"Feeling better, Princess?" Terry asks. "She was a bit Brahms and Liszt earlier," he explains to the others.

"Much better," I tell him. "I'm going home."

"Home!" Winston sighs, and the air is suddenly full of sound of steel bands.

"One day!" Ali promises himself, and I can almost smell the jasmine.

"I'll miss you all," I say.

And I mean it. If not with understanding, then at least with kindness, all these men have stepped a little way into my silent land of age and loneliness.

"We'll miss you, too," Terry replies. "Bound to, aren't we?"

"Drive on," I say. I'm speaking to Yuri, but I'm still looking at the three friends I will never see again.

I feel the car pull away.

"Don't go now, Princess," Ali says, and I can tell from his expression he's searching for some reason to make me stay. "We've got a special offer on stewing steak," he shouts after me as we turn the corner.

I wonder how my daughter will feel – about me, about herself – now that her revolution is just as dead as mine. And

311

will I still be able to love this ageing woman who was once a tiny helpless baby in my arms?

There will be other challenges, too. Confronting my past. Observing a Russia which is in my bones, but which I can no longer claim as mine.

"It will be very hard going home," I tell my dead husband. "Did I do the right thing?"

"Of course you did, my dear," he answers reassuringly. "You've always been a fighter – why stop now?"

We are on Kilburn High Road, but already my mind is back in my motherland, the wide steppes, the busy streets of Petersburg.

My aches and pains have disappeared. I imagine myself riding a wild Cossack pony again. I know I couldn't really do it – but I *feel* as if I could.